FOREVER
ALEXA

BOOK FOUR IN THE *BODYGUARDS OF L.A. COUNTY* SERIES

CATE
BEAUMAN

First Print Edition: May 2013

ISBN-13: 978-1484943083
ISBN-10: 1484943082

Editor: Liam Carnahan

Cover and formatting: Streetlight Graphics

DEDICATION

To all those who are lost

ACKNOWLEDGMENTS

Thank you Liam Carnahan, the BEST editor on the planet, for your excellent work. I don't know what I would do without you and Invisible Ink Editing.

A huge thank you to Lieutenant John Reese from the Loudon NH Fire Department, Misty Rose, and Deputy Chief Corey MacDonald, Esq. for lending me your expertise.

CHAPTER 1

February 1995

Alexa turned up the television, struggling to focus on the cartoon she loved instead of the whiskey splashing about in Mom's half-empty bottle of Johnny Walker. Her sister sat next to her on the lumpy cot they shared, clinging to her side like she'd done since they were told to get in the backseat of the car a week ago.

Abby giggled as Tommy, Chucky, Phil, and Lil found themselves caught up in another disastrous backyard adventure. Her smile faded when their favorite show went to commercial. "Lex, I'm hungry," she whispered close to Alexa's ear.

Alexa glanced at their more-than-half drunk mother, then turned to Abby. "We'll eat soon," she murmured, terrified mom would hear and realize she'd stolen twenty-five dollars from her almost empty wallet. She pressed her clammy, trembling fingers to the folded bills in her jean pocket as her own belly growled, despite her nerves. Mom forgot to feed them. She always forgot to feed them when she drank.

Alexa stared out the grimy motel window at the bright yellow arches across the way. Her mouth watered as she thought of ketchup and grilled meat, of soft white bread and salty pickles she couldn't wait to sink her teeth into. They hadn't had a meal since lunchtime yesterday. Soon, she promised, when mom passed out.

It was only a matter of time.

She snuck another peek over her shoulder at the tears trailing down mom's cheeks and willed her mother to close her eyes. Maybe she would finally be brave enough to pick up the ugly, green phone and call Gran. Gran showed her how to make a collect call, 'just in case.' Even at eight, Alexa knew what 'just in case' meant—it meant exactly this.

Why couldn't mom be like she used to? Everything had changed when Alexa was in first grade. Mom and Dad had yelled at each other, and then he went away. They moved out of the big house with the pretty pink room, and mom stopped taking care of them. Now she cried all the time and drank her yucky brown drink that made her talk funny or sleep.

When Alexa was in second grade, a woman came to school to tell her she and Abby would be moving to her Gran's apartment while mom went to a special hospital. Everything was better after that. Gran smelled nice and cooked good food, even though the bones in her fingers were twisted and her body hurt most of the time. Gran taught her how to play the piano, and she read to her and Abby every night. Alexa didn't mind that she had to do the laundry or brush Abby's hair or get all of the groceries when the special van came to take them to the store. Gran sat in a neat scooter and let Abby steer while she drove.

Mom came back sometimes, but she stayed at the hospital a lot—and that was okay. Alexa's stomach always hurt when she was around, and it made Abby cling to her and Gran. Mom wasn't beautiful anymore. Her long black hair, just like hers and Abby's, was no longer shiny and she never brushed it. She didn't tuck them in at bedtime or take them to the park, either.

When Alexa came home from school on Tuesday, the

van was there to take Gran to her doctor's appointment. Mom waited until Mr. Worthington drove away, then she made her and Abby get in the car she borrowed from the neighbor so they could go get ice cream. But they never went out for ice cream, and they never went home to Gran. She wanted Gran; she missed her so much. After she tucked Abby in at night, Alexa would stare at the phone in the light from the window or turn her face into the pillow and cry. She wanted to go home.

The empty bottle hit the ugly, orange carpet with a thud, and Alexa jumped.

"Lexy Lou, get me another," mom slurred, wiping her nose with the back of her hand.

Abby clutched Alexa's arm as their mother began to sing.

"It's okay, Abby." She turned the TV up louder. "Watch Rugrats."

"Hey, turn that down! Don't you know a good song when you hear one?" Mom laughed hysterically until she sobbed.

Abby pulled the blanket over her head, and Alexa rushed to her feet. She grabbed the full bottle of Johnny Walker on the table and brought it to the bed. "Here." She wanted mom to drink more so she would go to sleep and leave them alone. Eyeing the phone again, she stepped back.

"Where you goin', Lexy Lou?" Mom yanked her to the mattress and entwined her in a hard hug. "Don't you love me anymore?"

Alexa slammed her eyes shut and tried not to breathe in her mother's terrible breath.

Mom clutched her tighter. "I said don't you love me anymore? Or are you like your dad? You and Abby went to live with your grandmother and left me—just like him." She sobbed louder. "Don't you want to be with me?"

Abby's sniffles came from under the blanket she clutched tight around her on the cot. Alexa wanted to go to her. Abby was only four; she didn't know what was going on. Sometimes she wasn't sure either, but she was the big sister. It was her job to take care of Abby. "Yes, I want to be with you." She squeezed her eyes tighter as she lied. "I like being here with you."

"Then hug me back."

Alexa wrapped her arms around her mother, waiting, hoping to be released.

"He left us. He walked right out the door and left us. Why did he *leave* me? Selfish bastard!"

Alexa's heart thundered, and her lips trembled as she struggled to hold on to her own tears. Why did mom ask her questions she didn't know how to answer? When would she let her go?

"I don't want to do this anymore." Her mother finally released her, but took her hand. "I love you, Lexy Lou. I love you my Abby Dabby. I want you to remember that this is all his fault."

Alexa cringed as mom plastered her cheek with slobbery, stinky kisses.

"All his fault, Lexy." Mom got to her feet and lost her balance, falling back against the bed. She righted herself, grabbed her full bottle, and staggered to the bathroom, slamming the door.

Alexa stood where she was, shaking, listening to the faucet turn on in the bathtub and her sister's quiet crying underneath the blanket. She looked at the phone and hurried to the cot. "Abby, come on out from under there."

"I want Gran." Abby pulled the blanket off herself. "I want to go home to Gran."

"We will. We're going to McDonalds first." She

stared at her sister's long, tangled hair and watery blue eyes—the exact same color as her own. "You can have a surprise—a happy meal."

Abby wiped at her tears. "A happy meal? You too? Can you have one too?"

She wanted one. She'd never had a happy meal. Gran couldn't afford to get them one. They didn't go to McDonalds or Burger King like the other kids in her class. "I'm too big for happy meals. You're just a kid, so you can have one. We have to go. It's getting dark and starting to snow."

Alexa tied her shoes, then Abby's. "Coat on, Abby."

Abby put on the pretty blue parka their neighbor had given her and struggled to zip it. "I can't do it."

"I'll do it." She bent forward and froze when the water shut off in the bathroom. Ears straining, she listened until mom settled in the tub.

"What's wrong?"

"Nothing." She wanted to get them away from here. "Let's zip you up. Like this, remember?" She shoved the zipper in place and pulled up.

"Gran tried to show me, but her fingers wouldn't bend."

"I'll teach you. Like Gran is teaching me how to cook." Alexa had started doing the cooking while Gran watched and told her what to do. Gran's hands were getting worse. They hardly worked at all now, but that was okay. She could do it. She liked to help Gran and Abby. Gran always called her 'the little mommy,' but when she said her joke, her eyes were sad. "Come on."

Alexa reached for the knob as something crashed to the floor and broke behind the closed door. She wanted to ignore the mess that surely needed to be cleaned up, but it was so quiet. Mom didn't sing or cry or say bad words the way she had last night when she locked herself in there. The silence left her more uneasy than the sounds of her mother's misery. "Abby, turn on another show for a minute."

"But I'm hungry, Lex. You said we were going to eat." Her eyes watered. "I want Gran. When can we go home?"

"Soon." She glanced at the phone. Mom was probably sleeping. Maybe she should call now, but what if mom came out? Mom said if she tried to contact Gran, they would never see her again. Licking her lips, finding her courage, Alexa walked to the phone, picked it up, and quickly slammed it back down. The fear was too much. The clutching in her stomach made her feel like she was going to throw up.

"Who are you calling?"

Alexa turned. "Watch TV and stop with all the questions."

"You don't have to be so bossy." Abby made a face and stuck out her tongue before she walked to the cot for the remote.

Alexa reached for the phone again and yanked her hand away. She needed to check on mom first. If she was asleep, she would call, and Gran could send Mr. Worthington and his van to the truck stop they were stuck at and pick them up. They would wait at McDonalds and eat their dinner just in case mom woke up and wanted to take them away again.

Dread filled her and her shoulders hunched as she took small steps to the bathroom door. What if mom started to cry and wanted to hug her? Cringing, she raised her hand and gave a gentle knock.

No answer.

She knocked again. "Mom?"

Nothing.

Although mom remained quiet, she wanted to see her asleep for herself. "Mom?" she whispered as she twisted the knob, afraid she might wake her. Alexa peered in

12

and blinked. She stared at her mother and breathed in the metallic scent that reminded her of the taste of a bloody lip. She took a step toward the crimson-colored water and the brown liquid pooled on the floor where the glass lay in shards.

Alexa's breath shuddered in and out as she walked closer. Mom's long hair was so black against the white of her skin and her purple lips. The cheerful sounds of familiar commercials filled the silence of the bathroom. Despite her horror, Alexa couldn't take her eyes from mom's slim naked body silhouetted in the deep red. As she stared, she knew it was blood—too much blood. Mom's chest didn't move, and her eyes didn't open.

Heart thundering, Alexa backed up and began to hum the song she'd learned in school about calling nine-one-one. Mom needed her to call nine-one-one. She looked at her mother once more before she closed the door. "Abigail, come here."

Abby's attention turned from the television to her.

"Sing with me. Sing about calling nine-one-one." Although the TV blared, it was too quiet in the horrid room.

"I'm scared, Lex."

"Don't be afraid. I'll take care of you. I'll always take care of you. Sing the 911 song I taught you."

Abby clutched her arm, and soon her shaky voice joined Alexa's. Without thinking, without knowing what she did, Alexa picked up the phone, still singing. She watched her own fingers press the numbers. "...you know what to do. Call nine-one-one, and we'll help you."

"Nine-one-one, what's your emergency?"

The woman's voice echoed in her ear as she continued to sing, her eyes transfixed to the bathroom door and the horror behind it.

CHAPTER 2

May 2014

THE WARM WINDS BLEW THROUGH **Alexa's window** as she sped north on I-270 toward home. She glanced in her rearview mirror and smiled as she glimpsed Olivia fast asleep, exhausted in her pink booster seat after their weeklong adventure. Focusing on the road again, she came to attention when a sign announced a rest area two miles ahead. She had to pee—bad. She'd been holding it for an hour, waiting, hoping her passengers would stir. Well, they were going to have to get up, because her bladder was about to explode. "Abby, wake up. We're stopping in a second."

Her sister blinked several times in the passenger's seat, yawned huge, and stretched. "Where are we?"

"About sixty miles from Hagerstown."

"Thank God. It feels like we've been in the car for *hours.*"

Alexa rolled her eyes and chuckled. "Ab, we've been driving for less than four, and you've slept almost the whole time."

Abby smiled. "Some of us require plenty of beauty sleep."

Scoffing, Alexa slid her a glance. The one thing Abby would never need is beauty sleep. Her little sister was a stunner. "I've gotta make a pit stop. My eyeballs are practically floating. See?" She quickly turned her head and widened them, illustrating her point. "Can you wake Livy?"

Abby peered in the backseat. "Let's let her sleep. She wore herself out. I'll stay with her while you do your thing."

Alexa glanced in her rearview mirror as she exited the interstate. The gray van she had noticed off and on throughout the drive was still behind them. "It's getting dark. There aren't many cars in the lot."

"Worry wart alert. Worry wart alert," Abby blurted out in her familiar, teasing robot voice. "Just go pee, Lex. Olivia and I'll wait here with the windows up and doors locked. Nothing's going to happen in the five minutes you'll be gone." She rolled her eyes and shook her head. "I'll even punch nine-one-one into my cell. I'll keep my thumb hovered over 'send' the entire time."

Alexa pulled into a spot as close to the facilities as possible. The sun was dipping along the horizon, the first stars winking to life. "I'm sorry, did you say you wanted to walk back?" She and Abby grinned at each other as she unfastened her seatbelt. "You sure you don't want to come?"

"Pee already, Lex," Abby said with an exasperated laugh.

"Okay, be right back." Alexa rolled up her window and shut the door, careful to lock her sister and daughter in, and hurried up the path to the bathrooms. She glanced over her shoulder and smiled when Abby made an exaggerated go-ahead motion, as if encouraging her to continue forward. Chuckling, she shook her head. She couldn't help being the mama bear. Some habits would never fade, no matter how old she and Abby were. She was the cautious one and Abby the free spirit—it was ingrained in their DNA.

Alexa pushed her way into the restroom and into a stall. With her bladder empty, she sighed her relief, yanked up her jeans, and washed her hands. She studied her face in the mirror, noting the slight hint of tan the week of sun had left on her fair skin. The mini-vacation had been the perfect kick-off to an exciting new adventure. Abby had a week-old college diploma in her pocket and two interviews lined up in Los Angeles. Alexa had eight blissful weeks away from her first grade classroom. Lazy, wonderful summer days to spend with her sweet little girl lay ahead of her.

Ready to get on with it, ready to get back to their lives, Alexa pulled the door open, took a step, and stopped short as her heart froze. Time stood still as two men in black ski masks dragged Abby kicking and screaming toward the gray van. From a distance, her sister's pleading, terrified eyes bore into hers. Staring, blinking, she finally ran forward as the horror of the moment truly sunk in. "Stop it! Leave her alone! Abby! Abby, no!"

Her sister twisted and turned, fighting a useless battle against big hands and powerful arms. Alexa skirted her car as the men stepped into the back of the van, taking Abby with them. Abby's pleading shouts for help echoed into the night until the door quickly closed and the van screeched off.

Alexa sprinted after the vehicle, screaming until she came to her senses and dashed back to the car. Olivia cried in the backseat, tears streaming down her cheeks.

"Oh, baby. Oh, honey." Alexa fumbled with Olivia's buckle. Her hands shook and her breath heaved as she freed her daughter from her booster and clutched her close, rocking them both on the edge of the seat. She reached forward and rummaged through her purse in the center console, searching for her phone. Grabbing it up, she dialed nine-one-one. Her eyes darted around the dark, desolate, parking lot, and her teeth chattered while her body shuddered in sheer terror.

"Nine-one-one, what's your emergency?"

"Someone took my sister," she gasped between panicked breaths. "Someone *took* my sister."

⟿⟾

It was well after midnight when Alexa let herself into her small home. On autopilot, she carried Livy to the couch, laid her down, and covered her with a fleece blanket, too terrified to put her daughter in her bed, or even let her out of her sight. With her arms empty and suddenly feeling cold, Alexa glanced into the moonless darkness boring through the windows. She hurried around the living room, quickly twisting the blinds and yanking curtains closed, before she turned on every light she could. It was so quiet—too quiet—in her little corner of the woods. Her house, tucked among the trees on the outskirts of town, always brought her comfort, but not tonight.

Head pounding, heart aching, Alexa sat down and pressed a hand to her nauseous stomach. She stared at the lists she'd made before her family left for their week of fun in Virginia. Abby's small graduation barbeque was supposed to be tomorrow night. She wanted to do more, so much more for her sister, but money was tight. Purchasing streamers, balloons, napkins, and a million other items had been her biggest worry just hours ago. Now she wished juggling a couple hundred dollars was her biggest issue.

Alexa rested her weary head in her hands. "My God," she whispered, still unable to believe that two men had snatched her sister away. Abby was really gone. This had to be a dream. Glancing up, she looked at Gran's piano in the corner of the small room, the fireplace with the decorative display of wood and candles in its center, and Livy's toys and books tucked away neatly in the antique box by the window. Alexa knew she wasn't asleep; she was in the middle of a nightmare, but she was wide-awake.

Tears trailed down her cheeks one after another as she sighed out an unsteady breath. "What am I going to do? How will I get her back?" Where did she *start*?

The police were doing everything they could. They'd released Abby's picture to the media along with the few details they had on her case, but it wasn't enough. There were too many questions and hardly any answers, even after the police interview. She'd clutched Olivia in her arms for hours while she gave the detectives a description of the van and the two muscled men in black masks and jeans who had grabbed her sister, yet she hadn't been able to give them a license plate number. She never looked as she ran after the Chevy. And although she'd racked her brain, she couldn't think of a single individual who would wish her sister harm. Abby didn't have enemies. Everyone loved her. She was so warm and fun.

Restless and too frantic to be still, Alexa stood again, wandering the room like a lost soul. How could she have forgotten to get the license number? She didn't even know what state the vehicle was from. She'd felt even stupider when she couldn't give the officers a make and model of the van until she searched the catalog they gave her. She'd let Abby down in so many ways, and as a result, Alexa left the precinct the way she had arrived—powerless and without her sister.

Alexa stopped by the mantel and stared at the photo of her, Livy, and Abby grinning for the camera in their winter gear. They'd had so much fun at the town's annual Christmas Festival months before. Lips trembling, Alexa gasped for air as she gave in to her depthless sorrow. She crumbled to the floor and wept, drowning in her fear. "Oh, God, Abby. I'm so sorry. I'm so sorry I let you down."

On the couch, Livy stirred. "Mommy?"

"I'm right here, honey." She took a deep breath and wiped at her eyes, struggling to steady her voice. "I'm right here." Alexa used the last of her reserves to walk to her little girl, sit on the corner of the cushion, and smile. "Close your eyes, Lovely Livy." She stroked her fingers through her daughter's soft, wheat-colored hair. "It's late."

"Where's Auntie Ab?"

Alexa's lip wobbled. How much did Olivia see? What did she remember? Would she be traumatized? "She's not here right now."

"Why did they make her cry, mommy?"

"Oh, Livy." Alexa scooped her up and cuddled her in her lap, sweeping her hair away from her forehead. "The police are going to bring her home soon." She had to believe it. As she held her daughter close, clinging, breathing in the comfort of her baby, she shut her eyes. At moments like this, the heavy weight of raising her child on her own, of having no one else to depend on, was crushing. "Let's get you to bed. You can sleep with me tonight."

"Okay, mommy." Livy kissed her cheek.

Alexa stood and carried Livy with her to check the lock. She struggled to push the sturdy wooden bench in front of the door and left the lights blazing before she grabbed her cell phone and purse, desperately hoping Abby would find a way to call.

As she climbed the steep stairs, Livy's breathing deepened, evening out. Alexa turned into her room and could only be thankful she'd forgotten to open the blinds before they left on their trip. She didn't want to face the shadows cast by the scant sliver of moon peeking through the increasing clouds or wonder who might be in the dark, watching. Shuddering, she flipped on the dim overhead light. She pulled the covers back and lay Livy down, gently tugging off her shorts, and covered her against the chill of the still, cool nights.

Alexa settled in next to her, fully clothed in her jeans and Virginia Beach t-shirt, hopeful the police would call and tell her to come pick up Abby. She didn't want to waste time getting dressed.

She stared at the pictures on her dresser. One of her and Livy moments after she'd pushed her daughter into the world. Livy's first birthday. Her first steps. Somehow the years had rushed by, and her baby was three-and-a-half. How did that happen?

She looked at the photos hanging on the wall—the last family picture before Gran passed so unexpectedly and the new frame with pictures of Abby in her college cap and gown. She was stunning, with long, glossy, black hair, her classic oval face and flawless complexion, those huge dark blue eyes dancing with energy and fun. Everyone had always said she and Abby could pass for identical twins, but Alexa's cheekbones were sharper, and she had a good two inches on her sister's five-four, willowy frame. Alexa closed her eyes again when the pain became too much. "Oh, Ab, please be okay. *Please.*"

Her cellphone rang, and she jumped. She grabbed the phone up in trembling hands and fumbled it. "Abby?"

More ringing.

Frowning, she looked at her phone, confused, before she realized the ringing wasn't coming from her cell but from somewhere in her purse. She reached forward, yanking her bag off the nightstand, and rummaged through until she discovered the small Verizon flip

20

phone. "Hello? Abby?"

"Guess again," the sexless computerized voice said.

"Who—who is this?" Her heart slammed in her chest as she realized she was talking to Abby's kidnapper. "Where's my sister?"

"I talk. You listen."

She struggled not to shout her questions, to demand answers, fearful that disobeying might harm her sister.

"You've already messed up, sister Alexa. You shouldn't have involved the police or the press. Now we have to up the ante."

They knew her name. Did they know where she lived? She rushed out of bed and peeked around the corner of the window shade. Her eyes darted about, scrutinizing the trees surrounding her home. "What do you want? I'll do anything."

The mechanical laughter erupting in her ear sent shivers along her spine. She stepped away from the window.

"Two hundred and fifty thousand by Monday morning—2 AM. Leave it in your savings account. We'll take care of it from there."

"But..." A quarter of a million dollars? Alexa paced about as cold sweat dripped down her back. She didn't have that kind of money, not even close, but she didn't dare say so. "Let me talk to Abby."

"I do the demanding, not you, bitch. Forty-eight hours. No more police. No more press. Silence will save your sister's life until we get the money. Keep your new phone handy if you want to see her alive." The line went dead.

"Wait. *Wait.* Hello?" Alexa sunk to the bed, listening to the dial tone, then sprang back up to pace the room again. Teeth chattering, she sucked in rapid breath after rapid breath. She had fifteen thousand to her name and not a penny more. What was she going to *do*? With unsteady fingers, she pulled the card the detective had given her from her pocket and dialed, then stopped abruptly. Would the kidnappers find out? "I don't know. I don't know what to do," she said out loud as she pressed at the throb in her temple. Every move might be the wrong one. Every move had the potential to harm her sister. Unsure, she stared at the paper in her hand, then shoved it away again. The kidnapper said *no one*.

Alexa studied the cell she'd been given, noting the full battery and three hundred minutes someone had put on the pre-paid phone. They had to have slipped it in her purse when they took Abby from the car. What other explanation was there? Whoever did this planned Abby's abduction carefully, of this she had no doubt. Whoever took Abby knew Alexa's name, what she drove, and more than likely that she was a single mother home alone in the small house in the woods.

She rushed to her door, shut it, and shoved the solid oak dresser in front of it. No one was getting in there with the heavy antique furniture in place. Despite her efforts to reassure herself, she grabbed the baseball bat she kept under her bed. She clutched the Louisville Slugger close as she sat on the mattress and leaned against the headboard, staring at her sister's picture, listening to every creak as the old house settled around her, until the sun's rays brightened the morning sky.

CHAPTER 3

"I'M SORRY, ALEXA. WE'VE RUN your credit. Although you're in good financial standing, you don't make enough to qualify for a loan of this size, especially with your mortgage and two car loans."

"I'll sell the house and the cars. I need this money, Mr. Macabee. I'll pay every dime back." It would take her the rest of her life and a second job—maybe a third, but that didn't matter. "I'll call the realtor right now. We can put the house on the market today. With the improvements I've made—the painting, the front gardens... I have to have this money," she repeated, squeezing her hands together in her lap, trying hard not to sound too desperate. She'd saved for the down payment for her tiny two-bedroom, one-bath fixer-upper for three years. The living room was just big enough for Livy to play, the simple furniture she'd refurbished herself, and her grandmother's piano she treasured. She'd give it all up in a heartbeat for Abby.

"Alexa, let me be frank with you, honey, and it's hard, especially at a time like this with everything you're going through. I've known you since you were a little girl. Your grandmother kept her money in our bank most of her life. Even if you sold the house and yours and Abby's cars, you still wouldn't qualify. You're a one-income household. With the loans you took out to help Abby with her schooling and the medical bills you're still paying after your Gran's last hospitalization... The monthly payments would eat up your entire salary and then some. Teaching's a noble profession, but it doesn't pay much."

Did he think she didn't *know* that? Each month was a struggle to stay afloat financially, but they were making it. As the last of her hope withered away, Alexa closed her eyes and took a deep breath against another torrent of tears. It was on the tip of her tongue to tell Mr. Macabee what the money was for. Surely he would find a way. He'd known her and Abby for as long as she could remember, but she didn't dare. The kidnappers said no one.

She glanced at Livy coloring in the Dora activity book she'd brought along. "Can you run my numbers again? There has to be something..."

Mr. Macabee's pudgy, lined face sagged as he sighed and took her hand. "Alexa, it won't do any good. If there were any way, I'd walk into that vault and hand it over right now. I may work and live in a small town, but I have my suspicions as to what this money's for, honey."

She gripped his hand tight and evaded his gaze. "I'm not sure what you mean."

"Honey, this isn't the way. Even if I could give you the cash, it wouldn't guarantee Abby's safe return. After you hand it over, they may very well ask for more."

Her fingers went lax and she pulled away. "I need her back, Mr. Macabee. I can hardly breathe without her." The heavy weight of living without Abby, of letting her down, was almost more than she could stand. She'd always taken care of her sister; she'd always taken care of everything. Gran's Rheumatoid arthritis had worsened rapidly, disfiguring much of her body, not giving Alexa much of a choice, but she'd never minded. Gran had given them a safe haven from her mother's mental illness.

"Stay in contact with the police, honey. Give them time to do their job. Don't give up hope. We're all praying so hard for Abby's safe return."

Nodding, Alexa struggled to swallow the lump in her throat. She stood up. "Please keep this between us. They might—they might..." She looked at Livy, unable to let herself think about what the kidnappers might do to Abby.

He nodded. "Of course."

Alexa gathered up crayons and shoved them in the box. She couldn't be here anymore. She wanted to lash out at Mr. Macabee, to yank him up by his over-starched collar and demand what she'd come for. He had piles of money just sitting in his vault, stacks of stupid green paper that could save her sister's life, yet he refused.

"Livy, honey, it's time to go."

"Okay, Mommy. Do you like my picture?"

Alexa crouched down, fighting to be in the moment with her little girl. She had to keep herself together for Livy. Everything had to stay as normal as possible. As much as she wanted to fall apart, she would never do to her daughter what her mother had done to her and Abby. "I definitely do. You did such a nice job staying in the lines. We should put this on the fridge when we get home."

Livy gave her a huge grin. Her father's grin.

"We'll tuck this away for now." Alexa closed the coloring book and put it in the small canvas bag. "Come on." She held out her hand, and Livy took it.

"I'm hungry. I want peanut butter and jelly for lunch."

They were low on bread, peanut butter, jelly, and everything else for that matter. They had to go to the store. Her sister was missing, but Alexa had to struggle to keep up with life as it continued to move on. "We need to stop off at the grocery store. You can be my helper."

"I'm a very good helper."

"Yes, you are. The best." Alexa walked out of Mr. Macabee's office and stopped. News vans and eager reporters waited on the steps outside the glass doors. Damn. They weren't supposed to *know*. How did they find her? Did they follow her here? The phone calls had started early in the morning. Now this.

Mr. Macabee stepped up behind her. "Alexa, honey, why don't you go out the back door? Give me your keys. Meet me down the block. We'll get you out of here."

Anger still coursed through her as she faced him, but that would do nothing for Abby. He was willing to help her avoid the press. She would take what little help he offered and find another way to come up with the funds the kidnappers were demanding. How to do that was the big question. The dread of not finding an answer in time curdled her stomach and sent her pulse pounding. "Thank you." She handed him her keys and concentrated on keeping her hand steady as her heart rate continued to soar. Picking up Livy, she hurried out the back door and rushed down the alley toward Old Main Street. She shoved her sunglasses in place and looked down, oblivious to the charm of the small town she'd always loved, avoiding eye contact with anyone she might know.

Within moments, Mr. Macabee showed up in her car, slowed down, and pulled to the curb. "They're full of questions, Alexa. They want this story. They might be able to help you," he said as he rounded the front.

Alexa opened the back door for Livy to crawl in to her booster. She leaned forward and buckled her daughter in. "I can't talk to them. Thank you again, Mr. Macabee." Alexa hurried to the driver's side as she looked down the street, watching one of the reporters watch her. "I have to go." She got in and drove off quickly.

As she made her way to the local grocer, Alexa glanced in her rearview mirror and relaxed a fraction when she saw no one was following. She yearned to turn around and go to the press, to beg for any help they were willing to give, but after the phone call last night she didn't dare. She couldn't afford to be seen anywhere near a reporter.

She and Livy would hurry through the store and get what they needed, then go home and lock out the world. She wanted to check in with Detective Canon and find a way to come up with the money.

Alexa took a right into the shopping plaza and pulled into a parking spot as close to the entrance as possible. She glanced around before she opened her door. The coast was still clear. She opened the back door. "Come on, sweetie, let's—"

"Excuse me, Ms. Harris. I'm Michael Pearson with News Twelve. Can I ask you a few questions about your sister's disappearance?" One of News Twelve's top anchormen ran toward her from the van that had screeched to a stop next to her car.

Alexa glanced into his hungry brown eyes as she pulled a blanket from the backseat and covered Livy's head. Then she scooped her little girl into her arms and hurried toward the door.

"Ms. Harris, can you think of any reason why someone would want to take your sister?"

Alexa quickened her pace as she tucked her face closer to Livy's head, hidden by the soft pink fleece.

"Was Abigail seeing anyone recently?"

"Ms. Harris isn't answering questions at this time," a man said as an arm wrapped around her shoulders.

Startled, Alexa whipped her gaze up to the vaguely familiar voice. Doug Masterson, a blast from her past.

Doug ushered her into the store, grabbed a cart, and

stopped when they stood well away from the windows in the produce aisle. His dark brown hair had thinned a bit, but he was still in excellent shape.

"Doug, thank you so much."

"You're welcome. I saw you get out of the car and watched that guy swarm in on you like the vulture he is. I heard about your troubles, Alexa. I'm sorry for it."

She glanced down as so many memories came crashing back, colliding with the hell of her present. "Thanks. I'm hoping they'll find my sister soon."

"We received the BOLO up in Pittsburg late yesterday afternoon. I was on duty. We're all keeping our eye out."

"I appreciate it." She wanted to tell him about the ransom demand and the phone she kept in her purse, to beg for his help, but she stayed silent as people she saw every day sent her curious glances from sympathetic eyes. No risking Abby. Afraid she might break her own rule, she blurted out the first question that popped into her mind. "What brings you down to Hagerstown?"

"My wife's family lives in Baltimore. We stopped off for a couple of things."

Alexa couldn't help but smile. Doug Masterson, Jack's old college roommate and notorious player. He'd graduated the year before her. It felt like years ago, but really it wasn't that many.

"I haven't seen Jackson in some time. Haven't talked to him either. You two keep in touch?"

Her heart clenched. "Uh, no."

"I see you have yourself a little one here." Doug tugged at the blanket as Olivia yanked the fabric from her head, grinning. Doug's smile brightened for a moment, then faded.

Alexa struggled not to turn, put Livy in the cart, and move away from the questions in Doug's eyes. "We should probably get to our shopping. It was nice to see

28

you again, Doug. Thanks for the help." She set Livy in the back of the cart and waited for her daughter to sit on her bottom.

"Alexa..."

She turned and met his shocked stare, knowing he recognized Olivia's sharply arched brows, dark blonde hair, bright blue eyes, and full mouth with a hint of cupids bow.

"I had no idea. He never said—"

"I need to go, Doug." She started toward the grapes.

"He's not in Pittsburg anymore."

Alexa stopped.

"He moved out to LA three years ago. He works for some fancy bodyguard firm now—Evan Cooke Security or something like that." He shrugged. "Just so you know."

"Thanks. Goodbye, Doug." She turned again, struggling to put the past away—where it belonged.

Alexa stared out the living room window, watching the sun hover closer to the mountains in the distance. The deep country dark would soon surround her house. The dread of another long, sleepless night tightened the muscles of her shoulders and jaw until they ached. She eyed the Louisville Slugger, now leaning against the side table, as she listened to Olivia's happy chatter filling the small space. Livy and her dolls were enjoying the tiny glass teapot Alexa had filled with milk, the apple she had quartered, and the graham crackers she set out for an impromptu after-dinner tea party.

"Mommy, come play with us. You can sit by Lucy."

Alexa turned and gave Livy what smile she could. "Maybe in a little while, sweetie."

29

"The graham cracker is very yummy." Livy held up the golden half of cookie, dangling it like a token bribe, before she took a big bite.

"It looks wonderful, but I have more work to do on the computer."

Livy turned back to her life-sized baby doll and bit Lucy's cracker too as the party began again.

Alexa desperately wanted to join in on the fun but couldn't. There wasn't time. She had just over twenty-four hours to collect an unattainable amount of money. Sighing, she twisted the blind closed and turned away from the window, wishing the media vans were still parked along the dirt road out front. At least someone would've been close by while she waited for daylight again. The fifteen-car pile up on I-81 North sent the reporters and their news crews scattering several hours before. The knocks at the door had ceased. Abby's disappearance had already been forgotten, and she had no choice but to keep it that way.

Alexa glanced at Livy before she sat down to the laptop she'd left on the coffee table. She'd spent the last two hours researching ransom and hostage situations while dodging non-stop phone calls from concerned friends, co-workers, and of course the press. She'd let the answering machine pick them up until the message box was full. She couldn't deal with the questions.

She stared at the article she'd read before she had to put the computer down and walk away. The information had been so troubling, so depressing, she'd had to stop. The odds of Abby coming home were dwindling with every minute passing. Mr. Macabee had been correct; if she could get the money and pay the ransom, the kidnappers were likely to demand more and kill her sister anyway.

Alexa closed her eyes and rubbed her fingers against

the throb in the center of her forehead. What was she going to *do*? The media wasn't an option. The police weren't either. So where did that leave her? She glanced at Livy again, wiggled her mouse, and typed *Evan Cooke Security, LA* into her search engine.

Hits for Ethan Cooke Security popped up instead. She followed the link to the website and studied the company's bold red and black insignia. *World renowned security firm, offering the best in close protection.* Alexa clicked the mouse again and her heart stuttered.

Jack.

There he was among several other well-muscled men in the professional group photo. She moved her finger to his handsome face and traced it as she clutched the charm dangling from her necklace.

"Excuse me. Can you help me?"

Alexa glanced up from the books she was checking back in to the college library computer system and lost her breath as she stared into fantastic blue eyes. "What can I do for you?"

"I have a ten-page paper due for one of my criminal justice classes in—" he glanced at his watch, "less than twelve hours."

She measured his charming smile and ball t-shirt stretched over broad shoulders and mounds of biceps. Her smile dimmed—another dumb jock. Why were the cute ones always a disappointment? She knew her eyes chilled as she answered. "Sounds like a personal problem. The Criminal Justice section is along that wall." She pointed across the room.

At ease and clearly unaffected by her scolding tone, he edged himself along the enormous desk. "So, do you practice that disapproving librarian look in the mirror?"

She refused to give in to her smile. "I might."

31

"You're too young to have that mastered. What are you, a freshman? I've never seen you before."

"I'm a sophomore, and I imagine you haven't. I spend a lot of time in the library." But she'd seen him—Jackson Matthews, junior, football star, frat boy, Mr. Popular with the ladies. Definitely not her type. Not that she actually had a type, because she'd never been on a date. Her grades were too important. Her scholarships were vital.

He grinned. *"I believe I was just insulted."*

She smiled this time and shrugged. *"Maybe."*

"You've gone and hurt my feelings, and I don't even know your name."

"Alexa."

"Alex," he held out his hand. *"Jackson Matthews."*

Her brow shot up as she stared at him. *"I know who you are. And it's Alexa."*

He stood and glanced at his watch again. *"I guess I should get to work. Maybe I'll see you around some time, Alex."* He flashed her another heart-stopping grin and walked toward the stacks she'd pointed out.

She let out a long, shuddering sigh and looked down quickly when he glimpsed over his shoulder and smiled.

The flip-top phone rang, startling Alexa out of her memories. She jumped and caught the laptop just before it crashed to the floor. Licking her lips, she set the computer on the coffee table and picked up the phone. "Hello? Abby?"

"Wrong again, Sister Alexa," the familiar mechanical voice said.

Her stomach clenched with dread. "What—"

"I said no press."

"I didn't talk to them. I swear I didn't. They followed me. Please don't hurt her. Please don't hurt Abby."

"I saw you on the news, Sister Alexa. Grocery

shopping. You look just like her. I had no idea we could've gotten two for the price of one."

She rushed to her feet, grabbed the heavy wooden baseball bat with a trembling hand, and hurried to the entryway to check the lock as her heart rate soared.

"You broke our deal. I'm docking you six hours. You're down to twenty. Tick tock."

"No, I didn't—"

"Twenty hours or we take Olivia next." The line went dead.

Alexa gasped for breath as a terror like she'd never known constricted her chest. Not Livy. Not her Livy. She collapsed on the bottom stair in the landing, listening to her daughter's sweet voice as she continued to play in the next room, oblivious to the danger and turmoil destroying their lives.

Alexa struggled to her feet as her body racked with uncontrollable shudders and tears rushed down her cheeks. They had to go; they had to get out of here. She shoved the heavy bench in front of the door as she had last night and dashed up the steps, yanking a suitcase from the small walk-in storage space. She rushed into Livy's room and pulled clothes from drawers and the closet at random, then hurried into her own room and did the same. She headed for the bathroom next, scooping toothbrushes and toothpaste into the travel bag she had yet to fully unpack from their trip to Virginia Beach.

Alexa started back downstairs but stopped when Gordon, the mournful-looking stuffed frog Livy had slept with every day since her birth, caught her eye. She snatched the melancholy creature off the bed and bolted down the stairs with the cumbersome luggage, setting it by the door. "Livy, we have to go somewhere, sweetie," she struggled to say, still fighting for each

33

breath as adrenaline coursed through her veins.

Livy looked up from her spot at her small pink table. She was dressed in the princess costume Abby had made her for Christmas. "I'm having a party, Mommy."

"I know, honey. I'm sorry, but we really have to go right now." She flipped her laptop closed, dropped it into its case, and grabbed her purse. Next she took several of Livy's books and shoved them into a small canvas bag. "Come on. Let's go."

Livy's bottom lip turned down and her eyes filled with tears. "Lucy wants to eat her apples. I want to play tea party."

"Later, honey." Alexa glanced out at the darkening sky through the edge of the blind. She wanted them long gone from their isolated home. "You can bring your princess dress with you."

Livy's eyes brightened. "Okay."

She held out her hand. "Let's go."

Two hours later, Alexa clutched Olivia's hand as they walked through Baltimore-Washington International, rolling the suitcase and booster seat behind them. She glanced around as they made their way to the ticket counter, fearful Abby's kidnappers were somewhere close, watching for the perfect opportunity to snatch her daughter away.

"Can I help you, ma'am?" The pretty blonde smiled from behind her computer.

Alexa peered behind her, spotting the two men dressed in black pants and short-sleeved tops standing by the enormous panes of glass, staring in her direction. She picked up Olivia and clutched her tight. Were they here for Livy? "Yes. I need to buy two tickets."

"And your destination, ma'am?"

What *was* her destination? She hadn't thought that far. Her only instinct had been to flee. There was nowhere to go and no one to pick her up on the other end. She and Abby had always had each other, but now she was on her own. She moved her free hand to her necklace and rested her palm against the triangular charm. "LA," she said in a rush. "Two tickets to Los Angeles, please."

"We have a couple of open seats on a redeye leaving in an hour."

She glanced over her shoulder. The men were gone, but that didn't mean Livy was safe. "Okay, we'll take them."

The agent told her her total, and she tried not to wince. This was going to eat into her already strained budget, but what choice did she have? Money meant nothing with Livy's life in danger. She pulled her credit card free and her heart ripped in two. To save her daughter, she was leaving Maryland and her sister behind.

CHAPTER 4

ALEXA CUT LIVY'S WAFFLE AS her daughter bit into another slice of banana.

"Mmm, good."

"Save some of those pieces for your waffles, silly girl." Alexa smiled and winked, trying desperately to hold on for Olivia. She hadn't slept in three days. The mental and physical exhaustion were taking their toll.

Livy grinned with her mouth full and her pretty blue eyes still sleepy.

"Here, sweetie, eat up." She pushed the plate of Belgian waffles in front of Olivia. "We have to leave after breakfast."

Alexa peered over her shoulder—a new habit—still fearful for Olivia's safety. She studied the man sitting alone in the corner sipping his coffee while he read his paper. Was he just another weary traveler catching up on the news, or was he here to watch her daughter? Had she been followed to LA? Alexa had lain in bed after they checked in to their hotel at two a.m., listening to every sound, terrified that the men who'd grabbed Abby would break down the door and snatch Olivia away. Even the chair she'd propped under the doorknob had done little to soothe her fraying nerves.

Alexa spooned up cereal and shuddered over the first bite. Her stomach was raw and her head aching with the beginnings of a migraine. She swallowed the whole-wheat flakes, fighting the need to gag. She couldn't keep Olivia safe or continue to function without food.

As Olivia shoveled fruit and syrupy bread into her mouth, Alexa pulled her laptop from her case and woke the computer from sleep mode. Ethan Cooke Security's webpage still filled the screen. She clicked the *meet our agents* tab and scrolled down. Jackson's bold blue eyes stared into hers. She skimmed his short bio: resident of LA for over three years, former Pittsburgh police officer, graduated with honors from Europe's most elite bodyguard school, top-ranking agent specializing in sight survey/risk assessment.

Her gaze wandered to his picture again. Time hadn't changed him much. He was still gorgeous, still perfect. His dark blond hair was shorter and cleaner cut than it had been when she knew him. His shoulders were broader, his biceps slightly larger. His tan told her he hadn't lost his love of the great outdoors.

She traced her finger over his arched brows; his square chin, a little more defined without the softness of youth; and his full lips with their hint of a cupids bow, remembering how they felt against hers.

"Thank you."

Alexa whirled from the stack of books when a firm body pressed against her back and a white rose appeared in front of her face. Her breasts brushed Jack's chest as she stared into eyes inches from her own. She cleared her throat as her pulse pounded, and she attempted to step back but slammed into the bookshelf instead. God, he made her nervous. "For—for what?"

A slow smile played over his mouth. "For this." He pulled stapled papers from behind him. "I nailed this assignment because you helped me." He stepped closer, and she was trapped.

"I—" she cleared her throat again when her word came out on a whisper. "I just pointed you in the

37

right direction."

"No, that was the first paper. For this one you sat down with me."

He'd come to the library every Monday, Wednesday, and Friday evening over the last month, doing his homework, talking to her, asking her for some sort of help or other.

"I think my parents might cry with joy when they see my grades this semester."

"It's amazing what you can do when you actually apply yourself."

He grinned and moved closer until she swallowed and pressed a hand to his chest. *"Let me take you out."*

A commotion erupted in the front lobby before she could answer. *"Yo, Jackson, let's go, man. It's party time."* The group of football players filing into the library followed up 'party time' with obnoxious hoots and hollers.

"I'll be there in a minute. Head on over without me," he tossed over his shoulder.

The room grew silent as his teammates left.

"Come on, Alex. Let me take you out."

She'd been ready to say yes before his friends came in and reminded her she and Jackson were from different planets. *"Sorry, I can't. I have to work."* She pushed at his chest, skirting away from the torturous pleasure of breathing him in.

"The library closed two minutes ago."

"I need to study," she evaded as she walked to the desk.

He followed. *"It's Friday night."*

She turned. *"Look, Jack, I—"*

"Jack?" He grinned.

She shrugged, embarrassed. *"Yes. If you insist on calling me Alex, then I'm calling you Jack. It's only fair."*

He chuckled. *"I think I'm half in love with you."*

She studied him as he said what she felt. He'd sucked her in from the beginning with his great looks, happy-go-lucky attitude, and that smile that made her stomach flutter every time he flashed one in her direction. But more than that, she was in love with his brain. To her surprise he was extremely intelligent and fascinating. Alexa dismissed Jack's comment as Jack joking around—like he always did.

"Come on, Alex."

"I'm sorry. I don't party. I have no interest in watching you get slobbering drunk while you act like an idiot along with the rest of your moronic friends."

He frowned and gave a chuckle. "Ouch."

She jerked her shoulders in frustration. If only they were different people. "I need to lock up. You should go."

"How about a slice of pizza and a walk?"

The idea of walking and talking with Jack on a cool October evening was a bit too appealing. She struggled for another excuse. "I—I don't have a jacket."

He pulled the black fleece he was wearing over his head. "Problem solved."

She stared at his tough athletic frame and disagreed. Her problems were just beginning. "Okay, Jack. Half an hour."

"Sold." He held out his hand, and she hesitated before she took it.

Thirty minutes turned into three hours. They strolled down the sidewalk to her dorm, still holding hands. This was the first time she'd walked the campus at midnight. She was always in her room by ten at the latest.

"So, was it painful?"

She glanced at him as they took the stairs to her building. "What?"

"Spending time with me."

"Anything's tolerable after a slice of pepperoni pizza."

He chuckled.

She grinned. "I had fun."

"Good." They walked up the last step to the glass double doors. Then, in a lightning change of mood, Jack's smile disappeared as he turned her to him and stared into her eyes. "I want to do this again. Go out with me tomorrow after the game. Come watch me play." His fingers tickled her neck as his thumb traced her jaw line. "I can't get you out of my head."

"I..." She couldn't think over the tingles of sensation coursing through her body. She'd never been touched like this before.

"Alex," he whispered as he moved closer and pressed his lips to hers.

The shock of firm warmth had her eyes widening, but she soon closed them. She gripped his solid forearms as his mouth sought hers again. His lips parted and his tongue met and brushed hers.

She forgot to be nervous as the pleasure of the moment quieted her busy brain. Jack pulled her closer, and she relaxed her grip, savoring his hard body pressed to hers. Hesitantly, she moved her palms over his firm biceps and rested her hands on his muscular shoulders. A small hum of pleasure escaped her throat as he combed his fingers through her long hair and his bold flavor consumed her. She wanted the sweet moment to last forever, but he eased away and smiled.

She'd never been kissed; she was completely inexperienced when it came to men, but as she stared into his eyes, captivated, she knew she would never want anyone but him. Caught up, Alexa pressed her hand to his cheek. "Handsome Jack," she whispered.

He skimmed his fingers over hers. "Go out with me tomorrow."

She nodded, unable to speak.

"I'm full, mommy."

Livy's plate brushed Alexa's knuckles. "Huh?" She blinked and looked at her daughter.

"I don't want any more waffles. My tummy's full."

"Oh. Okay." Alexa shook her head, determined to put the past away and focus on her little girl. She picked up a napkin, dipped the corner in the paper cup filled with water, and wiped the sticky syrup from Livy's cheeks and chin.

She berated herself as she cleaned up the small mess they'd left on the table. She couldn't afford to get lost in memories while her family was in danger. Livy and Abby were her only priority. She glanced at Jack's picture one last time, scribbled down the address for Ethan Cooke Security's office, and closed the laptop. "We need to get going, honey." Her twenty-hour deadline was quickly coming to an end. She was running out of time to save her sister.

As they walked to the elevator, Alexa gripped Livy's hand, waiting, expecting someone to follow. She sighed her relief when the doors slid closed and they remained alone. Livy giggled and grabbed her stomach as the elevator began its quick ascent. "My belly's giggly."

Alexa smiled. "We're almost there." When the doors opened, she peered out, ready to scream if necessary. They were still alone. She hurried them down the hall and let them into the third-story room. Safely inside, Alexa secured the chain and shoved the chair back under the knob, then gathered their items together and pulled the travel tote from the suitcase. "Livy, we need to brush our teeth, then you can watch a cartoon for a couple of minutes."

"Okay."

She glanced at the door, then she flicked on the

bathroom light and stared at her drawn face, pale complexion, and weary eyes. She couldn't go into a place of business like this. If she wanted to be taken seriously, wanted help, she would need to appear professional, as if she had herself together, not like she was one shaky step away from a nervous breakdown. The fear from that alone had her gripping the counter. She met her own eyes in the mirror and reminded herself that she wasn't her mother.

"I'm ready, mommy."

"Okay. Come on up." She lifted Livy to the counter. "Let's brush those pearly whites."

With Livy's teeth clean and her face properly washed, Alexa pulled her cosmetics from the bag—the full arsenal would be necessary today. She applied powder foundation, blusher, eyeliner, mascara, and lip-gloss, masking the worst of her fatigue. "Better. Not great, but better," she muttered as she shoved her items away. She smoothed down her fitted white short-sleeve top and gray tailored slacks over her slender frame—professional and sleek. She appeared strong and capable, even if she didn't feel it. She turned off the light and the glint of her necklace caught her eye. She twisted the triangular charm until it rested on her back, then she grabbed her tote. Livy's favorite Nick Jr. cartoon was ending as Alexa stepped from the bathroom—perfect timing. "Time to go, Livy."

"Where are we going, mommy?"

"To visit...a friend." A man who'd been her whole world for two and a half years of her life. But that didn't matter anymore—couldn't, yet as she stared at her pretty little girl, a miniature of her father, she knew it would. Their lives were about to be ripped apart—again. This wasn't how it was supposed to be, but this is the way it was. She never thought she would see Jack again, but Abby's disappearance and the threats against Livy changed that. She needed help. His help. There was nowhere else to turn. With few options, she gathered the luggage, took her daughter's hand, and walked out the door.

One more plane change, three more hours, and he would be home. He was ready. Jackson sat back in his seat, waiting for the airline to announce his flight. The two-week checkup on the Appalachia Project had been more than enough for him. The locals were downright pissed that the Feds and agents of Ethan Cooke Security were messing in their business. He'd been shot at twice deep in the back woods of eastern Kentucky. The working environment was hostile and dangerous at best. He didn't envy his co-workers continued stay.

His phone vibrated against his hip as the attendant called flight 2885 for Los Angeles. He glanced at the readout, grinned, and pressed 'talk.' "Hey, Ev."

"Hello, gorgeous. Should I still expect you home this afternoon?"

"Give me four hours and I'm all yours."

"I've got big plans. I can't wait to show you what I've done around the house."

"Can't wait to see it. I have to go. We're boarding. I'll see you soon."

"Love you."

"You too."

Jackson powered off his phone and pulled his boarding pass free, thinking of Evelyn. They'd dated off and on over the last year. When he came back from Mexico three months ago, they picked things up again. During a long weekend away in April, he decided to take the plunge and ask her to move in with him. Evelyn was beautiful and intelligent—a paralegal for one of LA's most prestigious law firms. They got along great, had a ton of fun, so why not?

After his return from Cozumel, he hadn't been able to stop thinking about his conversation with Hailey on the beach. While Hailey had worried she and Austin wouldn't work things out, he had realized he'd been stuck on one woman for too long. Alex had moved on with her life, but he'd never let her go. Four years of regrets and longing was more than enough.

If he still thought of that stunning smile, those dark blue eyes, and the endless yards of soft black hair, he chose to ignore it. Evelyn loved him. This was his chance to look to the future and leave the past behind.

Jackson took his seat on the plane and buckled in, deciding he would stop off for a bouquet of flowers before he headed home.

CHAPTER 5

A LEXA'S STOMACH TWISTED INTO PAINFUL knots as the elevator climbed higher. The ride to the thirty-fourth floor dragged on for ages—or so it seemed. She tapped her foot in a rapid beat, trying to alleviate the worst of the anxiety wreaking havoc on her system. The dread of the messy scene she anticipated was almost unbearable. *God, what am I doing?*

The elevator beeped, and Alexa jumped as the door slid open. She took Olivia's hand and they stepped into the lobby. She glanced at the information plaque on the wall and immediately recognized the bold black and red insignia of Ethan Cooke Security among the other businesses listed. Suite 3405. Squaring her shoulders, she led Livy down the hall, rolling the suitcase and booster seat behind them. They approached the office door, and Alexa took a deep, shuddering breath, then wiped her damp palm on her slacks and grabbed for the knob. "Here we go," she said to Livy with a smile she didn't feel.

"Here we go," Livy repeated.

They stepped into the receptionist's area, and Alexa fought the urge to turn around and flee. She gripped the luggage handle tighter, struggling to remember her purpose over the drumbeat of her heartbeat echoing in her head. This was about Abby and Olivia—only Abby and Olivia.

The pretty brunette in her trim navy office attire smiled. "Good morning. Can I help you?"

"Um, yes. I was wondering if I might be able to speak with Jack—" Alexa shook her head. "Jackson Matthews. It's urgent."

"I'm sorry, Mr. Matthews is out of town until later today."

A new kind of dread ripped at her stomach as she realized her last hope had just died away.

"Would you like to leave a message for him? If this is an emergency, I'd be happy to page his company phone."

Now what? Alexa could barely think over her racing mind. "When—when did you say he would be back?"

"Let's take a look." The receptionist's fingers flew over her keyboard. "Mr. Matthew's flight should arrive right around 12:30."

By the time Jack landed, it would be four-thirty in Maryland. That barely left her any time to find a way to save her sister and protect her daughter. What was she going to do? She couldn't go home. They would find her—if they hadn't followed her already. She didn't have any family to turn to. There was no place else to go.

The reality of her dire situation and stress of the last three days snuck up to overwhelm her. Her throat constricted and her head went light as small black dots floated in front of her eyes. "I'm sorry. I need to sit down," she said weakly as she rushed to the leather furnishings across the reception area, pulling Olivia with her.

"Ma'am, are you all right? Let me get you something to drink." The receptionist leaped up from her seat and hurried to the mini-fridge, grabbing a bottle of water. She twisted off the cap. "Go ahead and take a sip. Mr. Cooke, could you come out here please?"

Alexa swallowed the refreshingly cool liquid and took a deep breath as Livy snuggled close to her side. "Mommy."

"I'm okay, honey." She wrapped her arm around her worried little girl and kissed her forehead. "I just need to rest for a minute." Officially at her breaking point, Alexa snuggled her daughter closer, refusing to give in to despair. She would be strong for Olivia. "Really, I'm all right," Alexa said to reassure the concerned, frowning woman hovering in front of her. "I'm sorry if I frightened you. Please don't disturb Mr. Cooke. We're going to go."

Alexa managed to stand up as a breathtakingly handsome man with black hair, gray eyes, and a fabulous physique stepped into the room. "Mia, what's going on?"

"Our guest seems a little unwell."

"I'm fine. I apologize for bothering you both." Alexa gripped the edge of the couch, struggling to stay upright, bound and determined to leave without causing any more of a scene. This had been a mistake, a monumentally *huge* mistake. Her desperation had made her rash and foolish. Why she thought Jack would be able to help her in the first place... Leaving without seeing him was for the best. "Come on, Livy. Let's go."

"I'm Ethan Cooke. Is there something I can help you with?"

"She's looking for Jackson," Mia supplied.

Mr. Cooke's gaze zeroed in on Livy. He did a double take before he met Alexa's eyes.

Alexa hurried for the door and grabbed the suitcase on her way past the receptionist's desk, realizing Mr. Cooke had already figured it out. "No, actually, we were just leaving. Again, I'm sorry we bothered you."

The door opened, and a beautiful blonde walked in, smiling at Mr. Cooke. "Hi." She extended her smile to Mia and Alexa. "Hello."

"Hi. If you'll excuse us, we were on our way out." She gave the blonde a small smile as she skirted past her and headed for the door, fighting with the uncooperative luggage and booster seat.

"Wait." Mr. Cooke rushed forward. "Please wait. Jackson will be back in two hours, three at the most. If you have an emergency, maybe I can help."

It was tempting, too tempting to tell him everything, to share some of the weight of the situation that left her floundering. She was in so far over her head, but what if he called the police? "No. No. Everything's fine. Thank you." She twisted the knob.

"Sarah, help me out here."

The blonde stepped forward and placed her hand on Alexa's shoulder. "We would love to—"

The flip-phone rang in Alexa's purse, and she stopped in her tracks. She rummaged through her bag frantically and clutched hold of the small cell when she found it and pressed 'talk.' "Abby?"

"Always so hopeful." The mechanical voice taunted.

Alexa glanced around at her audience, then turned away. "Let me speak to her," she whispered. "Let me hear that she's okay."

"Get me the money, Sister Alexa. You're running out of time."

"Wait." But the line went dead. Alexa squeezed her eyes shut, desperate to hold her tears at bay. She couldn't crumble now, not with everyone watching. She clutched the doorknob in a vice grip as she fought for composure.

A gentle hand rested on her shoulder again, and Sarah spoke. "Please, come sit down for a minute."

Alexa shook her head. "I really can't," she choked out.

"Jackson's a good friend of ours. We'd like to help you until he gets back."

Alexa turned, meeting her kind blue eyes. "I appreciate it, but we were on our way out. I need to

get us a hotel room and book us a flight for first thing tomorrow." Where they would go and what they would do now, she had no idea. She needed the night to think everything through and find a way to secure more money than she would ever see in this lifetime. She needed a couple hours to rest. Her body begged for sleep.

"Why don't you come home with me? We have a little girl, Kylee, right around your daughter's age, and a five month old, Emma. Kylee's three-and-a-half."

"I'm Olivia and I'm three-and-a-half," Olivia supplied with pride.

Sarah crouched to Livy's level. "We have a big swing set and a huge playroom Kylee would love to share with you."

"Mommy, I want to play with Kylee." Her eyes brightened with excitement.

Alexa stared down at her little girl. How could she say no when her daughter had so little joy to look forward to? When would she have another opportunity to play with someone her own age? Alexa glanced at Ethan Cooke, recognizing him from the group picture he and Jack had posed in with several other bodyguards. She looked at Sarah, who she assumed was Ethan's wife. These people weren't dangerous, of that she was sure. Olivia would be safe in the Cooke home. For an hour she wouldn't have to look over her shoulder or worry that someone was going to snatch her little girl away. She could *think*. "Okay, we can play with Kylee."

"I have my own princess dress. Auntie Ab made it for Christmas." Olivia grinned—her father's grin.

Alexa winced as Sarah's gaze flew from her daughter to Ethan. She glanced at her wristwatch. They would stay and play with Kylee for a little while and be gone before Jack ever knew she was here.

Jackson's plane touched down with a sway and rush of breaks. He gathered his carry-on as the jet taxied down the runway. They were early—only five minutes—but it beat the hell out of being late. He wanted home, his own bed, but more than that he looked forward to making good on an idea that struck him thirty minutes before landing. Evelyn was going to love it.

An hour later, after hurrying through the airport and stopping off to pick up 'the surprise,' he sped along Ten West, checking his messages.

"Jackson, it's Ethan. Give me a call as soon as you can. It's important."

He wanted to ignore Ethan for twenty-four hours and forget the demands of the job for one night while he spent a quiet evening alone with Evelyn, but if Ethan said it was important, it was important. Jackson dialed Ethan's direct line as the small fur ball in his lap yipped. He scratched the eight-week-old golden retriever/lab mix between the ears. "We're almost there."

"Cooke."

"It's Jackson. What's up?"

"You home?"

"On my way." He merged on Highway One.

"Can you stop by the house first?"

"Not really. I have something for Evelyn."

"There's a woman there with Sarah. Her daughter's playing with Kylee. She came to the office looking for you. Said it was an emergency. I think she's in some sort of trouble."

A woman with a kid? "Who the hell is she? I don't know a woman with a kid. What's her name?"

"She was pretty close-mouthed. I've been in meetings since she and Sarah left. I haven't had a chance to call and check in. Her daughter introduced herself as Olivia."

"Olivia... Olivia..." He racked his brain trying to place a woman with a daughter named Olivia. "It's not ringing any bells, man."

"Jackson, Olivia looks just like... Why don't you drop by real quick? The lady was hell bent on leaving. You might've already missed her, but like I said, she's in trouble."

Jackson let loose a sigh. "I'll stop in. Thanks, man."

"Take a couple days. I downloaded your reports on the Appalachia Project—very thorough. We'll meet at nine Tuesday morning."

"Sounds good." Jackson hung up. "Son of a bitch." It was tempting to assume the mystery lady had already gone on her way, but curiosity got the better of him. A woman with a daughter named Olivia? He had no idea.

Minutes later, Jackson pulled through Ethan's gate and waited for the wrought iron to close behind him before he continued down the drive. He rolled to a stop behind Sarah's sedan, and his new pup sat up in the passenger seat, tongue lolling. "Let's go solve a mystery," Jackson said in an excellent imitation of Scooby Doo. The puppy yapped and licked Jackson's chin. Grinning, he scooped the dog up and got out. "You liked that, huh?" The pup yipped again. "Damn, you're cute. Evelyn's going to melt when she gets a look at you. You're major brownie points, man, but not if I'm late." Jackson punched his home number in to his phone and started toward the door.

"Hello?"

"Hey, Ev. I'm in town but I'm running a little behind."

"Okay. When do you think you'll be here?"

"I'm making a quick stop by Ethan's. I'm thinking half an hour, maybe forty-five minutes at the latest."

"Hurry, gorgeous. I'm waiting," she purred.

CATE BEAUMAN

"Give me twenty, Ev." He hung up, eager to get this impromptu visit over with, and rang the bell. Moments later, Sarah answered.

"Hi, Jackson." Sarah smiled. "Who do you have there?"

"This is Mutt. I picked him up from the SPCA. He's a surprise for Evelyn."

"Oh, well he's a sweetheart."

Bear and Reece, Ethan and Sarah's golden mastiffs, rushed to the door, sniffing the air.

"Hey, boys!" He extended his hand, giving the huge, well-trained dogs the customary rub behind the ears. He'd spent plenty of time with Bear and Reece on more than one assignment. "Do you guys smell fresh meat?" Jackson grinned. "Let the socializing begin." He held Mutt down for Bear and Reece to sniff. Mutt began to tremble as big black noses investigated every inch of him. Mutt let out a frightened yip and peed in Jackson's hand. "Well, son of a bitch."

Sarah burst out laughing. "Come on in, Jackson. Let's get you cleaned up. I'll take Mutt." She grabbed Mutt from Jackson's one arm hold. "Boys, go out and play," she pointed outside, and the dogs ran off like a shot.

With the commotion over, Jackson stepped inside and glanced at his watch. "Sarah, what's going on? Ethan called and said some woman stopped by the office looking for me—now she's here?"

"Yes, she's on the couch."

"Hold on." He walked into the bathroom and scrubbed his hands, rinsed, and wiped them on the towel. "Better." He flashed her a grin before they started down the hall. "Who is she? Ethan said—" Jackson peeked in the living room, trying to catch a glimpse, and stopped dead. He couldn't believe his eyes. "Alex," he

52

muttered in disbelief. Alex was here, asleep on Ethan and Sarah's couch. He looked at Sarah. "Alex is here."

"Yes, she is. She's in trouble, Jackson. She needs help."

He walked further into the room, still in shock. "Jackson, are you okay?"

"I don't... I'm not..." He shook his head as he stared at Alex. She was no longer just beautiful. The years had turned her amazing looks into something striking. Her cheekbones were more defined, and her lashes went on for miles. He'd forgotten how impossibly long they were. And her hair, it was different, still straight and shiny black, just longer. He stepped closer, desperately wanting to touch and run his hands through her silky locks the way he used to. The rest of her body was as glorious as he remembered—willowy and perfect in her form-fitting clothes. In a matter of seconds, four years vanished.

"Should I—should I wake her up?" He asked, shaken, unsure of what to do as the woman he'd loved for most of his adult life lay before him, restful in sleep.

"You might want to. She planned to leave a couple of hours ago, but I didn't have the heart to wake her. She was just holding herself together at the office. She's exhausted and on edge. We didn't have much of a chance to talk. I went to get us some iced tea and sandwiches; when I came back, she was asleep. I'm not exactly sure what's going on, but I know her daughter's absolutely adorable. She's a smart little thing."

He crouched down next to Alex and breathed her in. She smelled the same, like vanilla and flowers.

"Mutt and I will go check on the girls. They're going to love him."

"Yeah, okay." He barely heard Sarah as he reached out, hesitating before brushing his fingers against Alex's soft, warm cheek. Never ever did he think he would do this again. "Alex," he whispered.

When she didn't respond, he swept the black tresses from her forehead and caressed his knuckles against her temple, taking her in, afraid he would wake up and she would be gone. "Alex," he repeated, and her lashes fluttered open. He stared into sleepy, dark blue eyes—eyes he knew as well as his own. He'd never been able to forget them.

"Jack." She brought her hand to his cheek, resting her palm against his skin as she smiled. "Jack."

Was this really happening? "You're here."

"Mmm."

He pressed his hand to hers and laced their fingers together, savoring the feel of her. He'd lived without her for so long. He smiled back. "Alex, what are you doing here?"

The dreamy look vanished from her gaze as she blinked and shot up to sitting position, yanking her hand from his. "Jack." She scurried up from the couch and stood. "What are you doing here? Where *am* I? Where's Livy? Abby." She rushed to the doorway in a panic. "Livy?"

She was three steps into the hall before he grabbed her arm and pulled her back. "Alex, you're still half asleep. Take a deep breath. Your daughter's okay. Sarah's taking care of her. Everything's fine."

She tugged herself free and glanced at her watch as she sat down on the edge of a chair, jamming her fingers through her hair. "Everything's *not* fine. It's 1:45. I'm almost out of time."

"Almost out of time for what?"

"They took Abby. Someone took Abby."

He hurried forward and crouched in front of her. "Who took Abby?"

She shrugged and rested her face in her hands. "I don't know who they are. They want a quarter of a million dollars in just a few hours or they're going to kill her, then they're coming to take my Livy." Her voice broke.

"Good Christ, Alex. Did you contact the police?"

"I did initially when I watched a couple of men drag my sister away at the rest stop, but not when they called demanding money two days ago."

"So, you got a ransom call Friday night?"

"Yes, although I guess it was technically very early Saturday morning." She spoke fairly calmly while she clasped her fingers together until her knuckles whitened.

He took her cold hand in his, wanting to comfort her. "What exactly did they say?"

"They told me if I talk to the cops or media, they'll kill Abby. I wanted to call the detective, but I didn't dare. I'm supposed to leave the money in my savings account. They said they would take it from there."

"What's our exact timeframe here?"

"They said the deadline was Monday. Two a.m."

"Okay. Let me make some calls." He stood, ready to get to work. They didn't have much time.

"It *was* Monday," she repeated. "Now I have until eight o'clock Eastern time tonight. They saw me dodging news cameras and docked me six hours as punishment." She sniffled, and a tear raced down her cheek. "They also said they would take Livy next. I don't know what to do."

Jackson rubbed his thumb and finger over his eyebrows as he stared at the floor. How the hell was he supposed to fix this in two hours? He remembered pretty little Abby. She'd always been so free and fun, much more relaxed than Alex, but she'd also had far less to worry about than her big sister. "Do you have the detective's number?"

"Yes, of course. His card is in my purse." She hurried over to the suitcase and child safety seat in the corner of the room and yanked up her bag, then pulled out the business card and flip phone. "The kidnapper has been calling me on this. They must've put it in my purse when they took Abby. The battery's running low." She handed off the cell with trembling fingers. "I should've called Detective Canon." She walked to the enormous picture windows facing the mighty Pacific. "I've been so scared—frantic. I didn't know what to do. There was no one to ask, no one to..." She shook her head. "Abby's going to die because I didn't do what I should have. My sister's going to die, and they're going to take my baby."

He stepped up behind her and placed his hands on her rigid, slender shoulders. "Everything's going to be okay, Alex. Let me make some calls." It more than likely wasn't going to be all right. They'd probably already killed Abby, or certainly would, but how could he tell her that? One step at a time. "Why don't you go find Sarah. The playroom's down the hall. I'll see what I can do to get this figured out."

She nodded and turned. "Okay. But I need the phone back. I have to keep it with me. They might call."

Shrieks of laughter echoed from down the hall. Suddenly Mutt ran into the room, tail tucked between his legs, as two bullets with blonde hair followed.

"Mutt, come here," Kylee giggled.

The girl with darker blond hair, shorter than Kylee and wearing a striped pink top and jean shorts, crouched down and peeked under the couch. "We just want to pet you, cute little puppy!"

Jackson got on his hands and knees in an attempt to rescue his dog. "Let's get him out of there. Out you go, Mutt. You can come with me." He pulled his trembling dog out from under the furniture and clutched the pup close to his chest. "There you go."

He smiled as the little blonde tilted her head up, grinning. His smile fell away as he stared.

"Mutt is cute. I like him very much," she said as she petted him. Her soft fingers touched Jackson's with each stroke. "He's just a baby. We have to be gentle," she went on.

This was Alex's daughter, Olivia. Olivia had his eyebrows and eyes, his mouth, his short nose that turned up at the tip just a touch, his hair color for God's sake.

"Alex?" He glanced from his tiny mirror image to her mother.

Alex's eyes filled as they met his.

Heart pounding, reeling from utter shock, he rushed to his feet. "Alex?"

Sarah stepped in the silent room. "Girls, let's take Mutt to the kitchen. We'll have a snack and get him a drink of water."

The girls clasped hands and ran off, making as much noise as they had when they entered the room. Sarah took Mutt from Jackson as he stared at Alex, the woman he'd yearned for, the mother of his child. "She's mine."

Alex said nothing as she tore her gaze from his and looked at the floor.

"She's mine," he snapped as embers of anger sparked to life.

She nodded. "Yes. Olivia's your daughter."

Although he'd seen her for himself, hearing Alex's confirmation was another jolt, adding to the flames of resentment. "How could you do this? How could you keep her from me?" He bit off each word.

She looked up as tears ran down her cheeks. "You

broke things off before I found out. If I was too much of a complication in your life... I didn't think you'd want her."

"I didn't want *you*, Alex." He spewed out a venomous lie. "I didn't want you. How old is she? How old is my daughter?"

"Three and a half. She was born on your birthday."

He turned away as grief mixed with furry. He'd had a daughter for three-and-a-half years—and yearned for her mother the entire time. They could've been a family. He could've had everything he'd ever wanted. Now they were both here in this house, but it felt like they were still miles apart. The ironic injustice knocked him back another step.

His cellphone rang. He glanced at the readout. Evelyn. He closed his eyes and reached for his phone. "Hey, Ev."

"Is everything okay? Where are you?"

"I'm still at Sarah and Ethan's."

"I thought you said twenty minutes."

"I know I did. Ev, I've run in to a few...issues. I won't be home for a while yet." He watched Alex turn to the window.

"Do you want me to come over? You sound upset."

Dear God, that was exactly what he *didn't* need. "No. I'll be home later. I'll explain everything then. I've gotta go."

"Okay. I love you."

"You too." He shoved his phone away.

Alex whirled around, rushed forward, and snatched the detective's business card from his grip. "Go home, Jack." She grabbed her luggage and started toward the hall. "Your 'issues' just cleared up."

He snagged her arm and yanked her back. "What are you doing? Where are you going?"

"This was a mistake." She moved her shoulder, attempting to free herself. "I shouldn't have come to Los Angeles. Let me go."

He tightened his grip, realizing he couldn't do as she asked. Now that she was here, he didn't know how he would let her go again. "Not yet."

"I don't have time for this. My sister needs help. I need to get out of here."

"So, what, I'm just supposed to let you walk away? That's my daughter laughing down the hall."

"I assure you no one knows that more than I do. I won't keep her from you, Jack, but I have bigger problems to deal with right now." She tried to pull free again. "I have to get to the airport."

A rush of panic surged through his veins. He was losing her again. "Like hell. You said they threatened to take Olivia. You're not thinking clearly."

Heat replaced the weariness in her eyes, and she took a step closer. "Don't you dare, Jack. Don't you dare insinuate that I would ever put my daughter in danger. I've been taking care of Livy all by myself since the beginning. We've done just fine so far."

And didn't that burn his ass? They would and could go on without him, as they had all along. Well, not anymore. "Where're you going to go?"

"I don't know yet. We'll probably travel for a while until the detective assures me it's safe to go back to Maryland."

"Come to my house," he blurted out. "I want you and Olivia to come to my house. Let me get to know my daughter while this mess gets straightened out. It could be months before it's safe. I'll help you with Abby. Give me a chance to be with Olivia." He desperately wanted to sit with that tiny little girl again and pet the puppy while she smiled at him.

"I don't think your wife will approve."

"Wife? I don't have a..." Evelyn. He kept forgetting about Evelyn. "Evelyn is my girlfriend."

"I can't imagine she'll be thrilled to have your college ex and long-lost daughter under her roof."

"Evelyn's an amazing woman. She'll understand after I talk to her." A small, nasty thrill coursed up his spine when Alex flinched as he complimented his current lover.

She shook her head. "This isn't a good idea."

Anger still ruled him as he pulled her closer. "You owe me, Alex." Their bodies brushed and their eyes locked. "You owe me three and a half years I can never get back."

She stared at him for several seconds, then nodded. "Okay."

"Let me call the detective and talk to Ev, then we'll go." He released Alex from his grip and walked off, trying to digest the huge change his life had just taken, while he struggled to ignore the familiar scent of vanilla and flowers that had haunted him for years.

CHAPTER 6

ALEXA RAN HER HAND ALONG Mutt's soft, golden fur as Jack drove his Lexus through yet another neighborhood. The Los Angeles area was overwhelmingly huge and the car ride painfully long and tense. She slid him a glance while she fought to keep her foot from tapping away her endless supply of nervous energy. Jack's brooding silence and furrowed brows made the uncomfortable drive almost unbearable. He was so *mad*. Jack rarely got angry—he was too busy being funny—but on the rare occasion he did, it wasn't pretty. Four years hadn't changed that.

"Mommy, are we there?"

Alexa peered over her shoulder and attempted a smile. "Soon, honey."

"I want to play with Mutt. Jack, I *want* to *play* with *Mutt*." Olivia brimmed with excitement.

Alexa winced when Jack seared her with a look as their daughter called him 'Jack.' Dear God, this was messy. As messy as she'd feared it would be.

"Just a couple more turns and we'll be home," he said.

Home. They were going home with Jack. This was so surreal. She'd imagined the three of them together more times than she could count, but now that they were, it wasn't the warm, loving experience she'd woven into dreams on so many lonely nights.

Livy had no idea the stranger with the puppy was her father. Jack had barely spoken since they left

Ethan and Sarah's estate, except to say tersely that the detective would call him back. They were going to a house where Jack's girlfriend waited for their arrival. No, this wasn't what she'd hoped for at all—not that she'd ever planned on any of this in the first place. After Jack broke things off, she'd fully expected to raise their daughter on her own.

Sighing, Alexa stared out the window, taking in the massive palm trees, bright in the warm California sun. She struggled to focus on anything but the unending complications of late. She'd worked so hard to give Livy and herself a quiet, simple life, free from the worries that had plagued her throughout her youth. She'd succeeded until their bubble of tranquility burst Friday evening at the isolated Maryland rest stop.

Moments later, Jack turned into a driveway, pulling up to a charming, smaller upscale house. The dark blue ranch with creamy trim was so pretty, its flower boxes bursting with bright white blooms—a woman's touch. Evelyn's touch.

The front door opened, and the stunning woman with shoulder-length black hair stepped outside, waving. Jack's eyes brightened, and a huge grin warmed his handsome face.

"Are we here, Mommy? Are we here?"

Alexa turned to her daughter and tried to ignore the twist of hurt Jack's reaction to his girlfriend caused her. He used to smile at her like that, but that was ages ago. She and Jack were long over. It was vital to remember that. "Yes, honey. Go ahead and unbuckle."

"Can I play with Mutt?"

"In just a minute." Jack took the puppy from Alexa's lap, barely sparing her a look. He stepped from the driver's seat and opened the back door for Olivia. "Come on. I want you to meet someone." He took Livy's hand,

and they started up the drive. Evelyn met them halfway. Jack handed her the small ball of fur, and her pretty brown eyes widened as she laughed and hugged Jack. He gave her a kiss before he picked Olivia up and said something to Evelyn as she smiled, then said something to Livy.

Alexa studied the couple Jack and Evelyn made. They looked good together. It would be hard for them not to; they were both gorgeous. Even in jeans and a navy blouse that accentuated sleek, sexy curves, Evelyn appeared every bit the smooth professional. And Jack was so different. His tailored khaki slacks and aqua-blue collared shirt were a long way from the denim and tight football t-shirts he used to live in. A lot had changed in four years. He'd grown up.

With a deep sigh, Alexa opened her door. She didn't want to do this. It would be so much easier to call a cab and head to the airport, but Jack was right; she owed him, and he could help her with Abby. And more importantly, Olivia was safe. With a final steeling breath, she closed the door and walked over to the commotion of her chatty daughter and yipping puppy, a smile pasted on her face.

Evelyn glanced up. "Hello. You must be Alex."

"Yes. Alexa," she amended as she took Evelyn's outstretched hand, staring at the truly beautiful woman measuring her. Perhaps it was petty to correct her, but only one person had ever called her 'Alex.' It would be better if Jack called her Alexa, too. 'Alex' ceased to exist years ago. "Thank you for having us in your home."

She nodded. "I hope you'll feel welcome. I know how important this is to Jackson." She circled her arm around his waist.

Alexa read the message loud and clear—welcome, but not *too* welcome. They were here because that's the way Jack wanted it. "Thank you."

"Let's go inside. Can I get you anything to eat?"

Her stomach jittered and clenched with nerves. Although she'd had nothing since the few bites at breakfast, the thought of food made her shudder. "Um, no thanks. Livy ate at the Cookes'. Sarah fixed her an early dinner. She's still acclimating to the time change."

Jack walked to the car and strolled back with the large suitcase, his own carry-on, and a bag full of items for the puppy.

Alexa rushed forward. "Oh, I can take my luggage." She wanted something in her empty hands.

"I've got it." He moved ahead to the house, not looking at her. His tone changed, and he smiled as he took Livy's hand as he passed her by. "Welcome home, Olivia."

Alexa's discomfort grew as she realized this would be Olivia's home on occasion. Livy was no longer just hers; she would be Jack's, too. And probably Evelyn's as well. Jack was serious about this woman. He'd moved on.

He held the door open and Evelyn carried the puppy inside. Alexa followed, stepping into the living room. Sea-foam-blue walls and dark, wooden furniture accented soft, creamy couches and beautiful nautical paintings. Area rugs over glossy wood drew out splashes of color in the art hanging about. Thriving plants set around the space, absorbing the sun. Alexa peered into the next room beyond and spotted the small table set for two. Crystal wine glasses still held chardonnay. White candles had been lit and blown out.

As Alexa glanced around the cozy space Jack and Evelyn had made, she realized she couldn't do this. She'd spent the last four years of her life loving, needing, and missing a man who'd stopped yearning for her so long ago. *I didn't want* you, *Alex.* Jack's angry words echoed through her head like a nightmare. He'd stopped wanting her that cold February night, and she'd never gotten over it. But as she stared down at Jack and Olivia, petting the puppy, smiling identical smiles, talking, she understood she hadn't had the right to keep them apart. She'd stolen something from both of them. Alex and Jack were over, but Jack and Olivia were just beginning. One had nothing to do with the other. Suddenly overwhelmed, Alexa pressed her fingers to her temple, trying to stem the stirrings of another headache. The small nap she'd taken had refreshed her a bit, but the slight recharge was quickly fading.

Evelyn laid a hand on Alexa's arm. "Alexa, are you all right? You're a little pale."

Jack's eyes snapped up.

"Yes. Yes, I'm fine. Thank you." She tore her gaze from Jack's and smiled at Evelyn, then glanced at her watch. She'd lost track of time. Forty-five minutes. She had less than an hour and no money for Abby's kidnappers. Her heart raced as heat rushed through her body. "I'm—I'm just going to sit down."

Jack stood. "I'll show you to your room. You look like you could use some rest." For the first time since he saw Olivia in the Cookes' living room, his voice gentled with concern.

"No. No, I'm okay. I should stay here with Livy. She might get nervous if I leave her alone in a house she's not familiar with."

They both glanced at Livy laying on the floor, talking to and snuggling with the puppy.

"Olivia's fine."

"I'm fine, Mommy." She beamed her confirmation.

"This way." Jackson winked at Evelyn as he picked up the suitcase and started down the hall.

Alexa peered into well-decorated rooms as they passed the kitchen, a bathroom, the master suite—all exuding elegant masculinity that fit Jack well, except for the candles still lit around the Jacuzzi tub in the master bath and quiet, ambient music playing from some distant stereo. She and Livy were interrupting an intimate evening.

Jack stopped at a spare room across the hall decorated with honey-colored furniture and sage-green bedding. "I hope this'll work for you and Olivia."

She hated his stiff voice and cool eyes as they stared into hers. Unable to bear it, she looked down. "It's lovely. Thank you. What—what did Detective Canon say, other than he'll call you back?"

"They're sending someone over from the FBI to put a trace on the burn phone."

Her brows furrowed. "Burn phone?"

"A throw away phone like the kidnappers gave you. If they call again, the Feds might be able to triangulate a signal and find out where the calls are coming from. Hopefully they'll get something. Otherwise there's nothing new."

There would be no comforting words from Jack. He would help her not because he wanted to but because he was too kind not to. "But time's almost up."

"Let them do their job, Alex. Someone should be here soon."

He walked further into the room and set the suitcase at the edge of the bed. She wanted to ask him exactly what the detective had said. Jack used to be a cop. They must have said more than what he shared, but he was already on his way out. "Jack, I don't think this is going to work," she said in a rush. "I think Livy and I should go."

"Why? Because this is hard on you?" He turned his back and disappeared down the hall.

Wearily, she rested her forehead against the smooth,

cool doorframe and closed her eyes, fighting back her tears. There was too much to think about—too many worries, and the weight was so heavy on her shoulders. Abby. Livy. She sniffed and swiped at the tear she wasn't strong enough to hold at bay. This *was* hard on her. The entire situation. What did Jack want from her? The decision she'd made had been the right one at the time, or so it had seemed. How could she have known Jack would want their child when he'd tossed away two-and-a-half years as if they'd been nothing?

Alexa wandered to the window overlooking the pretty backyard with its small flower garden, charming fountain, and a little patio complete with wicker furnishings. Physically spent and emotionally drained, she collapsed on the edge of the bed.

Jack had ended everything so abruptly. He'd devastated her and broken her heart beyond repair. Jack had been her first love—her only love.

"The blue sweater or the black?" she muttered as she walked down the sidewalk, clutching her coat closed against the frigid February winds, distracted by thoughts of packing for her long weekend at Jack's. She glanced up as she approached her dorm and grinned as she spotted him sitting on a bench in the dark.

Heart soaring, she ran to him and gave him a hug and a quick peck on the lips. "Jack, what a surprise. I didn't know you were coming. I was just going to my room to call you while I packed." Her smile faded as she looked into his stony eyes and realized he wasn't hugging her back. "What's wrong? Are you all right?" She sat down next to him, her leg brushing his, and he jumped up, whirling to face her.

"Alex, I can't do this anymore. It's not working."

Confused, she stood. "What? What's not working?"

"I can't keep driving down here. Two hours one-way... It's too much. He paced back and forth with fast, jerky strides. "You can't keep spending the little money you have on bus fare to come see me."

She'd never seen him like this. "Where's this coming from? Come on. Let's go inside where it's warm." She took his hand. "I'll make us some hot chocolate, and we can talk."

"No." He yanked away.

She dropped her hand and stared at the stranger before her as he shoved his fingers through his hair.

"There's nothing to discuss. This isn't working for me anymore. It's just not. We need to move on. I'm so swamped, so fucking overwhelmed with my life right now. I can hardly keep my head above water. I had no idea being a cop was going to be this hard. The paperwork alone... I can't think. I can't fucking think."

"Why didn't you tell me you were feeling this way? Have you talked to your boss?"

He scoffed. "I'm not in college anymore. I can't sweet talk my way out of real life, Alex, like I would with a paper. I need to concentrate on my job—and only my job."

His words were sinking in and her breath backed up in her throat as the first dredges of panic bloomed. A simple conversation wasn't going to fix this. "I'll come home with you." She tried to grab his arm, but he jerked away. "I'll quit school. This doesn't matter to me. I love you. I want to be with you. We'll figure this out together."

He shook his head. "It's over, Alex."

Heart crumbling, she grabbed his wrist and tugged on the leather of his jacket, desperate to make him understand as the finality in his voice crushed her. "Come with me, Jack. Help me pack. I'll get a job. I'll help with half the rent. We can make this work. I just need to be with you. I—"

"No." He yanked her against him. "You're almost done. I won't let you do this. I won't be responsible for you not finishing school. You're not going to throw your life away for me."

Tears raced down her face as her breath sobbed in and out. "Please, Jack." She pressed her hands to his cheeks.

"It's over, Alex. Over. We're finished. Do you hear me? Finished." He ripped her hands from his face and turned away. "I don't have room for you in my life right now."

She struggled to breathe as she realized his mind was made up. Without any warning, they were through. She stared at his back, sick and trembling. They weren't getting married after she graduated as they planned all along. They weren't going to live together and share their lives as they'd dreamed. After tonight, they would go their separate ways and never see each other again.

Jack turned and faced her as tears streamed down, unstoppable. "I'm sorry, Alex. You have no idea how sorry."

She looked into his eyes, knowing this would be the last time, and saw the regret as she swiped at her damp cheeks. Anger grew somewhere beneath the unimaginable grief. "Two and a half years and that's it? You're sorry?"

"Alex." He touched a lock of her hair.

"No, don't." She shoved him. "Don't touch me. I don't understand this. I don't understand you. I love you, Jack. I love you so much. How can you do this? How can you just throw it all away?"

He said nothing as she choked on sorrow and wiped at her eyes.

"Alex—"

"I don't want to hear anymore." Turning, she ran blindly, disappearing into the night.

"Knock, knock."

Alexa whipped her head around, still reeling from her painful memories. She looked at the man who'd crushed her heart as he held their sleeping daughter in his strong arms.

"She conked out next to the puppy."

"Bring her on in." Alexa rushed to the head of the bed and pulled the covers back. "Go ahead and lay her down. I'll change her in to her pajamas."

She hurried to the suitcase, struggling with the turmoil of the past and present as Jack laid Olivia on the crisp white sheets. She didn't know how much more she could take. Focusing on her daughter instead—the one bright light in her life—she pulled free Livy's lavender-colored jammies and stuffed frog and walked back to kneel next to Olivia as Jack sat on the edge of the mattress. "You don't have to... You don't have to stay. I've got this."

He held her gaze until she looked down and gently pulled Livy's shirt over her head, replacing it with the short-sleeved top. She unsnapped her tiny jean shorts next and tugged them off, trading them for the light cotton pants. Her eyes darted to Jack's as she struggled to calm her nerves. "She's worn herself out. All the traveling and playing with Kylee."

Jack reached out and brushed the bangs from Olivia's forehead. "She's so beautiful, Alex. She's so smart and sweet."

Alexa stared at the big, masculine hand moving tenderly over their daughter's face and down her arm to her fingers. "Livy's my treasure." She smiled and grabbed the stuffed animal from the floor, tucking the mournful frog under Livy's arm.

Jack fingered the light green, webbed foot. "Gordon," he murmured. "You kept Gordon."

She picked up Livy's shirt and folded the pink, striped cotton, needing to keep busy. "I couldn't throw him away. He was the only thing I'd ever had won for me at a carnival."

"I had to chuck that damn football more times than I should've. That game was rigged."

She folded Livy's shorts next. "You probably paid double for him what we would have if we'd bought him at the store."

"You wanted him. I wasn't leaving until you had this pathetic looking thing."

A small smile ghosted across her mouth as she looked up and realized he was smiling too. She swallowed as a rush of longing snuck through her defenses. She'd never been able to resist Jack's smile. "Livy has always loved him. She's slept with him since day one."

He held her gaze as he continued to toy with Gordon's foot. "Why didn't you tell me?" All traces of the happy memory vanished as his eyes sobered and his voice radiated with pain.

"Because I never wanted her to think, for even one second, she was someone else's burden."

"Goddamn," he whispered and stood to brace his hands on the window frame. "I've missed so much. I've lost so much time."

Alexa got to her feet and walked to him, hesitating before touching his shoulder. "I'm sorry, Jack. I thought I was doing the right thing for both of you. For all of us."

He faced her. "I didn't get a say. I'm so fucking pissed. I'm so sad. I want to hate you for this, Alex."

She stepped closer to the agony radiating in his eyes, even though it would've been easier to step away. "Do you think the past four years have been easy? Do you think I didn't want a typical family for Olivia and myself? *You* walked out on *me*. Out of nowhere you changed everything. Was I supposed to have tracked you down three weeks after you told me you didn't want me anymore and that I didn't fit in your life and tell you we were expecting a child?"

He pressed his hand to his forehead. "I don't know."

"Well, I didn't either. All I knew was you were gone and I had a baby to raise. After the initial shock wore off, I was thrilled. I've never regretted her for a second. Not one. She's brought nothing but joy to my life."

"She's so perfect, so articulate." He looked at Olivia again and smiled. "She's amazing. I'm still shocked she's mine."

"She's very bright. She's so much like you, Jack. There's rarely a day she doesn't make me laugh."

The room grew silent as they both stared at the child they'd made.

"Did you finish school?"

"Yes. After you… After everything, I had a hard time. I struggled to keep up with my classes and student teaching. Luckily my professors were very kind. I thought I was tired from stress, but I soon found out I was pregnant. Olivia gave me a reason to keep going, even when I didn't want to."

"Alex." He trailed a finger down a wisp of her hair.

She stepped away from his familiar gesture. The emotions swirling through the room were too strong. She couldn't afford to make any more mistakes. "Everything worked out. I finished school and went home and took a job at the local elementary school—first grade. Gran helped me with Livy. So did Abby. They were my rocks."

"How? How did it happen? You were on birth control."

"I was. Remember that nasty sinus infection I'd had? The doctor thought the pregnancy could have been a result of the antibiotics she prescribed me. They don't always mix well. We should've been more careful."

"What are we going to do? I want to know her. I need to."

"I—"

The phone rang on his hip. Jackson scanned the readout. "It's the detective. I'll be right back." He stepped from the room and walked down the hall as he answered.

She glanced at her watch. Three thirty. Half an hour and the ransom was due. The day had rushed by in a whirl, but she was no closer to a solution for Abby. There were no new answers, nor was there a quarter of a million dollars in her account for the kidnappers. She'd been so wrapped up in her own problems; she hadn't concentrated on her sister's.

Alexa sank to the bed and stood again, restless. Maybe she could convince the kidnappers to extend the deadline. They could have the money she had in her savings now—a drop in the bucket compared to what they demanded—but they could considered it a down payment to buy her a little more time and let Jack work with the police to figure this out. If the FBI was able get a trace on the phone, they might be able to save Abby before it was too late. She had to believe they would find a solution. But what if they didn't?

At wits end, she moved to the window, staring out at the rocky canyons in the distance. So much was up in the air right now; so many problems hurdled her way all at once; too much lay on the line. She couldn't keep up. Despair and helplessness stewed together until she thought she might explode. She glanced down at her watch, staring as the seconds ticked by. Jack stepped back in the room, and she whirled. "So?"

"So far they're running with dead ends. They've seen the same MO with a couple of cases over the last several months. They have a vice team tracking down leads.

They think they're close. That's all Detective Canon will share right now."

"They aren't telling you anymore than they told me, which is a whole lot of nothing. I'm sick of hearing their PR crap. I want to know what they know about my sister." She swiped her hair back and sighed as she stared at the ceiling.

He stepped closer and touched her arm. "We're all hoping they'll call again so we can get a trace. That's our best option right now. Detective Canon said Agent Marway will be here within minutes to set up the equipment."

"What if it doesn't work?"

"Let's see if it does. I put in a few calls to Pittsburg and talked to Dougie Masterson, my old roommate. This is a Maryland case, but information gets passed from precinct to precinct. He's going to keep his ears open. We just have to wait and be patient. They need a little more time."

She flung her watch up to his face. "We're almost *out* of time, and my sister's still out there somewhere. I have no idea where she is. I don't know what they're doing to her. Is she hungry? Is she hurt? Is she—is she alive?" She pressed her hands to her face as her voice broke, unable to bear it.

"Come here." He pulled her close and wrapped his arms around her.

Alexa stiffened, hesitating, before she gave in and rested her head on his solid shoulder. She closed her eyes as Jack settled his chin against her hair. How many times had they stood like this? How many times over the years had she yearned for him to hold her just like this?

"I know this is hard, Alex. I can't even imagine. They're doing everything they can."

She relaxed a fraction and returned his embrace, absorbing his warmth and strength. "I let her down. I've failed her in so many ways. She's so young. She has her whole life ahead of her. I left her, Jack. I got on a plane and left her when she needed me most."

He tilted her chin up. "You left to protect Olivia. She wouldn't have wanted it any other way. Olivia's safe here. So are you. Abby loves you as much as you love her. She would understand."

Her eyes filled, and she struggled to blink away her tears, but not before one escaped. "I need her back, Jack. I need her home."

"I know." He ran his fingers through her hair, and her eyes fluttered closed. Here was comfort. Here was everything she'd been without. "Jack," she whispered as she clutched at his hips, absorbing all that he offered. "I'm so afraid."

The pads of his fingers skimmed her jaw, her temple, leaving her skin hot wherever he touched. "You don't have to be. I'm right here."

"I thought you might like—" Evelyn froze in the doorway.

Alexa's eyes flew open, and Jack yanked himself away.

"I'm sorry." Evelyn walked off with her tray of lemonade and finger sandwiches.

"Ev." Jack hurried after her. "Ev, wait."

Evelyn shut herself in the master bedroom just as the doorbell rang. Alexa could hear Jack swear as he went to answer the door.

Alexa sat on the porch swing, staring into the dark. Crickets sang as she rocked the glossy wooden bench back and forth, her nerves stretching ever tighter. It had been *hours* since her deadline passed, so why hadn't the kidnappers called? She'd dreaded the creepy mechanical voice over the last two days, but now she prayed she would hear it again.

She picked up the flip phone Agent Marway had fitted with a portable monitoring device and stared at the blue bars, relieved that the battery had been given a full charge. Agent Marway reassured her— several times—that the FBI would be able to trace any incoming calls at the Bureau and would follow up on new leads immediately. She just had to remember to do her part—wait for the cell to ring three times before she answered and keep the kidnapper on the line for as long as possible.

She was ready—more than ready—to do what she could; they just had to *call*. Sighing, she set the phone back in her lap and tried to find comfort in the warmth of the night and the stars shining bright and beautiful above. Jack's neighborhood was quiet, and the mountains lit up by the city in the distance soothing. She glanced to the window, looking into the room where Olivia slept. She could see her daughter's tiny form cast in shadows from the bathroom light she'd left on. Alexa stopped swinging when Jack, clad in black gym shorts and a white t-shirt, stepped in the room. His tough, athletic frame hovered over their daughter. He sat on the edge of the bed.

She studied Jack as he picked up Livy's hand and held it in his. He was in love with his little girl. The adoration had been unmistakable after he'd moved past the shock. He wanted to know his daughter; he deserved to. And Olivia deserved to know him. If she could take the time back and tell him from the beginning... She shook away the regret. They could only start now, but 'now' had its own complications.

Leaning against the swing, she played back the scene from earlier this afternoon. She'd been foolish to let Jack touch her again; she'd been stupid to forget that being in his arms could only bring pain. One moment of weakness had caused so many problems. Evelyn had stayed in the master suite since she dashed away with her tray of refreshments. Jack shut himself in the bedroom seconds after Agent Marway left. As Alexa made her escape to the fresh air, she could hear Evelyn's quiet crying echoing through the door.

Sighing, Alexa closed her eyes in a moment of surrender and drifted as she tried to figure out what to do next. A hotel room would probably be better— something close... The phone rang in her lap, startling her. Alexa jumped and scooped it up, staring at the *unknown name, unknown number* that popped up every time the kidnappers called. She struggled to keep her breathing steady as she hovered her finger over the talk button, waiting for the next ring, then the next. That was three. "Hello?"

"Sister Alexa, where's the money?"

She stood and began pacing back and forth frantically as the nerves she'd struggled to keep at bay flooded her instantly. "I'm still working on securing the funds. You can have what's in my account now."

Mechanical laughter filled her ear. "Do you think I'm playing games?"

"No, no, I—"

"Say goodbye to your sister."

"Lex?"

Alexa froze as her sister's voice trembled with fear. "Abby."

"Oh, God, Lex. I love you. I love you."

Before she could respond, Abby's terrified screams echoed through the phone, and then there was silence.

"Abby? Abby?"

"We're coming for your daughter next." The line went dead.

"Abby!" Alexa no longer held the phone to her ear as she shouted her piercing wails into the receiver. "Abby!"

Jack rushed out the door. "Alex, what is it?"

Fighting for her breath over her helpless terror, she ran toward the latch on the gate. The wild, overwhelming horror consuming her body forced her to flee.

"Alex." Jack grabbed her arm and yanked her around. "Alex."

She clawed to get away. "They killed her. They killed her while I listened."

He gripped her close as she collapsed to the ground in hysterical tears.

"Come here. Come here," he murmured against her hair as he held her, rocking her in his lap.

"She's dead, Jack. Abby's dead." She pressed her face to his chest, letting her torrid emotions run free.

"Hold on to me. Hold on to me, Alex."

She did, clutching, trembling, sobbing, listening to Jack's comforting murmurs close to her ear. His hand ran up and down her back in soothing strokes until eventually he picked her up. She had no idea how long they sat in the grass while she cried as she never had before. Minutes? Hours? At some point, her tears dried, and she found herself resting her cheek against Jack's solid shoulder and staring at the tall wood planks of the fence. Somewhere along the way, disbelief had replaced her horror. Nothing seemed real as she drifted in and out of the present.

Abby couldn't be dead. She was only twenty-two. She had job interviews to get to, a life to build. This was all some sort of horrid mistake. Was Jack really holding her? Had she finally cracked? Her mind whirled between Jack, Abby, and Olivia.

"Olivia," she said listlessly as he carried her down the hall to her room. "They're coming for Olivia."

"She's safe, Alex. They can't touch her here. I won't let them. We won't let them." He set her on the bed and crouched next to her. "Where are your pajamas?"

What did he say? Why couldn't she keep up?

"Where are your pajamas, Alex?"

"My pajamas? I—I don't know."

"Okay."

He walked to a drawer, opened it, and came back with one of his t-shirts. "Put this on."

She stared at the white cotton, paralyzed.

"Come on, Alex." He tugged her to standing. "You need to close your eyes and get some rest."

"Is Abby dead? Is she really gone? She kept screaming and screaming. Then she stopped." Grief threatened to come back and swallow her as tears rushed down her cheeks, unstoppable. "I told Gran I would take care of her. I promised her I would." She shuddered, her breath ragged.

"This isn't your fault." He wiped tears away with his thumbs. "None of this is your fault."

"I didn't save her. I didn't save, Abby."

"Let's get you into bed." He unbuttoned the top button of her fitted blouse as she stared at him. "Come on, Alex. Help me out here."

"I can't sleep. I don't want to sleep. She screamed. She was terrified."

He undid the next button, then the next, his warm skin skimming hers as he tugged her shirt away. He yanked up the white t-shirt and pulled it over her head. "Take off your pants."

She glanced down and fiddled with the snap in the dark shadows of the room, her fingers shaking. "I—I can't get it."

He heaved out a sigh, then pushed her hands away, unfastened the snap, and tugged on the zipper. Her slacks pooled on the floor, and he stared into her eyes. "Get into bed."

"Okay." She took a step, looked at Livy, then stopped as she heard her sister's screams again. "I'm so afraid for Livy, Jack. I'm so afraid. I don't know what I'll do if they take her away."

Jack stepped up behind her and pulled her side of the covers back. "Look at me."

She turned.

"No one's taking our daughter, Alex." He skimmed his hands down her arms. "No one's taking her away. Trust me. Let me handle this. Let me take care of you both for awhile."

She'd taken care of Livy, of herself, of Abby and Gran for so long. "I don't know how."

"Take the first step. Get into bed and rest."

She nodded and lay down on her side, pulling Olivia close. "Don't turn off the bathroom light, 'kay?"

"Okay." He stretched out next to her, leaning his back against the pillows, and crossed his ankles. "I'll sit with you for awhile."

"Thank you." The warmth of his body seeped through her borrowed cotton shirt as she snuggled her little girl, listening to her steady breathing. There was no comfort in holding her baby close, only the stark terror that she was next. How would they take her? Would they pull her into the back of a van like they did Abby? Were they watching Jack's house right now? "Are the doors locked?"

"Yes."

"Maybe I should go check." The thought of walking through the dark was more than she could stand, but losing Livy was worse. "What about the windows?"

"I have a security system and a gun." He took her hand and she clutched it "My house is safe. You and Olivia are exactly where you're supposed to be. Try to get some rest."

She closed her eyes, still holding on to Jack, certain she would never sleep again.

CHAPTER 7

J ACKSON OPENED HIS TIRED EYES and looked down. He wasn't dreaming. Alex and Olivia were really lying in the guest bed next to him. He stared at his beautiful little girl, asleep, wrapped in her mother's arms, and smiled. They'd just met, but he loved her. She was so bright and amazing. He was still in awe that he and Alex had made her.

His smile faded as his gaze wandered to the woman who'd walked back into his life and turned his world upside down. Her beauty was still a sucker punch to the gut. Even in sleep, snuggled up in his simple white cotton gym shirt, she took his breath away. He'd tried like hell to remain unaffected throughout the afternoon but failed miserably. Alex was as potent now as the day he laid eyes on her in the college library. She'd knocked him flat—plain and simple. Four years apart hadn't changed a damn thing.

He'd never felt an instant attraction to anyone the way he did Alex. Women had thrown themselves at him back in his glory days, but he'd had to work to win Alex over. She'd been so serious and sweet—perfect for him. He'd wanted her from the first moment and never anyone else after. Alex had made a man out of him, and he'd walked away.

Jackson reached over and stroked Olivia's soft cheek as his regret ate him whole. As much as he wanted to be angry with Alex, he couldn't. He alone destroyed the best part of his life the night he let her run off devastated.

Could he really blame her for not sharing the news of her pregnancy?

If he could go back and change it, he would. God knows he'd paid for his mistake every day he'd had to live without her. He'd gone back for Alex, but it had been too late.

"What the hell are you doing, Jackson? What are you thinking? She won't want to see you." The worrisome thoughts plagued him as he raced down the interstate to the college. Despite the tension clenching his belly, he drove on.

He had to do this. He needed to apologize and tell her he'd been a fool. If only he'd taken the time to think before he messed everything up. Hours before he ended their relationship, he'd pulled his gun on a robbery suspect for the first time. It had freaked him the hell out. Life right now freaked him the hell out. Everything was so hectic and crazy; the responsibilities were overwhelming. Why did he think pushing Alex away was the answer?

Now she was gone, and he was miserable. The last two months had been hell. He wanted her, needed her—was lost without her.

He pulled into a parking space across the street from her dorm. The calendar announced early spring's arrival, but the piles of snow told a different story. "Alex, I'm sorry. I love you," he muttered, practicing what he planned to say. "I didn't—"

The words froze on his tongue, and he gripped the steering wheel tight when she pushed through the glass door of her building and stepped on the sidewalk. God, he missed her. She was so beautiful bundled in her navy blue coat with her white scarf tied at her neck.

He grabbed the handle on the Jeep and opened the door. Heart pounding, he cupped his hands around his mouth to yell her name, but stopped when a guy came up behind her and said something next to her ear. Alex threw her head back and laughed. Jackson stared, shocked, as the full-throated sound carried across the air and the man took her hand. Blinking his disbelief, he watched them walk away.

He sat in the Jeep long after Alex disappeared down the street, realizing he'd lost everything.

Jackson rubbed a hand over his heart, attempting to banish the raw ache of the still-painful memories. He'd been a coward, and as a result ruined everything years ago, but Alex was here now, and she needed him. He planned to be here for her every step of the way.

Sighing, he toyed with the ends of her soft hair. She broke his heart when she wept for her sister. Her desperate tears had brought him to his knees. Alex and Abby had always been close. They shared an unshakable bond that came from the ashes of a tough childhood. Alex had been as much Abby's mother as her sibling, which would only make her grief that much worse.

He'd meant what he said when he told Alex she and Olivia were right where they were supposed to be. Nobody knew Alex the way he did. No one could help her through this time the way he would. But first he needed answers. He thought of Abby's bright blue eyes and free spirit. What the hell had she gotten herself caught up in? Abby's abduction hadn't been random; she'd been a planned target. The burn phone was testament to that. Whoever took Abby did their research. They knew about Alex and Olivia; more than likely, the kidnappers knew everything about them.

Alex and Olivia were as much targets as Abby had been. Over his dead body would they meet the same fate. No one was going to touch his daughter or get to Alex. His new mission in life was to make sure the fuckers paid.

With a last brush of his fingers through Alex's hair and a final look at his daughter, Jackson stood. He needed to talk to Detective Canon again and get in on the case. He'd put up with the double talk and non-answers a few hours before, but that would end now. He walked out of the room and frowned when he noticed the light on under his bedroom door. Twisting the knob, he stepped in and stopped, staring in disbelief. "Ev, what are you doing?"

"Packing."

"I see that." Hurrying to where she stood, he pulled the blouse from her fingers and took her hand. "Why?"

"Oh, Jackson, why do you think?" She grabbed the light pink top and set it in one of the many open suitcases.

He jammed his fingers through his hair, hardly able to keep up with another emotional crisis. "I thought we were okay, Ev. You said we were okay. I know I'm asking a lot of you right now, but please don't go."

"I've had time to think this afternoon. I can't compete with your past. Quite frankly, I don't want to." She put a pair of folded slacks in another bag, hanger still in place.

He dropped his hand. "Compete with my past? I'm not asking you to. You have to give me some time to adjust here. This is hard on all of us."

"I want them to go to a motel." Evelyn yanked a drawer open and pulled free several pairs of frilly silk panties.

He frowned, surprised by the heat behind her words. "That's not an option."

She whirled away from dresser. "Why?"

"Because they're in danger. Abby's abductor killed her while Alex listened tonight. They threatened to take Olivia."

Evelyn's shocked eyes met his as she gasped. "My God, Jackson. That's awful."

He walked to her and settled his hands on her shoulders, desperately wanting her to stay. "Yes, it is. She's going to need a friend. I can't just walk away. We have a daughter. I know that's not fair to you, and I know this isn't what you signed up for, but this is where we're at."

"You're in love with her." She blinked back tears.

"No." He shook his head vehemently, needing to deny the truth. Alex was here. He planned to help her out, but Evelyn was his chance to move on. He and Alex shared a daughter, a past, but it was doubtful they shared a future. He couldn't spend the rest of his life yearning for what he could never have. "No, I'm not."

"Yes, Jackson, you are. You and I have dated off and on for just about a year now. I thought we were moving in the right direction, but then I saw the way you look at her. I want that. I want to be with someone who looks at me the way you do her."

"What are you talking about? How do I look at her?" How *did* he look at Alex? No different than he did any other beautiful woman, he assured himself.

"As if she's your whole world."

"No." He shook his head again and closed his eyes as the arrow hit the mark. But still he needed to deny. "Alex *used* to be my whole world. She *used* to be everything."

"She still is." Evelyn pulled away and zipped her full suitcases.

The commotion woke the sleeping puppy. Mutt yawned, stood, and began to sniff around.

"Ev, please stay." His voice rang with an edge of panic. "Please stay and give us all a little time to get used to this."

"I can't." Her voice shook as she set the luggage on the floor and snapped cases on top of cases. "Do you realize you've never told me you love me?"

"Yes, I have."

"No. I tell you I love you. You always say 'you too.' I've never heard the words. Now I know why. They belong to someone else."

He took her arm, desperate. "Evelyn, please. They belong to you." He wanted nothing more than for that to be true.

She let loose a humorless laugh as tears trailed down her cheeks. "Even now, when it's all on the line, you can't say it." She yanked away, ignoring Mutt as he jumped at her leg. "Goodbye, Jackson." She wiped at her eyes.

"Ev. Ev, I'm sorry."

"Me too." She pulled her enormous cases behind her and strolled out of his life.

Jackson absentmindedly rubbed the puppy curled in his lap while he stared at his office phone. Evelyn was gone. She actually left. Just like that, she'd packed up her clothes, her scented candles, and whatever else she'd placed around the house and took off. It was as if she had never been here, as if they hadn't lived together for almost six weeks. His whole life had changed in a matter of a day, and she hadn't given him a chance to adjust. They'd been building something steady and strong, and now it was over.

So why wasn't he devastated? Why didn't he feel torn in half the way he did when he saw Alex with the man on the sidewalk? He and Evelyn had good chemistry. They had fun. Their relationship was easy—maybe *too* easy. He hadn't realized he'd never told her he loved her until she pointed it out. Why?

Because he didn't.

Jackson closed his eyes. He definitely didn't love Evelyn. He'd wanted to. He'd *tried*. God how he'd tried, but Alex was always there in the back of his mind. He leaned his head against the soft leather of his chair as the weight of despair crushed him. Would Alex haunt him forever? Would he always love someone he couldn't have?

Alex was here in his house—asleep in his bed. She had carried his child, but that hardly guaranteed them a future. He'd read her weary eyes and nervous, jerky body language while they tucked Olivia in to bed. Alex's shield was up, and it would be hell on earth trying to knock the layers away. He had damaged a piece of her and destroyed her trust. He wouldn't get it back easily.

Sure, she had leaned on him throughout the day, but she was vulnerable, at rock bottom. Alex would bounce back soon enough. She wouldn't stop until she had justice for her sister. Alex was a fighter. He had broken her heart, yet she'd carried on with her life just fine and raised their little girl without him. He loved her, always had, always would, but that didn't mean much if the feelings weren't mutual.

With a sigh, Jackson picked up the phone. He couldn't change the past. And the future... They would have to take that a day at a time. Alex needed help now. He would concentrate on the present for a while. He punched in Detective Canon's office number and waited. It was six a.m. on the East Coast. Canon was probably there.

"Detective Canon."

"Detective Canon, this is Jackson Matthews. We spoke yesterday about the Abigail Harris case."

"Yes. What can I do for you?"

"Several things, but let's start with the call Alexa Harris received at one a.m. Pacific Time. Did you boys get a trace?"

"I'm afraid I'm not able to share that information with you."

Jackson adjusted Mutt in his lap as he raised his legs and crossed them on the desk. He might as well get comfortable. This was going to take a while. "Oh come on now, Detective, give it a try."

"I've already told you what I can, Mr. Matthews."

"Which was a whole lot of nothing."

"I'm sorry."

"Sorry's not good enough. I was a cop myself for two years—Pittsburg PD. Now I work for Ethan Cooke Security—Los Angeles Branch. Risk Assessment Specialist. Go ahead and look me up."

"Mr. Matthews—"

"You can either be straight with me right here and now, or I'll go around you. I still have plenty of connections out east."

Detective Canon let loose a heavy sigh. "Mr. Matthews, you're backing me into a corner."

"Someone's threatening my three-year-old. I'll back you off a cliff if that's how I'll get answers."

The sigh again.

This time a humorless smile curved Jackson's lips.

"The feds called me shortly after five—one a.m. your time," Detective Canon began. "They triangulated a signal half an hour north of Baltimore at one of the inlets on Loch Raven Reservoir. A team of agents along with a group of our men went to check it out. They located the phone and dusted for prints. Came up with nothing. They brought in search-and-rescue dogs, who followed a trail of tire tracks for a mile before they lost Ms. Harris's scent. The feds had the cadaver dogs search the area and follow the same tracks, but they didn't alert, so that's something. CSI made a mold of the tire tracks and any footprints found at the location."

"That's a lot of action. Break it down for me."

"Despite the nature of the abductors' last phone call, there's a strong possibility Abigail Harris is still alive."

Jackson sat up in his chair, and Mutt yipped his startled surprise. "Run that by me again."

"CSI assures me that if Ms. Harris had been killed in the area, which the phone call alluded to, her remains would've begun their decomposition process right away. The cadaver dogs utilized are a Quantico trained team—the best the FBI has to offer. They can pick up on fresh remains almost immediately after death."

"So Abby's alive?"

"More than likely. As I said when we spoke earlier, we've seen this MO on three other occasions over the last six months. The ransom piece is new, but the method of abduction is dead on. Alexa Harris shared with us in an interview Friday evening that she remembered a van following her off and on throughout the day as they traveled home from Virginia Beach. In all four kidnapping incidences, young women have been taken by two men who rush from a tan, silver, white, and now gray van. The only difference between Abigail Harris's case and the other three is the burn phone. This is the first time the kidnappers have attempted contact with the family."

"So let's go with the theory that Abby is alive and the same people who abducted three other young women have also taken her. Why would they want to make contact with Alex? What's changed?"

"Nothing. My gut's telling me this is a diversionary tactic. A vice team spotted one of the victims last month in a strip club in DC, then again in Baltimore. Immigration and Customs Enforcement ran several raids—without luck. Now they know we're on to them."

Jackson's stomach sank as the pieces started fitting together, but he would let the detective play it out. "You lost me. Who knows you're on to them?"

"The Mid-Atlantic sex ring. Our vice teams are putting in overtime at some of the seedier strip clubs and prostitution joints in the Baltimore/DC area. They're getting closer to blowing this thing wide open. The FBI and ICE as well as the Baltimore and DC PDs are working a joint taskforce to bring this group down. They're big and dangerous. An agent was made yesterday. They found him floating in the Potomac last night."

Dread quickly replaced unease. "Son of a bitch." The situation was more dire than he'd imagined. A sex ring had a bead on his family. "Sex trafficking? Are you telling me Abby may be caught up in sex trafficking? That doesn't make a damn bit of sense."

"Doesn't have to, Mr. Matthews. They see what they want and take it. But that's where we hit our dead end. We haven't been able to find the common denominator. Why were these girls targeted and taken? *How* were they targeted? We've been through their computers, cell phones, have talked to close friends and family. None of the typical avenues we check are coming up as a green light. Nothing fits. Nothing matches to string the four victims we know of together. Until we figure that out, we aren't bringing anyone home."

Jackson rubbed his fingers over his brow and closed his tired eyes. "So, what's the next step?"

"We'll continue to search for leads until we can take this operation down. Our biggest objective right now is focusing on the major players. I want them wrapped up with a goddamn bow. Zachary Hartwell, CEO of Starlight Entertainment—he's our number one man, dirty fucker. He's smart, slippery, lawyered up, and he's mine. The Commissioner and DA are breathing down my back to bag him on something that'll stick."

Jackson recognized a personal vendetta when he heard one. "That could take months, even years. What does that mean for Abby and the other victims?"

"It means were working our asses off to get them home."

"But not until Zachary Hartwell takes the fall."

"I'm doing the best I can here, Mr. Matthews. We're all doing the best we can. I'll keep you up to date with any new developments."

"Thank you, Detective." Jackson hung up and scrubbed his hands over his face. "What a fucking nightmare," he muttered. Kidnapping to murder to sex trafficking. If this latest development in Abby's case was the road they would be traveling, it was bound to be long and ugly. If Abby was still alive, she was going to be a mess when they found her—if they found her. The call had been made north of Baltimore an hour ago. She could be anywhere by now.

He stood, wanting to talk to Ethan and begin formulating a plan, but it was late. First thing in the morning he would start making his calls. He wouldn't be leaving Abby's fate in Detective Canon's hands. Jackson read between the lines just fine. Abby and the other young women weren't on his list of priorities unless they were going to help him bring down the Mid-Atlantic sex ring, which was highly doubtful. Abby was taking a backseat to politics and pretty promotions. That wasn't acceptable.

He twisted off the gooseneck lamp and started down the hall, carrying the snoring puppy. How was he going to tell Alex? How could he get her hopes up with news that Abby might be alive only to dash them with the rest?

He turned into his room and laid Mutt on the small bed he'd made out of a couple of spare blankets. Mutt gave him a half-hearted tail wag before he rolled to his back and went to sleep. "You definitely have the right idea," Jackson muttered as he stood and pulled off his shirt, tossing it across the room in the general direction of the hamper. Abby's situation was bad, as bad as it got, but his hands were tied for now. He needed access to Ethan's fancy computers before he could do anything more.

Yawning, he sat on the edge of his bed, ready to rest his exhausted mind. A few hours of sleep for everyone would only help in the end. He settled himself against the pillow and closed his eyes until Alex's sniffling and unsteady breaths registered. He got up and walked across the hall. "Alex?"

"I'm okay. Go ahead and get some sleep."

Her words came out in between tearful shudders. She was anything but okay. Sighing, aching for her, he made his way to her side of the bed and sat down. "I was hoping you were going to get some decent shut-eye."

She sat up, sniffed again, and pulled a tissue from the box by the side of the bed. "I tried. I dozed off for a while. She swiped the tissue over her damp cheeks and blew her nose. "Is this real, Jack? Is Abby really gone?"

He closed his eyes in defense against her shattered gaze. How the hell should he answer? He needed to tell her. It was better to get it over with. "I talked to Detective Canon."

Alex tossed the tissue in the trash.

"He shared some interesting news."

She paused as she reached for another tissue. "What did he say?"

"Alex." He took her hand. "There's a chance…" He blew out a breath. "There's a chance Abby's still alive."

She clutched his fingers in a vise grip. "What?"

"Detective Canon and a team of Federal Agents believe Abby might be alive."

"Detective Canon told you she's *alive*?"

He nodded, watching her struggle with disbelief. "Could be."

"I don't understand. How? I heard them kill her. Her screams just stopped. God. God." Her lip wobbled, and she pulled her hand free to cover her face. "I can't stop hearing her scream. I think that alone might destroy me."

He moved closer, wrapped his arm around her slumped shoulders, and pressed her head to his chest. "I'm sorry, Alex. I'm so sorry I'm messing with your emotions like this."

"I don't know what to do anymore. I can hardly breathe. I have such a heavy weight on my chest. I keep replaying the phone call—that computer voice, the creepy laugh, the silence."

His arm tightened around her as he struggled to find a way to tell her the rest. Clenching his jaw, he looked at the ceiling. "They don't have anything conclusive one way or the other, but evidence from the scene of the trace is pointing to her being alive."

She looked at him again. "I don't understand."

"The cops were able to triangulate a signal from the call. Detective Canon said Baltimore PD and the FBI rushed to the location—a reservoir north of Baltimore. They found the cell phone, some tire tracks, and footprints." Now the part he'd been avoiding. "They brought in search and rescue dogs and picked up Abby's scent but lost it."

"So how can they say she's alive?"

He fisted his hand at his side. "The cadaver dogs they brought in followed the same trail and did a search of the area. They didn't alert to human remains."

Alex flinched as a tears spilled down her cheek.

He desperately wanted to take her pain away. "That's a good thing, Alex. As morbid as it sounds, that's really, really good."

"They could be wrong."

"Or they might be right."

"I can't... I can't let myself believe."

"This is a lot to take in." And there was so much more.

She stared into the dark for a long time. "They were hurting her. If she's alive, they're hurting her."

He kissed her hair and pulled her tighter against him. How could he possibly describe to her what Abby was probably living through? "We're going to do everything we can to find her."

"How long?"

"I don't know." He brushed his fingers through her black, silky hair. "Tell me about the van that took Abby."

"I told the detectives everything."

"But you haven't told me."

"There's more, isn't there? What else did Detective Canon say?"

He'd stalled as long as he could. "Do you remember the van that followed you on the interstate?"

"Yes. They found the van?"

"No, but three other young women were pulled into vehicles similar to the one that drove off with Abby. The vans have been different colors each time, but all of the victims were grabbed the same exact way."

"The similarities the detective kept talking about but wouldn't expand on..."

"Exactly. One of the teens that was taken before Abby has been spotted in some pretty rough areas of

Baltimore and DC. At strip clubs."

"Strip clubs?"

"Yeah." He was making this so much harder by trying to protect her from the truth. "Alex, Abby may have been kidnapped by traffickers."

"Traffickers?" She frowned. "Drug traffickers? Abby doesn't do drugs."

This was worse than he thought. Alex was so naïve. "Sex traffickers. They steal young girls and boys, young women….and use them as sex slaves."

Horror filled her eyes as she stared into his, shuddering out each breath. Color vanished from her face in the pale glow of the bathroom light. "No."

"Detective Canon—"

"No." Alex scrambled from the bed, ran to the bathroom, and shut the door.

Jack rushed to his feet and gave a quick knock against the wood. He stepped in without bothering to wait for a response. Alex sat on the lip of the tub and stared at the tiled floor as tears coursed down her cheeks. He walked to her and knelt before her.

"I think I'm going to be sick."

"Take some deep breaths."

She attempted one, then shook her head. "Detective Canon's wrong. He has to be. I don't know which thought is harder to live with—Abby dead or Abby suffering."

"I'm sorry, Alex."

"I just don't understand any of this. Sex trafficking and strip joints. Ransom calls… If they didn't kill her why did they want me to think they did?"

"People eventually stop searching for the dead. The police have their hands full with the living."

She clenched her hands. "I'll never stop searching, Jack. Never. I won't stop until I find my sister."

"If she's out there, we're going to bring her home."

He had to believe it. He needed Alex to believe it too.

She met his eyes as tears fell faster and her breathing grew shaky again. "I—" She shook her head as she began to weep. "I'm so lost. I feel desperate, like I'm going to start screaming and never stop. I feel like I'm breaking into a million pieces. I love her so much; I can't stand the thought of someone violating her."

He pulled her to the floor and sat her in his lap as he leaned against the tub. "I wish I could take this away. I wish I could make it better. If there was anyway…" He rested his chin on her head and breathed in wildflowers and vanilla. "Let me help you. Let me help Abby. Tell me about her days before they took her." He rubbed her back as she fought to steady herself.

"What do you want to know?" She tried to sit up.

He held her where she was, tucked against him, safe, her cheek resting on his naked shoulder. He continued to trace gentle circles over her slender back. "Give me a rundown of her last six months. What did Abby do for fun?"

"She didn't really have time for fun." Alex's voice was dull as she played with the hem of the white shirt she wore, exposing more of her smooth, slender thighs. "She'd been so busy getting ready for the fashion show her design class had three weeks ago. Abby's creations are amazing. That's how she lined up the job interviews in LA. Everyone loves her stuff. Her clothes are so chic and fun. They're so…Abby. We didn't talk a whole lot, just here and there when she wasn't at the studio or running from class to class."

He rubbed his cheek along her soft hair. Alex's fingers stopped fidgeting, and her body finally relaxed against his. "Was she dating anyone?"

"No. As I said, she was pretty obsessed with making her big splash in the fashion world. She was thinking

97

'now or never.' She mentioned going to dinner a few times with a photographer she knew."

"What's his name?"

"Who?"

Her voice grew groggier by the minute. He wanted her to sleep but needed her answers. "The photographer."

"Abby called him Renzo. She never said a last name, just Renzo."

"How often did they go out?"

"I think a couple times, maybe four or five. He travels often. I remember her saying that. She said they had a lot in common, but I never got the impression they were serious."

"Renzo," he repeated as he stared at the bathroom sink. The modeling and fashion world was often targeted by traffickers. He'd start with Renzo and see where they ended up. "Did she ever tell you where they went on their dates?"

"No, I don't think so. Nothing's coming to mind. As I said, it never seemed serious. They were just friends—at least that's the impression I got."

Alex's head rested heavily on his shoulder as her breathing evened out. He wanted to sit here, just like this, holding her while she would let him, but that wasn't what she needed. "You need to rest, Alex. You need to sleep."

"I can't."

"Let's try." Jackson got to his feet, bringing Alex with him. He settled her on the mattress and covered her as he sat on the edge of the bed and gave her a small smile. "Close your eyes."

"You don't have to stay. I'll be okay."

It was starting. She was already pulling back. "Just for a couple minutes."

"Olivia will be up soon." She took his hand, squeezed.

"Go sleep, Jack."

She didn't want him there, but he wanted nothing more than to stay. With no other choice, he stood. "I'm right across the hall if you need me."

"I know."

He held her gaze for another moment, then walked from the room.

CHAPTER 8

A LEXA GAVE HERSELF ANOTHER PASS in the mirror. She'd done her best with her makeup and hair, even though her heart wasn't in it. Hopefully the fitted, dark blue, sleeveless sundress she'd unpacked two weeks ago was dressy enough for an afternoon wedding.

She smiled at Livy twirling round and round in her pale lavender and white striped dress. Her shoulder-length golden curls flowed about with her constant motion. She hadn't realized she'd packed this outfit of Livy's in her rush to flee the house all those nights before.

Twelve days had passed since the kidnapper's last call. Twelve long, agonizing days had crawled by while she waited for news of a sighting of her sister—or her sister's body. The police phoned Jack a week ago with news of a woman's size seven shoeprint found at the scene by the reservoir—Abby's size—and tire tread consistent with a large SUV, but that was all the information they had. There were too few answers when so many questions remained.

"We should put on your sandals, Livy. We have to go."

Jack tapped on the doorframe. "Hey, you ready?"

"Yes, I guess so." He was so handsome in his light gray suit and tie. The pale shade brought out the boldness of his baby blues and accentuated his muscular build. Alexa had done her best to ignore his looks over the last two weeks. She'd struggled to remain unaffected while she and Livy shared his home.

The days weren't so much the problem. His job kept him swamped and stuck in his office. It was the evenings, when the three of them sat down to dinner— as if they were a typical family, or when they walked the beach or went to the park so Livy could play. Their current arrangement was too much like the dreams she used to weave on lonely nights. In the moments when his smile made her heart beat too fast or his sweet, humorous ways made their daughter laugh, Alexa would remember the frigid night in February not so long ago.

But recalling painful memories didn't always help. Although four years had changed Jack, so many pieces of him remained the same. He was still kind and funny and everything she had ever wanted, but admitting so was foolish and one step down a road she could never travel again. She wouldn't be letting her guard down around Jack anytime soon.

He frowned. "You guess so?"

She shrugged and gave him an apologetic smile. "I don't think I'll be very good company today. Are you sure you don't want to give Evelyn a call? Perhaps she'll reconsider." Guilt still plagued her, knowing she'd caused Jack unhappiness.

"Alex, we've already been through this—several times."

"I know, but I feel terrible."

"You shouldn't."

"But I do. Why don't *I* call her? I'll explain that I have no intentions of trying to steal you away. Livy and I can stay at a hotel close by. You still might be able to work this out."

"It's done."

"I—"

"Done, Alex." His firm tone left no room for argument. His moody eyes brightened as he peered in to look at

Livy. "Who's that pretty girl with the curls in her hair?"

Smiling, Livy stopped her spinning and grabbed hold of the edge of the bed, struggling to keep her balance. "Mommy curled it with the iron. Don't touch it. It's *hot*."

He grinned. "Check, don't touch the curling iron. Are you ready to play with Kylee?"

"Yes." She beamed. "Can we bring Mutt?"

"Wouldn't leave home without him. I want our shoes and my furniture in one piece when we get back."

"Are you sure Sarah won't mind?" Alexa checked the battery on the flip phone, then she dropped it in her purse. She kept it close at all times, hopeful it would ring, praying she would hear her sister's voice once again.

"Nah, Mutt can hang with Bear and Reece while Austin and Hailey say their 'I dos.' Maybe they can teach him some manners."

Mutt ran out of Jack's room carrying a gym sock in his mouth.

"Speak of the devil." Jack crouched down for the sweet puppy. "And I do mean devil." He ruffled the pup behind the ears. "Come on, let's get out of the house for awhile. It'll be good to be around some great people for an afternoon." He stared at her as he scooped down and picked up Livy.

The Cooke grounds were spectacular. The endless yard and rambling house with a view of the Pacific and city beyond—perfect. Alexa had been oblivious to the beauty the last time she was here, but she appreciated it now. She breathed in the warm summer breeze blowing through the open windows, carrying hints of the sea. Even from this height, the water could be heard thundering against the rocks far below. She stared in awe. What would it be like to wake to the rush of waves every morning? How amazing would it be to look out at the buildings of Los Angeles lit up in the dark? "Ethan and Sarah have their own little piece of paradise."

Jack smiled as he rolled to a stop behind two gorgeous sports convertibles—a red honey and a silver Mercedes. "Yeah. I've offered to trade houses, but Ethan's so damn selfish."

She grinned.

"Mommy, can I unbuckle?"

"Yes, sweetie, go ahead, but don't get out until we have a handle on Mutt."

"Okay."

Alexa stepped from the car and opened Livy's door once she was certain Jack had Mutt secured in the crook of his arm. She glanced around, taking in the spectacular transformation of the west lawn. A massive tent ate up much of the lush, green grass. Huge cascades of blue, purple, and white blooms decorated the space in pretty concrete pots. The effect was elegant and fun.

"I'm ready, mommy." Livy danced about, bursting with excitement. "I want to play with Kylee." Livy had been unable to talk of much else since she sprang out of bed at five in the morning.

"I know, sweetie. I know you do." She crouched next to her little girl, smiling, attempting to smooth one of her flyaway curls.

"Mooommeee, come *on*." Livy spun in a circle, then another, sending Mutt into a fit of yipping puppy barks.

Alexa sighed as she watched her quick repair job vanish with Livy's busy movements.

"I'm thinking you might want to give up on that."

Alexa rolled her eyes up to Jack as she stood. "I officially give up."

He chuckled and set Mutt down. "Liv, should we find Kylee?"

"Yes!" She jumped up and down, beside herself with anticipation.

"Are you sure?" Grinning, he lifted Livy under the arms until they were eye to eye.

"Yes!"

"Are you really sure?" He poked his finger into her belly, sending their daughter into a fit of wild giggles.

"Yes! Yes!"

"Let's *do* this." He started toward the house.

Alexa stayed where she was, watching Jack take exaggerated steps that had Livy bouncing about in delight. It melted her heart to see them this way. Livy had lost out on so much.

He stopped at the door and turned. "You coming?"

"Uh, yes." She looked around and discovered Mutt watering a shrub. "Come on Mutt." She gathered him up and took the steps to the entrance.

Jack didn't bother to knock; instead he opened the door and they stepped into chaos. Kylee screamed her delight down the hall when she spotted Livy. The two friends grabbed hands and squealed all the way to the playroom.

"Good Christ," Jack winced as he rubbed at his ear. "I'm going to need a hearing aid by the time this day is over."

She smiled at Jack. "They're little girls—busy, excited little girls at that. Better make that appointment right away."

He shrugged. "At least they'll sleep good tonight."

"I'm coming right now. I have the veil in my hand," a petite, gorgeous, and quite pregnant woman with huge green eyes said into her cell phone as she hurried to the stairs in her strapless, blue, thigh-length dress.

"Hey, Jackson. Hello." She smiled at Alexa. "Welcome to pandemonium," she called behind her.

"That's Morgan. She's Hunter's wife. He and I work together."

"Oh. I wonder if I could be doing something to help?"

"Let's find out."

Mutt squirmed to get down.

"Hold that thought." He scratched Mutt behind the ears, then he opened a door, set the puppy on the floor, and closed it. "We'll let Bear and Reece run the show for a couple hours."

Alexa bit her lip, worrying. "Do you think he'll be okay? Bear and Reece are so big."

Jack smiled. "They're beasts, but they're sweet—unless you're a bad guy. They're going to help me train Mutt. Minus the shoe incident, the chewed up boxers and socks, and the piss on the living room rug, he's a great dog. We might be able to use him for security."

"Oh." She couldn't picture the small bundle of fur barking and snarling at a criminal.

"Let's go meet everyone." He took her hand, but she hesitated. Jack held her gaze, challenging, she knew. She'd been careful to keep her distance since the night he comforted her. Touching Jack brought back too many memories, too many raw emotions, but it didn't have to. This was the perfect opportunity to show them both—but mostly herself—that a simple gesture didn't have to be anything more than that.

"Let's go." She pulled him toward the laughter and commotion in the living room. They stopped in the doorway, and Alexa blinked. She'd never seen so many gorgeous, muscular men in one space.

"Matthews, glad you could make it." The groom grinned.

"Congratulations, man." Jack let go of her hand and

gave the tall, muscled giant with kind, dark green eyes a 'guy' hug, rough back slaps and all. Stepping away, Jack captured her hand again. "Everyone, this is Alex," he shook his head. "Alexa Harris. Alex, that jerk over there is Hunter. You've already met Ethan. And the guy getting himself hitched is Austin."

She smiled. "Nice to meet—"

Olivia rushed into the room. "Perfect timing." Jack snagged her up. "And this is Olivia, our daughter."

Alexa studied each of the men, holding her breath, waiting to see the scolding judgment in their eyes. Surely word had made it down the grapevine that Jackson's long-lost college girlfriend was back with the child she'd kept from him. She relaxed when Hunter, the golden God with the sexy dimple in his chin, stepped forward and tugged gently on one of Livy's curls.

"Nice to meet you, squirt."

Smiling, Olivia shied and turned her face into Jack's neck.

"Way to go, Matthews. She looks just like you." Another slap to the back.

"Morgan and Hunter are expecting their first baby in August—a little boy," Jackson supplied.

"Congratulations." Alexa gave Hunter another smile. "We just watched your wife zoom upstairs. She's stunning."

Hunter grinned, his eyes bright with pride. "She's not bad. I'll keep her around."

Alexa chuckled. "That's very kind of you."

"Oh, good. Another set of hands." Sarah rushed into the room, flushed and beautiful in her bold blue dress, identical to Morgan's, holding a pretty, cooing infant. "Alexa, would you mind taking Emma?"

"I can take her." Ethan stepped forward.

"No, you can't. You're due for pictures in—now. All

of you, out on the deck. The photographer's waiting."
She took two steps, shooing them out the door with her
free hand.

Alexa walked over and took Emma from her frazzled
mother. "Hello, sweet girl."

Emma grinned and drooled.

"Shoot, I forgot her burp cloth." Sarah pressed her
fingers to her temple.

"It's okay. I'll find one." Alexa snuggled Emma close,
breathing in baby powder. "Oh, she's so perfect."

"And she's due to eat soon. She's going to get fussy.
I put some breast milk in the fridge. I hate to do this
to you."

"I've done it before." Smiling, Alexa nudged her head
toward Livy, who was still giggling in Jack's arms.

"Of course you have. I'm sorry." She shook her head.
"Things are a little hectic right now. We're thirty minutes
from the official 'I-dos.'"

"Come on, Olivia," Kylee called from the hall. "I'm
getting my dress on."

Livy's eyes widened, and she scrambled out of her
father's arms. "Kylee's princess wedding dress!" She
dashed off.

"I need to help with that." Sarah hurried from
the room.

"Is Livy in the way?" Alexa called.

Sarah stopped and whirled. "No, she's actually a
help. I might keep Kylee in one place with Olivia here."
Sarah disappeared around the corner.

On cue, Emma's grins turned to tears as soon as
Sarah vanished.

"Are you hungry, honey? Should we get you a bottle?
Kitchen's that way, right?"

"Yeah. I'll show you." Jack started to follow.

"Oh, you don't have to. I'm pretty sure I remember.

Emma's going to have a little snack, maybe a little nap."
She kissed the baby's soft forehead.

"I don't mind."

She'd done everything in her power to avoid spending
time alone with him. Over the last two weeks, she'd
made sure Livy was never far away. When Livy went
to bed at night, Alexa stayed in the guest room with
her, perched at the small writing desk, typing away on
her laptop, researching missing person's cases similar
to her sister's. Perhaps her retreat was cowardly, but
she would do what she had to do to make it out of this
situation whole.

They stepped in the kitchen as Emma's fussing
turned in to lusty cries. "It's okay, sweetie." At ease with
the baby in her arm, she filled a bowl with hot water,
pulled the bottle from the fridge, and set it in the water
to heat.

"Why don't you just put it in the microwave? It'll
be faster."

"Because the microwave destroys the nutrients in
the milk." Alexa smiled down at Emma, cooing to the
pretty baby with the black hair and soft blue eyes.

"Ah, well, you learn something new every day."

Alexa pulled the bottle from the bowl, shook the
liquid, and tested it on her wrist. "Just right. Here you
go, beautiful girl."

Emma's cries turned to noisy swallows.

"Much better, huh, sweetie?" She played with Emma's
tiny fingers. "I miss this. I miss this so much. Livy used
to..." Her smile vanished, and her gaze whipped to
Jack's as she realized her mistake. "I'm sorry."

He stared into her eyes as he brushed his fingers
over Emma's hair. "Let's bring her up to the nursery."

She nodded and cursed herself a thousand times for
being so careless as she followed Jack up the stairs to

Emma's gorgeous room. Pale greens and pinks accented sweet little chicks and beautiful pine furniture. "Look at this. It's amazing."

"Wren, Ethan's sister, decorated it. She fixed up my house too. Hell, she's played with all of our places. She's an interior designer."

"She does an excellent job. Emma, you're a very lucky little girl. And look at this view." She stepped to the window and sighed, studying the waves crashing against the cliffs in the distance. "It's breathtaking. I love the ocean. I love watching Livy dance and play in the waves. We don't get to the water as much as I would like back in Maryland. We're always so busy with Livy's tumbling classes and my lesson plans. Groceries and laundry. Time gets away from me."

"We can go more often if you want. The beach is just a couple miles down the road."

She'd forgotten herself in her pleasure. "That's okay. You have a lot going on with work."

"Forgot to be careful and keep it all bottled up."

Surprised, Alexa turned. He still knew her so well.

He leaned his shoulder against the frame of the crib, the picture of relaxation, until she focused on his eyes.

"I'm not sure—"

"Yeah, you are. We both are. You tell me what I want or need to know about Olivia and Abby, but you're off limits—a closed book."

Her back went up. "That's right."

"Can I hold her?"

She stared at him, frowning, unable to keep up with the abrupt change in conversation. "Of course." She walked to him and handed off Emma.

Jack sat in the rocking chair, setting an easy rhythm with his legs. "She's getting so big. She's such a pretty thing."

Apparently the tense moment had passed. "Yes, she is." She continued to study Jack. He was so handsome, so tough and masculine, yet gentle and attentive as he smiled down at the baby in his arms. Alexa clutched the edge of the crib, drowning in waves of regret. "I stole a million moments like this from you and Livy."

He stopped rocking and looked at her.

"How can you stand it? How can you be so kind to me when I took that from you?"

He held out his hand. "Come here."

She shook her head and stayed where she was. "You didn't want me, but that didn't mean you didn't want her. I was wrong, Jack. I was so wrong."

He settled Emma at his shoulder and burped her. "Come here, Alex."

Giving in to her heart, she walked to him and took his outstretched hand.

"I messed up our relationship, Alex. I did this."

"No." She couldn't let him take all the blame.

"Give me some of it back. Tell me what it was like. What was Olivia like?"

"Perfect. Amazing. She was amazing." Alexa smiled, getting lost in her memories. "She was such a peanut when she was born. I remember the first time I held her. I was terrified but so in love. I stared at her perfect little face and saw so much of you."

Jack clutched her hand tighter. "You used our names."

She nodded, stunned that he remembered. "Yes, I used the names we picked out on those silly occasions we would dream. I wasn't going to. It hurt too much, but then I saw her and I knew she had to be Olivia Grace."

"Alex."

She shook her head in defense against the gentleness in his voice and the pain in his eyes. "Every moment was beautiful—has been beautiful," she went on before he could say anything more. "Even the days and nights when I was so tired and scared and had so many plates spinning in the air... She's been my joy."

"I'm sorry I wasn't there. I'm sorry you went through it alone."

"I wasn't alone. I had Gran and Abby. They were great. Abby came home on the weekends. Gran helped as much as she could, but she was in so much pain."

"You were taking care of Gran and Olivia *and* working full-time."

Alexa shrugged. "I did what I had to. She gave up so much for me and Abby."

"When did she die?"

"A couple years ago. She passed mercifully quickly. I made it to the hospital with just enough time to tell her I loved her and to promise her I would take care of Abby. She told me I should find you. That was the last thing she said." Alexa dropped his hand and walked to the window. Touching him was too much right now when her defenses were down.

Jack laid Emma in her crib and stepped up behind her. "Alex." He turned her to face him. "Alex, I..." He frowned and snagged his finger against the chain of her necklace, tugging at the charm half hidden under her top.

"Jack, don't." She took a step away and stared into his eyes as she clutched her hand around the small piece of gold.

"Stop." He grabbed her arm and pulled her back. "Let me see."

She pressed her lips firm and tightened her grip. "Leave it alone."

"You—you kept it." He removed her fingers curled around the chain and toyed with the triangular charm.

"Alex, you kept it."

She turned and stared out at the rough waters. She had no choice but to tell him the truth. "I couldn't take it off."

"Do you... Do you always wear it?" He brushed his hands down her arms.

"Yes." She closed her eyes, struggling to remain unaffected by the warmth of his touch. "Please don't."

He pulled her against him. "All this time... The last two weeks... I didn't notice." The heat of his breath feathered her neck.

"I didn't want you to," she whispered.

"All this time," he repeated next to her ear as he clasped their fingers.

This was a mistake—a huge mistake, but she couldn't pull away.

The door opened. "We're starting... Oh, excuse me." Sarah stepped back out and shut the door.

Coming to her senses, Alexa freed herself and hurried to the crib.

"Wait."

"No." She gently picked up the sleeping baby. "You don't want this."

"Don't tell me what I want, Alex."

"Okay, I don't want this. You're caught up."

"Damn straight I'm caught up."

She shook her head vehemently. "You don't get to be. You don't get to do this. We can't go back. We can't make mistakes because of old emotions and memories." Although she spoke to Jack, she was reminding herself. She'd melted under his touch. This couldn't happen again. She yanked the door open and stepped out, almost crashing into the bride. "Oh, oh, I'm so sorry." She clutched Emma closer.

The bride smiled, fully, beautifully. She was stunning

in her simple A-line organza gown. The empire bodice matched her bridesmaids' dresses. Los Angeles was definitely home to 'the beautiful people.' Alexa hadn't seen anything different yet.

"No, problem." The bride's honey-colored eyes twinkled with excitement.

"You look wonderful." She adjusted Emma in her arms as the baby nuzzled closer.

"Thanks. I'm Hailey." The bride held out a well-manicured hand.

"Alexa." She took it and shook.

"There's the bride."

Hailey's smile grew impossibly wider when Jack enveloped her in a hug.

"You're stunning." He kissed Hailey's cheek. "I think you might just knock Austin on his ass."

"I already did." Hailey chuckled and poked him in the stomach.

"You got me there." Jack winked and hugged her again. "Congratulations, beautiful."

"Thank you." She held him a moment. "Thank you so much for everything," she whispered as her tone grew serious and she looked at him.

He nodded and skimmed a finger over her cheek.

There was an unmistakable bond between Hailey and Jack.

Hailey drew away, and her eyes brightened once more. "Alexa, I want to spend some time with you later, but first, there's something I have to do."

Hailey's sweet excitement was infectious, and Alexa grinned. "Don't let me stand in your way."

"Nothing could. I'm getting *married.*" She did a little boogie. "I still can't believe it. I'm actually marrying Austin Casey."

"Not a nerve out of place in this one," Morgan joked

as she came up behind Hailey. "Come on, Bride. Let's do this *before* baby Phillips arrives. For someone who's so excited, you're sure taking forever." She pulled Hailey toward the stairs. "Ethan's waiting to walk you down the aisle."

The hall was silent again as the wedding party headed downstairs. Alexa followed in her attempt to avoid Jack.

"Alex, wait."

She stopped, blew out a breath, bit her lip, and turned. "We need to get Livy and find our seats."

He stared at her, nodded, and they went downstairs.

Dusk darkened the cliffs beyond as the DJ rolled into his next song. Jackson smiled as he watched Olivia and Kylee laugh and dance about in their pretty dresses. Their cheeks were flushed and their cute hairdos long since tangled by the blowing Pacific winds. They were having a hell of a time. Olivia would always have a friend when she came to visit.

His smile dimmed as the thought depressed him. Now that he had his daughter with him, how could he let her go? He didn't want to share her on vacations and every other holiday; he wanted her living in LA every day. He loved having Olivia in his home, loved being surrounded by her energy, clutter, and noise. She had only been in his life for a couple of weeks, but she was by far one of the two best things that had ever happened to him.

Scanning the bustling crowd, he searched for the other. He spotted Alex across the tent, standing in the glow of several candles. She too seemed to be hitting it off as she talked and laughed with Hailey, Sarah, and

Morgan. This was the first time she'd appeared remotely happy since he woke her on Sarah and Ethan's living room couch. It was good to see a bit of sparkle in her eyes again. The last two weeks had been hell for her. He'd heard her quiet crying and endless pacing late into the nights but kept his distance, because that's what he knew she wanted.

He hated that he wasn't able to make her laugh the way Hailey was now, the way he used to. When they'd first started dating, he'd had to coax her into relaxing and letting herself have a little fun. The burden of too many responsibilities had taken their toll. Helping her ill grandmother raise a teenager while trying to work and maintain her scholarships had been more than any twenty-year-old should have to deal with. Every smile he'd teased from her in the beginning had been a small victory. It wasn't all that different now. He'd seen a few of her stellar grins, but not nearly enough. She was too weary around him, too stiff and guarded. It was going to take more than two weeks to move past the damage he'd caused in their relationship.

Jackson continued to study her—the way her glossy black hair shined in the dim light, the way her eyes widened with surprise before she threw her head back and let loose her full-throated laugh. "My God," he muttered as the familiar sound sent him reeling. She was so damn beautiful. Would he ever get used to it?

Hailey said something and Alex responded. Jackson's focus sharpened as she reached up and touched her necklace—a habit he'd noted throughout the evening. She'd kept it and had never taken it off, she'd admitted, albeit reluctantly. While dinner had been served, he hadn't been able to take his eyes off the charm—intertwining loops that created an ornate triangle. He hadn't noticed it several nights before when he helped her undress, only the glint of a chain against the smooth skin of her neck. Would he have helped Evelyn pack if he'd known the gold twists of the charm were facing her back? There had to be something left between them if she wore the gift he gave her all those years before.

"Open your present." He held out a rectangular box, wishing they were anywhere but in his trashed room at the frat house. The blaring music from down the hall, even with the door closed and locked, didn't exactly set the scene he'd been going for, but he hadn't been able to wait for the special dinner he'd planned.

She hesitantly took the box he'd painstakingly wrapped in frilly, flowered paper. "You didn't have to get me anything."

"Of course I did. You only turn twenty-one once, and besides, I just missed your birthday when we met last year." He loved surprising her with little things. She never expected them, which made giving them more fun.

"Thank you."

He grinned. "You haven't opened it yet."

"I know, but…" Smiling, she shook her head and bit her lip as she peeled the paper away.

Uncustomarily nervous, he shoved his hands in his pockets and took them back out as she lifted the lid.

"Oh, Jack," she gasped. "It's beautiful." She freed the shiny gold necklace and let the chain dangle between her fingers, then she caught the charm in her hand and studied the intertwining knots. "I've never seen anything like it."

"I was kinda going for one-of-a-kind. You know, symbolic."

"I love it." She took her eyes from the jewelry and met his. "I really do."

FOREVER ALEXA

"Good." He relaxed his shoulders and touched her jaw. He'd wanted the gift to be perfect. "Good," he repeated. "Let me help you put it on."

They turned to the mirror on his closet door. Alex lifted yards of silky black hair away from her long, slender neck and he was instantly surrounded by the intoxicating scent of flowers and vanilla. "So, what does it mean?"

He struggled with the small clasp. "The jeweler said the charm has many meanings—religious and so forth, but the loops are what caught my eye." He secured the chain in place and met her gaze in the mirror as he slid his hands down her arms and laced their fingers. "I like how they go on forever." He kissed the back of her neck. "That's what I want. I want forever with you, Alex." He watched her eyes fill. "I love you."

She turned and pressed her hand to his cheek. "I've never been given anything so special. Thank you."

"You're welcome." He locked his arms at her waist. "Happy birthday."

"I love you so much, Handsome Jack," she whispered.

Caught up, he pressed his lips to hers, and the tender kiss soon turned hungry. Need sent them instantly to the floor where clothes were tossed aside. Sighs and gasps filled the air as minutes passed. Eventually, Alex straddled him, moving with him while the charm of her new necklace caught hints of the light as it swung back and forth against her naked chest.

"Hell of a party," Tucker Campbell said as he sidled up next to Jackson.

Jackson took a long swallow of his beer, fighting to bury the past that snuck up to catch him off guard. "Austin and Hailey know how to have a good time."

"They look happy."

Austin pulled his gorgeous bride against him and kissed the top of her head as he wrapped his arms around her waist and joined in on the conversation with Alex, Morgan, and Sarah.

Jackson took another pull from the bottle, ignoring the tug of envy. "That they do. A new house, wedding, and a two-week honeymoon in Tahiti. Doesn't get much better."

"I'm betting they come back with more than that to look forward to—pools going around the office for baby dates."

Jackson shook his head but wasn't surprised. "Sick bastards. You'll bet on just about anything." Every agent had been victim to the odds at one point or another. "Last week it was atomic hot wings..."

"Tony shit himself for days after that one." They both chuckled. "But this is a sure thing. I'm more than willing to take a pot of easy money. Hailey loves Ethan's kids. It's no secret she wants her own. Austin will do anything to make her happy. You're just bitter that Collin's still bopping the ditzy blond. Should've held out for a couple more weeks."

There was an easy logic to this. Sighing, Jackson pulled his wallet from his slacks and tugged out a one hundred dollar bill. "I'm in. Put me down for the third week of next March. First babies usually come late."

Grinning, Tucker slid the crisp bill in his front pocket. "We're going to burn in hell."

Jackson swallowed more beer. "The whole office is burning with us."

"So, how's Alexa's sister's case going?"

"Slowly." And just like that, they were back in professional mode. "Haven't had anything new since the shoe and tire prints."

"Did you run the photographer? What's his

name? Renzo?"

"Dead end. He had an alibi the evening Abby disappeared. His credentials are legit. He works for Face. That modeling agency's the real deal. Travels a lot internationally. No criminal record, no connection whatsoever to Zachary Hartwell that I could find."

"What's your overall impression?"

Jackson turned to his good friend and fellow bodyguard. "That Abby and the others are fucked. Detective Canon and the FBI have tunnel vision. They want Zachary Hartwell and whoever else he's playing with. The cops can't find the common denominator linking the women, but something tells me they aren't looking all that hard. They're waiting for their big break, and Abigail Harris isn't it."

"Let me know if I can do anything."

"Thanks, man." Tucker looked like he belonged on the cover of Men's Health, with his pretty face and tough build any man would be envious of, but he was cop through and through. He'd been a lead detective with LAPD before he gave up police work to join Ethan's security firm. "I want to take Alex and Olivia back to Maryland for awhile. Get in touch with my old connections and dig into this myself. I'm not getting anywhere waiting around out here."

"Like I said, hit me up if I can help."

"You'll be the first."

"Alexa's a beautiful lady."

Although Tucker's comment was harmless, it rubbed Jackson the wrong way. He knew other men looked at her. It drove him crazy thinking someone else had touched her. "Always has been."

"Your daughter and Kylee are having fun."

Jackson grinned as he looked at Olivia. "Yeah, they are."

"Congratulations."

"Thanks." His smile faded. "It's a fucking mess." No pretenses were needed here. He and Tucker had been to hell and back over the last few months on several dicey assignments.

"I take it Evelyn's no longer in the picture."

"Guess not. She packed her bags and walked out."

"You're taking it pretty well."

He shrugged and glanced at Alex. "I don't know how to take anything these days. Shit's piling up faster than I can shovel."

The music slowed.

"What are you going to do about it?"

He gripped his bottle tight. "Couldn't tell ya. She doesn't want anything to do with me. She needs my help and is giving me a chance to get to know our daughter..."

"What do you want?"

"Her. I never stopped wanting her."

"She's right over there."

Alex stood feet away, but she might as well have been back in Maryland. "It's not that simple. I messed it up—messed *her* up."

"Guess you should probably fix it."

He sure as hell planned to try.

Wren Cooke walked by, petite, stunning, and exotic with her smoky gray eyes and long, curling black hair.

Tucker took a step in her direction. "Hey, Cooke, let me do you a favor and dance with you."

Wren stopped as she glanced over her shoulder and rolled her eyes. "Let's not and say we did. I don't dance with cops."

Tucker looked around, his hazel eyes heating with challenge. "You're in luck. I don't see one." He pulled her into the crowd of dancing couples as they continued to argue.

Jackson shook his head and set down his beer. He could never tell if Tucker and Wren wanted to rip each other to shreds or jump each other's bones. Probably both.

He decided to take a page from Tucker's book as he walked across the floor, spotting Alex staring out at the cliffs. Tucker was right; she was here. What the hell was he waiting for? He'd respected her need for space—maybe too well. If he kept staying out of her way, he'd never make amends or win her back—and, ultimately, that was the goal. He'd been persistent all those years ago when Alex barely gave him the time of day, but in the end his stubborn determination had paid off. It was time to move past the guilt of his mistakes and take back what he wanted. He moved to her side and gave her a gentle bump with his hip.

She jumped. "You scared me."

"Sorry."

"I should check on Livy."

He snagged her hand as she turned away. "She's fine. She and Kylee are having a blast. We should dance."

"I don't think so."

He pulled her against him despite her hesitation and wrapped his arms around her slender waist. "See? Not so bad."

She pressed her hands to his chest. "Jack."

"It's not so bad, Alex." He held her gaze as the wind twisted the curls in her hair.

Sighing, she followed his lead.

"Are you having fun?"

She looked down and fiddled with the end of his tie. "More than I should be. I feel so guilty smiling and laughing when my sister's..." She shook her head.

He tightened his grip, hating that the light had vanished from her eyes. "She would want you to smile,

121

Alex. We have to believe she's out there. We're going to find her. I won't stop searching until we do."

"I'm too afraid to let myself hope. I can't—" Her fingers curled against his shirt. "I can't forget the way she looked at me while they dragged her to that van. I keep trying to remember something important I might have missed, something that will break her case open and bring her home, but nothing comes."

The agony in her voice ripped at him. "It's not that simple, Alex. Not even close."

"I want it to be."

"I know. I wish it could be." He stared out at the city beyond, at the lights winking to life in downtown LA. "I've been tossing around some ideas. I think it might be time to head back to Maryland for a while. My hands are tied here. I want to dig into Abby's case and see what I can come up with on my own."

Alex stayed silent.

"What do you think?"

"I want to say no. What kind of person does that make me? I want to keep Livy here where it's safe. I feel like I'm sacrificing my daughter to save my sister, and vice versa." She huffed out a breath. "I can't do this." She pulled away and walked back to the balcony.

He stepped up behind her and rested his palms on her shoulders. "Can't do what?"

"This." She made a sweeping motion with her hand. "I can't dance with you while people laugh and rejoice all around us. I can't act like my life is normal. If Abby's alive... What are they doing to her, Jack? Are they pumping her full of drugs to keep her quiet? Are they selling her? I can hardly stand it. She's so beautiful and bright. She has job interviews lined up with two of LA's top fashion designers. Who will she be if we get her back? Will she end up like our mother? Nothing's going to be the same for her again."

He stroked his thumbs along her skin. "You have to believe she can overcome. If she's even half as strong as you, she's going to get through this. Abby will still be beautiful. She can still work for the top fashion designers in LA. This doesn't have to change that."

"But she'll be different. She won't be *my* Abby—the Abby from two weeks ago—and it breaks my heart."

He breathed her in as he eased himself closer and gripped her hands in his, offering comfort. "Let me help you. Let me take you and Olivia back to Maryland. I've already talked to Ethan. He and Sarah are going to take care of Mutt while we're gone. We can leave tomorrow if you want."

Her fingers clutched his. "I'm scared. I'm afraid to go and afraid to stay."

"I'll be with you every step of the way." He pressed his lips to her temple, unable to stand her pain.

Her breath shuddered out as she leaned against him.

He rested his chin on her head and closed his eyes. "I—" His cellphone vibrated on his hip. He wanted to ignore it but instead took his phone from the holder and glanced at the readout. "It's Detective Canon."

Alex tensed.

"It might be nothing."

She lifted her head and turned until their eyes met. "Or it could be everything."

"One step at a time."

Alex pressed her lips together and nodded.

He answered. "Hello, Detective Canon."

"Mr. Matthews, I—"

"I'm sorry, Detective, can you give me a second?" The thundering waves made it difficult to hear.

"Certainly."

"Come on." He took Alex's hand and held his phone

up in signal to Ethan and Sarah to keep an eye on Olivia as he pulled Alex with him into the quiet of Ethan's gym "Better. I apologize again, Detective."

"No problem."

"What can I do for you?"

"We may have had a sighting of Abigail Harris."

He gripped Alex's hand tight. "That's excellent." 'Sighting' he mouthed.

"A concerned citizen snapped a photo on their phone and e-mailed it over. The picture's pretty grainy. I'd like to send it your way. Hopefully Alexa can help us verify."

"Send it over. We'll give it a look. I'll call you right back."

"What's going on?"

"They might've spotted Abby. Someone took a picture. Detective Canon wants you to take a look."

"Of course." She stood close as Jackson opened the e-mail and enlarged the image of a slim woman stepping from one dark passenger van to another.

Alex moved closer. "The picture's so dark and blurry. I can't really tell."

"Come with me." He took her hand and hurried to Ethan's office. "We'll open this on Ethan's computer." He opened the attachment on Ethan's state-of-the-art equipment, enhanced the photo, and played with the image. "It's still not great."

Alex moved close to the screen, squinting, studying. "The woman's built like Abby, but she doesn't have long hair."

"It could be up under her hat, or they may have made her cut it."

"I don't know." Her voice vibrated with frustration. "I can't tell if that's her."

"Let me try something else." He cut-and-pasted the willowy woman from the photograph onto a blank

124

background and enlarged and enhanced until the figure was too big to fit the screen. "We'll study little bits of her at a time and see if there's anything we recognize."

He moved the image to start at the woman's sandaled foot. "Does she have any tattoos or piercings we could be looking for?"

Alex shook her head. "No. No tattoos or piercings."

Jackson traveled up the woman's jean-clad legs until he came to a blurry hand.

"Wait. Wait. That ring. The silver ring on her thumb. Abby has one. She always wears it."

The image was so fuzzy it was hard to make out any patterns or features on the band. "Does it have any gems?"

"No. It's smooth. The ring was Gran's. Gran's finger was bigger than Abby's, so Abby wears it on her thumb."

"This is good. Let's see if there's anything else." He moved the image over a slender arm, noting several bruises on the bicep.

"Oh, that looks so sore." Alex's brows furrowed with her concern.

"Do you want a couple minutes?"

"No." She shook her head and stared at the computer again. "Keep going, Jack."

"Give yourself a second."

"We don't have a second. Abby needs my help right now. Move to her shoulder. She has a small mole I forgot about."

Jackson moved to the frame, and Alex gasped. "Abby. That's Abby."

"Let's be sure." He centered on the woman's face. It was difficult to tell from the angle of the photograph. The woman looked down. The black cap she wore was in the way.

"There's definitely a similarity. This has to be her.

125

Let's call the detective. Now that they've seen her, they can go get her." She laughed. "Abby's coming home." She gripped him in a hug. "Thank God. Oh, thank God."

He pulled back and held her at arms length. "Alex, it's not necessarily that easy."

Her smile dimmed. "They know where she is."

"A concerned citizen spotted her on a dark street stepping into a van. Let's back up a step and call Detective Canon."

She turned away.

"I'm sorry, Alex. I don't want you getting your hopes up."

"Just make the call."

He stared at Alex's rigid shoulders as he picked up his cell and dialed.

"Detective Canon."

"Detective, it's Jackson Matthews. Alex is pretty certain the picture is of her sister. She recognized the ring on Abby's thumb and a small mole on her left shoulder."

"Excellent."

"So where does that leave us?"

"That's the tricky part. The picture was from late last night. The citizen sent it to us a few hours ago."

"Son of a bitch." He jammed his fingers through his hair. "Why did they wait so long?"

"Couple of guys from a bachelor party. They didn't realize they had the photo until they woke from their drunken stupor earlier this afternoon. One of them thought they recognized the woman as Abby from the pictures the media's been flashing."

"Well, where was the bachelor party?" He picked up a pen, ready to write down a name.

"That's problem number two. They did a pub-crawl. The group bar hopped throughout the night—all over Baltimore. None of them remember taking the photograph. We've taken their phones and have all the pictures. There are quite a few. We're going to try to make heads or tails of them and hopefully track down some sort of location. We're also going to follow their credit card transactions. I have men on it right now."

Jackson leaned back, closed his eyes, and clenched his jaw. Their break had already fizzled. "Keep me informed if anything else comes up."

"Will do."

Jackson pressed 'end' as he stared at the ceiling and set down the phone.

"They don't know," Alex said quietly. "They don't know where she is."

He rubbed his fingers over his brow. "They're working on it. We have to be patient."

"Stop saying that!" She whirled. "I'm so sick of hearing it. Be *patient*, Alex. They're *working* on it, Alex. We're going to *find* her, Alex." She pressed her palms to the desk. "What if we don't? I can't take this anymore." She rushed to the door and twisted the knob.

"She's alive." He stayed where he was, his voice calm despite his frustration. "We know she's alive and somewhere in Baltimore. The picture was taken last night."

"But she's suffering, Jack. She's in danger. You saw her arm. Do you think I don't know what they're doing to her? I've been researching when Livy sleeps." Her weary voice wavered.

Jackson stood and walked to her. "I know it doesn't seem like it, but this is a step in the right direction. This picture came with potential leads."

She rested her head against the door. "Such as?"

"Although none of the men remember taking that exact photo—"

She cut him off with an exasperated laugh. "That's a lead? They took a picture and they don't even remember doing it? What good does that do?"

He took her hand as it flopped from the knob. "Plenty. They took several photos and bought alcohol with credit cards. The authorities need to connect the dots. Answers are coming, Alex. Not as fast as we want them, but they're coming."

"They might move her."

"We have to hope like hell they don't."

She covered her face with her hands.

He tugged them away. "Come on, we'll go say our goodbyes, get Olivia, and head home. We'll book our flights for sometime tomorrow. I'll call my parents."

Her eyes widened. "Your parents?"

"It's not safe to go to your place. We have no idea if they're watching the house. No risks. There shouldn't be a link between you, me, and Olivia. They might know you're in LA, but they have no idea where. You're credit card trail stopped after your flight and the night at the hotel. They'll have no idea we're with my family."

"Lost in the shuffle."

"That's right. My parents will be thrilled to see you again."

"I'm not so sure about that. I kept them from Livy."

"Mom didn't talk to me for two weeks after I broke things off with you. She loves you like crazy. I want them to meet their granddaughter face to face. This is the next step, Alex. We need to go. I can't do anything more for Abby here."

She nodded. "Okay. We'll stay with your family—if they'll have us."

"They will." He brushed the hair from her temple. "I need you to hang in there."

She put a restraining hand around his wrist, halting

his movement. "I'm trying. I want her back. I need her back."

He reversed their positions so that he held her wrist in his hand. "Whatever it takes. We'll find a way to bring her home."

"Thank you. I'm sorry I snapped at you."

He shrugged. "No biggie."

"I'm grateful for all you're doing."

He tightened his grip against her wrist. "I don't want your gratitude, Alex."

"You've got it anyway. I'm thankful you're willing to help me after everything that's happened." She frowned. "Why does saying so make you mad?"

"Because I feel like you're giving me a damn pat on the head." Why was he making this into such a big deal? She said thank you. "Let's get Olivia." He dropped her arm and reached for the doorknob.

"Wait a minute." She snagged his arm this time. "I don't understand what just happened. You're helping me with my sister and have given Livy and me a place to stay. There's nothing wrong with being thankful. I don't know what else you expect me to feel."

And *there* was the problem. She had him tied up in knots. The scent of flowers and vanilla was making him crazy. He *wanted*, *needed*, and she was thankful. Enough was enough. He pressed her to the door, sandwiching her against him and the dark solid wood. "I want you to feel what I do, Alex." He skimmed his fingers over her jaw and rubbed the pad of his thumb over her bottom lip. "Just for one second, I want you to feel the way I do."

"I—" The word came out on a trembling whisper.

"One second, Alex." Their breath mingled, and then he captured her mouth the way he'd been yearning to for years.

She stiffened and pushed at his chest. Despite her protest, he held her still, waiting as he sensed her hesitation. Seconds passed before she moaned and curled her fingers into his shirt, pulling him closer and parting her lips.

Like a starving man, he dove deep, savoring the sweet flavor he'd craved and gone without for too long. Tongues collided and teeth scraped as the moment spun out. He held her face in his hands, nipped her full lip, groaned, then took them both under for more. How had he lived without this?

"Jack." Alex eased back, still clutching at his shirt. "Jack, we can't do this."

He stared at her swollen lips and flushed cheeks, wanting to disagree. Her eyes told him he only had to lean in again and take, but he wouldn't get them where he wanted by pushing his advantage. Alex would need time to realize she could trust him again before they could move forward. With a last brush of his fingers along her jaw he stepped away. "Let's get Olivia and go home."

CHAPTER 9

ALEXA STARED OUT AT THE dark blue waters of the Chesapeake as Jack drove the rental car along the Bay Bridge. It had been ages since she crossed the twenty-mile stretch to Kent Island. Her house in Hagerstown was only two hours from the Eastern Shore, but she hadn't been able to make herself come back to one of the places she loved most.

There were too many memories wrapped up in the pretty creeks and quiet marshlands not far from Jack's parent's home—Christmases celebrated; long, lazy summer days in the sun; dreams woven that never came true. She never intended to come here again.

As the Hyundai bumped over the smooth metal beam transitioning them from bridge to land, Alexa pressed a hand to her unsettled stomach. Jack assured her several times that they weren't followed from LA and that no one was waiting at his parents' place to take Livy, but she still worried. She hadn't been able to shake the persistent unease since they'd parked Jack's car at LAX and left the safe anonymity of his home. Baltimore wasn't far away, nor was DC. They were closer to Abby—hopefully—but Livy was now a target again. The dread of constantly looking over her shoulder was back with a vengeance.

Jack merged off the busy highway and turned right. They passed a bank and the diner that served the best French fries she'd ever tasted and the strip mall she and Jack's mother used to stroll through. Eventually they made their way to the cozy streets of the familiar neighborhood. She breathed deep, fighting to calm another flutter of anxiety. They were just about there.

The anticipation of seeing George and Carol was almost as overwhelming as her fear for her daughter's safety. The hitch of guilt still plagued her as she remembered the bits and pieces of the phone call she'd overheard Jack have with his parents several nights before, when he called to tell them they were grandparents. It only lasted moments, then he'd hung up and moved to the living room with his laptop and accessed Skype. His mother's weeping echoed through the room when Livy sang and danced in front of the webcam for her grandparents. Alexa had to leave when Jack's own eyes filled with tears.

Grammy and Grampy had 'visited' with Livy everyday via the computer for the last two weeks. They'd all missed out on so much. Not only had Alexa robbed Jack and Livy of time together, but also Livy and her grandparents. Yet they were ready to welcome her into their home with open arms.

Moments later, Jack pulled into the pretty, flower-lined driveway Alexa remembered so well. A rainbow of pansies filled the concrete planters separating the asphalt from lush yard. She studied the calm blue of the inlet several steps down a grassy embankment, the boats sailing by on their way out to open waters, and the large two-story clapboard, catching herself before she sighed. The tiny apartment she'd shared with Gran and Abby had been full of love, but this place had always felt like home.

When Jack brought her here for the first time, she'd worried what his family might think of the poor girl from subsidized housing making her way through school on a full ride. Their house had screamed classy, quiet wealth, but their warmth had settled her nerves instantly. "It's still the same. It's so beautiful. I've missed coming here."

He gave her an easy smile. "We've missed having you."

Jack had been more relaxed since their steamy kiss in Ethan's office two day ago, which left her more on edge. She had tried her best to avoid him with her usual tactics, especially after they'd practically eaten each other alive in a foolish moment that never should have happened, but Jack was always in her way.

How was she supposed to forget his bold, familiar taste and the way those firm lips felt pressed to hers, or the *heat* that still sparked between them, when he wouldn't leave her be? Keeping Livy close didn't work. He just stayed and played, making their daughter laugh—and her too.

Escaping to her room at night had proved fruitless—he followed and sat too close at the tiny desk while she breathed him in and felt his muscular arm rub against hers as he helped her track down information on cases similar to Abby's. And he kept touching her—little brushes here and there that set her skin humming and yearning for more. It was almost as if Jack had declared a silent war to wear her down—and he was winning.

"Ready?" He winked.

"Sure."

"Let's go." He skimmed his knuckle along her chin.

She studied him, frowning. "What are you doing?"

"Getting out. We've been sitting all damn day." He opened his door.

"That's not what I—"

"Is that my baby?" Carol Matthews stepped from the screen door, pretty with her chin-length blonde hair and blue eyes so similar to Jack's. "It *is* my baby. And Alexa."

"Mom." Jack hurried up the steps and hugged his mom, spinning her once while she laughed. "I've missed you."

"I've missed you too, sweetie. Where's my grandbaby?"

He grinned. "What am I, chopped liver?"

"No, but you're all grown up with that rough stubble on your cheeks and chin. I want to hold my sweet darling girl, but not before I give my other sweet darling girl a big hug." Carol eased away from Jack and ran down the steps like a woman half her age. "Alexa Harris, I've missed you to pieces."

Alexa held on to the petite woman dressed in khaki shorts and a striped green top. She'd always envied Jack his wonderful, warm mother. Secretly she'd considered Carol her own. "I missed you too, Carol."

"Carol? You're going to hurt my feelings if you don't call me Mom. A few years away shouldn't change a little thing like that." She winked. "I had the piano tuned for you, just in case you want to play. Now, where's my Olivia?" She moved to the car and peered in the backseat, all but rubbing her hands together with anticipation.

"Why aren't you angry with me?" Alexa's eyes widened as she realized she said out loud what she'd been thinking.

Carol turned back to her. "What good would that do? You're here now, right? You and Jackson will patch everything up and move on, as you should've all along."

Jack winced and cleared his throat. "Mom."

"I'm not meddling. This is for the two of you to figure out. Now, let's get our little princess inside and ready for dinner. Dad's grabbing lobster. He had a meeting on the golf course. He'll be along any minute." Carol opened the door, unbuckled Livy from her booster, and grabbed her up in her arms. "Oh, oh, I'm so in *love*. She smells so good. Jackson, she looks just like you."

Livy blinked her eyes open.

Alexa stepped over and smiled at her confused little girl, caressing a finger over her forehead. "Livy, we're at Grammy and Grampy's house."

"I want to go on the bridge." Livy yawned and stared at Carol.

"She fell asleep before we made it to the bridge," Jack supplied. "That's all she talked about on the plane."

"We'll go on the bridge tomorrow, my sweet little Livy."

"Are you my Grammy?" Livy stroked her fingers over Carol's face.

Carol's eyes filled. "Oh dear, I'm going to get drippy."

Livy grinned. "Grammy's going to get drippy."

Carol let loose a watery laugh. "Grammy has some surprises for you. She went shopping today just for her beautiful grandbaby."

"I love to have surprises. They are my favorite."

"Good. Let's go inside. Your mommy and daddy can get your things." Carol started for the steps.

"Jack is my daddy. Mommy said so."

Alexa wrinkled her nose and winced as Carol paused mid-step.

"Yes, Jack is your daddy," Carol confirmed as they went inside.

Alexa walked to the trunk, waiting for Jack to join her. She smiled when Livy's delighted screeches echoed through the screen door. "I guess your parents feel duty-bound to spoil their granddaughter."

"It's a grandparent's prerogative." He popped the trunk. "She has a lot of time to make up for."

Alexa's smile vanished as his comment compounded her guilt.

"Shit, Alex. I'm sorry." He took her hand and squeezed. "I didn't mean anything by that."

"Don't worry about it." She pulled away and grabbed

the handle of her suitcase.

"Alex—"

"You have every right to be angry. I'm angry with myself."

"Hey." He turned her to face him. "We've already talked about this. There's plenty of blame to pass between the two of us, but it doesn't seem to do much good. We need to move past this. I'm sure as hell trying."

"Yeah." She desperately wished she could give Jack and his family back the time they'd missed. Alexa looked to the embankment, to the tall marsh grasses waving in the breeze, the calm waters beyond, craving the serenity the view had always brought in the past. "I'll get mine and Livy's stuff in a couple minutes. I'm going to clear my head."

"Okay." He took a step in her direction.

"Alone, Jack. I need to walk alone." She grabbed her purse from the front seat, too afraid to leave the flip phone behind, and started to the back of the house without looking at Jack. She was drowning in the messy emotions crowding her. Ten blessed minutes by herself would do her some good. She stepped to the graying, weathered boards of the dock and moved to the end, then she sat and stared out at the diamond twinkles on the water from the sun and the pretty wooded area a couple hundred yards across the inlet. The landscape had barely changed over the years. If only she could say the same about her life.

Sighing, she closed her eyes and breathed deep, trying desperately to focus on the tranquility nature offered. Fish splashed about as frogs croaked and a gust of salty air twisted a lock of hair against her cheek. Time slipped away, and her heart rate slowed. For the first time in two weeks, she found a true stirring of peace.

She opened her eyes again, smiling, and gasped when a great white heron only a few feet away soared to the sky. "Beautiful," she murmured, captivated. She wanted to show Livy. She wanted her little girl to experience all the joy she'd found here along the Eastern Shore.

More settled, she stood, ready to get back to Livy and catch up with Carol. She took two steps, and the cellphone rang. Habit had her reaching for the flip phone first, but the window on the small, prepaid cell stayed dark. By the third ring, Alexa freed her own phone. *Unknown name. Unknown number.*

"Oh, God." Was it the kidnappers? Her finger shook as she pressed 'talk.' "Hello?"

"Lex," came a trembling whisper instead of the horrid mechanical voice.

"Abby? Abby, is that you?" A woman cried in the background—not her sister. "Abby?"

"Help me," came the whisper again. "Help me, Lex."

"I don't know where you are. Where are you?" She pressed her hand to her ear, drowning out the extra noise, waiting for the dull, quiet voice to give her the answer she needed most. "Where—" She jumped, startled, as a huge commotion erupted on the other end of the line and men shouted. She could hear something crashed to the ground. "Where are you, Abby? I need to know where you are."

The line went dead. "No!" Not again. Not *again.* "Abby!" The dial toned buzzed, and she chucked the phone up the embankment as a burst of frustrated rage consumed her. Breath heaving, she gasped for her next gulp of air and stood perfectly still. Hot, fat tears spilled down her cheeks as she lost yet another opportunity to save her sister.

"Her heart's heavy, Jackson. Her eyes are so sad and troubled."

He glanced at his mother standing by the large picture window overlooking the bay as he sat on the floral area rug next to Olivia. "She's going through a lot."

"I can't even imagine. Are they any closer to finding her sister?"

He absentmindedly placed the miniature couch in the living room of the pretty new dollhouse his parents had purchased. "I don't think so. Leads keep coming in, but they fizzle before they go anywhere."

"Poor darling."

"She's hanging in there. Being back on the bay will be good for her. She's always loved it here."

"I'm glad she has you to help her through this. Alexa's too used to dealing with everything on her own."

He grunted as he looked at Olivia. Alex didn't know how to let anyone help. She'd grown up handling more than her fair share and sailed into adulthood doing the same. When they dated, it had taken her months to unbend and lean on him. He could only assume it would take even longer this time around.

What would Alex say when she realized he'd paid off the last of her Gran's medical bills and the two loans she'd taken out to help her sister with school? He imagined she was going to be seriously pissed, but she would have to get over it. He got a peak at the balance in her checkbook several nights before as she paid her bills at his kitchen table. She'd barely had anything left by the time she finished. Alex deserved to be taken care of for once in her life. He'd be damned if anyone was going to get in the way of him doing so—including Alex herself.

"How's Evelyn handling all this?"

His gaze flew to his mother as she turned to face him. "She's not. She left."

She nodded. "Evelyn is a nice young woman, but she's not for you."

"Mom," he warned.

"I already told you I wouldn't meddle. You're a grown man, but you can't blame me for hoping you and Alexa will find a way to work things out. She's the best thing that ever happened to you. Now you have a daughter to consider."

His mother wasn't telling him anything he didn't already know.

She came to sit on the rug with him and Olivia and ran her fingers through her granddaughter's hair. "She's beautiful, Jackson."

He smiled. "I love her beyond words."

Olivia looked up from the doll and miniature cat she made talk in different voices. "I love you, Jack. You're my daddy."

His heart swelled as he grabbed her up and set her in his lap. "Maybe we can work on you calling me Daddy instead of Jack." He nuzzled her neck and made her giggle.

"Okay. I will call you Daddy. Jack is your big people name, like Alexa is mommy's big people name."

He grinned. "That's right." He looked at his mother. "Have you ever met a smarter kid?"

"I'm a very smart kid," Olivia agreed as she crawled out of his lap to play with her dolls again.

Jackson chuckled. "And modest too. You must get that from your mother."

His mom laughed. "I made a salad and some rolls, but I should start the water to boil for the corn. Your dad will be home any minute. Olivia, do you like corn on the cob?"

Her eyes widened. "It's yummy. I help mommy peel the green stuff away."

"Would you like to help Grammy?"

"Yes. I'm a great helper. The best!" She stood and took Grammy's hand.

Jackson chuckled again and shook his head. "Liv, we need to work on your self-confidence."

"There's nothing wrong with a good self-esteem is there, my Livy?"

"No, Grammy." Olivia smiled as they left the room. "What's a good slef-esleem?"

Jackson laughed as he stood. God, he loved his little girl. He walked to the window and watched Alex sitting on the dock, wanting nothing more than to be out there with her, holding her close and enjoying the evening together as they had so many times before. But that would take time. Lots of time. He was making progress—slowly. He'd stepped up his game since their kiss in Ethan's office. She'd melted in his arms. There was definitely something between them still. He just had to keep her off balance until she realized she could trust him with more than her family's safety. He *would* win her back, and when he did, he was never letting her go.

Down the hall, Olivia's lively chatter mixed with his mother's laughter. Now was as good a time as any to get in Alex's way again. They'd made so many great memories here; it was time to make more. Alex stood, and he smiled. "Perfect. Hey, Mom, I'm going to check on Alex. We might take a little stroll."

"I think that sounds wonderful, honey."

So did he, liking his idea more and more. He turned as Alex did and hesitated, facing the window again when she frantically searched her purse. She pulled the small flip phone from her bag, and his stomach clutched. "Son of a bitch." He ran through the room and down the hall, pushing past the screen door.

"I need to know where you are."

Alex's frantic pleading carried on the breeze, and he sprinted down the grassy hill.

"No! Abby!"

He dodged the phone she threw as he ran to her. "Alex." He took her stiff, trembling arm while tears poured down her cheeks. "What's wrong? What happened?"

Alex stood where she was, gasping for each breath.

He wrapped her in a hug. "What happened?" he asked again.

"She called," she said between shuddering gasps.

"Abby called you? Are you sure it was her?"

"A woman was sobbing in the background. Men were shouting, and something crashed to the floor."

"Alex." He took her face in his hand. "Are you sure it was your sister?"

"She was whispering. She's afraid. She needs my help. She needs me to help her, but I can't."

Tears still poured, but she wouldn't give in to the sobs straining for release. "Okay." He cocooned her against him and brushed his fingers through her hair. "We'll figure this out. I'll contact Detective Canon. Did a number come up on your phone?"

"Nothing. There was nothing."

He clenched his jaw as he laid his cheek on top of her head. There wasn't a damn thing they would be able to do. "We're going to get her."

"Right." She pulled away and swiped at the drops still falling down her cheeks. "Of course we will." She took a step toward the house as she sucked in steadying breaths.

What the hell? He snagged her arm and turned her

141

back to face him. "Where are you going?"

"To the house." She wiped at her face again.

Puzzled, he studied her, watching her pull herself together. "You're upset. Take a minute. I don't—"

"I can't do this anymore," her voice broke, but she shook her head and shored herself back up. "I can't. We're getting nowhere. Abby's out there *somewhere*. She's trapped in hell. That's what I got from that phone call. She's trapped and needs my help and there's not a damn thing I can do about it." She hurried up the uneven wooden planks and disappeared behind the dip of tall marsh grasses.

Jackson stared into the deepening dusk for a long time before he had his boiling frustrations under control. Alex was exactly right. Everything she'd said had been dead on. There wasn't a damn thing they could do but wait.

Jackson scrubbed his hands over his face as he sat back in his father's office chair. The cool breeze rushing through the open window felt like heaven to his weary body. He'd been on the phone for hours talking to Detective Cannon and Doug Masterson, his old college roommate and current Pittsburg police officer. The detective documented Abby's attempted contact but could offer nothing new. Dougie, however, had come through big time. He finally had something solid to work with.

Stretching, Jackson stood and switched off the light. Bedtime. He would run with the leads he'd been given after a few hours of shut-eye. He walked down the hall to his old bedroom and stopped with his hand on the knob. The distant sound of piano music carried up the stairwell. "What the hell?" he muttered. It was after one thirty in the morning.

He peeked in the guest room across the hall and glanced at Olivia fast asleep with Gordon tucked under her arm, but Alex was gone. Retracing his steps, Jackson moved past the home office and down the stairs, following the weeping notes flowing from his mother's Steinway.

Jackson slid open the pocket doors leading to the family room and silently stepped in. Alex sat in the shadows of the dim space, her hair stirring in the breeze. One of the burgundy spaghetti straps on her pajama top had slid down her shoulder, leaving her smooth skin bare. Her eyes were closed while her fingers moved over the keys—the picture of serenity, yet the mournful song told a different story.

He'd forgotten how well she played—her Gran's last student before her arthritic fingers curled into gnarled, useless balls. He leaned against the wall, mesmerized, lost in Alex's beauty and pain, knowing he should leave. This moment was for Alex alone. She rarely played for anyone, but he couldn't make himself go.

He stared as the song carried on, until Alex's hands stilled and the last note died away. She blinked her eyes open and gasped. "Jack."

"I thought you'd gone to bed."

She shook her head. "I couldn't sleep."

The gentle gust of wind molded the silk of her top to small, firm breasts. He wanted to go to her, to free her of her burdens, but stayed where he was. "I wish there was—"

"I'm fine," she said too sharply.

Alex had managed to hold herself together after her small breakdown on the docks. She'd eaten a bite or two of her dinner and smiled while carrying on with conversation, as if the trauma of her sister's whispered pleadings for help never occurred. In a short period of time, Alex had buried her agony, but her tense shoulders and wrenching eyes told him the pain was hiding close to the surface. "It's late."

"I know." She noodled with the keys. "You spoke to Detective Canon."

"Yeah." He sighed, not wanting to talk about Abby's case until he had something to tell her one way or the other. But Alex wouldn't settle until she had the latest update.

"What did he say?"

"Not much."

Her fingers stilled, and she set them on her lap.

He struggled not to stare at her smooth, slender legs or her inviting lips he wanted to devour again. "But I talked to Dougie. He was a little more helpful."

Her eyes flew to his.

"The taskforce compiled a list of strip joints and nightclubs they watch regularly for trafficking activity. Rumor has it women caught up in the sex ring are shuffled from nightclub to nightclub and strip joint to strip joint—makes it nearly impossible for the authorities to keep up with who's who, where each girl is at, and who's there because they want to be. Credit card receipts verify that the men from the bachelor party visited a few of them. Doug slipped me the list."

Alex's gaze stayed on his, but she still said nothing.

He steamed out a breath through his nose, wanting some sort of reaction. Alex had completely closed herself off again. "Abby was being ushered into a van from the back or side of a building. We have to assume the place is one of the establishments on the list."

"Why? She could have been anywhere. The men went to several bars, right?" All traces of optimism were absent from her voice.

"Yeah, but many of the places don't really jive with what we're looking for—sports bars, family-type eateries. As the night carried on, the bachelor and his buddies' taste went downhill. They ended up in some pretty rough areas of Baltimore."

"Okay." She stood from the piano bench.

"Okay?" He'd expected her to say many things, but 'okay' wasn't one of them.

"Okay," she repeated as if that were the end of the story and started toward the pocket doors, looking down.

"Hold on." He stepped in her way.

"I'm tired and ready for bed." She attempted to skirt around him.

He grabbed her arm. "I told you I have a lead and you're going to sleep?"

"That's right. Excuse me." She yanked free.

He grabbed her again.

She fought his grip. "Stop it."

"Don't shut me out." He took hold of her shoulders. "*Talk* to me."

She stilled. "What do you want me to say?"

"I want you to tell me you're not giving up."

"I'm not giving up. You have a lead—maybe. I can't keep getting my hopes up. I can't keep thinking that 'this one' will be *the one*."

"It probably won't be," he admitted. She turned for the door again on a huff of breath, but he whirled her back. "I'm not going to lie to you. I'm not going to give you empty promises. The bachelor and his friends partied like fucking rock stars. My list of places to look into is a mile long. The businesses that may or may not use trafficked girls are all glossed up and completely legit on paper, but it's a box to check off—one way or the other—and a step, hopefully, in the right direction."

"And what if it's not?" Her voice broke.

He took her cheeks in his hands. "What if it is?"

She closed her eyes and sniffed.

"Look at me," he whispered, reining in his own frustration. "Look at me, Alex."

She met his gaze.

"The only promise I can make to you in all of this is if we get a break, *when* we get a break, I'm going to do whatever it takes to bring Abby home. We're bringing Abby home."

"We have to." Her lip trembled as she clutched his arms. "We have to. She's afraid. She's in so much pain."

And so was Alex. He rested his forehead against hers, hardly able to stand it. "*God*, I hate this."

Her breath trembled out.

"I'll start looking into this tomorrow. I'm going out after Olivia's in bed."

She gripped him closer. "I'm coming with you."

He pulled back. "No."

"Of course I am."

"Alex, it's not happening." He was ready to fight her on this. "This is dangerous. A lot of those clubs are in really shitty areas."

"You can't expect me to sit back and do nothing." The determined light was heating her eyes.

"I can expect you to stay here and be safe. Besides, you look too much like Abby. That's a huge risk for both of you."

"Fine."

"I'm not going to let—fine?" He frowned, studying her. She was giving in too easily. When Alex had her mind set on something, it was damn near unshakable.

"You're right. I don't want to put Abby in any more danger."

He continued to hold her gaze, waiting for the catch.

"We should get to bed. Livy will be up before long."

"Alex." Why did he have a bad feeling about this?

"Thank you." She slid the doors open and left. "Good night."

"Yeah, no problem." What the hell was she up to? His stomach twisted with unease as his eyes followed her up the stairs. Whatever it was, he knew he wasn't going to like it.

CHAPTER 10

A LEXA HELD LIVY'S HAND AS they followed the amazing scent of cinnamon and coffee down the stairs to the kitchen.

"Morning, Grammy and Grampy." Olivia bolted for Jack's dad. "I'm awake now."

"So I see." George settled Livy on his lap at the table and smiled at Alexa. "Good morning."

Exhausted after another night of fitful snatches of sleep, she attempted a sunny smile as she sat down. "Good morning."

Carol slid a steaming cup under Alexa's nose. "I made you the hazelnut decaf you like so much—a spoonful of sugar and a splash of milk included."

Touched, she smiled fully this time as she breathed in the heavenly aroma. "Thank you, Car... Mom. I can't believe you remembered."

"Of course, sweetie." Carol placed a huge platter of her freshly baked homemade cinnamon rolls on the table—Alexa's favorite. "I remember all sorts of things. My heart broke when you and Jackson decided to go your separate ways."

Nodding, Alexa bit her tongue. She wanted to remind Carol the decision to end their relationship had been Jack's alone, but what purpose would that serve? "Is Jack still in bed?" She picked up her mug and cupped her hands around the warmth.

"Good grief, no, honey. He was up and out of the house at sunrise."

Alexa frowned as she set down her cup. "Jack left? Where'd he go?"

"He said something about meeting up with someone or other." George snagged a cinnamon roll and met his wife's stare as he put the icing-laden bread on a plate. "One roll isn't going to kill me, Carol."

Her brow shot in the air. "Let's hope not." She turned her attention to Alexa. "George's cholesterol was a little high at his last doctor's visit."

Alexa studied Jack's father. Five-foot eleven and health-club fit; light brown hair going gray at the temples; handsome, ruddy complexion; blue eyes friendly and alert—he appeared healthy to her. George looked better than most men half his age, and he was still shy of sixty. "You look wonderful."

"See now, Carol? I look wonderful." He winked at Alexa and grinned. Jack had his father's smile, great sense of humor, and outgoing personality. So did Livy.

"Besides, Livy wants to share some of Grampy's breakfast, doesn't she?" He pulled another plate from the small stack and set it in front of his granddaughter.

"Yes, I do. You can have a bite, Grampy. I will eat the rest."

Laughing, George hugged Livy tight. "Now, that's my girl. A hearty appetite's a fine thing."

Alexa chuckled and sampled her coffee, savoring the rich flavor. "Cinnamon rolls are a special treat, but Livy's definitely not picky, are you, pumpkin?"

"I like lots and lots of food. I try new things," she preened.

"Yes you do." Alexa kissed her finger and touched it to the tip of Livy's nose before she glanced at the digital clock on the stove. Seven-thirty. Why didn't Jack tell her he had a meeting this morning? "Did Jack mention what time he thought he might be back?"

"No. He mostly grunted his way through breakfast." Carol grabbed her own cinnamon roll. "He was grumpy as two constipated bears. I don't think he slept well."

Alexa sipped her coffee again and made a sound in her throat. Did last night's conversation keep him up, too? She was trying so hard not to get her hopes up about the new lead Jack had stumbled on, but it was difficult. This one actually seemed like it could go somewhere. She had every intention of being by Jack's side when he left tonight, even if he was dead set against the idea. She was as determined to go as he was that she stay behind. Abby's terrified whispers still echoed through her mind, breaking her heart. She wouldn't sit back and do nothing while her sister suffered. She had yet to work out exactly how she was going to bring Jack around, but she would.

"So, Jackson said you're teaching first grade."

Alexa snapped back to attention and looked at George. "Uh, yes. I do. I love it. The kids are so much fun, and the hours are perfect for Livy and me."

"You're wonderful with children. You've done an excellent job with Olivia. You must be a very special teacher," Carol added.

Alexa smiled. "That's quite a compliment coming from a veteran. You're still teaching math?"

"Can't imagine doing anything else."

"And the drama club? Do you still do that?"

"Drama club," she scoffed. "High school *is* a drama club, but yes, I'm still involved with Maryland's brightest actors—head of the department now. I have boxfuls of supplies in the den from our last competition—didn't get around to bringing them back yet." She shrugged. "I have all summer."

"Competition? I always thought of drama club as school plays."

"Oh, it is, but it also means hitting the road to do small skits for nursing homes, hospitals, and competition."

"Very interesting."

"And time consuming, but I figure while George is busy selling his insurance, I might as well stay occupied too. Now that the boys are grown and so far away, I have the extra time. The students are very talented. We win quite often. Helps keep us in wigs and greasepaint."

Alexa reached for a roll and stopped. "Wigs?"

"Oh, all kinds. Blond, redhead, you name it. The kids are wild about their fake hair. They say it helps them immerse themselves in their roles." Carol rolled her eyes and smiled.

Alexa grabbed the gooey, cinnamon-y bread as an idea started to take hold. "Do you have wigs in your boxes in the den?"

Carol frowned. "Sure, sweetie."

"Huh. Will it bother you if I take a look?"

Carol stared at Alexa as if she'd lost her mind. "Be my guest."

Restless, thoughts whirling, Alexa got up, went to the fridge, and poured Livy a glass of milk. Then she grabbed the Tupperware container filled to the brim with green grapes. "I may have to go out later this evening—after Livy's in bed. Would you be willing to keep an eye on her if I do?"

"Of course, but I thought you and Livy were staying close to the home front for the next little while."

"Mmm." She walked back to the table. "Livy, have some milk and fruit with your roll, sweetie."

Alexa ran the hem under the needle one final time and snipped the bobbin thread as she freed her new skirt from the sewing machine's arm. She nibbled her lip and eyed the denim, scrutinized the length before she pulled it on, snapped the button, and zipped.

She hurried over to the three-sided mirror in Carol's beautiful sewing space, which had a view of the bay, and swallowed as she studied her appearance. Abby was the designer in the family but she hadn't done half bad. The clinging white tank top with a plunging neckline left nothing to the imagination. Her tight jean skirt stopped three inches below her ass cheeks. She'd used a heavy hand with the eyeliner and mascara, giving her lake-blue eyes a large, sooty look to play up the dark blond wig and add to the party-girl effect.

"Hopefully this works," she muttered. While Olivia had taken her afternoon nap, Alexa studied pictures on Google Images, trying to determine what women wore out for a night of bar hopping and clubbing. She'd never done either. While her college roommates had partied, she'd busted her butt to keep her scholarships and worked at the library to send what money she could home for Gran's constant stream of medical bills.

She slid on her sandal-heels and scrutinized her face. There was no way she could be mistaken for Abby looking like this. She opened the door, peeked in the hall, and made a dash for the room she and Livy shared, closing herself in. She smiled down at her exhausted daughter and smoothed the sheet over her sprawled, sleeping form.

Bedtime had never been easier after the excitement of the day. Livy was typically a night owl, but not this evening. The afternoon boat ride had been a thrill for both of them. Alexa forgot how much she missed the wind in her face as the powerboat glided along the choppy water. Watching Olivia help Grampy steer the sweet watercraft had been such a special moment.

And the soft shell crab... Livy had her first taste when they docked at a local dining spot a few miles from the house. Alexa chuckled as she remembered how Livy's nose had wrinkled with her dislike, but the grilled hot dog and chocolate ice cream had gone down just fine.

Although their lives had been turned upside down, Alexa couldn't be sorry Livy was getting the opportunity to get to know the rest of her family. The Matthews were such good people.

A light knock sounded at the door. Alexa kissed Livy on the forehead and tucked her daughter's beloved stuffed frog back under her arm, then she grabbed her purse and turned. She took a deep breath as she smoothed down her skintight clothing and walked to the door. "Here goes nothing," she muttered and twisted the knob.

"I'm going to head..." Jack's eyes went huge as he looked her up and down. "What the *hell* are you wearing?"

If she wasn't in for the fight of her life, she would've laughed at his shocked expression. "My clubbing outfit."

"Your—your *what*?"

"Shh." She glanced over her shoulder, afraid they were going to wake Livy. She opened the bedroom door fully so George and Carol would hear Olivia if she called. Then she grabbed Jack's hand, pulling him down the hall as she continued. "My clubbing outfit. I'm coming with you."

He stopped short. "No, you're not. We've talked about this."

"You told me I wasn't going because Abby and I look too much alike. We don't anymore. I'm coming to help find my sister."

"I also said this was too damn dangerous. It's not happening."

Her brows winged high. It was time for the big guns.

"You take me or I go myself."

He smirked at the challenge. "You don't know where I'm going."

Damn. She hadn't thought of that. The argument was supposed to have ended with her threat. Now what? She shrugged, then began to rifle through her purse, searching for her phone. "Where's my phone?"

He pulled her cell from his back pocket. "I took it with me today—had the lab boys see if they could get a trace on the call from yesterday."

"Did they?"

"No. Abby must've called from another burn phone."

She swallowed the familiar taste of disappointment as she reached for her cell, more determined than ever to tag along.

Jack held it out of reach. "Why do you want this?"

"Because I pay the bill." She made another grab, but Jack moved again. "Give me my phone, Jack."

"Why?"

She steamed out a breath and glared. This was *not* going the way she planned. "Because I'm calling a cab."

Eyes hot, he shoved the cell in his back pocket and leaned close to her face. "No fucking way." He spaced out each word on a dangerous whisper.

"Don't talk to me like that." She shoved him. "Get out of my way." She stormed down the stairs.

"Where are you going?"

"I'll use one of the landlines. I'm sure if I ask a cabbie to take me to a strip club in Baltimore, I'll end up where I want to be." Her stomach fluttered with unease. She didn't want to go without Jack, but pride pushed her on.

"Damn it, Alex. Why do you have to be so stubborn?" He followed behind.

A smug smile spread across her lips as she continued down the steps. Maybe all wasn't lost. She hurried in the den, and her smile disappeared when Carol gasped. Alexa wrinkled her nose as she looked at Jack's stunned and staring parents snuggled on the couch with a bowl of popcorn, a movie playing on the TV.

"Honey, what on earth?"

"Alex, wait a minute." Jack hurried in after her. "Excuse us," he said as he pulled her into the living room. "I want you to stay here."

She shook her head and brushed at the strands of dark blond that stuck to her glossy lips. "I can't."

"Yes, you can. Go change into...*clothes*. Watch a movie with my parents."

"I want to help, Jack. I need to."

"I get that, but this is nowhere near safe. I've been straight with you from day one, and I'm telling you this is dangerous."

"No more dangerous for me than you."

Brow raised, he looked her up and down. "You're playing with fire going anywhere dressed like that."

"I'll fit right in. I researched my outfit online."

"You—" His eyes softened as he smiled. "You researched?"

She saw her opening and took his hand. "Please, Jack. *Please.* I have to help Abby. I'm going crazy sitting here waiting for someone else to rescue my sister. I need to be able to tell myself each and every day that I've done *something* to try to bring her home. Would you be able to sit patiently by if someone had Will? Wouldn't you do anything for your brother?"

He closed his eyes and sighed. "Low blow."

"Whatever it takes, Jack. Please take me with you tonight."

He stared at her, jaw clenched, breath steaming from his nose. "You have to stay with me."

Detecting a glimmer of hope, she yanked him into a

hug. "Thank you."

He eased her back and ran his hands down her arms. "I'm serious, Alex, right with me."

"I'll be stuck like glue." She hugged him again, her relief huge as she stared at him, eyes level in her heels. "See? Like Elmer's."

He grinned. "I'm thinking more like Krazy Glue."

She wrapped her arms tighter and hooked a leg around his jean-clad hip. "This would probably draw too much attention." She grinned back as he chuckled.

"Probably." He clutched his hand on her thigh, keeping her in place. Heat replaced the humor in his gaze. "You're bound to cause a riot dressed the way you are."

Her heart kicked into high gear as his thumb stroked lazy circles against her sensitive skin, making her shiver. His hungry stare held her captive. How many times had he looked at her in just that way while they made love? "Whatever it takes," she murmured.

He fingered the golden strands of her chin-length wig, and his palm brushed her jaw. "I'm going to miss running my fingers through your hair tonight."

Need tugged and pulled at her center. His mouth was an inch from hers. She was desperate to taste him. "I..."

"We need to go." He let go of her leg and stepped away.

"I—Yes." Her brain had turned to mush as her hormones raged. "Okay."

He took her hand and walked with her back to the den where his parents sat, once again tuned into their movie. "Mom, Dad, we're going to head into Baltimore."

"Can you still watch Livy?" Alexa struggled not to squirm as George and Carol stared.

"Of course, but sweetie, why in the world are you dressed like—like *that*?"

"I'm...immersing myself in my role."

"Dougie Masterson gave me a couple of places to check out in the city—Abby's case."

"Honey, I don't think it's safe to be going out like that."

Alexa pressed her lips together. "Typically I would agree one hundred percent, but tonight I'll blend in."

"It seems dangerous."

Carol sounded just like her son. "I need to find my sister, Mom. I have to try. I'll have Jack close by to keep me safe. Abby has no one. We might find her."

"We could," Jack squeezed her hand. "But more than likely not, Alex. I don't want you getting your hopes up."

She met his gaze. "I stopped getting my hopes up several days ago."

Jack pulled her against his side and kissed her forehead. "Let's go see what we can dig up."

She closed her eyes, trying to block out the comfort his habitual gesture brought, but not before noting George and Carol's quick glance at each other. She eased herself away from Jack. "I'll have my phone on me." She plucked her cellphone from Jack's back pocket and tossed it in her purse. "If you need anything or have any questions, don't hesitate."

"Livy will be fine. You two be careful."

Jackson drove north toward the bright lights of Baltimore and glanced at Alex's smooth, toned legs—again. How the hell was he supposed to concentrate on *anything* with that killer body of hers distracting him?

"You know, I'm actually feeling pretty good about tonight." She smiled.

He loved seeing her bright eyes and warm smile without the strain, but she was getting her hopes up. "I want you to keep in mind that this is a first step.

Surveillance takes time."

"But it's a step, right? You even said so last night."

"Yeah, but—"

"Shh." She pressed her finger to his lips. "I'm not getting my hopes up. I know how you think. It just feels good to be doing *something* that might help."

He swallowed as a swift punch of desire clutched his stomach. Those eyes—so big, so dark and sexy. He could stare into them for days. He wanted to yank off that horrible wig and run his fingers through her hair. And her smooth, silky skin; he needed to touch her everywhere. She was hardly wearing anything. He could pull over and have her naked before he took his next breath.

She'd churned him up, and her barely-there clothes didn't have a damn thing to do with it. When she'd held him close with her leg wrapped around him, he'd seen glimpses of the past. She'd grinned at him, *for* him, while they joked. He wanted that back, craving the fun and lightness they used to share so long ago. Alex was twisting him up.

Clenching his jaw, he stared ahead and took the exit for downtown. They were minutes from their first stop, Club Jerhico—a strictly nightclub atmosphere. He planned to ease Alex in to the night slowly. She had no idea what she was in for. Some of the spots they would visit were little more than skeezy pits of naked, strung-out women. For that alone he'd wanted her to stay home. Alex had done thorough research on the hellish conditions her sister was more than likely living in, but pictures on a computer and printed police documents were a far cry from actually experiencing it firsthand. After tonight, there would be no way to protect her from Abby's grim reality. "Did Abby ever go clubbing?"

"Uh, I don't think so. That's not really her scene. Why?"

He shrugged. "Just playing with the pieces, trying to make them fit."

"Which pieces exactly? There are a million."

He pulled into the parking garage and rolled down the window, grabbing the ticket the machine spit out, then driving forward. "The police still can't find the tie that connects Abby to the other victims."

She unbuckled as he turned into a parking space. "What if there isn't a connection between the girls and Abby? What if the cases are unrelated? The police could be chasing down leads to nowhere."

He killed the engine and looked at her. "My gut tells me they're on the right track. The abductions are too similar. There has to be something to it."

"But what? I just don't see it."

"Well, let's break it down, starting with the first three victims."

She turned in her seat, facing him. "I've read everything I can get my hands on about the girls. Even *their* cases aren't necessarily similar. The first two girls have the most in common: broken homes, a lack of supervision, mothers with substance abuse issues, absentee fathers, etcetera, etcetera, but not Kristen Moore."

Alex had done her homework. He didn't expect anything less. "She had a different home life, but there are definitely parallels," Jack said. "Kristen's parents are loving, quality individuals, but divorcing. She was taking the separation hard and getting herself into trouble as a result. All of the girls' friends reported sneaking into nightclubs on more than one occasion, so that's a connection right there. You add that up and we get three troubled young women, fractured home lives, and the Baltimore club scene. That's the dot connecting three identical abductions."

Alex frowned as her busy brain worked. "Okay, I can see your point, but once again, how does that bring us around to Abby? Other than the actual kidnapping— the vans and the two men grabbing her—the cases don't sound even remotely the same to my sister's. Abby isn't into the club scene. She has a great head on her shoulders. She's confident, driven, and successful in her own right. She has a degree in fashion and a minor in business. She doesn't need a man to make her feel good about herself. We had a terrible home life—no doubt about it. The mother with serious mental health and addiction issues...and eventually suicide; the non-existent father. But that was so long ago. Money was always hard to come by, but somehow Gran pulled it off with her meager social security checks. Our first few years with my mother left little impact, especially after the counseling. Gran raised us to be strong, independent women."

"I loved your Gran. She was amazing. She did a hell of a job."

Alex smiled. "Yes she did." Her smile dimmed "And that's what makes this so much worse. We've all worked too hard for this to be it for Abby."

"This isn't the end of her story, Alex. That's why we're out here tonight."

She blew out a breath, fluttering her fake blond bangs. "You're right."

"One of the most important things we can do for Abby is keep an open mind. After my conversation with Detective Canon today, I know the authorities are seriously considering a lure."

"A lure?"

"Yeah, someone who seeks out the ideal 'candidate'— tells them what they want to hear, promises them love, fame, drugs—whatever it takes—before they bag 'em."

160

"See, again, that doesn't fit with my sister. She's not the 'ideal candidate.' Abby lived in Federal Hill with three other fashion majors. Maggie, one of her roommates' father, owned the row house they stayed in. It's a beautiful place—very upper class. They split the utilities four ways. It was very reasonable. Abby did a bit of modeling here and there to pay for her classes and room and board. She didn't need anyone to promise her love, money, or drugs. That wasn't what she was after. Abby isn't a party animal like you were. She's obsessed with her sketchpads, sewing machine, fabric, and mannequins. She was usually at school, a fashion show, home with Livy and me, or working on her art."

"Would she have gone to a club if one of her roommates wanted a friend to tag along?"

She shrugged. "Maybe, but I can say without a doubt she wouldn't have been a regular. When you knew Abby, she hadn't discovered her passion yet. She was still finding her way."

Jackson grinned. That was an understatement. "Abby was pretty relaxed about school."

Alex chuckled. "'Relaxed.' I like that. Gran and I certainly pulled a few hairs out over Abby's nonchalance. But that was before Gran's downstairs neighbor started making Abby's senior prom dress. Halfway through, Ms. Beesley fell ill and was hospitalized. Gran tried to work on the gown, but with her hands the way they were, it was impossible. She called me once, upset because she was afraid Abby wouldn't have anything special to wear. My skills with a needle and thread are passable at best. I was pregnant, exhausted, and stressed out with student teaching and finding a job, but I told her I would come home over the weekend to see what I could do to help. Gran called me the next night and said not to worry about a thing. Abby finished the whole dress and

161

added a flourish or two of her own. From then on, Abby was obsessed. She applied to schools and sent designs along with her applications. Despite her grades, they accepted her. She's amazing, Jack. Gran was so proud."

"She was proud of you both."

Alex took his hand and squeezed it, smiling. "She was, but Gran and Abby shared something…a little bit different. I think I was always more guarded with my feelings. I was my mother's first, whereas Abby was always hers." Her smile dimmed, and she pulled free of his grip. "I'm so glad Gran's not here to deal with all this. It would've broken her heart."

He took her hand back and stroked his thumb over her knuckles. "You've had a right to your 'guard,' Alex. You dealt with more than any one person should have to. I'm sorry you and Abby are going through this. If I could make it go away…" He wanted her to smile again.

"You've been just what I've needed. I don't know how I'd be getting through this nightmare without you." She pulled his hand to her face and rested her cheek in his palm—an old gesture that surprised him and gave him his first inkling of hope.

He brought her fingers to his lips and kissed them. "Let's see what we can find out tonight."

She nodded. "Okay."

Twenty minutes later, after a two-block walk, Jackson gripped Alex's hand as they made their way through the mobs of people dancing to the pounding bass and multicolored lights of Club Jerhico. He scanned the alarmed exits and noted the hordes of patrons surrounding the bar. There was no way in hell Abby was here. There were too many opportunities for escape among the chaos. This was either a dead end or a front for lures. He would give them half an hour to figure it out before they moved on.

Alex slammed into him when he stopped. "Sorry." She stepped back. "So, what are we looking for?"

He pulled her against him. "First and foremost, we need to blend. If something's going on here we don't want anyone figuring out we've noticed. Keep your eyes open for under-aged girls and men hanging around them."

"It's so crowded." She glanced over her shoulder and started to turn. "How are we supposed to tell?"

Despite her outfit, Alex screamed 'fish out of water.' "Just dance with me for a little while."

"How can I find my sister if we're dancing?"

"We're blending while we look, remember?" He took her hands and wrapped them around the back of his neck as he found his rhythm to the hammering beat.

She stared at him for several seconds. "I'm not much of a dancer."

"I haven't seen you try. I'm doing it, aren't I?"

"Yeah, but you're an athlete. You look good whenever you move."

He grinned. "Are you hitting on me?"

"What?" She blinked several times. "No. No, of course not. I was just saying..."

He laughed. "I'm kidding. Lighten up." He pinched her chin gently. "Dancing is part of our cover. Give it a try."

She licked her lips and imitated his movements. Within minutes her shyness vanished and she was smiling. "This is kind of fun."

Despite her initial hesitation, she had decent moves. His mouth watered as her willowy body brushed and bumped his. He scanned the crowds and glanced at several men watching her. Maybe Alex dancing wasn't such a good idea after all. Her short, tight skirt barely covered her. The thin, clinging top she wore showcased her tiny waist and a provocative hint of smooth creamy breasts. She'd pulled off 'sexy' a little too well.

"Over there."

"Huh?"

She pressed her body to his and leaned in close to his ear. "Behind you."

He shivered as her breath heated his neck and his fingers touched her hips.

"There's no way that girl is twenty-one. She's not even eighteen."

Jackson glanced over, spotting at least twenty women.

"That guy's all over her," Alex said in a disgusted hiss. She eased back and stared into his eyes as Jackson casually turned them in the direction she spoke of.

He scanned the crowd. "I don't see her."

The song changed, slowing, but grew louder.

"What?" she yelled, shaking her head.

He leaned in as she had. "I don't see her."

She turned her head in the girl's direction and raised her hand to point. "She's wearing—"

"No, Alex. Here. Look at me." He took her face in his hands. "You're gonna blow it."

"You're right. Sorry."

"Just focus here. I'll check it out again in a few seconds." He trailed his fingers over her jaw.

She clutched at his waist. "What are you doing?"

"Blending. Looking like everyone else." The masses of men and women crowded around them, held each other tight. "What does she look like?" He traced his thumb down her neck and paused on her hammering pulse, then he continued down to her collarbone and toyed with the triangular charm resting against her chest.

"Um, she's..." Her lids fluttered closed as he made his way back up. "Brown hair." Alex opened her eyes, locking on his. "She has brown hair."

He was taking advantage of the situation but didn't

care. She looked so different in her wig, but she smelled the same—vanilla and flowers. He brushed his mouth along her cheekbone and pressed his lips to her temple. "What's she wearing?"

Alex's fingers wandered to his hair. "She—I—I can't think when you touch me like this."

He clutched her ass over the little denim covering it, yanking her against him, and snagged her bottom lip, tugging gently, wanting to devour her whole right where they stood. God, she was driving him crazy.

"Jack." The heat of her breath warmed his skin as she whispered his name.

He turned them a fraction to the right and spotted the young girl with brown hair out of the corner of his eye. "Is she wearing a blue skirt?"

Alex's brows furrowed. "What? Yes. Yes, and a white, sleeveless top."

He studied the pretty brown-haired girl, for surely she was still a girl—no more than seventeen—take a piece of paper from a good looking, well-built man easily five to ten years her senior. "Her friends are cruising over. I think they're leaving." He rested Alex's head on his shoulder and turned slowly in a dance that matched the rhythm of the music blasting through the huge space, watching until the group of four girls disappeared in the crowd toward the exit. "They're leaving."

She pulled her head from his shoulder. "Well, thank God. How are they—"

"Hold on." He took his phone from his pocket and moved until he framed the darkened, blurry image of the man in the screen. "Smile."

Alex did as she was told. He snapped the photo.

"Why'd you do that?"

"I'm getting a shot of him. I'll send it to Ethan and see if he can make anything out of it."

Seconds later, the man vanished into the mob of dancers.

"He makes me sick. I'm so sick." Alex started to move into the crowd.

Jackson grabbed her hand before he lost sight of her. "Hey, wait a minute."

"I can't." She whirled. "How are they getting in here? Even with a fake ID, it's clear she isn't of age."

"Come on." He walked with her through the noise until they stepped out the door and into a cloud of cigarette smoke.

Alex coughed as she fanned her hand in front of her face. "We need to call the police." She reached into her purse.

He tugged her toward the direction of the parking garage. "Let's stroll for awhile."

"The police—"

"No police, Alex."

"But he was taking advantage of her."

"And what should we tell them? This place is a Disney movie compared to where we need to go, Alex. That guy hit on someone he shouldn't have. He gave her a phone number—again, pretty G-rated. Unacceptable," he added when Alex steamed out a breath. "But G-rated nonetheless."

"Okay, so no cops. But I'm still angry."

He kept quiet as they made their way along the sidewalk in the balmy summer air. This wasn't going to work. "We should go home."

"What?" Alex stopped in her tracks. "No. We can't."

"I think we have to."

"But it's only eleven. We haven't even started looking for Abby."

"You're right, we've barely started looking for Abby and you're already worked up. It's going to get so much worse."

"I can handle whatever I need to."

He stared at the fierce determination darkening her eyes. "One more stop, Alex. You show me you can keep it together at the next club, or you're finished."

"You can't—"

"I can and will. This isn't some action flick or suspense novel. The people who have your sister aren't fucking around."

"I'm aware of our reality, Jack. Take me to the next place. I can handle it." She stormed down the sidewalk.

He stared, sighing, then started after her. They might just make it through the night if the hard light stayed in her eyes instead of the sad vulnerability and outrage he saw moments before.

CHAPTER 11

A LEXA PEEKED AT JACK'S WATCH—TWO in the morning. She'd lost count of the bars and clubs they'd ducked in and out of over the last few hours. They stayed at some spots for mere minutes, other places longer, but this club was different. They had been here for almost an hour. She had no idea what compelled Jack to stay, but she trusted his instincts.

Her eyes burned and her throat was dry and irritated from the clouds of smoke surrounding them as they sat. She eyed the glass of water Jack ordered her, yearning for a sip, but didn't dare. The establishment—and that was a loose term for it—didn't appear to be overly worried about the city's health codes. Who knew what types of diseases waited on the rim of the filmy glass?

Bright pink lights showcased dancers sliding on or gyrating against poles to loud hip-hop. The young women were scantily clad in various colored g-strings.

Alexa stared at the stage entrance and exit, too sick inside to watch the women exploit themselves for another second. Was this what Abby did night after night? She struggled not to turn away as a dancer shoved her crotch in a man's face while he threw bills on the stage. Alexa's sense of urgency to rescue her sister only increased after Jack brought her to the first strip joint. She'd never consider herself a prude or sheltered, but maybe she was—sheltered, anyway.

Alexa looked down at her lap when a college-aged kid waved a fifty in the air, and a mostly naked brunette left her pole to crouch and press his face to her breasts. His tongue flicked out, lapping, to the hoots and encouragement from the group he'd come with, before an intimidatingly bulky bouncer dressed in black pushed the over-eager man away.

God, *God* this was awful. She wanted to tell Jack she'd had enough, but she sat where she was. Abby didn't get a choice. Her sister had no free will to leave a life she hadn't chosen. If Abby endured this each night, she sure as hell could sit here too.

Who would Abby be when they brought her home? Would the trauma send her down the road their mother had taken? Would her sister drown herself in an abyss of alcohol and depression until she couldn't take it anymore? Would she walk into a bathroom and find Abby dead in a bathtub full of blood and water, the way she had her mom?

Alexa squeezed her eyes shut and clenched her fists against the horrid memory. Abby was so bright and talented. Gran had worked hard to erase the neglect and distress of their early childhood. Alexa needed to believe Abby would be strong enough to overcome this too.

Did Abby know she was searching for her and that she would never, ever give up? Alexa clamped her fists tighter until they ached, willing her sister to *feel* her—wherever she was out there. Abby wasn't here. She hadn't been in any of the places they'd gone to. Alexa took a deep breath of stale, smoke-filled air and struggled not to give in to her tears. Jack had tried to prepare her for the conditions she would see. He'd urged her several times not to get her hopes up, but her unyielding need to believe that they would soon free Abby from her nightmare didn't allow her to listen. Although she'd tried to remain cautiously optimistic, a small piece of her had been convinced they would find her tonight.

"Hey, you ready to get out of here?"

Alexa continued to stare at her thighs, afraid Jack would see the sorrow in her eyes. He knew her too well. "Yes. Let's go."

"Come on." He took her hand and they stood.

They started toward the exit, weaving their way through the tables full of men and women. Alexa glanced around once more, taking everything in—the dancers circling the poles, the men transfixed and staring, the darker hallway off to the side of the stage leading to closed doors, but there was no Abby.

Jack pushed open the door and she took a step into the night. "You said—"

"Stop." He pulled on her hand.

Frowning, she met his gaze as he tugged her back into the noisy room. "What is it?"

"I think I just saw Abby."

She whirled. "Where?"

"Going into one of the rooms down the hall."

Without thinking, Alexa rushed ahead.

Jack caught her by the elbow and squeezed hard until she gasped and halted. "What are you *doing*?" he hissed close to her ear.

"I—Abby's here."

"I *think* she's here," he bit off.

"We have to do something. We have to get her and take her with us." She glanced back to the hallway, fighting the urge to pull away and yell to her sister that this was almost over.

"Look at me."

She met Jack's cool eyes, surprised by the chill she'd only seen once before on a cold February night.

He pulled her several steps away from the door and the bouncer. "If you want to see your sister again, you'll calm down. This is make or break, Alex. If they even think we've seen her, they'll pull her out of here before you can blink and put her on a plane to some place that makes this shit hole look like paradise."

She took a deep breath and pressed her lips firm, trying to settle her racing heart. "You're right. I'm sorry. You're right." She had to pull herself together. This wasn't the time for hysterics. Abby needed her to be strong. "What are we going to do?"

He studied her, then nodded. "We need to find seats—closer to this side of the stage."

"Okay."

They weaved through the crowds again to an empty table.

"Should we call the police?"

Jack shook his head. "The rooms off to the side are usually used for private dances. I'm going to try to get a positive ID before we do anything. You'll have to stay here."

She wanted to go and see Abby for herself but knew that wasn't an option. "Okay. If it's her how will we get her out?"

"We won't."

Shocked to the bone, her eyes flew to Jack's. "What do you mean we won't? You promised me that when we got our break you were going to do whatever you had to do to bring her home. This is our break, Jack. I can't leave here without her."

"Look around the room. Do you see the bouncers at every door, next to the stage, and at the end of the hall?"

Alexa's gaze darted to each of the large men dressed in black, covering all potential exits. Abby was possibly no more than fifty steps from where they sat, and she couldn't help her. "Jack," her voice broke. She cleared away the weakness. "There must be something. There has to be a way. The police."

"One step at a time. Let me make a positive ID first." He took her chin between his fingers. "Listen to me, Alex, and listen carefully. Don't do anything stupid. Don't move from this table. Don't go to the bathroom, the bar, or outside. Keep your phone in your purse and *do not* call Canon or 911. Understand?"

Who was this cruel stranger? She pulled free of his grip. "Yes."

He stood and walked to the bar.

What happened to Jack? In a matter of seconds he'd gone from supportive to hard and distant. She watched as he spoke to the bartender and pointed to the rooms in the back. He shook his head and shook his head again. It wasn't long before the bartender signaled to one of the bulky men in black.

The bartender said something to the man before the bouncer nudged his head for Jack to follow. She met his gaze and watched as he disappeared down the dim hall beyond.

The bouncer opened the door to a dingy room. "No touching the ladies, or I'll have to punch your face in."

Jackson nodded and took his seat in the folding chair, noting the holes in the plaster-cracked walls as he breathed through his mouth. The place smelled like shit.

The knob twisted and a redhead stepped in. Not Abby.

"Hold up. I said the black-haired girl."

The bouncer folded his arms and tilted his head. "What's wrong with Strawberry?"

"For fifty fucking bucks I want what I paid for." Jackson looked the young redhead up and down. If she was eighteen, he was eighty. "Sorry, sugar, redheads don't do anything for me."

Strawberry glanced at the bouncer, then at the floor as she stepped from the door.

"I was gonna bring some pals here for a bachelor party next week, but if you guys can't deliver—" Jackson started to stand.

"Hold your fucking horses. She's coming."

He settled again, wound tight from the wait. He was worried about Alex out in the lounge by herself among the slime of Baltimore. He couldn't shake the anguish haunting her eyes. She'd stared at him in disbelief when he told her they would have to leave Abby behind—if she was even here at all. His mind raced as he tried to think of a way to get them both out safely, but he had to remember his own words: one step at a time. Confirmation first.

The door opened and Abby walked in wearing a tiny red bikini. Her small, firm breasts spilled from the ill-fitting top. The stringy bottom left little to the imagination. Jackson clenched his jaw as their eyes met, the recognition instant. He held his breath when she paused mid-step, afraid Abby might blow it right then and there. Things would get bad quickly if she ruined his cover. "Now this is more like it." He grinned. "What's your name, sugar?"

"Fawn."

"Fawn?" He nodded and winked. "I've been looking for someone just like you, honey." Son of a bitch he felt like a fucking perv, even with the double meaning. This was Alex's little sister. She'd grown into a stunning woman.

She glanced down before their eyes met again and she straddled him with her pretty, slender body.

He swallowed, sick from the entire situation as she ground herself against him, rubbing her breasts over his chest. *I'm sorry, Abby. I'm so sorry.*

She reached her arms behind her neck and tugged on the tie to her top as she stared at him, her eyes pleading. Jackson wanted to reassure her and give her some piece of comfort, but he could only hold her gaze while the bouncer stood in the corner watching their every move.

The thin straps of her bikini fell forward. Abby moved her hands to her back to unhook the last piece of flimsy fabric while she gyrated against his crotch.

He couldn't take any more. Forgetting the rules, he grabbed her arms and squeezed gently. "Leave it on."

The bouncer stepped forward. "I said don't touch the lady."

Jackson held up his hands before he got kicked out. "Sorry. Leave it on, Fawn. Tits aren't my thing. Your ass however... Take off the bottom."

Her brow shot up in the same go to hell expression he'd seen on Alex's face a hundred times before. Dear Christ, she was Alex's mirror image, and she was suffering.

"That's not part of the service, fucker," the bouncer sneered. "There're girls on every corner around here."

Jackson shook his head and shrugged. "I guess this'll have to do. Do you dance often, Fawn?"

"I—"

"She ain't gettin' paid to talk. Times up."

Jackson pulled a fifty from his wallet and handed the bill to Abby, full well knowing they would take it from her as soon as she left the room.

Abby stood and held his gaze as she walked to the door.

"I'll be thinking about you, Fawn. I'll be back." He winked and smiled as she left, and he got to his feet, wanting to see where she went.

"What's your hurry?" The bouncer stepped in front of him, blocking the exit.

He shrugged. "Don't have one."

Thirty seconds passed before the asshole moved to the side.

Jackson opened the door and peered about, but Abby was gone. He made his way down the hall, listening, trying to figure out where the dancers went after they finished their 'performance'.

"You had your dance. Time for you to go." The bouncer walked behind him, following him to the main lounge.

"Guess I can't win. First, I was in too much of a hurry. Now, I'm not fast enough."

"Just walk, asshole." He gave Jackson a shove on the shoulder.

It was tempting to turn around and punch the shit out the man who was more fat than muscle, but he spotted Alex at the table, fending off the advances of some guy.

"I said no thank you." She shrugged away from the same kid who'd had his face in the dancers boobs just a few minutes before.

"You know you want to," Frat boy slurred.

"I assure you I definitely don't." She started to stand.

Jackson stepped up to the table. "Beat it."

Frat boy stood from his lean on the cheap plastic and overbalanced, catching himself on another patron before he fell. "What's it to you, pal?"

"She's with me."

"Are you his girl, sexy?"

"Uh, yes." She stood and wrapped her arm around his waist.

"I'll fight you for her." Frat boy stumbled forward.

He didn't have time for this shit. Jackson sidestepped Alex and yanked the little punk up by his sweaty t-shirt.

"Get the hell out of here before I knock you out."

Two of Frat boy's friends hurried over and pulled him from Jackson's grip. "Fuck, Dustin, what the hell? Sorry man." With their apology, they slung their arms around Dustin's shoulders and started back to their table center stage.

Jackson glanced around the room, noting more than one bouncer looking in his direction. "Come on. Let's get out of here." He grabbed Alex's hand.

She tugged away. "Did you see her? Was it Abby?"

"I'll explain in a minute." He took her hand again and pulled her toward the exit, reading her hesitation perfectly. She had no intentions of going anywhere without her sister. He would put a call in to Canon as soon as they were safely in the car and out of earshot. "Come on, Alex." He yanked her through the door as Abby stepped into the darkened hallway dressed in jeans and a t-shirt, her long, black hair tucked under a ball cap, accompanied by two well-muscled men with shaggy beards and crew cuts.

Alex clutched his arm as she struggled to turn. "Oh, Jack, there she is. I see her. She sees me. They're walking her down the hall. They're taking her away."

He wrapped an arm around her waist, forcing her to face forward as a bouncer eyed him. "Keep going, Alex," he said next to her ear. "Keep walking. They're watching us."

She did as she was told. "I can't leave her here, Jack." Her breath shuddered in and out. "I can't just walk away."

"We don't have a choice." He propelled her forward and scanned the parking lot, keeping his eyes open for muggers. They were in one of Baltimore's worst areas. He unlocked their doors when they stopped at the rental car. "Get in."

"Please, Jack. Please." Her eyes filled as she clutched his hand.

She was killing him. "Get the hell in, Alex, before we have more problems to deal with." He opened the door for her when she made no move to do so herself and gave her a small shove. "Now."

She sank to her seat.

"Fucking *A*." He slammed her door, seething with helplessness. They were too late. He'd wanted to call Canon and get someone from the taskforce over here, but Abby's handlers and the drunk fucker had ruined his plan. If he hurried, he might be able to follow them back to their stash house.

Just as he opened his own door, he spotted trouble heading their way. Three men appeared from the shadows just steps from where he'd parked. Not good. Bending quickly, Jackson pulled the .9 mm Sig from his ankle holster and took aim in their direction. "Former cop, boys. I'm not really up for any games tonight. Keep your hands where I can see them and get out of here."

The men held up their hands. "Hey, man, we're just walking by."

"Walk faster."

They hurried toward the bold pink lights of Lady Pink, and Jackson got in, locked the doors, and started the car, then placed the pistol in the center console. "Buckle up."

Alex stared at him as he pulled on the street and took an immediate right into the back alley of the strip joint. Bold, colored graffiti painted dirty bricks, trash spilled from dumpsters, but no one was here. If they brought Abby out this way, they were long gone. *Goddamnit!*

A rush of anger flooded his veins as he threw the automatic into reverse, backed out of the narrow lane, and accelerated on the quiet, mean streets, slowing for traffic lights instead of stopping. He reached for his phone as they merged south on the interstate and dialed Detective Canon's office line, waiting, steaming out a breath when he was sent to voicemail. Hanging up, he tried Cannon's cellphone. Same thing. With a calm he didn't feel, he left his message. "Detective, this is Jackson Matthews. It's 2:45 Wednesday morning. I've just left a club in downtown Baltimore, Lady Pink, where I saw Abigail Harris and another potentially trafficked young woman. Please get back to me as soon as possible." He hung up, swore, and tightened his hands on the wheel. Abby had been right *there*. He glanced at Alex and caught her eye before she turned to the window.

"Alex."

She didn't answer.

"Alex, we—"

"Leave me alone, Jack." Her voice was a cool slap.

He rolled his neck, trying to relieve the tension. "Alex, I—"

"I don't want to talk right now."

He ground his teeth in defense against the pain radiating in her voice. "Fine."

The last thirty-five minutes of their ride passed in brutal silence. Thank God they had less than ten to go. Jackson counted down the miles as they traveled the Bay Bridge to the island. He glanced Alex's way again. She hadn't moved. He drove through the quiet town, turned into the sleepy neighborhood he'd grown up in, and sighed as he pulled into his parent's drive.

Alex reached for the door handle as he shut off the engine.

He grabbed her hand before she could make her escape. "Hold on."

"I don't want to hold on." She wouldn't look at him.

178

"Alex, we had to—"

"We left her!" she exploded. "We left her there! I saw her. She saw me. She watched me walk away. My *God*! What must that have been like for her?" Alex flung her wig to the floor as her breath tore in and out. She yanked herself free of his hold and rushed from the car.

He whipped his door open and headed her off at the front of the vehicle. "Wait." He pulled her against him. "We're going to get her, Alex."

"Oh stop it!" She shoved at him. "Just stop! She was right *there*, Jack."

"So were fifteen bouncers. She had two handlers all her own. How were we going to get her past them? Do you think they were going to let us take her hand and walk away?"

"I don't *know*." She freed herself from his grip and hurried toward the docks. "All I can think of is the way she looked standing next to those horrid men and the way her eyes held mine. She's a *prisoner*. You promised me, Jack. You promised me we would do whatever it took when our break came. That was it. That was our shot to get my sister the hell out of this."

He took two steps after her, and she whirled. "Don't follow me."

"Of course I'm going to follow you. You're upset."

"I don't want you," she spewed and kept walking.

Jackson stopped short as her verbal sucker punch hit the mark. He turned and headed back to the house but hesitated when her quiet sobbing echoed on the early morning air. He closed his eyes and jammed his hand through his hair. "Goddamnit." Guilt and regret were eating him alive. He'd wanted to take Abby away from that hell too. If she had been in the alley with the two men as he'd hoped, he would've grabbed her. How could he make Alex understand that they had to walk away? Even with his weapon, he'd been no match for more than a dozen bouncers.

He stared into the dark, listening to her quiet agony as a boat motored by in the distance. Despite what she said, he couldn't leave her. Sighing, he walked to the end of the dock and stared down as Alex hugged herself tight and rested her forehead against her knees in the moonlight. Her gentle, muffled weeping destroyed him. He sat next to her and hesitated, then hooked his arm around her shoulders. "I'm sorry, Alex. You have no idea how sorry. I tried to think of a way to get Abby out of there."

She leaned against him and wrapped her arms around him, clinging. "Oh, Jack, I know that. I do."

He pressed his lips to her hair.

"What are we going to do?"

He stroked his fingers along her spine and stared into the dark. "Call Ethan. Talk to Tucker, the former detective I work with."

She swiped at her eyes as she looked at him. "What about Detective Canon and the taskforce? They can get her now that they know where she is."

"I don't know." He hadn't even wanted to call Canon after the meeting they had several hours earlier. His instincts had been dead on when it came to the officer's priorities—Abby's rescue wasn't one of them.

Alex sat up, breaking their embrace. "They can get her, Jack."

"I'm going to talk to him as soon as he calls me back, but this whole situation is pretty damn complicated. They want Zachary Hartwell, CEO of Starlight Entertainment. All of Hartwell's establishments, from the classy to the trashy, are under constant surveillance, including Lady Pink. My gut is telling me that unless they can run another raid and nab some of Hartwell's bigger players,

Abby's going to wait."

"But she's being victimized right under their noses. How can they let that happen? They're supposed to protect and *help* the innocent."

"ICE—Immigration and Customs Enforcement steps in from time to time when they're certain they can rescue a few, but the small potatoes they arrest in the operation are taking the fall instead of the people higher up in the feeding chain—the guys they want. Every time the authorities run a raid, the ring gets smarter and sneakier. They learn from their mistakes and become more cautious, making it even harder for law enforcement to crack the ring wide open. It's a catch-twenty-two: help one or two verified victims or save several, maybe even hundreds, by waiting and hitting the organization where it hurts."

"What does that mean for Abby?"

"It means it's time for me to start making things happen myself. No more waiting around. Now that we know where Abby is, I'm going to see if Tucker can come out for a few days and give me a hand."

"Abby can't wait that long. She needs help now."

"She may have to. We'll only have one chance." He pulled her against him, needing the comfort as much as he wanted to give it. "If we don't do this right, Alex, you'll never see her again."

Her lips trembled as she stared up at him.

"Damn that's harsh, but I don't want to lie to you." He held her tighter and traced the wet trail her mascara left along her cheek. "I know Abby sounded awful on the phone, but she's hanging in there. I saw her, touched her, talked to her."

She closed her eyes and clutched his hand against her face. "What did she say?"

"Nothing, but her eyes told me volumes. She might

be afraid, but she's tough. She knows, Alex. Abby knows we're coming. That'll keep her going until we can get to her."

"Do you think so?"

He nodded. "I told her I'd be thinking about her and that I'd be back. She understood what I meant."

Another tear spilled over. "I'm sorry, Jack. You've done nothing but help me, and I've been so unkind."

He caught her tear with his thumb and shrugged. "I can handle it."

"But you shouldn't have to." She touched his cheek as she stared into his eyes. "Thank you," she whispered and feathered her lips over his. Alex held his gaze and moved in again.

He wrapped his arm around her, holding her tight. The shock of her mouth warm and willing on his was exactly what he'd been waiting for. He knew he should pull away and stop Alex's advance, but he was a prisoner to his own needs. He *needed* Alex.

Groaning, hungry for more, he deepened the kiss, relishing her flavor as her tongue sought his. He tightened his grip around her waist and helped her move until she straddled him, his legs dangling off the dock. He ran his hands up smooth thighs, skimmed the edge of her denim skirt, and continued up, kneading her firm ass through her silky panties, tugging her closer.

She gasped and clutched at his shoulders. "Jack," she murmured. "Jack," she repeated while she peppered kisses along his jaw and neck.

He tilted his head back and closed his eyes as her fingers played through his hair. He'd missed this—the way they were together when nothing but emotion ruled. Alex forgot to be shy and serious when she was in his arms. He eased her back and held her face in his hands. "I've missed you." He kissed her forehead. "All this time, I've needed you."

She curled her fingers into the waist of his shirt as their gaze held, and her small breasts heaved against his chest with each rapid breath.

He pulled her mouth back to his, starving to taste her again. Would he ever get enough? A purr escaped her throat as he tugged the loosened elastic from her hair and threaded his fingers through long shiny black locks, surrounding him in the familiar scent of flowers and vanilla.

"Jack. Jack, we have to stop. We have to go in," she said against his lips.

He wrapped his arms around her tiny waist. "Come to my room the way you used to." He nipped her chin. "I want to be with you."

She shook her head. "I need to get in to Livy. We've been gone for so long."

He physically ached from wanting her. It was on the tip of his tongue to ask her again, but she was right. They'd been gone for hours and were both exhausted. He didn't want their first time together to be a quickie at four in the morning. When he had Alex again—and he *would* have Alex again—he planned to make up for every second he'd been away for the last four years. He'd waited this long; a few more days wouldn't kill him—probably.

He touched his lips to hers. "Let's go in and check on Olivia. I'll give Tucker a call." He scooted back from the edge of the water and stood with Alex still wrapped around him.

She dropped her legs to the dock and stepped away, breaking their embrace.

"We should try to get some sleep." He held out his hand, waiting, testing, studying her in the moonlight. Where did they stand now that the heat of the moment passed?

"I'm tired." She hesitated ever so slightly before she reached out and took the hand he'd offered.

They were definitely getting somewhere. For the first time since he watched her vanish into the dark February cold, he believed he might get back everything he'd thrown away so carelessly.

❦

"What are you doing, Carol?"

Carol glanced over her shoulder toward her husband's deep, sleepy voice in the dark as she walked to the open window. "I'm just making sure everything's all right. I hate hearing them argue so. They used to laugh. She made him so happy, George. They made each other happy."

"They'll either work this out or they won't. Meddling won't help. It'll probably make things worse." He rolled to his side.

"Oh, phooey. A mother's worry isn't meddling." She peeked around the edge of the curtain as Alexa shouted that she didn't want Jackson and he turned and started toward the house. "Go to her," she murmured. "She doesn't mean it."

A small smile touched Carol's mouth when he stopped and shoved his hand through his hair—a gesture of frustration she knew well. Her poor baby. He was hurting. They both were. They loved each other; it was plain as day, but Alexa was leery. She had every right to be. And Jackson was fumbling and unsure— understandably. He'd messed up.

Carol pressed her lips firm in frustration when Jackson didn't budge from his spot. They weren't going to get anywhere at this rate. This was his chance to change everything. She wanted more grandbabies. "Come on, son," she whispered. "Don't make the same mistake twice." She sighed her relief as Jackson walked to the docks and sat down beside Alexa, who was curled up with her arms wrapped around her knees. Her quiet, painful crying tore at Carol's heart.

Jackson hesitated, then put his arm around her. Within seconds Alexa clung to him and Carol pressed her hand to her chest, to the swell of hope. She knew she should give them their privacy, but another second couldn't hurt. It'd been too long since she'd seen her son at peace. He'd been a fool to push Alexa away all those years ago, but she was here now with their precious little girl. Perhaps with some time...

She clutched at the curtain and sighed when Alexa kissed Jackson. He dove in, pulling her into his lap. She drew the fabric over the window and turned to her husband. "I think it's going to be okay, George. I think everything might be all right."

"They'll find their way, Carol." He held out his hand. "Come back to bed now. Livy will be up with all of her sparkle before too long."

She got in on her side and held George's hand as she looked at him in the shadows the moon cast about the room. "He hasn't been happy without her."

He kissed her forehead and made her smile. "I know. Close your eyes now."

CHAPTER 12

J ACKSON PLOPPED DOWN IN HIS father's office chair, utterly drained. The quick shower to rinse off the cigarette stench from Lady Pink helped a bit, but not enough; the last two and a half weeks were starting to take their toll. He needed sleep—a couple of solid hours to take the edge off, but first he had to talk to Tucker. The return call he'd received from Detective Canon seconds after he said goodnight to Alex still boiled his blood. The fucker.

Abby was in dire straits, yet Canon's big concern was Jackson blowing the investigation by interfering in police business. It had been tempting to tell the good ol' detective to suck ass right then and there, but that wouldn't help the situation. He needed to keep the lines of communication open with the authorities for Abby's sake.

Scrubbing his hands over his face, he leaned his elbows on the desk. Goddamn, this was frustrating, and, if he was honest with himself, completely overwhelming. Alex was depending on him to bring her sister home, and now that the writing was officially on the wall with Canon, so was Abby. He could no longer wait around for the detective and his taskforce to act. She didn't have that kind of time. The ring would move her before long. He hadn't had the heart to remind Alex that the traffickers would shuffle their 'product' around to new cities and even new countries to keep the authorities off their tails. Abby was officially in a now-or-never situation.

With a weary sigh, Jackson shrugged against the uncomfortable weight compounding on his shoulders. Abby was hanging in there, but for how long? He had to make something happen immediately or nothing would happen at all. Abby would soon be lost in an endless hell of prostitution, pornography, and everything else that came along with the injustice of sexual exploitation.

He sat up and struggled to gather his sluggish wits while he stared at the phone. Call Tucker, then sleep. At this point, he was useless to everyone without a few hours of shuteye. He picked up the receiver and winced as he glanced at the time. Tucker wasn't going to be happy. He listened to the first ring, then the second, and faced the bay, staring out at the dock he and Alex had been sitting on half an hour before.

"Hello?" Tucker answered groggily.

"Did I wake you?"

"Jackson?"

"Nothing gets by you."

"What the hell, man? It's two in the morning. I just got off duty forty minutes ago."

The movie premiere. He was supposed to have worked that. "Sorry. We found Abby."

"What?" The sleepiness in his friend's voice vanished. "She's home?"

"I wish." He stood, teeming with frustration. "Alex and I saw her at some shit hole strip joint on the southeast side—Lady Pink. She gave me a lap dance for my trouble." He squeezed at the back of his neck, still sickened by the memory.

"Wish I could say congratulations. What can I do to help?"

He knew he could count on Tucker. "I'm hoping you can give me a hand out here for a couple of days and help me figure this out. I met with Detective Canon earlier this morning. No. Wait. Shit. What the hell day is it?" He shook his head, gathering his jumbled thoughts. "Earlier yesterday morning. The taskforce still isn't doing much more than surveillance. I called him about Abby and another possible victim called Strawberry. She had to've been sixteen, possibly seventeen, and that's a stretch. Of course Canon jumped up my ass about procedure and messing up the investigation, but he didn't have a whole hell of a lot to say about getting Abby out of there."

"In a nutshell, what's the status?"

"I got the official bullshit runaround—Vice will check it out and they'll keep the area monitored. Basically, they aren't budging until they have Hartwell wrapped up with a pretty red bow."

"Sounds about right."

Jackson sat back down, watching black fade to dull pink along the horizon as predawn began to chase away the night. "I also think there may be a potential luring situation going on at one of the clubs Alex and I were at. That probably needs to be looked into, but I left it alone. If Canon's taskforce is monitoring, they're aware."

"Let me talk to Ethan. I have a few days off coming up. I'll be on the next available flight out."

"I had to leave her, man. With the fucking scum of the earth." He balled his hand at his side as he relived the last few minutes at Lady Pink. "Alex saw her. She begged me to bring Abby with us." He squeezed his eyes shut as Alex's pleading to help her sister echoed through his head. "I don't know what this'll do to her if we missed our opportunity." He didn't know what it would do to him.

"We'll talk when I get there and figure everything out."

"Do you want me to pick you up?"

"No. I'll get a rental and directions when I land."

"I don't know how to thank you."

"I'll think of something expensive."

Jackson grinned when the phone buzzed in his ear. Thank God for great friends. Having Tucker in on this for a couple of days would be a relief. He twisted the chair around to the computer and fired off an e-mail to Ethan, attaching a copy of a dark, poorly shot picture of the man he and Alex had seen talking to the young girl at Club Jericho. Hopefully Ethan would be able to clean up the image and search the data banks. Maybe he could dig up something on the sleazeball. He couldn't be certain there was a connection to Abby's disappearance, but no potential lead was worth overlooking.

Jackson blinked his blurry, tired eyes and got to his feet, more than ready to turn his mind off. He craved his bed and oblivion. He opened the office door and stopped short of knocking Olivia over.

"I'm awake now." Livy rubbed her sleepy eyes.

"I see that." Jackson glanced at his watch again. "Liv, it's really early."

She smiled. "I'm not tired anymore."

He picked her up and kissed her forehead as he walked toward the bedroom. "Why don't we go lie down for a little while longer? You can snuggle up with daddy."

She pressed her hands to his cheeks. "I want to play with my dollhouse."

Jackson stared at his bedroom door longingly and caught a glimpse of Alex asleep in the guest bed across the hall. He looked at his little girl eager to play with her new toys and sighed. "Let's go play with your dollhouse."

She grinned. "I will be the people. You can be the doggie and the kitty. I'm sharing. Sharing is a very nice thing to do."

He nuzzled her neck, breathing her in, more in love

189

every second, and made his way back down the hall. "I can't argue with you there. Daddy needs to make some coffee before I play with the doggie and kitty."

"Okay."

He yawned as they started down stairs.

∘⤜⧉⤛∘

Alexa sat at the sewing machine creating her outfit for the evening—the black top she'd transformed into a halter would hug her curves and stop just above her midriff. The accompanying skintight jeans and red wig she'd found were bound to make a statement. Carol's box of props was coming in handy. She would blend in perfectly with the patrons of Lady Pink.

Hopefully after tonight she would never have to go to that vile place again. This evening was the official first step in ending Abby's nightmare, and Alexa was ready. She and Tucker were due to leave at seven thirty. Now that they knew where Abby was, surveillance was the goal. Tucker wanted to see for himself the bouncers, bartenders, and potential exits. Alexa would be his prop girlfriend while she made another positive ID on Abby when her sister came from one of the retched rooms down the dark hall.

Jack and Tucker felt it better that Jack stay home with Livy, especially after his little scene with the drunk college kid. Two nights in a row might seem suspicious to the bouncers, and there could be no mistakes. They were too close to bringing Abby home. With any luck, Tucker and Jack would take her sister back late tomorrow night. Abby would be in her arms in less than forty-eight hours, though even that seemed like too long.

Her sister's pleading eyes flashed through her mind

as she remembered the two men lording over Abby as if she was their personal possession. Alexa shook her head as the memory curdled her stomach. Instead, she clung to Jack's words, trusting that he was right—Abby was hanging in there. Her sister was strong. She knew they had found her and that they were coming. Hopefully she was as comforted by that, as Alexa was herself.

There would be so much to do after they brought her home. Abby would need to see a doctor and perhaps visit with a psychologist to help her cope with her ordeal. It would be best—safer—if they all went back to LA for a while. Abby would probably feel more secure with hundreds of miles separating her from Baltimore and the men who'd taken her. And it would be good for Livy and Jack. They needed more time together. But she, Abby, and Livy would have to get their own place. They couldn't stay with Jack anymore. Sharing meals and sleeping across the hall from him wasn't a good idea. She winced as she thought of her strained budget. Renting an apartment, even something small, would cost a fortune in LA, but she would find a way. If anyone could stretch a dollar, it was her. She was letting her guard down around Jack again, and that couldn't happen.

Alexa sighed as she ran the needle along the final hem. She shouldn't have kissed Jack, but she'd been powerless to do anything else. He'd been so comforting and sweet. His eyes had pleaded with her to be strong. She'd only meant to say thank you when she touched her lips to his, but even that had been a mistake. The spark of need had consumed her instantly, and the years vanished. It had been so easy to forget and let herself *feel*. Twice now she'd let herself do too much feeling and not enough thinking.

Even as she chastised herself, a surge of butterflies

danced in her belly as she remembered his clever fingers skimming her thighs and his rough palms kneading at her butt, pulling her against him. He'd definitely wanted her, and she him. Her heart and body had begged her to give in to the pleasure she knew they could bring each other, but thankfully her brain had begun to function again after the initial shock of having Jack's hands on her.

Jack was a dangerous man. From the first time he kissed her so long ago, he'd enchanted her, putting her under his spell. When she was in his arms, need ruled and everything else was forgotten. Four years proved nothing had changed. Even hours later, she still ached for him and throbbed to have him fulfill her. Her craving for Jack was overpowering her need to remember the way he'd hurt her. That alone sent her heart trembling. This couldn't happen again. She wouldn't let it. Eventually the summer would end. Abby would probably stay in LA to start her career, but she and Livy would have to come back. Their life was here. Her job was here. Rolling around in the sheets with Jack would do nothing more than scratch an itch and complicate an already impossible situation.

Alexa eased off the presser foot and lifted the needle from her halter-top, then snipped the bobbin thread. This wasn't where her mind should be. She needed to concentrate on Abby and Livy—only Abby and Livy. Two kisses from Jack, and the feelings they stirred were only as big as she chose to make them. She'd yearned for Jack before; she would again. As long as she remembered that they were finished, she could deal with it. They were attracted to each other—of course they were—that probably wouldn't ever change, but that didn't have to mean anything more than pheromones.

She stared at the creation she'd made, then pressed

her face into the shirt with a frustrated groan, knowing full well she lied to herself. Jack would always matter too much. She would have to keep her distance if she was going to survive this time.

Something crashed to the floor, and Livy screamed. Heart thundering, Alexa rushed to her feet and raced down the stairs before it registered Livy was shrieking in delight. Her screeches dissolved into deep belly laughs when Jack growled. Alexa stopped on the bottom step, trying to catch her breath, while Jack chased Livy on all fours until their daughter pushed at his waist and he collapsed in a heap.

"I got you, grumpy, growly dog." She screamed again when Jack opened one eye.

"Grumpy, growly dogs like to catch little girls named Olivia." He grabbed her, rolled to his back, and held Livy high above him and she laughed. "Maybe I'll have you for snack." His triceps bulged as he lowered her nose to nose.

"No, growly dog! No, don't eat me!" Livy pressed her hands to Jack's mouth.

He made a biting motion with his lips, making Livy giggle and him chuckle.

"Maybe growly dog should throw you in the air." As he said it, he tossed Livy high and caught her. Jack did it once more, then grabbed her up in his arms and sat up, hugging their delighted little girl.

Alexa's heart melted right then and there. Her yearning for Jack had nothing to do with pheromones or magic spells; it was love—plain but not so simple. She'd always loved Jack, but never as much as she did right now.

His muscles bunched as he squeezed Livy tight and kissed her forehead. His gorgeous face brightened as his exhausted eyes held Livy's and they grinned at each other.

"Handsome, Jack," she murmured as she unconsciously clutched the charm on her necklace.

Jack's gaze left Livy's and locked on hers. Her pulse pounded and her heart raced as heat flashed in his suddenly serious eyes, rendering her defenseless to their potent effect. The triangular points of the charm bit into her hand as she squeezed, struggling against overwhelming emotions.

A slow smile spread across his face, this time just for her. Traces of sweetness mixed with hints of desire, sending a wave of goose bumps over her skin. She swallowed as Livy crawled out of Jack's lap and ran to her.

Alexa bent down and picked her up. "Sounds like you're having fun."

"I am. Will you read with me?" Livy rested her head on her shoulder. "I miss you, Mommy."

"Oh, sweetie, of course I'll read with you." She kissed Livy's cheek as guilt snuck up to grab her. She'd been so distracted with Abby's situation, and Livy was paying for it. She'd never spent an evening away from Olivia before like she did last night. Typically they spent all their free time together, usually snuggled up with books or a board game or playing at the park.

"Grammy brought new books about the princesses."

"We should probably read them." She kissed Livy's other cheek. "Jack, why don't you go catch a nap. You look exhausted." She walked with Livy to the living room, plucked up the three new books Carol had purchased, and sat on the couch with her little girl.

Livy settled herself in the crook of Alexa's arm as she always did.

"Which one should we start with?"

"This one." Livy pointed to the pale pink hardback.

"Do you mind a joiner?" Jack stood in the doorway, his tired eyes bloodshot.

"Jack, you need—"

"Come listen." Livy held out her hand.

Jack joined them on couch, sitting on the end cushion.

"You can't see the pictures, silly goose." Livy tugged, and he scooted closer.

Alexa moved her shoulder when his side brushed her arm. She didn't want to touch him right now. Too many feelings left her unsettled.

"Mommy, your hair is in my eyes."

"Sorry." She sat up taller, trying to accommodate both Livy and Jack.

"How about this." Jack kicked a leg over Alexa, and Livy and lay against the plush arm of the beige couch. Alexa stiffened as he pulled her back to his chest. After a moment's hesitation, she settled against him. What choice did she have?

Jack moved Livy, and she rested on both of them. "There. Better. Much more comfortable for everyone."

Alexa glanced at Jack as she struggled to remain unaffected by the coziness of their situation. She'd dreamed of moments just like this all the years she and Livy had done without him. She couldn't do this. She tried to sit up. "Jack, I think—"

He pulled her back. "We should get to the story." He settled his arm at her side and brushed Livy's bangs from her forehead with his other hand. He winked at Alexa and smiled. "Come on, Mommy. We want to hear about those princesses. Right, Liv?"

"Right."

She stared at him a moment longer, realizing he knew exactly what he was doing. Alexa followed her daughter's lead and rested her head against Jack's solid chest. His breath heated her temple as she opened to the first page and brought the enchanted world among the pages to life for their little girl.

⁓✺⁓

Jackson sat on the floor by the bathtub, relaxed with his legs outstretched and crossed at the ankles, his feet bare. His jeans were covered with small, dark spots from the occasional splash as Olivia played with the princess water toys his mother bought. He smiled as Liv sent the redheaded doll down the magical waterslide. Grammy hadn't missed a trick.

With his parents off to a dinner/dance benefit and Alex and Tucker leaving soon, he and Olivia would be on their own for the next several hours. He tried to ignore the whisper of nerves. They would be fine. She was just a little girl—his little girl. How much trouble could they get in?

"We should probably wash your hair, Liv. The water's getting cold."

"It's very warm water. I like my princesses." Olivia picked up the blond doll and sent her down the shimmering slide next.

Inspiration struck, and he smiled, impressed with his own genius. "Your princesses have beautiful, clean hair. Princess Liv needs beautiful, clean hair too."

"Princess Livy doesn't like to get her hair washed. The water hurts her eyes."

Jackson's smile disappeared as the mutiny in his daughter's heated stare registered. Now what the hell was he supposed to do?

Alex popped her head in the room. "It sounds like someone's having fun in here."

Olivia glanced up and beamed. "Grammy has

good toys."

Alex chuckled. "Yes she does." She stepped further in, and Jackson struggled not to swallow his tongue. Her jeans hugged her slim curves like glory. The tight, black top she wore stopped several inches above her waist, showing off the smooth skin of her midriff. "I thought I should come in and make sure everything's okay before Tucker and I head out."

Jackson tore his eyes from her sexy stomach. "Yeah, Liv and I'll be just fine." He was mostly sure of it, even if he didn't have a clue how the hell he was going to convince a three-year-old that she really *did* want to get her hair washed. Pride kept him from asking for help.

"Mommy, stay and play princesses. It's very fun." Livy danced the redheaded doll around for her mother's benefit.

Alex crouched down next to the tub. Her small, firm ass brushed Jackson's knee, and he clenched his jaw. "I wish I could stay home and play, sweetie, but I have an important appointment tonight. I'll only be gone for a little while. You and Daddy are going to have such a good time."

"Daddy said he's going to wash my hair." Livy frowned at him, and Alex smiled.

"It only takes a minute, Livy. Head back, eyes closed, and ears plugged. Right?"

Olivia's frown deepened.

Oh, shit. This was *not* how he wanted his first solo evening to start.

"Do you want me to wash her up, Jack?"

Yes! "Nah, I've got it." He swallowed as Alex eyed him. "You sure? We've gotten hair washing down to a pretty painless science."

He shrugged. "We'll be all right. Me and Liv have to figure it out some time."

"Okay." She leaned in and kissed Livy's nose. "Mommy will be back later. Have fun. I love you." She stood and directed her attention to him. "I'll have my cellphone if you need *anything*."

"Wait, Mommy, one more smoochie."

Alex crouched down, her butt touching his knee again as she puckered up. Livy kissed her. "Kiss daddy too. He's my daddy."

Alex's gaze flew to Jackson's. "Livy, Daddy doesn't want me to kiss him."

"Yes, he does." Smirking, Jackson sat further up, more than willing to take advantage of this opportunity. He hadn't stopped thinking about their impromptu make out session on the dock since it happened. She'd done her best to keep her distance throughout the day, but he wasn't about to let this moment slip by. "Daddy wants mommy to kiss him right here." He puckered his lips and pointed to his mouth as Alex stared him down with unamused eyes.

"Come on, Mommy. Daddy wants you too," Olivia said in a singsong voice.

Jackson leaned further in, and Alex met him halfway. She pressed her lips to his in a chaste kiss, and their little girl giggled. As Alex pulled away, he grabbed her arms and she lost her balance, falling into his lap. "We should probably try one more. Liv got two kisses. It's only fair."

Livy giggled again. "It's only fair, Mommy."

He touched her lips to his as Alex's heated eyes continued to stare at him. He added more pressure this time, holding her still until her mouth gave against his. He eased back and brushed his fingers through her hair. "Be careful tonight. Stay with Tucker."

She nodded. "I will. I have to go. Tucker said he had a call to make. He should be finished by now, and I still

198

need to take care of my wig."

Her body tensed beneath his hands, and worry filled her eyes. He hated seeing it there. Hopefully tonight was the beginning of the end. "You'll have to tell me if blonds or redheads have more fun."

She smiled as she stood. "I'll let you know later." She turned to Olivia. "Bye, sweetie. I'll be back in a bit."

"Bye mommy."

Alex closed the door behind her as Jackson glanced at the bottle of tear-free shampoo. It was now or never. "Time to wash your hair, Liv."

"No, daddy. No."

She looked at him with such pleading desperation; he almost told her they didn't have to. "We'll be quick." He picked up the plastic cup floating in the water, filling it to the brim. "Head back, Liv. Close your eyes. Plug your ears."

Livy squeezed her eyes tight, tipped her head, and screamed as Jackson poured the first cup of water over Olivia's shoulder-length blond hair. Dear Christ, it sounded like he was torturing her. Why didn't he just let Alex do this? He held his breath as he scooped and dumped the next cup over her pretty golden locks. Livy let loose another scream despite him being careful not to get the water on her forehead. "Liv, it's not that bad. It's really not," he tried to reassure them both.

Five long minutes later, Jackson rinsed the remaining suds away. He grabbed a towel and wiped at Olivia's face, even though he'd done a hell of a job of keeping the water from going into her eyes. "You can open your eyes, Liv. We're finished."

Olivia blinked them open and smiled. "That didn't hurt. You're a great hair washer."

Flushed from his success, he grinned. This was going to be a piece of cake after all. If he could make it through hair washing hell, he could handle anything. "Thanks. Let's get you out of the tub. You're turning into a raisin."

"A raisin." She beamed at him. "I like raisins. They're healthy for my body."

He helped her stand, wrapped a towel around her, and plucked her from the bath. Jackson brought her to the bedroom and was happy to see that Alex left Olivia's pajamas laid out. "Okay, Liv, let's get you dressed." Then what?

"I can do it myself. I'm a very big girl now."

He raised a brow as he studied her. She sounded like she was fifteen, not three. She was growing up so fast. He'd already missed too much. "Well, by all means then." He sat on the bed and looked out the window as Olivia pulled on her yellow and pale purple polka-dotted top. He watched a small motorboat rumble by with a young boy sitting in the back with a fishing pole in hand, and an idea struck. "Liv, have you ever gone fishing?"

"No," she said as she pulled up her little shorts.

"Do you want to?"

"Um, yes I do. But I don't know how."

"I could teach you."

She smiled. "Okay. I like to learn new things. That's why I'm such a smart girl."

He chuckled. There was that modesty again. "Come on, Liv. Let's go fishing." He took her hand and walked to the kitchen, opened the fridge, and grabbed a hunk of his mother's bleu cheese.

"Pew." She plugged her nose. "That's stinky."

He grinned. "Sure is. Fish love smelly cheese." He hoped. They would save worms for another day. He didn't know how Olivia would feel about watching him bait a hook with anything other than food. "Let's go get a pole."

"Can I hold it?"

"Sure, but I'll help. We have to be careful of the hook. It's sharp." They stopped off at the garage and grabbed one of the fishing poles he and his brother had used when they were young boys. "Are you ready?"

"I want to catch lots and lots of fishies."

"Let's see what we can do." Dusk was settling in. If they could stay quiet enough, they would hopefully snag at least one. "We have to be nice and quiet or we'll scare all the fish away."

"Nice and quiet," she repeated in a whisper as they made their way to the end of the dock.

"Sit right next to me, Liv. The water's pretty deep."

She did as she was told.

"Now I'm going to put a hunk of this smelly stuff on the hook." He grabbed a chunk of the offensive bleu cheese and secured it in place. "You can help me cast off, and we'll see if we get anything." He settled Olivia on his lap. "Ready?"

"Yes." She grinned as she put her small hands on top of his on the pole, and he cast off. The hunk of cheese made a plop as the line sunk.

Livy rested her head on his chest and looked up. "Where's the fishy?"

He smiled. "It takes a few minutes. We have to be patient." He tweaked her nose with his free hand.

"I like Grampy's boat. He let me drive to the hotdog restaurant."

Jackson glanced at the cabin cruiser tied to the dock. He'd missed Olivia's first time out on the water. Instead of enjoying an afternoon with his family a couple days ago, he'd been stuck in Detective Canon's office trying to get to the bottom of Abby's disappearance. "Maybe we can take the boat out again soon."

"I want to drive some more."

"I think we can make that happen. Do you—" The pole jerked, and he gave a small yank, securing the fish on the line. "Liv, I think we got something. Help me bring it in." He wrapped her hand around the reel, helping her turn the crank against the weight of the fish.

Seconds later she gasped as they pulled a bluefish free from the water.

"Look! Look! A fishy! I caught a fishy!"

Jackson's heart filled to bursting at the excited pride in his little girl's voice. This was their moment, their memory. He'd missed so much, but this would always be theirs. "Yes, you did. You caught your very first fish, Liv."

They reeled the fish in further and he made a grab for it. The elongated body, the length of his hand, flapped back and forth, sprinkling them with small drops of water. "Stay right here, Liv. Let me get him off the hook."

"He moves a lot." She shrunk back against his chest.

He grabbed hold of the cool, wet body and removed the hook as gently as he could. "Do you want to touch him?"

Livy hesitated, then slid a finger over the fish's side. "Slimy."

"A little bit."

She moved to touch again.

"Stay away from his mouth, honey. He has pretty sharp teeth."

Livy yanked her hand back.

"You don't have to be afraid. Touch him once more then we'll let him go. He can't breathe unless he's in the water."

"But I want to keep him."

"He's too little. His mom will be looking for him."

"Like Nemo. But Nemo's daddy was looking for him."

He'd never seen *Finding Nemo*, but he agreed. "Yeah, like that."

Livy touched the blue-grayish scales once more. "Bye, Nemo. Go find your mommy."

Jackson threw the fish back. He looked down at Olivia as she glanced up. "Nice job."

"I'm a great fisher."

"You sure are." He winked at her as he set the fishing pole on the dock.

Livy turned in his lap and wrapped her arms around him. "I love you, daddy."

He pulled her close and held her tight as he rested his cheek against her hair. His throat tightened as a wave of emotions flooded him while he held his daughter in the warm summer air. "I love you too, Liv. So much."

She gave him a kiss. "Will you read to me about the princesses?"

He stared at his little mirror image, filled to the brim with adoration. "Yeah, let's go read about your princesses. Then it's time for bed."

"Will you snuggle with me? Grammy and Grampy's house is very scary at night."

"I can't think of anywhere else I'd rather to be." He picked up the fishing pole in one hand and held Livy in his other arm as they walked back to the house.

CHAPTER 13

TUCKER OPENED THE DOOR FOR **Alexa, and they** entered Lady Pink. The smoke choking the space was just as bad as last night, and the bright neon lights highlighting the stage no less tacky. She hated being here knowing that Abby was stuck in this hell hole, but that was going to change tomorrow.

Alexa scanned the area, keeping an eye out for her sister. Abby wasn't on stage dancing—thank God. As much as she wanted to see Abby, she wasn't sure she would be able to sit idly by while her sister was forced to exploit herself. There were only a handful of customers, unlike the last time, but her stomach still shuddered with disgust as two pretty young women— barely dressed—swung themselves around the poles while men sat by the stage, staring. "She must be back in one of those rooms," she said close to Tucker's ear, afraid her voice might carry even though loud pop music blared through the speakers.

"Let's find a seat." Tucker led them to a table with a decent view of the bar, stage, darkened hallway, and the two visible exits. Tucker plunked himself in a chair and slung his muscled arm over the back, appearing relaxed, as if this was just another ordinary night at a strip club. He almost blended well in his jeans, Baltimore Orioles t-shirt, and matching ball cap worn backwards, but his looks made it impossible for him to go unnoticed. Tucker Campbell was magnificent, maybe even beautiful, with his long eyelashes; slow, arresting grin; and buff, chiseled body. In the hour and a half they'd been together, Alexa noticed that people looked twice at Tucker Campbell—men and women alike.

All business, Alexa pulled her chair close to his. "So what should we be looking for?"

"We need a count—"

"What can I get you two?" A topless waitress dressed in a bold, yellow g-string stopped at their table. Alexa forced herself to look at the once pretty face gone hard, caked in makeup, instead of stare at the floor like she so desperately wanted to—not that the waitress was paying her any attention.

"Two Buds," Tucker answered with a friendly, inviting smile.

"You know, I give a hell of a private dance, baby." The waitress winked and skimmed a finger down his well-toned arm. "You say the word and I'll be sure to add in a little something extra. Just tell Tony you want Blondie to show you a good time." She gestured to the bartender, who was pouring a scotch and water.

"If I wasn't here with my lady, I'd be game, honey." He looked Blondie up and down, devouring her with his appreciative, hungry gaze.

Blondie spared Alexa a glance, then strutted away.

Alexa stared at Jack's friend as Tucker transformed from 'sleaze' back in to the respectable former detective she'd walked in with. "Very smooth."

He shrugged. "Gotta play the game."

"You play it well."

"The criminal element can spot a cop a mile away. I've only been off the force nine months. I imagine I'm still wearing a few layers. Figured I should bring my A-game."

"Mmm." Alexa studied the man who would help Jack bring her sister home, still trying to figure him out. He was sweet to Livy, fun with Jack, and kind to her, but he always seemed... a step removed. Even when he smiled, his dark hazel eyes remained guarded.

Blondie came back with two beers. "Here you go, hot stuff." She smiled another invitation as she set his bottle down.

"Thanks." Tucker traced the pad of his finger over Blondie's knuckles. "You dancing tonight?"

"Later."

He nodded while he continued to seduce Blondie with his gaze. "My buddy was here the other night."

"Oh?" She purred. "Is he as good looking as you?"

He shrugged. "The ladies certainly don't run away. He's got a thing for long, black hair."

"What about you?"

He glanced at Alexa and dismissed her, then gave his full attention back to their waitress. "Red heads are okay, but I prefer blondes."

Blondie touched her tongue to her top lip. "Well, aren't you in luck."

"My buddy's getting himself hitched." He shook his head mournfully. "Who the fuck knows why, but I wanted to do it up right for him. He couldn't stop talking about Fawn. Is she dancing too?"

Blondie's flirty smile vanished. "I don't worry 'bout nobody but myself." She tried to tug her hand free.

Tucker kept hold of her fingers even as one of the enormous bouncers started making his way to their table. "That's too bad. Cause I was thinking about you and me and my buddy and Fawn."

Alexa struggled not to squirm as the bouncer came closer. They were going to get kicked out. They couldn't help Abby if they had to leave.

"Fawn's not here."

Alexa no longer focused on the bald man with the

ring in his nose when Blondie's words sunk in. "What—"

"When is she working again?" Tucker interrupted smoothly.

Blondie gave a jerky shrug. "Like I said, I don't worry 'bout nobody but me."

The hulking man stopped at the table. "Don't touch the lady," he said to Tucker.

Tucker let go of Blondie's hand. "We're just talking."

"You don't talk with your hands. Get back to work," the bouncer said to Blondie.

Abby isn't here? She has to be. I saw her just hours ago. Alexa stared at her bottle of beer as her eyes filled. She struggled to keep her breathing steady as wave after wave of despair threatened to drown her.

"You keep your hands to yourself, pal, or you're outta here." The bouncer walked back to his post by the bar.

Alexa clenched her hands in her lap, trying to ward off the trembling. "What are we—what are we going to do?"

"Wait here for a while."

Alexa met Tucker's unreadable eyes. "But Abby's gone."

"I don't believe everything I hear." He touched her arm. "Hang in there, Alexa. We know she was here. Right now we need an idea of how many bouncers they keep on the floor and how many disappear down the hall. How long do the dancers dance before they switch off? Even if she's gone now doesn't mean she won't be back tomorrow night or the next. It's not uncommon for the rings to rotate the women—keeps the cops off their tail. Tonight's a perfect example. Jackson tipped off the taskforce about Abby, less than twenty-four hours later and she's gone. It's hard to raid a place if a suspected victim isn't in the same spot night after night, right?"

Alexa nodded despite her hopelessness. Tucker made complete sense, but how many times had she heard something like this? They should've taken her last night. They should've called the cops immediately instead of waiting for a positive ID. Someone could've come to help before the men took Abby away. What if Abby didn't come back tomorrow or the night after? Sighing, Alexa stared down the darkened hallway, willing her sister to appear as she had only hours before.

One hour ticked into three, and Alexa sat in her spot, methodically counting bouncers and dancers and keeping track of the women coming and going from the hallway—none of whom were Abby. Blondie had been telling the truth; her sister wasn't here.

"I'm pretty confident I have their pattern. It hasn't varied. Ten bouncers—including the two that stay in the hall, three dancers, six waitresses, and two girls that handle the rooms," Tucker said before he took a sip from his second bottle of Bud. "We should go."

"But what if she shows up? It's still early."

"That's highly unlikely, and we can't stay 'til last call, especially if we have to keep coming back. The last thing we want is to start drawing attention. Despite your outfit, you don't blend in here. Jackson and I will come back tomorrow."

Everything Tucker said was right; in her heart she knew that, but it was a struggle for Alexa to push her chair away from the table and stand. Even though Abby wasn't here, Alexa felt as if she was abandoning her sister again.

Tucker slung a supportive arm around her shoulders, and they headed for the door. Her gaze darted about the room as she desperately hoped Abby would appear like she did before. She and Tucker moved by the bouncer they'd passed to enter, and her heart broke as she was forced to turn and step through the exit. Where was Abby? Her breath caught in her throat as she struggled to keep the helplessness at bay.

"Excuse me," she murmured as she bumped into a man among the crowd hanging out around Lady Pink's entrance.

"We'll come back tomorrow, Alexa."

"I know." But that didn't help Abby tonight.

"We're making progress."

She couldn't stand to hear another empty line of consolation. "Please, let's just go." Each step to the car was a struggle. The headlights flashed twice when Tucker hit the button on the key fob. Alexa reached for the door handle and sighed out an unsteady breath as she looked around, staring into the shadows wearily, remembering Jack pulling his gun on three men. She'd never heard Jack's voice low and dangerous like it had been in that moment.

"Yo, Renzo," the outside bouncer called.

Alexa whipped her head around as a tall man gave the bouncer a knuckle bump. "Renzo," she whispered as she studied him, cast in the neon pink lights of the sign.

"What is it?" Tucker stepped closer.

"That man talking to the bouncer. His name is Renzo. My sister went out on a few dates with someone named Renzo."

"The photographer, right?" Tucker shut his door, hit a button on the key fob, and the lights blinked again. "Take off your earring."

She tore her gaze from the entrance as Renzo disappeared inside. "What?"

"Take off your earring. We just realized you lost it. We should go in and look around."

Catching on, Alexa took off her jewelry and shoved it

in her pocket as they hurried back to the door.

"My lady lost her earring."

The bouncer eyed them both. "So?"

"So, we want to go in and find it."

"It's one of my favorites." Alexa gave the bouncer a tease of smile as she looked up from under her long, sooty lashes.

"Fine." He moved out of the way.

Tucker grabbed Alexa's hand as she bolted inside.

"Take it easy," he warned as he reined her back to him.

"I want to see him. This is too much of a coincidence."

"I agree, but we need to play it cool."

It was hard to remain calm when every instinct told her that the man laughing and joking with the bartender had something to do with Abby's disappearance.

"Look for your earring, Alexa."

She tore her gaze from the well-built man in his designer jeans and navy short-sleeve polo shirt as she pretended to look under their table. She snuck another peek at Renzo while she moved the chair she'd been sitting in. He was definitely Abby's type. His charming grin and dark Italian features certainly would've caught her sister's eye.

Could he really be the guy Abby had gone to dinner with a handful of times? Was he the one Abby felt she had a lot in common with? Renzo didn't seem to fit in here in his expensive clothes and appealing smile any more than she and Tucker did.

As Alexa pushed the chair in, Blondie sidled up to the bar for the drinks the bartender poured. She placed a beer bottle and vodka tonic on a tray as Renzo moved to her side and said something close to her ear. Blondie's fingers tightened on the glass and she turned to leave. Renzo grabbed her wrist and yanked her back around.

Blondie flinched when he tugged her forward, causing the beer bottle to topple on the tray. His eyes changed and the features of his handsome face contorted into something mean.

Alexa clutched the back of the chair as her heart pounded. That man had the answers to Abby's kidnapping. She turned to Tucker. "He did it. He took Abby."

"Okay."

How could Tucker be so calm? "He knows where my sister is," she tried again, wanting Tucker to feel the same urgency she did.

"Let's get out of here and go back to the house."

She looked at Renzo one last time as he took a seat on an empty stool, memorizing every feature of his face. Another waitress came to the bar, eyeing Renzo wearily. When she turned with her tray full of beverages, he pinched her naked butt cheek. The tray crashed to the floor, and Alexa whirled while Renzo's laughter mixed with the bartenders. "I'm ready." There was nothing more they could do for Abby tonight, but she knew in her heart that Renzo was the key to bringing her sister home.

Tucker pulled up to the curb in front of the Matthew's house forty-five minutes later. The drive back had passed in a blur of Tucker's non-stop questions. She'd racked her brain, trying desperately to remember the few details Abby had shared about her dates with Renzo. In the end, she simply hadn't paid enough attention. Abby's mention of her nights out with the photographer hadn't thrown up any red flags, nor did they make Alexa think that the handful of encounters were anything more than casual dinners.

Were there clues in Abby's e-mails or planner? Certainly there had to be something. The authorities took Abby's laptop and cellphone, but Alexa still had Abby's day planner. Surely there was some mention of Renzo she had missed. She'd read each page a thousand times with no luck, but now that she knew what she was looking for, she would try again.

Tucker yanked on the parking break as Alexa whipped off her seatbelt and opened the door. She pulled off the ugly red wig she'd forgotten about and hurried up the front steps, using the key Carol had given her. On a mission for answers, she rushed up the stairs and down the hall. As she reached for the doorknob to her room, Tucker took a right and shut himself in George's home office. She opened her door and came to a stop three steps inside. Jack slept in her bed with Livy snuggled in the crook of his arm. So many emotions swamped her: love, longing, despair. How many times had she hoped for this? How many nights had she lain awake, dreaming of her daughter knowing her father?

Everything about Jack and Livy was as it should be. There was already a strong bond between Jack and their little girl, despite the years apart. So why did she want to cry?

Because she needed Abby. Nothing would be exactly right until Abby came home. She couldn't move forward without her sister. Her heart was torn in so many pieces; she couldn't begin to put it back together until Abby was safe.

Alexa stared a moment longer, then tiptoed around the half-wall to the small sitting area with the view of the water. She rifled through her carry-on until she found the black leather book chock-full of Abby's past and future plans. She plopped herself on the edge of the plush couch as the refreshing breeze blew off the bay and through the open windows. Alexa painstakingly read each phone number in the contact list, placing a small red dot next to any name she didn't recognize. First thing tomorrow morning, she would start calling to find out who was whom.

Several minutes later, she started the tedious process of reading each hour of Abby's day, staring in December of last year. By the time she made it through late March, she teemed with frustration. Although the details of Abby's dates with Renzo had been sketchy, she was positive Abby had gone on at least two by that point. So why wasn't his phone number or the name of the restaurant they visited together scribbled down? There was *nothing*. Abby was so meticulous with her schedule—she was too busy not to be—but other than *dinner* written in a rectangular box blocking off the hour between seven thirty and eight thirty on March 15 and March 28, there was zilch to work with. Dinner *where*? Dinner with *whom*? She had an idea, but she needed solid facts.

Alexa steamed out a frustrated growl and started her own list of things to do. She would call her sister's roommates again and find out what they remembered about Renzo. Focusing on the calendar again, she scanned April and the first three weeks of May, noting three more *dinner* blocks from seven thirty to eight thirty. Those *had* to be the date nights. With no more answers than she started with, she shut Abby's planner and stared at her laptop.

The police had taken Abby's laptop, but could she still access the e-mail account? She'd never tried, fearing she might damage some sort of vital evidence, but she was willing to try now. The authorities weren't spending their time trying to help Abby; their only interest was

Zachary Hartwell. Nibbling her lip, she typed in Abby's username and password. Seconds later, Alexa's screen filled with hundreds of unopened e-mails. She scanned two pages, recognizing many of the senders. The few addresses she didn't recognize, she opened. Most were from contacts in the fashion industry offering words of hope for a quick and safe return. Alexa sniffed and wiped at her eyes. Her sister was so well loved.

She pulled a tissue from the box on the small end table and dabbed at her nose as she tried to pull herself together. Sentiment wasn't going to help Abby. She took a deep breath and got back to work, scrutinizing each sender once more. She backtracked into Abby's opened mail, but she still couldn't find anything from Renzo. "What the *heck*?"

Sighing, she rubbed at her temples. The guy wasn't a damn ghost. She'd seen him in the flesh herself—unless she'd jumped to a major conclusion and the Renzo at Lady Pink wasn't the person they were looking for. "No. No." She rested her face in her hands, afraid she would scream out her anger as she hit yet *another* dead end. Of course he was the right Renzo. The coincidence was too perfect. "Okay." She flexed her fingers before she typed *Renzo* in the search bar of Abby's account. A box reading, *No messages matched your search*, popped up. She tried *Lorenzo* next. The message popped up again. She flopped back against the cushion of the couch. What's his last name? Why hadn't she asked Abby? It was such basic information, yet she didn't have a clue.

One more try. She typed *Renzo, Baltimore fashion photographer* into Google. Several hits filled the screen. She clicked on the first and discovered that *The Renzo* was a posh restaurant overlooking the water, located not far from Abby's old row house. She clicked on the next hit with *Renzo* and *fashion* in it. A paper had mentioned a small fashion show the restaurant had hosted several weeks back, but that wasn't what she was looking for. After scanning five more hits with similar results, she gripped the edges of the laptop as her breath rushed in and out, hot tears filling her eyes. She set her computer down with great care, fighting the urge to throw it to the floor and watch it crack in to pieces, as she struggled with her unfamiliar rage. She'd never felt as helpless and angry as she did right now. For every step they gained in the investigation, something stood in the way to slow it down.

Alexa stood and walked to the window. The steady breeze and sounds of the night did little to soothe her. She needed Abby's cellphone. There was probably a text from Renzo, or at least a number, but the police still had it. Jack or Tucker would have to call the detective and have him check. She pressed her head to the window's wooden frame, trying to get a grip on her raw emotions. The inability to do anything more than wait on others was becoming too much to bear. There had to be something else she could be doing.

"Alex?" Jack stirred in the bed beyond the half-wall.

"Yeah."

The mattress squeaked with his movements. She didn't turn to face him as he walked from the other side of the room. She was afraid she might lash out. No matter how she tried, she couldn't bury the spark of resentment wanting to burst into flames. He'd promised her he would bring Abby home, but he hadn't. Abby had been right in front of them, and he watched her walk away. He protected people for a living, but he didn't protect Abby. Shamed to the marrow, more tears filled her eyes.

"How'd it go?"

"She wasn't there."

"She wasn't... Where's Tucker?"

She shrugged. "In the office."

He rested his warm, calloused hands on her shoulders. "I'm sorry, Alex."

"Sorry doesn't do Abby much good," she bit off, unable to hold it all back.

Jack's fingers tightened against her skin, but then he dropped his hands.

She squeezed her eyes shut. "She was there last night. We should've called Detective Canon right away. You should have tried to take her."

"No, I shouldn't have. We already talked about this."

"I'm so sick of talking." She whirled. "Everyone wants to talk, but nobody wants to act. My sister needs *help*."

The room filled with tension as Jack held her gaze but said nothing.

"We saw a man named Renzo tonight."

Surprise flickered in his eyes. "What?"

"A man named Renzo came to Lady Pink as we were heading to the car. I heard the bouncer say his name."

"Son of a bitch." He jammed a hand through his hair. "I need to talk to Tucker."

"Renzo knows where my sister is. I *know* he does."

"Let me talk to Tucker. I'll put in a call to Ethan."

"What about Detective Canon?"

"No."

"Why?" she asked with exasperation. "He's in charge of Abby's case."

"And how many times has he called you with new leads?" His voice lowered as his eyes heated. "I can waste time listening to him rip me another asshole for getting in the way, or I can get moving on this. We've uncovered more in twenty-four hours than the police have since she disappeared. Canon has to follow procedure. I don't. I've already told you they aren't going to act until they have the key players of this ring. Let Ethan do some digging into Renzo. Let me and Tucker work the angles on this for a day or two. If we can't bring anything else around, I'll call Detective Canon."

"Abby can't afford to wait."

"She also can't afford mistakes. There aren't any easy answers here, Alex. As much as you don't want to hear it and I hate repeating it, you're going to have to be patient."

Patient. If she was told to be patient one more time... She turned again and stared hard out the window. "They've already moved her. How long until they send her away? We tried your way last night, Jack, and look where that got us." She bunched her fists at her side, hating herself for being so mean. None of this was his fault. "I'm sorry, Jack. I—" She turned and he was gone.

She took a step toward the door but stopped and sat on the couch instead, lying against the cushion. What was she *doing*? She was hurting the only person who'd stood by her through this ordeal. When Jack came back from the office, she would sit him down and apologize, but as the minutes ticked by and she waited, she fell asleep.

Jackson rapped his knuckles on the door of his father's office and peeked in.

Tucker gave him a 'come on in' signal with a jerk of his head while he spoke on his cellphone. "Run that and let us know what you get. Yeah, we're going back tomorrow night. Okay, later." He set his phone down and propped his feet on the edge of the desk, ankles crossed. "I take it you spoke with Alexa."

"Oh, we talked." Jackson clenched his jaw and

217

plunked his ass on the arm of the couch. The angry hurt in Alex's eyes and barely controlled fury in her short, cutting words bothered the hell out of him. "Abby wasn't at Lady Pink. Renzo was." He steamed out a long breath and stood again, too restless to be still. "Goddamnit." He rubbed his fingers against his forehead. "Abby wasn't fucking *there*. Alex is pissed."

"So, she's pissed." Tucker shrugged. "You made the right call last night."

Jackson walked to the window and stared out at the dark waters. "Yeah, I guess."

"You guess?" Tucker dropped his feet from the desk. "Were you going to fend off a dozen bouncers with your fists, or better yet draw your weapon, shoot a couple of the bastards, and go down for murder? Don't be stupid enough to take that on, Matthews."

Jackson let loose a humorless laugh and shook his head. He knew he'd done the right thing for both Alex and Abby—deep down he did, anyway. The odds of getting them out of Lady Pink safely had been nil, but that didn't make any of this easier. Abby was still being held against her will, and Alex's heart was broken. "I can deal with her anger. God knows she's been mad at me before. But when she looks at me with those eyes..." He bunched his fists. "They're so fucking sad. I can hardly stand it."

"This is tough, man. I don't envy your situation. All we can do is keep at it."

"I know." He turned back to Tucker, struggling to push his last 'conversation' with Alex from his mind. "Tell me about Renzo."

"He's in this up to his eyeballs. My fucking spidey senses started tingling as soon as I saw him. They still are."

"Same Lorenzo Cruz I was investigating back in LA?"

"Yup. I pulled up his information again—couple of speeding tickets, but no criminal record. He's clean according to the law, but I look forward to Ethan's take. There's more to this guy than we're seeing. We just need to give Ethan time to dig. He said he'll get back to us tomorrow night at the latest."

Uncustomarily edgy, Jackson scrubbed his hands over his face. "All this waiting is making me ape shit, man."

Tucker shrugged. "It's part of the game. You know that."

He did, but this was the first time the waiting affected someone he loved. Alex was being torn to pieces. The torture was unbelievable. "What am I going to do if I missed our chance? This whole thing is worse now that I've actually seen her and talked to her and touched her. Abby's fucking gorgeous. She and Alex could be twins. They're going to use and abuse her until they kill her..." Jackson stopped, and his gaze flew to Tucker's steady, impenetrable stare as he remembered. Abby's case couldn't be easy for Tucker to work. So many pieces were cruelly similar to Tucker's twin sister's unsolved murder. He'd been so wrapped up in Alex and Abby, he'd never stopped to think of the horror Tucker had lived through several years ago. "I'm sorry, man. I wasn't thinking."

Tucker gave Jackson his trademark shrug. "They're probably rotating her. She'll be back."

Jackson nodded, understanding that the subject had been dropped as quickly as it had been brought up. Tucker rarely spoke of his sister or the tragic circumstances behind her death.

Tucker stood. "I'm thinking I'll spend tomorrow spot-checking Renzo's house, his place of business, etcetera. Hopefully I'll have a few things to add to whatever

Ethan finds. I have no doubt he'll uncover something. This guy's in deep. The waitresses are afraid of him. He knows the bartenders and bouncers. I can't figure out why a guy who looks like him and has a career like his would be hanging out at a place like that unless he had something to gain from it."

"Definitely raises a few flags. Now we have to figure out who he's working with and see if it leads us back to Hartwell. This could be big."

"Might be." Tucker stretched his arms as he walked to the door and opened it. "I'm fucking beat. I'm going to bed. Tomorrow's going to be a long one."

CHAPTER 14

ALEXA BOPPED HER LEG UP and down while she sat in the moonlit living room, waiting. She glanced at the clock—again. It was three thirty in the morning. Where *were* they? She picked up her phone from the coffee table and started punching Jack's number in for the fourth time, but stopped herself before she hit the last digit. She set her cell down and wandered to the large picture windows facing the bay, nibbling her lip. She'd texted Jack at midnight for an update, and again at one. When she received no response, she tried to call and was immediately sent to his voicemail. "They're busy. That's all."

But what if they weren't? She turned from the window and swiped a loose strand of hair behind her ear, growing more frantic with every passing minute. What if they were in trouble? Maybe the bouncers figured out that they weren't there to ogle naked women. Or maybe Jack and Tucker saw their chance to take Abby, and something had gone terribly wrong.

Alexa pressed a hand to her jittery stomach and tried a deep, calming breath. "They're fine. They have to be." But maybe they weren't. "Damn it, Jack. Be okay," she whispered, and bit her thumbnail.

Guilt compounded her worry as she thought of her last conversation with him. She'd been so unkind and way out of line. None of what was happening to Abby was his fault. Although Jack had said he could take her abuse, she'd had no right to dish it out. She desperately needed to apologize and make things right, but first he had to come home. Jack and Tucker had already been gone when Livy woke her at seven. They hadn't been back since.

Alexa looked at the gorgeous grandfather clock and closed her eyes as she rested her butt on the arm of the couch. Five minutes. Had it really only been five minutes? She would give them until four, then she was calling Detective Canon. She reached for a copy of *People* and twisted on the lamp on the side table. Absently, she flipped from one page to the next, listening to the antique timepiece in the corner of the room tick the seconds away.

Could tonight be the night? Would Abby finally come home? Perhaps Jack and Tucker had taken her to the hospital for an evaluation, but certainly Jack would've called to tell her. Or maybe they followed the van that transported women back and forth from the clubs to the stash houses. Or what if—

She whipped her head up, on full alert when a key was shoved into the lock and the front door opened. "Oh, thank God." She tossed the magazine aside and hurried to the entryway. "You're okay." She threw her arms around Jack and held on, despite the cigarette smoke covering his clothes. "You're okay," she repeated, resting her head on his chest. "I was so worried."

His arms came around her. "Sorry. I didn't know you were still up."

"I couldn't sleep." She peered over his shoulder to the front steps. Abby wasn't waiting in the shadows to be welcomed. She met Jack's stare and struggled with her disappointment.

Tucker skirted around her and Jack. "I'm going to follow up with Ethan and see if he found anything else." He gave Alexa a nod. "Good night."

"Tucker, thank you so much." She gave him a small smile.

"You're welcome." He turned and disappeared up the stairs.

She returned her attention to Jack. "So, how—how did it go? How's Abby holding up?"

He played his fingers through her hair and held her gaze. "Alex—"

She read the apology in his eyes, and her stomach sank. "Abby wasn't there."

"No."

She'd tried to prepare for the possibility, but she'd been so sure everything would work out this time. "Abby's gone," Alexa said, more to herself than Jack as she stared at the floor, trying to absorb another crushing blow. Did the ring ship her sister off to some faraway city, or worse, another country?

"We have to keep believing she's coming home." Jack held her tighter and pressed his cheek to the top of her head as he stroked his hand up and down her arm. "Ethan called us on the drive back. He found some stuff—a couple of websites he's looking into. The details are still coming in, but if there's a lead, Ethan'll find it. He's excellent at what he does."

Alexa wanted to find comfort in another possibility, but the last dredges of hope had finally vanished. "That's good," she said with more enthusiasm than she felt. She untangled herself from Jack's grip, afraid that if she looked at him, she would burst into tears. "I—I should probably get to bed." She cleared her throat, steadying her voice. "Livy will be up soon." She turned and hurried up the steps, fighting to keep her breathing steady and suppressing her need to sob.

The front door shut, and seconds later Jack followed. Alexa picked up her pace, desperate to lock herself in her room and relieve the consuming ache alone.

"Alex, wait a second."

She shook her head as she stepped to the plush carpeting of the upstairs hallway. She was almost there.

"Alex, wait."

"I can't," she choked out as she reached the threshold of the guestroom and gripped the knob, attempted to close herself in. But Jack pressed his hand to the door before it shut.

"Alex."

She held her weight against the wood. "Please, Jack. I just need—"

"To let me in." He gave a sharp push, dislodging her from her spot, and stepped inside.

She walked to the small sitting area, keeping her back to him as he closed the door and followed.

He snagged her arm and turned her to him. "Alex, *talk* to me."

What could she say? So many thoughts were swirling about—apologies, regrets, disappointments. Finally she looked into his eyes and saw what she'd wanted to avoid—embers of anger and hurt. "Oh, Jack," she said on a ragged breath and folded herself around him. "I'm so sorry. I'm so sorry I blamed you."

He sighed as he returned her embrace and kissed the top of her head. "Come sit with me." He tugged her to the couch, still holding her against him.

She clutched at the arm of his t-shirt, listening to the steady beat of his heart, trying to hold back the worst of her pain. Jack already felt bad; she wasn't about to make it worse.

"Let it go, Alex." He stroked her hair away from her cheek.

She shook her head. "I'm fine." She pressed her lips firm against the lie. "Really. I got my hopes up again, that's all." She tensed her grip on him as a sob snuck up and surprised her.

He lifted her chin until she looked at him.

A tear fell, and her lips trembled as he held her gaze. It was no use. "I—I needed her to be there, Jack."

"I know." He kissed her forehead. "I know you did."

"I can't stop wondering if the other night was the last time I'll see her." Another tear spilled, and she swiped it away, trying hard to keep herself together.

"I won't let it be." He caught the next tear.

"I've done the research. The odds aren't working in our favor. Each day that passes..." Her breath rushed out again. "I'm sorry." She didn't want to cry in front of him.

"Don't apologize. This is hard. It's killing me watching you suffer this way." He skimmed his fingers along her temple. "I wish I could take it all away." His hands found their way into her hair. "I wanted to take her with us, Alex. I did. I keep running the scenario over—"

"Please don't." More tears tracked down her cheeks as she shook her head and pressed her hand to his cheek. "If you could've, you would've. I really do know that. You've been here for me. You've been nothing but honest and kind, yet you keep taking the brunt of my frustrations, and it's not fair."

"I can handle—"

"No. No," she repeated and framed his face with both hands. "You shouldn't have to. I can see how much this is hurting you, too. This isn't just about me and Abby."

"But that's all I care about." He framed her face as she did his. "All I care about is you, Alex. You're all I've ever cared about."

Her heart stuttered as they breathed each other's breath.

"I have to make this better. I need to make this

okay for you. Every time you cry for your sister...it rips me up."

"I'm sorry—"

"Don't." He moved in and captured her mouth with a light brush of lips. "Don't," he whispered again and eased in for more.

Powerless to do anything but respond, she closed her eyes as he kissed her again. Gentle comfort turned hungry as his tongue sought hers and she wrapped her arms around his neck. Time spun out while she held Jack close and absorbed his familiar taste. There was no past, no future, only now, and she wanted nothing but him.

"I can't walk away," he murmured against her lips as he played his fingers through her hair. "I need you."

"I don't..." Her eyes fluttered closed as he skimmed her jaw. "I'm not..." She let loose a shuddering sigh, cutting off the last of her own uncertainties, as his tongue darted out to caress the sensitive spot just below her earlobe. She slid her hands along his strong shoulders while the heat of desire warmed her skin and he made his way back, retracing his steps with gentle kisses, stopping at her chin and nibbling.

"I need you, Alex," he repeated.

Her stomach fluttered with tugs of yearning. She wanted this as much as he did. "Yes," she heard herself murmur as she pulled him closer, waiting for his mouth to consume hers, sure she would never get enough of his flavor. Just this one time she would give in to what she'd craved for the last four years.

"Alex, I—are you... God." He gripped her against him and groaned as he dove in.

A whimper escaped her throat as he tipped her head back, plundering, devouring until she was sure she would melt right then and there. She clutched at his arms, holding on, ready for what Jack would bring.

He eased away, his breathing labored. "Are you sure? Are you sure you want to do this?"

She stared at the man she'd loved for years and nodded. "Yes." Regrets would be for tomorrow. Tonight she wanted to *feel*. "Yes, I want to be with you." She met his lips. "But we don't have a bed. The headboard in your room is on the same wall as your parents'."

He smiled. "You noticed that too?" He grabbed the blanket from the back of the couch and tossed it to the floor. "Somehow we managed a time or two without one."

Their first time had been on a blanket by the lake on a cool October evening. "I guess we did."

"This is right." He kissed her. "Being together this way seems right."

She nodded, knowing he remembered too.

Jack moved to the floor and spread the blanket over the plush carpet. He took her hand and pulled her to him, thigh to thigh, breasts pressed to his chest, and sent her reeling with another searing kiss. Minutes passed, and his palms moved down her naked arms, over her back, leaving a trail of desire wherever he touched.

Wanting her hands on him, she pulled his shirt free of his jeans and yanked it up and over his head. She held his gaze as she traced the smooth lines of his six-pack, making his muscles jump and quiver.

Giving as good as he got, his eyes held hers as he pulled her sleeveless nightshirt up and off. "My God, Alex," he groaned as he stared and brought her closer.

Hot skin collided with hot skin, and her breath caught in her throat. "I never thought this would... I never thought we would be here again."

"We never should've been apart." His rough palms traveled the sides of her waist, leaving goosebumps in their wake as he nibbled at her neck. "I've missed you,

Alex. I've missed talking to you and touching you." He nipped her shoulder. "I've craved you."

His words seduced her as he roamed, feathering his lips over her skin, trailing moist heat over the swells of her breasts. Fingertips traced and teased. His tongue circled her nipple until it grew hard. He suckled and flicked, and she exhaled with a quiet moan.

How had she lived without this? How had she made it through years of her life without Jack touching her? "Jack," she said as the familiar tug started low in her belly, a sensation she hadn't felt since the last time they were together. She wanted nothing more than to be joined, to feel him deep inside her. "Jack," she said again as he moved to her other breast, slowly, lazily, sending her closer to the edge.

It had always been like this—every time since the beginning. Even when he'd unlocked this secret world to paradise for the first time, it had never occurred to her to be shy or afraid. All she thought of was him, and he simply made her *want*.

He continued his exploration, stroking at her ribs in his languid pace. She clutched at his hips. How could he take his time when she was burning from the inside out? Needing, craving release, she rubbed at his jeans and discovered him ready below the barrier of denim. He steamed out a breath and moaned as she reached for his snap and pulled, found the zipper, and tugged.

He clutched her ass, pushing her against him, making it impossible for her to reach in and grab him. "Easy, Alex." He laced their fingers together and drew her hands behind her back. "One step at a time."

Her chest heaved with each breath. She was a volcano ready to erupt, and he wanted to take his time. "I don't think I can. I haven't been... I need to... It's been so long. Take me right now."

228

He clutched her fingers and pressed kisses to her throat. "When you put it like that, I'm not sure I can argue."

She pushed her head back, giving him room to explore. "Don't argue. Definitely don't argue. Fast this time. I need you," she begged.

He set her hands free and skimmed her hips before traveling up her front. "This time? Are you planning on another? I'm not twenty-four anymore." Humor lit his hungry eyes.

"Let's just worry about now. My God, touch me. I really need you to touch me. I forgot how much you make me want—make me crazy the way you used to. Do that thing with your fingers." She took his hand and shoved it into her pajama bottoms. "Please."

"I'm not sure I remember."

She was about to implode and he was teasing her. "Yes, you do. You did it all the time."

"It might take me a couple of minutes to get it right."

She gasped, ready to explode. "Then you better get started."

He grinned as he pulled his hand from her shorts and tugged them off along with her panties. "I don't recall you being this aggressive. This is definitely new."

"Take advantage. Sometimes you should take advantage." She wrapped her arms around his neck and pressed her breasts to his chest.

"I guess maybe I should."

"You absolutely should," she said and snagged his bottom lip between her teeth.

His mouth went hot on hers as he dragged her onto his lap and she wrapped her legs around him. "What about Olivia?" he asked breathily. "She's just in the next room."

"She's a deep sleeper." She reached up and turned

229

off the dim light on the side table. "She'll sleep 'til morning." Her whispered words were muffled against his neck as she plied him with kisses. She eased back and looked at his gorgeous face cast in moonlit shadows as she feathered her fingers through his thick hair and he stroked her inner thighs. "Hurry, Jack. Hurry and take me."

"I thought you wanted me to do this first." He pushed two fingers deep inside her and moved in a rhythm that sent her flying.

She jerked from the shocking pleasure and rocked her hips as she muffled her cry against his muscular shoulder. He eased her back, and she arched up as he continued on. "Oh my God, Jack. Oh my God." Shuddering, whimpering, she gasped and bucked as he brought her to peak for the second time before he pulled her up and she sagged against him, resting her cheek on his damp chest, breathless and weak from the onslaught of powerful sensations.

Jack's heart pounded and he let out a heavy breath as he hooked his arm around her and settled his chin on top of her head. "So, was that right?" He kissed her hair. "Did I remember?"

She smiled and met his gaze. "It must be like riding a bike."

He chuckled, but then his smile disappeared. "I want to be with you, Alex." He stroked her back and kissed her sweetly. Tenderness replaced any sense of urgency, and the reality of their situation quickly cooled the heat of the moment.

"Jack, wait." She pressed her hand to his chest. "I wasn't thinking clearly. I'm not on birth control."

He brushed his hand down her arm. "I don't have any rubbers."

"This isn't very responsible."

His mouth moved to her shoulder. "We can still screw around a little."

"That's true." She closed her eyes as his teeth and tongue coaxed a moan from her throat. "Lean back." She tugged at his jeans and boxers until he was free. She wrapped her fingers around him and smiled when he tensed.

He kissed her as she continued to play him and his mouth heated on hers as he struggled with his shuddering breaths. They lay down and rolled, and he settled on top of her. Jack reached down and pulled his jeans the rest of the way off. "Better."

"Mmm. Much better."

He looked into her eyes and smoothed the hair from her forehead. "We never did spend much time just screwing around."

She smiled again. "For the first couple of months we did. You were so patient and sweet. But then you took me to the lake and showed me how it could be. We never stopped at third base after that."

"I prefer a home run."

She chuckled. "Who doesn't?"

"I like this. Being with you like this. Seeing you smile. Touching you. Feeling your body under mine." He pressed his lips to hers. "I never got over you."

She looked away, wanting the serious moment to pass, hoping to keep things light.

"I want you back, Alex." He skimmed her jaw with his thumb. "I want you and Olivia the way we should have been all along."

His words shocked her as she stared into the intensity of Jack's blue eyes. Her heart pounded as fear and want left her paralyzed. For years she'd dreamed of hearing Jack say those words. Now that he had, she was terrified. "This is too much." She pushed at his chest, trying to free herself. "I can't think about this right now. We can't go back, Jack." She pushed again, but he held her still.

"I don't want to go back. I want to move forward."

She closed her eyes and fisted her hands tight. "Please stop."

"I can't."

She shoved again. "I don't want to talk about this."

"We need to. I wasn't going to push. I was going to give you time, but now that we're here. Now that we're laying here like this—"

"No."

He took her hands and pulled them over her head, trapping her more fully against him. "Maybe this isn't fair—"

"When was it ever fair?" she hissed, struggling to free her hands. "You left me. Without any warning you just up and walked away from everything."

"I came back for you," he said in a rush.

She froze. "What?"

"I came back, but you had already moved on."

"I never—what are you talking about?"

"I was miserable without you. I missed you. I needed you. I knew I'd made the biggest mistake of my life, so I went back to try to fix it. I'd assured myself that if I could make you understand that I was freaked out about the big, bad real world you would forgive me. I wasn't going to leave until I had you back. I pulled into the parking lot across from your dorm and was getting out to find you when you came out from the lobby. You were in your blue coat. You had a white scarf tucked around your neck. You were so fucking beautiful, and I couldn't get my breath. I was about to yell to you when some guy—I think it was Pete—came up behind you and said something close to your ear. You laughed, your big, loud, throaty laugh it took me months to tease from you, and he grabbed your hand. All I could do was stare. I knew then that we were finished, and I wanted to die right there. I didn't know how I was going to live the rest of my life without you."

He'd come back for her. She squeezed her hands tight against his as she absorbed the heartbreaking truth. If she had looked toward the parking lot or if Jack had hollered before Pete walked up to surprise her, everything could have been different. "Why—why are you telling me this?"

"Because I need you to know."

"There was never anything between Pete and me. He was there for me when I needed a friend. There's never been—there's never been anyone but you."

He frowned. "But I saw—you two were—"

"Friends."

He closed his eyes and rested his forehead on hers, sighing. "All this time. We've wasted so much time. I messed everything up. I ruined us and missed out on my daughter's first years. My God." He released her hands and pulled away.

She couldn't stand the agony radiating in his voice and from his eyes or the cool emptiness he left behind as he lifted his body from hers. "Stay here." She looped her arms around him. "Lay here with me, Jack."

"I can't."

She kissed him, wanting to take away his pain. "Stay here." Her heart thudded in time with his as their mouths met again. His tongue entwined with hers, and his hands found their way to her hair like they always did. Tender moments passed as they offered each other comfort, and he eased back and stared down.

"Stay," she whispered.

Nodding, his breath heated her skin and he moved

to her neck, then her collarbone, before he came back for a searing kiss that left her melting.

She skimmed her fingers down his muscular waist, settling them there, reveling in his powerful body covering hers.

Urgent touches replaced gentle caresses as he took her breast in his mouth, and she moaned, clutching at his shoulders. The throb in her center spread through her belly with a liquid pull, and her skin tingled. She knew she should stop him as he moved to feast at her other breast, but she closed her eyes and surrendered to the pleasure he brought her instead.

"I love the way you feel, Alex. I love the way you taste." He reached down, teasing aroused skin, and groaned as she whimpered. "God, you're so wet. I have to have you. I have to be with you," he shuddered out through quaking breaths.

She did nothing to stop him as he pushed himself into her. She gripped his shoulders, crying out. Finally. Finally... Her body moved with his in a dance they'd mastered long ago. This was all she wanted—Jack moving with her, inside of her, making her feel what she hadn't since the last time. They were playing with fire with their lack of precautions, but she no longer cared about responsibility as they both climbed higher and higher. He moved faster, and his breathing grew shallow as he teetered on the edge.

She arched her hips higher, taking him deeper as he held her gaze, shuddering with his powerful movements. He thrust once, twice more, and came with a deep groan. Alexa followed, clutching at Jack's shoulders, stunned by the currents of pleasure coursing through her center as he held her captive with his bold blue eyes.

Moments passed. They continued to stare as their heart rates steadied. "I've wanted this," he whispered

234

while he combed his fingers through her hair. "I've wanted you just like this for too damn long."

She smiled, still holding him tight.

"This was right, Alex. Making love with you again was exactly right."

She wanted to regret the last hour, but she didn't. Even with the new complications this would surely bring, this was the first time she felt truly settled since he'd walked away. Just for a little while, she would let herself enjoy it. She smiled again as she skimmed her finger along his ear. "Yes, this was right."

He touched his lips to hers. "I meant what I said. I want you back. I want you and Olivia to come home with me. If we just made another baby, I won't be sorry."

Her smile vanished as the easy moment disappeared and her fear came rushing back with a vengeance. "No. This is moving too fast. You aren't giving me time to catch up. Livy and I live here, Jack. We have a house here. My job is here. One evening of passion doesn't change that."

"I have a home for us. We can find you a new job. There's an elementary school right down the street. Or you can stay home if you want. Ethan pays me well."

"I can't think about this right now—babies, taking Livy away from the only home she's ever known. I like being with you, I miss being with you, but we need to take this one step at a time."

"I think we're several steps *behind*. Livy will be happy living wherever you are. I want my daughter in my life, not just on school vacations and holidays. I want her with me every day. She told me she loved me last night. I taught her how to fish, and she told me she loved me. Now that I have her, I can't live without her."

She knew this was bound to come up sooner or later, she just hadn't planned on it being while Jack was still nestled inside of her. "I think—"

"I still love you, Alex."

Her mind blanked as his declaration sank in. "No. No, Jack." She pushed at his chest, much harder than before. "Let me up. I need to get up right now."

He cupped her face in his hands. "I made a mistake. I made the biggest mistake of my life the day I walked away from you."

"Jack, please let me go."

He moved so that she could free herself. Her fingers shook as she yanked her shirt over her head and pulled on her shorts. She was completely unprepared for this conversation. She'd always loved him, but that didn't change the way they had ended. "You can't expect me to alter my whole life because of, because of this." She made a sweeping motion with her hand. "We had sex, and now you want to live together and make more babies?" She shoved her hair behind her ear. "I can't— this is completely—" She huffed out a breath, frustrated by her jumbled thoughts.

"Alex, I just came in you. That's a big deal. There are consequences."

"I'm very aware. That wasn't our best idea. I won't lie and say I regret it. I'm far enough along in my cycle that we should be okay, but it can't happen again."

"I agree—one hundred percent. My goal isn't to trap you into something by getting you pregnant again. I don't want you thinking that."

"I don't."

"Good. But in the interest of full disclosure, I do want more Livy's running around."

"No more. I can't do this." She snapped the blanket up in her panic as he stood. "I can't do this," she repeated as she folded the soft fleece.

"You had to know I still have feelings for you."

"Yes, I suppose I did. But love... I just—*God.*"

"Why is that so hard to wrap your mind around?" He grabbed his boxers, pulled them on, and pulled up his jeans.

"Mommy?" Livy called. "Mommy?"

"I'm right here, sweetie." She hurried through the door toward their daughter's panicked voice. "It's okay, honey."

"The light's off. It's scary."

Alexa gathered Livy close as Jack switched on the dim light on the side table. "There you go, sweetie. It's not so scary now." She kissed her little girl's forehead. "Let's lay back down."

Jack appeared in the doorway of the sitting area.

"Daddy, I want you." Livy held her hands up for him.

He sat on the edge of the bed, and Livy crawled in his lap. "I'm scared. The monsters are going to get me."

"There aren't any monsters, Liv." He enveloped her in a hug, and Livy clung to him.

"They live in the closet."

Alexa rolled her eyes, still fully regretting the day she let Livy watch that supposedly friendly monster movie. "Sweetie, remember, there are no such thing as monsters. The monsters in the movie were nice."

Livy buried her face against Jack's naked chest.

He looked at Alexa as he rubbed a soothing hand over Livy's back.

"We watched a movie that was supposed to be for kids her age. She's been terrified of the dark ever since. Livy, why don't we snuggle up and get a little more rest?"

Livy tightened her grip around Jack. "I want daddy. Daddy will keep the monsters away."

"I'll lay with her for a few minutes."

Alexa nodded. This was another moment Jack and Livy had every right to. Livy deserved to know the comfort of her father chasing the monsters away.

"Come on, let's go back to sleep for a while." He lay down and settled Livy in the crook of his arm. "Close your eyes, Liv. Daddy won't let anything hurt you."

"Okay, daddy. I want mommy too. Lay with me too, mommy."

Alexa hesitated for a moment, wanting to give Jack and Livy this time, but their little girl was pale with terror. "Of course, sweetheart." She crawled to the center of the bed and lay down on her side, stroking her daughter's cheek. "Go to sleep, Lovely Livy. Mommy and Daddy are right here."

"Closer, mommy. I'm so scared."

Alexa scooted forward until her knees touched Jack's, and they cocooned their exhausted, terrified baby between them. She reached for the sheet and pulled it over all three of them. "Think of good thoughts, Livy. Think of driving the boat with Grampy or playing with your new dollhouse or fishing with Daddy," she whispered.

Livy's eyelids drooped. "I caught a fishy. The cheese is stinky," she slurred.

Jack grinned. "We used bleu cheese for bait," he said softly.

Alexa smiled. "Pew."

His grin widened. "That's what Liv said." His smiled disappeared as he stared into her eyes. "I'm sorry."

"Jack, I—"

"I'm sorry this is the first time I've been here to comfort our daughter in the middle of the night."

She closed her eyes, unable to handle the regret in his voice.

"I'm so damn sorry I walked away from you and left you to do this by yourself."

She met his gaze again. "You didn't know, Jack."

"But I would have if I hadn't been so stupid. I've regretted it every *single* day."

"Why? Why did you do it?" The question she'd longed to ask since that cold night in February slipped out before she could stop herself.

"Because I was overwhelmed and afraid, which doesn't make any sense." He reached out and brushed the hair back from her temple. "That night... I was freaking out. I'd pulled a gun on a robbery suspect for the first time, and it scared the shit out of me. I still can't figure out why I thought pushing you away was the best way to deal with it."

They continued to stare at each other, blinking in the moonlight. "I don't know what to say. I don't know what to think or feel. I would've helped you."

"I've been pissed at myself for four years. I never got you out of my head, Alex. You've haunted me. That laugh, those eyes. I ended up leaving the force after a while, because I couldn't stand knowing you were two hours away and no longer mine. I felt like I was dying a slow, painful death. Dad knew someone who knew somebody out in LA who was hiring for some bodyguard firm. He encouraged me to give it a try, to get the hell out of here and get on with my life. Ethan hired me, and I dove into my job. I went to Europe for a while and worked my ass off to become one of the best in my field, but no matter where I went, no matter what time of day or night, I couldn't leave you behind."

"What about Evelyn?"

"She was my attempt at moving on. She loved me, and I wanted to love her. I tried to love her, but she wasn't you."

She captured his hand and pressed his palm to her cheek. They'd lost out on so much. "I'm scared. I'm scared to let myself feel again."

"What can I do? What can I do to show you how much I love you?"

Hearing Jack say that again brought her as much joy as terror. She'd learned to live her life without him. She'd found a way to move on and make a home for herself and her daughter. How could she just hand him her heart again? "Let me breathe for a while. There's so much going on. I can't think about my future, or Livy's or much of anything else until Abby comes home."

"Okay." He looked down at Livy and kissed her nose. "Will she be all right? She was so afraid."

"Yes. Now that she's snuggled up with you, she'll sleep just fine."

He yawned. "We both need to get some rest. I'm not sure what you want me to do here."

"Close your eyes." He wanted it all, but this was what she could give him for now.

He held her gaze. "Are you sure?"

"Yes."

Jack wiggled out of his jeans and drew Livy more solidly in the crook of his arm. "Good night, Alex." He took her hand and laced their fingers, the way he always had when they fell asleep together so long ago.

The old gesture brought her comfort more than fear, so she shut her eyes. "Night, Jack."

CHAPTER 15

J ACKSON NUDGED OPENED THE DOOR to his father's office with his shoulder, carrying two steaming mugs of his mother's spectacular coffee in his hands. "I thought I would find you in here."

Tucker glanced up from his laptop.

Jackson handed over one of the mugs. "Sorry I bailed on you last night. Alex was pretty upset, then Liv needed me."

"I ended up heading to bed. Ethan didn't have anything new when I checked in." Tucker leaned back in the comfy leather chair, holding the cup close to his nose, breathing deep. "Damn, this smells like heaven." He swallowed and groaned. "I want to marry your mother."

Grinning, Jackson sat on the edge of the desk, sipping the hot, strong brew, and sighed. "Nobody makes coffee like mom." He drank again, eager for the kick of caffeine. Despite sheer exhaustion, he'd only slept in snatches while he lay with Alex and Olivia. He hadn't been able to shut down his mind. There was too much to think about between Abby's case and the abrupt change in direction his relationship with Alex had taken.

So much for slow and steady. In a matter of an hour, he and Alex had gone from cautious friends to full-on lovers again. He kept waiting to regret their lack of precautions and his confessions of love, but he didn't. How could he? The woman he thought he would have to live without had been wrapped around him, warm, naked, and completely with him—touch for touch and kiss for kiss. He hadn't been able to get enough.

Hints of Alex's vanilla scent still clung to his skin, even after a shower. He and Alex had taken a huge step in the right direction, but he wanted more; he wanted everything, and they had a long way to go. When the heat of passion cooled, her guard had gone back up. Alex was still leery; she was waiting for him to hurt her again. It would take time for her to realize he wouldn't be walking away. He had a lot to make up for, even more to prove, but first they had to find Abby. With another deep sip of his coffee, Jackson pushed Alex to the back of his mind and focused on her sister. "Did Ethan come up with anything we can use?"

"You could say that. We just hung up about twenty minutes ago. Apparently he didn't find much in Canon's files, which was what he was searching when I called him early this morning. So he took a detour through a few of the ICE agent's files instead."

Jackson choked on his next swallow. "Ethan hacked into Immigration and Customs Enforcement? Fuck, man, that's Homeland Security."

Tucker shrugged. "If anyone can cover his tracks, it's Ethan."

Jackson shook his head. "Ballsy bastard. So, what'd he find?"

"He thought it interesting that ICE and Canon's taskforce are monitoring a couple of the dating websites in the Baltimore area. Baltimore Dates seems to get a little more scrutiny than others. A few red flags have been raised over some of the ladies frequenting the site—pretty young foreigners looking for their ticket to the States. Maybe there's something to it—more than likely—but then again, maybe not. You just never know."

"Sounds interesting."

"Ethan was intrigued enough to dig deeper, because," Tucker shrugged, "that's what Ethan does."

"Naturally." Jackson crossed his ankles, getting comfortable. Tucker would get to his point eventually.

"Just for shits and giggles, Ethan decided to play with that new facial recognition scanner he's all hot and bothered about and entered Abby's photograph, along with the other young women recently kidnapped, into the system. He got a hit on Kristen Moore, the teenager who disappeared a month before Abby did."

Jackson's brow shot up as he sat up straighter. "No shit."

"She had a profile—LoveGoddess17. Her information has since been erased, but whoever wiped it clean wasn't aware that Ethan Cooke, Super Computer Geek, would be flying in for a look-see."

"How could they've figured?"

"Exactly. Kristen looks pretty damn different from the missing posters her parents plastered all over the city and news. In those pictures she's virginal—an innocent schoolgirl. Here she's blonde, brown-eyed, and beautiful and *definitely* doesn't look like she just turned seventeen." Tucker turned the laptop. Kristen was indeed all of those things.

"Certainly has the three B's."

"Not to mention a recent track record for running away and a turbulent home life. Her parents decide to call it splits, and she starts looking for trouble. She was the perfect mark." Tucker turned the computer back in his own direction. "She and someone with the profile name Crazy80 had a few conversations, which Ethan was more than happy to copy for our benefit and send along."

"Son of a bitch." Jackson set his mug down as he

stood and walked to Tucker's side of the desk. Finally they were getting somewhere. "Let me see."

Tucker handed over the printed sheets.

Jackson skimmed the first couple of conversations between Kristen and 'Crazy80'. They did the typical get to know you dance with casually flirty questions and answers. Crazy80 bragged about his career in the fashion industry. Kristen shared her plans to get out of Baltimore and move to New York, where she wanted to start her modeling career. She ranted about her parents and their divorce and her desire to be far away from them. "Crazy80's a fucking pro. He keeps things nice and vague, but Kristen sure as hell is willing to spill."

Tucker leaned back in the chair and crossed his arms. "He structures his responses with double talk. It seems like he's saying something, but really he's not saying a goddamn thing. Kristen eats up the sympathy he dishes out while she feeds him more information about herself. Pretty classic fishing."

Jackson grunted as he continued scanning through the chats. Crazy80 had definitely played this game a few times. Poor naïve Kristen didn't have a chance against declarations of strong feelings and deep connections and promises of a glamorous career. Jackson flipped to the next page and clenched his jaw while he read the rest. "So they met?"

"Looks like."

"Fucking-A," Jackson muttered as he shook his head and continued. Crazy80 and Kristen's date had been magical, something special. Crazy80 wanted to meet with Kristen again and make all of her dreams come true. Jackson frowned as he struggled to decipher Tucker's chicken scratch notes at the bottom of the page. "Jesus, Campbell, where the hell did you learn to write? Olivia probably has better handwriting."

"Where'd you learn to read? It says 'Kristen disappeared a week after the last web contact.'"

Jackson looked up and met Tucker's stare. "He's one of their lures. Who the hell is Crazy80?"

"That was my take, and we're not sure. Ethan's working on that right now, but really, he could be anybody. Photoshop a picture of whoever the hell you want into the profile, make something up, and bam— you're Crazy80. Whoever he is, he's smart. He's been careful to use public access computers at the university and public library."

Jackson nodded and scanned the conversations again. "And we're sure on the time frame between Kristen's disappearance and their last 'date'?"

"Absolutely."

"And remind me why the cops never figured this out."

"If Kristen didn't access her Baltimore Dates account at home, there wouldn't be any record in her computer's history. According to the information we have, she was in and out of her parents' house for much of the month before her disappearance. Her mother called the cops several times to report Kristen as a runaway. Kristen may have the three Bs, but she's also a fucking mess."

"This whole *thing's* a fucking mess." Jackson handed the papers back to Tucker. "Refresh my memory—last known whereabouts?"

"Half a block from her friend's apartment building— Ellwood Park area. She'd been crashing there because she couldn't stand her mother, then out of the blue she decided she wants to take the bus home. Her friend encouraged her to stay, but Kristen wouldn't. Next thing you know, the same friend is calling nine-one-one saying she saw two guys pull Kristen into the back of a van."

"Ellwood Park? At night? By herself?"

"I'm at a loss for words, man. Kids are stupid. They think they're invincible."

"But doesn't it strike you as risky on the kidnapper's part to yank some kid up from the sidewalk like that at what, ten o'clock? I know the area's bad news, but still..."

Tucker shrugged. "Crappy neighborhood. Nobody gives a shit. There weren't any other witnesses, or at least no one else came forward. Seemed to work for them. Their method has worked for them every time, whether it be ten at night or four thirty in the afternoon, like with Abby."

Jackson made a sound in his throat and took another sip from his mug. "Did Ethan find a profile on anyone else? What about Abby?"

"No. At least not yet. He's still digging, but this is a damn good lead."

Jackson nodded. "I agree. When we find out who this guy is, it'll only be a matter of time before he leads us to Abby."

"I'm going to talk to a friend on the force out in LA, see if she'd be willing to play decoy. I think we should set up a profile of our own. We might get a hit."

"Good idea—"

The knock at the door cut Jackson off. Alex peeked her head in and met his eyes. "Am I interrupting?"

"No, come on in." Jackson's stomach clutched as she sent him a smile. Damn, she took his breath away. Despite Olivia waking them four hours after they lay down, Alex appeared rested. Alex smiled again while he stared at her in her snug blue jeans and light blue Sagawa Elementary PTO t-shirt, remembering the way she'd come alive in his arms before the sun came up. They had burned up the sheets more times than he could count in their college days, but it had been different last night; *they* had been different last night. Each touch and taste had meant more. He had taken their relationship for granted before. He would never make the same mistake again. "Where's Liv?"

"She wanted Grammy to French braid her hair so she could be a *real* princess for the annual Matthew's Neighborhood Barbeque this afternoon. I guess my regular braids aren't good enough." She chuckled.

He grinned. "A princess wants what a princess wants."

"This is true." She moved closer to the desk. "I thought I would pop in and see if Ethan had any more news on those websites."

"Actually, he found a few things. Tucker and I were just discussing it."

"That's great."

He loved watching her eyes brighten. "We're looking into a couple of dating sites Detective Canon and his taskforce keep an eye on."

She frowned. "But what does that have to do with Abby?"

"Honestly, we're not sure yet, but we can't afford to overlook anything."

"What about Renzo? I thought you said you had something." The light had vanished from her eyes.

"We do, but this doesn't necessarily have anything to do with Renzo. That'll take some time to figure out."

"Oh." She sat on the couch by the fireplace with a barely perceptible huff.

"One of the young women who vanished before Abby had a profile on Baltimore Dates. She was corresponding with someone on a regular basis up until the week she disappeared. The conversations follow a pretty classic pattern used by somebody fishing for a victim. This has sex trafficking written all over it, Alex. We haven't connected all the pieces yet, but this has

247

serious potential." Maybe it was unfair to get her hopes up, but he truly believed this might be their big break. A bump on the right card could bring the whole house tumbling down.

"Abby wasn't into online dating. She tried it once a couple years back. Her first and only experience turned out to be a disaster. The guy she went out with was an obnoxious chauvinist. She left the restaurant through the kitchen, and that was the end of that. Besides, Abby doesn't have any trouble attracting a date if and when she wants one."

"I'm sure that's true, but there's a connection somehow. Kristen converses with a potential lure in a sex ring and disappears a week later in an identical way to your sister. There's definitely something here." He looked at Tucker, who nodded his agreement.

"I guess." She stood and started toward the door. "I'll have to take your word for it."

He snagged her hand as she moved passed and pulled her to him, slinging his arm around her waist. "Take my word for it." He ran his hand up and down her back as he looked her in the eye. "This is the first time we have a serious lead to follow. Answers are waiting for us somewhere in cyberspace. Trust me on this."

"Of course I do."

His hand stilled on her back. "Good." He brushed his lips over hers. "Keep it up."

Her fingers curled into his shirt. They both knew he wasn't speaking of Abby's case. He held her gaze as Tucker's computer made a pinging noise, alerting them to a new e-mail.

"From Ethan," Tucker said. "He sent us—well, son of a fucking... Take a look at this." Tucker turned the laptop. The grainy image Jackson had snapped of the man dancing with the underage girl at Club Jericho had been cleaned up and filled the left side of Tucker's screen. Another cropped photograph of the same black-haired, brown-eyed man filled the right side.

"Bingo," Jackson muttered. He read aloud the small caption attached at the bottom. "This is Tim Monroe. He's a freelance fashion photographer with numerous connections in the modeling industry. According to Ethan, Tim and Renzo's names overlapped on several different occasions—they worked several of the same runway shows, snapped photos at many of the same shoots. Oh, and isn't this interesting. He also has a profile on Baltimore Dates. This is the picture on the right." He flicked his finger toward the screen. "Of course, Ethan couldn't find anything overly alarming in his interactions with women eighteen years of age or older, except on more than one occasion he's checked out the foreigners Canon's taskforce keeps an eye on." He looked at Tucker.

Alex leaned closer to the laptop, studying Ethan's latest e-mail. "What does this mean exactly?"

"It means we've got a few big coincidences here. Tim Monroe has an eye for young girls and foreign women, *and* he has a connection to Renzo. He also has a connection to the same dating website Kristen was affiliated with. Ethan's going to have to do some more work."

Alex stood straight. "Is Tim Monroe the one who was corresponding with Kristen?"

"We can't be sure. Monroe's profile name is PhotoShop, but the person who potentially lured and arranged Kristen's disappearance is Crazy80."

"Then how can you say this is connected? What if Tim Monroe just happens to have a profile on Baltimore Dates? Baltimore is a large city; it's not that hard to fathom. Many singles look for love online."

"True, but not all singles are professionally connected to a man who was dating your sister just a few weeks before she disappeared. And how many do you think go to clubs to flirt with young girls when there are literally hundreds of legal adults surrounding them. If Monroe is looking for love, he isn't looking in the right places—unless he's a trafficker." Jackson's excitement built as he glanced from Alex to Tucker. This was going to be their big break. "I'm willing to bet my house that Tim and Renzo have something to do with Abby and Kristen's disappearance."

"Then let's call Detective Canon." Alex reached for the landline.

Jackson settled his hand on top of hers, holding the receiver in place. "Not yet. Give us some time to toss this around."

"We're *wasting* time by 'tossing this around.' You're theory makes perfect sense."

"I'm with Jackson on this one," Tucker supplied. "I don't see dissecting the angles as wasting time. The taskforce would definitely check out what we pass along, but unless they find a solid connection between Cruz, Monroe, and Zachary Hartwell, they're not going to touch it. Plus, Canon will just get bitchy knowing we still have our noses in on this when he's told Jackson to back off. Cops are real bastards that way."

Temper darkened Alex's blue eyes. "Well that's unacceptable. This isn't a game of yours or mine. My sister is suffering."

Jackson pulled her rigid hand from the phone and held it in his. "Now that we have something absolutely solid... We won't give up until Abby's home, Alex. I promise." He gave her icy fingers a gentle squeeze. "Tucker's going to call one of his former co-workers, a detective with LAPD, and ask her if she's willing to be our decoy—off the record."

"Decoy?"

"Yeah, you know, set up an account on Baltimore Dates and pose as a young woman traffickers would find interesting."

"I'll do it."

He could only stare as Alex's words froze his heart. "No."

"Yes." She yanked her hand from his grip. "This is a great idea."

"Forget it. Absolutely not." His heart now shuddered as trickles of unease grew to full bloom.

"Tucker's friend lives in LA. I'm right here. I want to do this for Abby."

"Melinda's a cop, Alex," Tucker interjected. "She does decoy work all the time."

"Melinda's sister isn't missing." She seared Tucker with a look.

"Drop it," Jackson snapped, recognizing the unshakable determination in Alex's voice. "We're wasting time arguing about something that isn't an option."

"Why?" She focused her frosty stare on him. "Because you say so."

"Damn straight. Case closed."

"But Abby's isn't."

"We won't get to the bottom of her disappearance any faster if we have to worry about your safety too. You're staying out of this. Tucker, call Melinda."

Alex held Jackson's gaze a moment longer, and then walked out.

Jackson stared down the hall while Tucker spoke to Melinda, feeling no better about the situation. Alex had let that go too easily, much like she did the night she'd convinced him to bring her to the clubs. There was no way in hell she was changing his mind this time. One wrong move is all it would take for Alex to find herself in as much trouble as Abby or Kristen Moore.

⸺◦◦◦⸺

Laughter and noise from the barbeque flowed through the open windows as Alexa shut the office door behind her. She leaned back against the dark, glossy wood, swallowing the vile taste of deception as she stared at Tucker's laptop and the small stack of papers beside it. Sighing, she closed her eyes. She *hated* what she was about to do, but she couldn't think of another way. God knows she tried while she nibbled BBQ chicken and mingled with guests in Jack's parents' backyard, but nothing had come to mind. Jack had left her little choice when he said no earlier this morning. No wasn't an option she could live with. Abby was lost out there. If this could bring her home...

She stood straight, huffing out a breath. She was wasting time. Who knew how long it would be before Tucker or Jack came up to check in with Ethan again? Alexa shoved away her regret as she walked toward George's beautiful antique desk, watching the breeze catch the edges of the printouts she intended to study. *This is for Abby,* she reminded herself when her pulse kicked into high gear. She licked her dry lips, knowing that once she started the wheels turning, there would be no going back.

She reached for the papers but jerked her hand away, standing perfectly still, as footsteps echoed on the stairs. Her breath came faster, and she glanced over her shoulder, staring at the doorknob, waiting for someone to enter. What would she say? She had no reason for being in George's office. Tucker or Jack would more than likely see through her phony explanations—her lies. Surely that was what she was doing—telling lies. She pressed a hand to her queasy stomach, struggling to ignore her guilty conscience, as whoever had come up the stairs went back down.

She was a hypocrite, plain and simple. She always touted the importance of telling the truth to Livy and her students, yet she was taking the first steps down the road of deception. Her shame only compounded when she caught site of Jack and Livy through the window, sitting in a lawn chair by the docks. Jack took Livy's dripping vanilla cone from undoubtedly sticky fingers and licked around the melting edges, then he handed it back to her. He was such a good daddy, such a good man, and she was going behind his back. "I'm sorry, Jack," she muttered as she clasped her hand around her necklace and looked away.

There was no one she wanted to hurt less. She loved him, but she loved Abby too. Her sister had slipped through their fingers. They were running out of chances to bring her home. How long would the sex ring wait before they shipped her overseas, if they hadn't already? Desperate times called for desperate measures, and what she was doing fell under that heading.

Bolstered by her justifications, Alexa reached for the papers again. She lifted the pretty shell Tucker used as a paperweight with trembling fingers, mindful to remember the order in which she took sheets from the stack. She scanned the first two pages—e-mail correspondences between Ethan and Tucker—and set them on the desk. She studied Timothy Monroe's Department of Motor Vehicles picture, and then moved on to the copy of his information from Baltimore Dates. "PhotoShop," she murmured as she read his profile name, interests, hobbies, and philosophies on life. Interesting, but not what she was looking for. She flipped again until she stared at the photo of the beautiful girl with blonde hair and brown eyes—LoveGoddess17.

Kristen looked different from the pictures Alexa had seen on the Missing Children's Websites and local news. Here she appeared older; the hint of desperation and defiance in her eyes was unmistakable, but she was just a baby—barely seventeen. A swift kick of anger melded with sorrow. This was so wrong. Everything about this entire situation was wrong for Kristen and Abby.

Kristen should've been home getting ready for a date to the movies or sunbathing by a pool with her best girlfriend, not dealing with the traumas of prostitution and sex slavery. Alexa slammed the paper to the desk, growing angrier by the second, and studied the shadowy photograph of the man known as Crazy80. The strong jaw and sharp cheekbones hinted at a handsome face, but it was hard to tell with his dark shades and ball cap pulled low on his head. He could be anyone, but he wasn't Timothy Monroe or Renzo. The features she could make out didn't fit either man, but that didn't mean Crazy80 didn't *know* Timothy and Renzo.

She tore her gaze from the mysterious face and read his generic profile. Next she read the conversations Kristen Moore had had with him. Her breathing grew shallow as she scanned the words of a young woman in crisis and the slimy promises of someone who knew what a girl desperate for love and attention would want to hear. "Bastard," she hissed as her eyes filled. Crazy80 was a bastard of the lowest form. He'd reeled Kristen in with false promises, and now she was paying the ultimate price.

The sticky clutches of guilt troubling Alexa lessened as she stacked the papers neatly and replaced the paperweight. She needed to do this. She had to help Abby and Kristen and as many other victims as she could. Hopefully this would be the beginning of the end for all of them. If the answers to her sister's disappearance were floating in cyberspace as Jack said, she was going to find them. She grabbed a sheet of paper from the printer and jotted down the Baltimore Dates URL along with the links to Timothy Monroe's and Crazy80's profiles, although the latter's had been disabled shortly after Kristen disappeared, according to the notes Ethan sent.

She shoved the paper in her pocket and glanced out the window again. She did a double take as she noticed the empty lawn chair. Where did Jack and Livy go? She scanned the crowds of people talking and laughing in groups around picnic tables or the small fire pit until she found them on the dock. Despite everything, a smile tugged at her lips. Jack held Livy on his lap, but a fishing pole had replaced the dripping ice cream cone in her hands. Alexa's heart melted as she stared at her baby girl smiling up at her daddy.

Forgetting herself, Alexa walked closer to the window, drawn by the sweet scene Jack and Livy made. He was so perfect and kind. "Handsome Jack," she whispered, as she had so many times before when he filled her heart to bursting.

He loved Livy. He loved her.

It was safer and certainly less scary to believe he'd said what he did because he'd been caught up in the heat of passion, but while they lay together in the wee hours of the morning, holding hands with their daughter snuggled between them, she'd had no choice but to accept that he meant every word. He'd never gotten over her; he'd never stopped loving her.

Alexa stepped back from the glass and sighed as she pressed her hand to the paper in her pocket. Would he be able to forgive her for this? From the beginning, their relationship had been built on trust. Would such a blatant deception ruin what they were working to get back? She needed to believe he would understand. She thought of her sister's screams of terror and whispered pleadings for help. "I'm coming for you, Ab. No matter what, I'm coming for you."

Turning her back to the window, she walked from the room and closed the door behind her.

"Night, night, Lovely Livy. I'll see you in the morning."

"Okay, Mommy." Livy puckered up for her kiss.

Alexa leaned in and pressed her lips to her daughter's. "Snuggle up, sweetie." She tucked the light cotton sheet up to Livy's chest.

"I want to write a book about fishing with daddy," Livy announced as Alexa settled herself more comfortably on the edge of the bed for their nightly bedtime chat.

"I think that sounds wonderful." She brushed Livy's soft bangs back from her forehead. "What will you say?"

"It's a surprise. I will draw the pictures, and you can write what I say for the words."

Alexa smiled. She'd introduced Livy to 'storytelling' as a diversionary tactic during a particularly long wait for a well-child checkup two months before. Livy had been wild about drawing her 'stories' ever since.

"I want to draw my fishies in the morning."

"It's a date. I can't wait. We'll get started right after breakfast."

Livy's grin turned into an enthusiastic yawn.

"I think someone needs to close their eyes."

"Don't turn off the light."

"I promise I won't." Alexa kissed her finger and touched Livy's nose. "Sweet dreams, my smart, beautiful girl."

"I love you, Mommy."

Alexa hugged Livy tight. "I love you too."

"I want to say goodnight to Daddy."

"He'll be up a little later. He's helping Grampy and a few of the neighbors put away some of the heavy tables and chairs."

"Don't tell him about my book. It's a secret present," she whispered conspiratorially.

"Cross my heart." Alexa winked as she followed her words with the appropriate action.

Livy yawned again and turned to her side with her stuffed frog—a sure sign that she would be down and out within minutes. "I don't know how to draw fishies," she said groggily.

"I'll show you." Alexa rubbed Livy's back and watched her eyes grow heavy. Her baby blinked once, twice, three times, and then her lids stayed closed.

Alexa stared at her pretty girl, wishing this was any typical evening, but it wasn't. She had stuff to do, things she wished she didn't have to. She touched Livy's arm and stood, regretting that she couldn't curl up and snuggle while she read a chapter or two in a good book. Instead, she walked to the window, watching Jack and Tucker help several of the older residents of the neighborhood stack large folding tables and numerous chairs into the back of pickup trucks. There were half a dozen vehicles down the block that needed to be unloaded.

Jack sat in the driver's seat of Mr. Farley's loaded-down flatbed. Tucker hopped in on the passenger's side. The break lights glowed bright in the dark, and then the truck took off down the street.

Alexa stepped back and hurried to the guest bathroom. She peeked at Livy, who was by now sound asleep, before she closed the door and began her work, detesting every second. Sighing, she looked at herself in the mirror, then plucked up the hair tie sitting on the counter and pulled her hair up in a tight ponytail. She wrapped her long mane of soft black locks around the elastic and secured the bun she'd made with bobby pins.

It was time for step two—the tricky part. How did she go about making herself appear several years younger than she was? She wasn't an old hag, but she certainly wasn't eighteen. Light on the makeup would probably be best. Alexa pulled powder, an eyeliner pencil, and other cosmetics from the drawer she had shoved them in and started her transformation. She powdered her face, then drew a thin line of dark blue across the edge of one eyelid, then the next. Beige eye shadow followed for a natural look. She brushed her lashes with several short sweeps of the mascara wand and examined the effect. Perfect. Her lake-blue eyes were huge. She applied a swipe of blush and heightened the fullness of her lips with clear, shimmery gloss.

Alexa unbuttoned her pale pink top until a hint of smooth, creamy cleavage peeked out from the black, clinging, spaghetti-strapped tank she wore underneath. She grabbed the chin-length blond wig she'd swiped from one of Carol's prop boxes and secured it in place. Closing her eyes, she took several breaths and opened them. She blinked at the prettily chic youngster staring back at her in the mirror. A slow smile touched her mouth as she tilted her head and glanced up from under her lashes. Flirtatious. Sexy. Naive. *Amazing.* Definitely not sixteen, but certainly not twenty-seven either. This could work. This just might work.

She picked up the digital camera she'd set on the counter before she helped Livy brush her teeth and aimed the lens in her own direction. She practiced her sweet, vulnerable look a few times before she snapped a picture. She examined the results, scrutinizing, making sure it was impossible to tell she was related to Abby, then took several more. She pressed the button again, trying for that desperate and defiant look, attempting to mirror the picture she had seen of Kristen.

Alexa glanced at the digital clock tucked in the corner on the granite countertop and winced. She had taken longer than she'd planned. Jack would be home before long, and she had so much more to do. Setting down the camera, Alexa pulled off the wig, crouched down, and shoved the fake hair to the back of the cupboard below the sink. She washed her face, scrubbing off the makeup she'd painstakingly applied, and changed into a long Ravens jersey. With her skin fresh and soft from moisturizer, she opened the door and stepped into the bedroom with her camera in hand.

Smiling, she walked to Livy, who was already tangled in the sheets. Alexa tugged on the blanket and gently pulled Gordon free from Livy's clutches, rescuing the frog from his one-leg dangle off the bed, and set the stuffed animal next to her daughter's side, knowing her restless little sleeper would reach for him when she moved again.

With Livy settled, Alexa hurried to the small sitting area and plunked herself on the couch with her laptop. She pulled free the piece of paper she'd stuffed in her pocket and typed the Baltimore Dates URL in to the address bar. Seconds later, a backsplash of the city, along with several pictures of smiling, attractive couples filled her screen. She blew out a nervous breath as she located the *Join Now!* hyperlink and pressed it. This was it—the official point of no return.

Her heart beat faster as she looked at the empty data fields waiting to be filled with her name, date of birth, e-mail address, and so on. She placed her fingers on the home row, licked her lips, and started to type the first few letters of her profile name, 'JennyLove,' but the framed picture of Jack on the side table caught her eye.

She froze, staring at a younger Jack grinning with a college football trophy in his hands. She remembered that night and the glory of watching Jack and his team battle their way to the division championship. Hundreds of students had rushed the field when Jack landed on his back with the winning catch, herself included. Among the sea of maroon uniforms and the chaos of exited fans, they'd found one another. He'd picked her up—sweaty and exhausted—and spun her while they laughed and plied each other with quick, enthusiastic kisses. So much had changed in the years since George took that picture of his son, but Jack's eyes were still the same—kind, friendly, and honest. "Damn," she sighed. "Please understand, Jack. Please understand that I have to do this." She rubbed at her stomach as it clenched with the newly familiar pangs of guilt. "Abby. Abby. Abby," she whispered as she tore her gaze from Jack's. "This is for Abby." Remembering her purpose, she buried the mix of messy emotions and settled in to create the profile she'd been planning for much of the day. With her fingers back on the keyboard, she typed 'Jennifer Carstens' as her name. Jennifer had just turned eighteen on April 12 and loved photography. She'd graduated from high school a month ago, and her dream was to become either a fashion photographer or model; it didn't matter as long as she worked in the industry. College was still up in the air. She wanted to spend a year traveling with her girlfriends before she made any major commitments. For fun she enjoyed taking pictures, anything adventurous, hanging out with friends, shopping, and partying.

Alexa read and reread what would be her new

identity—if she actually got a hit. Hopefully this was good enough. Hopefully her plan would work. She'd been careful to add the pieces most lures appeared to look for—youth, naiveté, a definite lack of direction, and desperation to be part of the fashion world. With nothing left to do, she uploaded the third picture she had taken of the dozen. The big, trusting eyes and flirty hint of smile matched Jennifer Carstens best—better than the rebellion shot imitating Kristen Moore.

Two doors slammed in the driveway; the sound ricocheted off the water. Alexa came to attention when Jack and Tucker's voices called out their goodnights to Mr. Farley. The old pickup reversed and drove away. Seconds later, the front door opened.

"Shoot. *Shoot.*" With her heart in her throat and her hand on the mouse, Alexa scanned Jennifer Carstens' profile one last time. Footsteps took the stairs in twos and walked down the hall, stopping outside her door. Afraid she would chicken out, she slammed her eyes shut and clicked *submit* with a trembling finger. She sat statue still, taking in deep breaths. It was done. She was officially a liar.

Knuckles wrapped lightly on the wood, and Jack poked his head in. "You're up."

Alexa opened her eyes and exed out of the site, then shut her laptop and stood. "Yeah." She cleared her throat when her voice came out weak. "Yeah," she tried again. She clutched her hands in front of her and immediately dropped them to her sides, afraid she was giving herself away.

Jack opened the door wider. "Do you have a second?"

"Sure. Come on in."

He stepped in, and her stomach fluttered with twinges of guilt and love. He looked so *good* with his black ball cap worn backwards. The white Ethan Cooke

Security t-shirt and carpenter shorts accentuated his muscular build. He glanced at the bed and smiled at their daughter. "She's out, huh?"

"Yeah, she was pretty tired. She had a fun day." But they didn't. Although she and Jack had cared for Livy together, and he had cheerfully reintroduced Alexa to many of the neighbors she met years before, hints of tension had marred an afternoon meant for celebrating the relaxing, carefree days of summer.

"I want to talk about earlier."

"Okay."

He closed the door. "Can we sit down?"

"Of course."

They walked to the couch and each took a cushion. Alexa gave Jack a small smile, then glanced down. How would she look at him day after day after what she just did?

"Alex, I'm sorry about this morning."

Her gaze flew to his. "Please, don't apologize."

"I lost my cool—"

She took his hand. "Please don't." She could hardly stand listening to the regret in his voice. "It's no big deal."

He gave her hand a squeeze. "Yeah, it is. You were thinking of Abby. I know how much you want to help her. The way I handled things—it was knee-jerk, and I regret it."

"I *have* to help my sister. Helping isn't simply a want." She desperately needed him to understand. "Any opportunity that presents itself... I have to do my part to bring her home."

"You are doing your part."

She shook her head vehemently. "No. I'm not doing nearly enough. After I saw her the other night... She was so close, and now she's gone."

"You've helped the authorities confirm a sighting

from the bachelor party pictures. You helped me *find* her."

"It's not enough." She stood, restless. "It will never be enough. No length is too far; no situation is too dangerous. I can't rest until she's standing here in front of me safe and whole again. How can I make you see? How can I make you feel this desperation I wake up with every day?"

"Alex—"

"No." He was trying to appease her, and it couldn't be done. "Sitting around waiting for everyone else to come up with answers... Depending on others—strangers no less... I'm used to taking care of her. I've been doing it for as long as I can remember." She paced back and forth. "Abby's my responsibility. I took care of her when my mother was too drunk and depressed to take care of herself. Gran and I raised my sister together. Abby needs me more than ever and I'm not there for her." She stopped at the window and stared out.

"Alex." Jack's solid arms enveloped her waist, and his chin settled on her head. "None of what's happening to Abby is your fault."

Instead of leaning back into his gesture of comfort, she held herself rigid. She didn't deserve any of the kindness he offered.

He pulled her more tightly against him. "This isn't your fault, Alex."

She wrapped her fingers around his forearms, intending to free herself from his hold, but she slid her hands down until they rested on his, then leaned in to his chest. Despite her betrayal, she couldn't walk away. "I should've done more. I should've done so much more. I didn't pay enough attention to the van following us. I never gave it any thought. When I saw them driving behind us or pulling ahead on occasion, I just figured they were travelers heading in the same direction. If we would've kept going instead of stopping..."

"They would've taken her regardless. It was only a matter of time. They wanted Abby, and they were going to have her."

"I didn't even get a license plate number—a *license plate* number, Jack." She closed her eyes as she huffed out a breath. Her ineptitude still made her angry. "Such a vital detail, and it never crossed my mind."

"You were in shock."

"I was shockingly stupid."

"Stop." He pressed his cheek to hers. "The information you *did* give Detective Canon linked Abby's case to the others. If you hadn't witnessed her abduction, we would have absolutely nothing to go on; besides, the kidnappers probably pulled off an exit or two up the road and moved Abby to a new vehicle altogether."

"But that would've slowed them down."

He shook his head. "Getting caught slows you down. This is an extremely organized operation. They weren't going to let something as simple and identifiable as a license plate or van color fuck up their plans."

She'd never thought of it that way, but then why would she? Her life revolved around the wants and needs of a three-year-old and her classroom full of first-graders. "Still."

"Stop, Alex." He turned her to face him. "I know Abby's in a terrible situation, but we're doing everything possible to get her out of it. He rested his forehead against hers.

"Jack."

"Even though things are bad, I'm thankful they aren't worse."

"How can you say that?" She yanked away from his hold. "My sister's being raped and God knows what

264

else. It doesn't get any worse than that."

"You're alive. Oliva's alive. You're both witnesses to a suspected multi-million dollar operation. They didn't have to keep you that way."

Alexa felt the blood drain from her face as she stared at him. "I guess I—I guess I never thought—I don't want to think... I need to sit down." She walked back to the couch on watery legs. Abby and Livy had been alone in the desolate parking lot for at least five minutes while she'd been in the bathroom. They could've hurt her baby while she'd been washing her hands and thinking her relaxing summer thoughts. "God, that makes me sick." She clenched her hands at her sides. "Even after all the cruelty we've read about and seen, I never thought about... She was trapped in her car seat. She had no idea what was going on. She's just a little girl."

"They don't care." He sat beside her and put his arm around her. "They don't give a damn about anything but their bottom line. That's why I want you to stay out of this. The stakes are too high. These people aren't messing around. Tucker's friend is going to handle the website. She's agreed to help us out. We officially have a decoy in place."

"But it's not a guarantee. The person we want has to take the bait. If two of us have accounts our odds will increase."

"True, but the risks to you aren't worth any of the odds. If they contact Miranda, they'll want to meet her. That's when a bust will go down."

"You could help me. We could do it together."

"No. We're finished with this, Alex."

"Abby deserves everything we can give her."

"Agreed. That's why Tucker contacted Miranda. I have absolute faith in her. She's played this game hundreds of times before. Rounding up creeps on the internet is how she makes a living."

Jack's confidence in Tucker's friend should've appeased her. "But—"

"I wouldn't be able to stand it if anything happened to you, Alex." He pulled her closer. "I can't handle losing you now that I've found you again."

She pressed her hand to his cheek. It was on the tip of her tongue to tell him, to confess everything, but her sister's desperate screams echoed through her head, and she stayed silent.

"I need to keep you safe. I love you."

Oh, Jack. She closed her eyes, unable to look into his.

He kissed her. "Are we okay?"

They were far from okay, but she nodded. "Yes, we're okay." *I'm so sorry.*

"What's wrong?"

She opened her eyes. "I'm worried about Abby."

He shook his head. "It's more than that."

"I want all of this to be over."

"We're getting closer. Tucker, Ethan, and I are definitely on to something."

"I know." Hopefully, so was she. It didn't matter who crossed the finish line first as long as the end result was having Abby home.

"You should go to bed. You're exhausted."

"In a few minutes."

"I can handle that." He moved back, resting against the cushion, bringing her with him. "So did you have fun today?"

This wasn't exactly what she had in mind. She wanted time to *think*—alone—about what she'd done, about what Jack had said. But none of it mattered. She planned to go ahead with her own decoy operation, no matter the risks. Sighing, she answered. "It was nice seeing everyone again. There were even more people here than the last time I came, and that's saying something."

He chuckled and shrugged. "What can I tell ya? Mom and dad like to entertain. But word might've spread that Alexa Harris was back—and so were her famous chocolate chip cookies." He smiled, winked, and kissed her temple. "We won't tell mom," he whispered. "It might hurt her feelings."

She gave him a weak smile.

"We should get to bed. It's late. Olivia will be up bright and early."

Alexa already knew she wouldn't sleep well with her conscience weighing heavy. "Yes she will. She's definitely a morning person."

He chuckled. "Olivia's a morning, afternoon, and evening person. She never slows down."

"This is true."

"Can I lay with you?"

"Uh, sure." How could she deny him such a simple request?

He stood and held out his hand. "I'm beat."

"I'm pretty tired myself." She reached out and took his hand as they walked to bed. Alexa settled in as Jack stripped out of his t-shirt and shorts and got in on his side. They both moved closer to Livy, much like they did the night before. He took her hand and pressed his lips to her palm. "See you soon."

"Good night." She clenched her jaw and closed her eyes, trying to ignore the fear of what would happen if Jack discovered the truth.

CHAPTER 16

J ACKSON BUCKLED OLIVIA INTO HER seat and gave her a kiss. "Have a good time, Liv."

"I'm going to see dolphins and jellyfishies and froggies and—and birdies that sing pretty songs." She bounced about in her excitement.

"Will you make me another story when you get home?" The surprise fishing story she'd gifted him with two days ago, wrapped with frilly purple ribbon and too much tape, still made him smile. His little girl made him a present. The four-page book stood on the shelf above his childhood bed in front of the numerous football and baseball trophies he'd collected over the years.

"Yes. Close the door, Daddy. I need to go."

He chuckled. "Yes, ma'am." He shut the door and turned to his mother. "Are you sure you're up to this? She's going to run you and Dad ragged."

"Somehow we managed with you and your brother. I'm just as excited to take her to the aquarium as she is to go." She gave him a kiss on the cheek. "What are you're plans for the day?"

"I have a date with Dad's office chair. We were planning to peruse the internet, answer e-mails, and enjoy long phone conversations while I search for more leads. We have a real love connection."

"You know, Tucker already left for the day, and we have a perfectly good boat just bobbing away by the dock over there. Perhaps Alexa would enjoy a ride."

Jackson looked at the sleek cabin cruiser, then his

mother. "That might not be a bad idea." In the three days since Miranda went live as their decoy, they hadn't received any hits on her account worth mentioning. Despite the hours of endless hunting, he, Ethan, and Tucker were spinning their wheels. The case was stalling again, and Alex was discouraged. If the contact Tucker was meeting with in DC didn't breathe new life into their dying lead, they would be back to the drawing board. Perhaps an hour or two on the water was what he and Alex needed. God knew a little time away from the endless game of phone tag could only make things better. Maybe he would float back to the dock with a fresh perspective.

"Your mother's full of good ones. There's a picnic basket in the fridge just waiting for someone to take it."

"You're the best." He wrapped his mother in a bear hug.

She hugged him back. "And don't you forget it."

"Never could." He eased away as the front door slammed. Alex came rushing out in khaki shorts and a white tank top.

"Sorry. I was on the phone with my boss. I need to say goodbye to Livy." She breezed past Jackson and opened the door, unleashing the noise and commotion of their eager daughter. But as she bent down to their daughter, he noted the worry clouding her eyes.

"Mommy, I need to *go*. Grammy is talking and it's taking so *long*."

"I know you're excited, but you have to be patient. Stay with Grammy and Grampy. Don't let go of their hands. Make sure you—"

"She's going to be fine, Alexa." His mom patted Alex's shoulder. "Try to enjoy yourself today."

Alex nibbled her lip. "Maybe I should come with you. The aquarium is so big, and Livy is very busy..." She stopped and sighed. "I'm being overprotective. She'll be all right."

"Of course she will." His mother gave Alex a bright smile. "I certainly don't think we have to worry about losing her, honey. A blind man could see that shirt and hair tie you dolled her up in."

Jackson glanced through the window at the florescent pink t-shirt Olivia wore, proclaiming that she was 'Super Cute!' in bold lime green letters. The matching green and pink bow wrapped around her sassy little ponytail was hard to miss.

"We always have the kids wear brightly colored clothes when we take them on field trips. It's easier to keep track of everyone. Better safe than sorry." Alex smiled sheepishly.

"Grammy, come *on*. Come *on*."

"Yeah, Carol, come on. I want to get there while there's still some parking available," dad said as he clicked his seatbelt into place.

"All right. Off we go." She opened her door.

"Don't forget, you have my number programmed in your phone, and I gave George a copy of Livy's Identa-Kids card."

Jackson took a step forward to pry Alex's white-knuckled grip from Olivia's still-open door.

"Alexa Harris, take a deep breath and back away from the car," his mother scolded lightly. "I've raised two boys and taught hundreds of kids. I haven't lost one yet."

She dropped her hand herself without Jackson having to intervene and shook her head. "I'm sorry, Mom. I'm just a little nervous with everything going on."

Mom gave her a hug. "Of course you are, sweetie. We'll guard Livy with our lives. Nothing but good fun is going to happen to her today."

"Thank you for taking her." Alex closed her eyes as she held on. "She's going to have fun."

Jackson smothered a smile as his dad started the car and pressed the gas pedal just a touch, revving the engine to make his point. If George Matthews was anything, he was punctual. This had to be driving him crazy.

"Yes she is. Now, I better get in or they're going to leave without me. Cranky old bear," his mother muttered as she took her seat.

"Bye, Lovely Livy. Have fun." Alex kissed Livy once more, closed the door, and returned Livy's enthusiastic wave.

Jackson pulled Alex against him and hooked his arm around her waist as they waved until the car disappeared down the street. "She's going to have a blast. This is good for her. She's been cooped up since we got here."

She rested her head on his shoulder. "I know. I'm just a little worried."

He tipped her face up to his, recognizing the tightness of unshed tears in her voice. "Alex."

She shook her head. "I'm being silly." She strangled out a chuckle as she wiped her eyes.

He hugged her, fully realizing how huge a toll this was taking on her. "I wouldn't let them go if I thought Olivia was in any danger. The kidnappers have no idea we're here. You're credit card trail stops at a hotel room in LA."

"I know." She sniffed.

"Olivia will probably get back an hour or two after we are."

Frowning, she looked up into his eyes. "What do you mean?"

"Stay right here."

"Jack—"

"Don't move." Jackson hurried up the steps and rushed to the kitchen. He opened the refrigerator and smiled when he spotted the big wicker picnic basket on the bottom shelf. "*Nice.*" He grabbed the pretty handcrafted basket his mother had packed more times than he could count, set it on the counter, and flipped open the top. His smile widened as he glanced at thick ham slices, fruit salad, a mixed green salad, rolls, chocolate cake, and a bottle of white wine with two crystal glasses. "Thanks, mom."

Flipping the lid closed, Jackson snagged the boat keys off the hook and headed for the door. He stopped at the stairwell and ran up, anticipating Alex. Moments later, dressed in blue swim trunks and a white muscle shirt, he opened the front door and shut it, locking up behind him.

"What do you have there?" Alex asked with a hand on her hip.

"A picnic lunch."

"That's very sweet, but it's ten in the morning."

"It won't be by the time we get to where we're going." He held out his hand, encouraged that she hadn't refused outright. "Come on."

She stood where she was, eyeing him. "And where's that?"

"You'll see. Come on," he said again when she still made no attempt to move.

"Jack."

He reached forward and snagged her hand. "Where's your sense of adventure? What happened to the woman who learned to let her hair down and have a little fun?"

"She grew up."

"So now that she's all grown up she can't have fun anymore?" He gave her a tug toward the grassy hill and dock below. "Come have fun with me, Alex. The way we used to."

She took a step with him and stopped. "I have to get my cellphone. What if Livy needs me? What if they get a break in Abby's case and Detective Canon calls?"

"It's in my back pocket." He turned his ass toward her.

"We don't have any sunblock."

"It's in here, along with your sunglasses." He motioned to the beach bag he'd unearthed from the guest closet and gave her another tug. "Come play with me," he encouraged again. "I've hardly seen you over the past couple days." He and Tucker had been in phone meetings with Ethan, Hunter, and Austin, dealing with Abby's case as well as briefings on several of Ethan Cooke Security's clients. The company was busier than ever with premieres and numerous other big events. Their agents were bogged down with no end in sight.

Tucker would only be able to stay a couple more days. Ethan could really use him too, but they all understood he wouldn't be going anywhere until they had Abby back.

"All right. I'll come play with you for a little while." She smiled fully for the first time since she'd knocked on the office door the morning of the big picnic. Something had been different. She'd seemed more tense and distant during the few snatches they'd been able to steal together. They both needed this time away. He was determined to make the most of it.

"Let's go then."

She'd needed this—the sun, the warm wind blowing on her face. Jack knew her so well...or Carol did. Alexa smiled. There was no way Jack packed the wicker basket full of beautifully presented goodies, which she'd put away in the mini-refrigerator below deck. But that didn't matter. It was the thought that counted.

Jack guided the big boat around the small peninsula miles from his parent's home and headed right. He glanced back from the driver's seat and smiled as he pushed the throttle full speed. He was taking her to their place—the desolate island fifteen minutes from the southeast tip of Kent Island. He'd brought her there the first summer she'd come to visit. There had been so many 'firsts' that magical July: her first boat ride, her first time making love in the brackish waters of the bay. Her stomach tingled with the memory.

The land grew distant as they headed further out. Seagulls flew overhead and swooped to the dark blue water below. She loved this and was beginning to realize how much she'd missed the relaxation a day on the Chesapeake could bring. It seemed wrong that her tense muscles were uncoiling, and she found herself relaxing when her little girl was not within eyesight or earshot. Still, there was a ball of anxiety in her stomach that wouldn't go away. Her sister was still being held against her will. and she continued to lie to Jack.

She checked Baltimore Dates every morning after Jack woke and left the bed they'd all begun to share. He no longer asked to join her and Livy. Late at night he crawled in on his side, took her hand, kissed her palm, and closed his eyes. She didn't have the heart to tell him he couldn't stay, especially when she found the web of deception growing stronger with every flirty reply she made to her increasing list of fans in her dating inbox. She'd had several invitations for a night out, which she'd politely turned down by saying she needed time to get to know her potential match. It was easier to string them all along until she could determine who was looking for a simple dinner out and who wanted more. Two men in particular set off alarm bells with the questions they asked and the comments they made, but it was impossible to tell if they were the same person who had posed as Crazy80. The men's profile pictures were as vague as Crazy80's had been when he'd been in communication with Kristen. The photos could have been of anyone.

With a sigh of frustration, she stared at the breathtaking scenery. Just because she wanted their mystery lead to contact her didn't mean he would. Every hour that passed without the hit they needed only heightened Abby's urgent situation. Before long, her sister would become a cold case. In many ways she already was. The cops had moved on to other kidnappings and crimes.

At least Doug Masterson kept his ears open for anything new for Jack. According to Doug, Abby hadn't been back to Lady Pink since the night she and Jack saw her. She or Miranda *had* to get a hit on their profiles; it was the only answer to moving Abby's case forward.

Alexa came to attention when Jack throttled back on the engine. The boat slowed on its approach to the small, tree-covered island. He glanced over his shoulder and gave her another smile. "Do you remember this place?"

He was so handsome with his hair disheveled from the wind. "Yes." She stood and made her way to him. "How could I forget?"

"I thought it might be nice to spend the day here, maybe do a little swimming, have a picnic, pretend the rest of the world doesn't exist for a few hours."

It would be hard not to worry about Livy or think about Abby or not feel guilty about her big lie, but she wanted to try for Jack. His weary eyes under amber-tinted lenses told her he needed a day to 'just be' as

275

badly as she did. "I think that sounds like heaven. I'm assuming you packed my bathing suit in your little bag downstairs."

"I was all for swimming naked, but since you never know when a boat is going to pass by..." He shrugged.

"I appreciate your sensibility. I'll be right back."

"Let me come with you. I'll help you tie your—"

"I think I've got it." She smiled and put a hand on his chest, stopping him.

"I don't know." He moved closer and kissed her neck. "Those knots can be pretty tricky. I would feel better if you let me give you a hand."

She lifted her head higher and closed her eyes, melting from the sun's heat and the sensations he sent careening through her body with his touch. "That's very generous and so selfless... Mmm." She lost her train of thought as his hands snuck under her tank top and cupped her breasts. "Jack..."

The hoots and hollers of a boat full of college-aged men went speeding by, interrupting their moment.

Jack looked up. "Bastards."

Alexa took the opportunity to step back.

"Kids these days." He shook his head mournfully. "They're so obnoxious."

She snorted out a laugh. "Oh, please. You were just as bad, if not worse."

"Maybe, but I had more *style*." He grinned as she rolled her eyes.

"I'm going down to put on my suit—alone, Mr. Style."

"Call me if you need any help."

"You'll be the first," she tossed over her shoulder, smiling. She heard Jack chuckle as she descended the three steps to the small galley. She wanted this day with him more than she'd realized. She wanted the laughter and fun they always used to have together; she craved it. For the next little while, Alexa was determined they would have it. Livy was fine. Abby wasn't... She shook her head. "Two hours," she said out loud. Perhaps they would take three before they boated back to the overwhelming problems of the real world.

Alexa changed into her dark red bikini and wrapped her ponytail in a bun, securing her hair with another elastic, then slathered herself in sunblock. Moments later she took the steps up to the main deck and stopped as a ball of lust curled in her belly. Jack was bare-chested, pumping air into a red inner tube. His sun-kissed skin and muscled arms and torso were a sight to behold. Why had she stopped him from coming down into the galley with her? Was she crazy?

He glanced up, and his hand froze on the pump. "Damn, Alex. You take my breath away."

"I was just thinking the same thing." It was still a struggle for her to be so frank. She'd been cautious to filter her thoughts over the last few weeks, making certain she didn't give away anymore of her heart than she wanted.

He smiled. "Should we take a dip? It's hotter than hell out here."

"Sure, but I bet the water's freezing."

"Let's find out." Jack plugged the red tube and grabbed the blue one he'd filled while she was downstairs, and they moved to the back of the boat. Jack set down the tubes and freed the small metal ladder. He sent the first few rungs into the bay. "Ready?"

"You go ahead. I plan to inch my way in."

"Ah, now where's the fun in that?"

Before Alexa could respond, he shoved at her lower back, propelling her into the water. She let out a shriek, then remembered to suck in a breath just before she met the cool dark blue. Seconds later, she surfaced, sputtering. "You are *so* lucky this water isn't half bad, Mr. Matthews." She wiped at her stinging eyes. "I can't believe you just did that."

"I can't believe you didn't *expect* me to," he said, grinning. "You were so close to the edge. Some people never learn." He tsk, tsk'd her while he shook his head.

Jack had a point—she *should* have learned. He'd shoved her in each and every time they'd gone out boating over the years. "Why don't you come in here and say that?"

"Are you gonna punish me?" He wiggled his brows, and she laughed.

More than willing to play, she swam to the edge and hoisted herself up enough so she could reach his leg. "Do you want me to punish you?" she asked in a sultry voice.

"If you're going to look at me and talk to me like that, you're damn straight I do."

"Do you like to be disciplined?" she purred as she stroked her fingers up the firm muscle of his calf.

"What do you think?"

"I think you should probably hop on in, Handsome Jack, but not before I do this." She grabbed a patch of his leg hair and yanked.

"Ow!" He jerked back. "Son of a bitch."

She fell into the water on a loud peal of laughter as Jack leaned down to rub the sore spot.

"Goddamn, Alex."

She laughed harder. "Maybe you'll think about that the next time you want to play dirty. We'll consider this your first round of conditioning."

He stopped massaging his calf. "Huh?"

"You know, like Pavlov's dogs—the bell rings and they drool. Now your brain will forever be reminded that if you push me into the water, I'll pull your leg hair. You

278

push, I pull. You push, I pull. Sounds pretty fair to me."

He grinned. "Is that your attempt at being funny, Alex?"

She smiled back. "Yes, it is."

"We'll have to work on that." He jumped in and surfaced seconds later. "This is paradise." He yanked her against him. "You pulled my hair for this?"

She wrapped her arms around the back of his neck as he treaded water, keeping them afloat. "You better believe it."

"But the water's not even cold."

"It's the principle of the matter."

"Ah, I see." He pressed his warm, slippery lips to hers. "I think I'll go grab one of those floats."

"You wanna grab the other for me?" She smiled sweetly and batted her lashes.

"I probably could." A mischievous light lit his eyes. "For a price."

"Nothing's free with you."

"I'm an enterprising kind of guy."

"What's it going to cost me?" She gripped him closer, enjoying the mood the afternoon was taking on.

"I'll probably need another kiss."

"I think I can handle that." She met his mouth with a short smacking kiss, knowing that wasn't what he had in mind.

"Nice, but I'm going to need something more. It's a long trip there and back with two floats."

She grinned. They were less than ten feet from the ladder. "Let's see what I can do." She grazed his chin, tasting the salty droplets clinging to his skin. Her lips teased the corner of his mouth. "How's this?"

"Getting better," he murmured as he pulled her with him to the ladder. "But you're holding back. I have to *feel* like you really want the inner tube." He skimmed his hands down her waist.

She shivered despite the sun boring down on her shoulders. "Oh, I want it." She captured his mouth, and the searing kiss spun out as tongue teased tongue. He gripped her ass, bringing her against him, heat to heat. Jack groaned, and she whimpered, as the kiss grew hotter. Growing bold, Alexa walked her fingers down his chest, his stomach, stopping at the waistband of his swim trunks. She slipped her hand into his shorts and grabbed hold, freezing mid-stroke as something bumped her foot in the depths of murky blue.

"Don't stop, Alex." He left kisses along her shoulder. "Keep going. You're making me crazy."

Whatever touched her foot brushed it again. She jerked it away and her eyes flew wide as the creature came back and nipped at her big toe. "Get out!"

Jack stopped dead and frowned. "What?"

"Get me out of the water, now." She practically crawled over him to get up the ladder. "Something tried to eat my toe."

He boosted her up to the small deck and followed. "It was probably just a fish."

She swallowed hard as she studied her foot, relieved that all five of her toes appeared as they had before she was pushed in the water.

"It was just a fish," Jack repeated as he crouched in front of her.

She shuddered as she thought of the sharks Livy was going to see today. "Or maybe it was Jaws moving in for a sample."

"Baby, he would've taken more than a tiny nibble, I can promise you that."

"You're such a comfort." She peered into the waves, searching for whatever had tried to eat her. "I don't want to go back in."

He smiled as he studied her. "Are you sure? We never got to the tubes." He put his hands on her shoulders. "I'll protect you from toe-eating fish if you want to try again."

"I would put my life in your hands any day—on land. The water, however, is a different story."

"Well, now you've gone and hurt my feelings." He sunk his teeth into her chin with a playful bite. "Since you don't want to swim anymore, how do you feel about lunch?"

She chuckled. "You and your stomach."

"So does that mean you feel good about eating?"

"Yes." She grinned. "I feel fine about it."

"Thank God." He stood and held out his hand.

She took it, and they went below deck.

⌒⌣⌒

Jack scooped up the last bite of rich chocolate cake and creamy chocolate frosting. "You want?" He held the fork out to her.

She shook her head. "No thanks. I'm stuffed."

"Half a piece of ham and a few bites of fruit... I'd starve to death if I ate like you."

"It's too hot to eat much." She raised her brow as he shoveled the cake in his mouth. "For some of us."

"What can I say, I'm a growing boy." He set down the fork. "*Mmm*, that was good." He picked up his wine and sipped. "You didn't drink any of yours. I thought you liked Chardonnay."

"I do." She shrugged. "But I thought I should play it safe, since we didn't."

He snagged her glass of golden liquid before it toppled as the boat dipped deeply, then he met her eyes. "Waves are getting a little rough. I thought we were okay."

"I'm sure we are, but like I said, I want to play it safe."

The empty cake container fell to the floor as the boat plunged again.

Jack stood and handed off the glasses. "Hold that thought. I'm going to pop my head above deck and see what's up."

"Okay." She clutched the small table as the boat swayed.

"Alex, I'm going to face us into the wind," he yelled down from above.

She set the glasses in the miniature sink and picked up the Tupperware, then she climbed the steps and blinked against the strong, cool winds rushing up to meet her. Her damp hair blew around her face, and she grabbed at the dark, loose strands as she stared at the wall of black clouds in the distance. "That doesn't look good."

"It's not great. We're about to get creamed," he said as the weather radio belched its warnings.

She moved closer to Jack, gripping the railings, struggling to stay upright. "We should head home. I'm worried about Livy. She's afraid of storms."

"Olivia's fine. My parents are taking good care of her."

"Still, we should go. I'm sure we can beat the front."

"That's what everyone will be thinking. The last thing we want is to lose visibility in the inlets with a bunch of morons racing for shore. Sit down for a minute." Jack circled the boat, catching a large swell of seawater, and they lurched forward. He drove a good two hundred yards farther away from the island and dropped anchor again. "This storm might get a little hairy before it's over, but it's moving fairly quickly. I checked the radar on my phone." Lightning flashed in the distance, and thunder followed. "Let's get below deck." He took her hand, and they gripped the railings as they maneuvered forward.

Jack closed the hatch, and the howl of wind ceased. The boat soared up on a wave and dipped low, sending them both hurtling toward the small bed. "Shit," he said as he grabbed her and turned, taking the brunt of their fall forward.

The boat creaked and popped, and Alexa clutched at Jack's arm as her heart pounded. "Is this thing going to break in half?"

"Nah. We're just gonna get tossed around a bit. I think the worst we'll have to worry about is a bruise or two and seasickness. Do you want some pressure bands for your wrists? Mom keeps them handy." The boat lurched again, and he snagged her around the waist before her hip connected with the table.

"No, I'm good."

"Come here. Let's lie down until this passes. We can watch from the windows."

She stared at him, searching his eyes. He didn't seem overly concerned.

"Relax, Alex. Dad and I were in a hell of a storm a couple years back that had us both on our knees praying when we weren't puking our guts out. This will be over before you know it. It's a pop-up that'll cool things off a few degrees." He crawled on the small bed and rested his head on a pillow. "Come watch with me."

The boat rocked violently. With few alternatives, Alexa gripped Jack's leg like a lifeline and started toward him.

"Don't even think about pulling my hair again."

She smiled. "You're safe for now."

He outstretched his arm, inviting her to lay with him.

She rested her head on his solid shoulder as her heart thundered along with the deafening booms beyond. A huge bolt of lightning splintered across the sky, and rain pelted against the circles of glass as the boat continued to sway. The purple hue tinting the portholes lent a magical feel to the violence just on the other side.

"Not so bad after all, huh?"

"No, not so bad." She glanced up at him. "But I hope Livy's okay. She's terrified of thunder. Maybe I should grab my phone—" She looked toward the small table, realizing her phone no longer rested on the wooden top. "Where's my cellphone?" She shot up to sitting, trying to scramble away to go in search of her lifeline to her little girl. "Livy might need me. Or Abby."

Jack pulled on her arm, bringing her back to him. "Alex, it's in here somewhere. If they need you, the phone will still ring. We'll find it then. Relax."

He made perfect sense. The phone would be easier to locate among the shambles of plastic dishes and odds and ends littering the floor if it was ringing. She took a settling breath and leaned back against him. "Sorry."

"Don't apologize for thinking of our daughter and your sister."

That settled her further. She looked to the storm-darkened trees billowing wildly in the wind on the small island as she breathed in Jack. "Thanks for bringing me to our place."

"This wasn't exactly what I had in mind." A deafening blast of thunder shook the cabin.

"Severe weather and shark bites—"

"Shark bites?" He interrupted. "It was a fish, Alex. Probably a minnow." He chuckled and pressed a kiss to her forehead.

She sat up on her elbow. "Are you making light of my brush with death?"

"You're brush with…" He laughed. "Hell, yes. I'm *definitely* making light of your brush with death."

She loved the sound of his deep-in-the-gut laugh.

284

"The years have made you hard and insensitive." She grinned as she squeezed his chin, looming close to his face.

Another rumble of thunder echoed through the cabin. A huge bolt of lightning spider-webbed across the sky.

"I think it's safe to say the years have embellished your imagination." He grabbed her chin much the way she still held his and pulled her closer. "The next thing you know—"

The boat dipped dangerously low, sending Alexa into a half-roll over Jack, and something fell to the floor with a crash. They stared at each other, wide-eyed, while Jack held her firm on top of him. Their hearts slammed in the same rapid rhythm. "Whoa," they said in unison.

"Are you sure we aren't going to break in half or capsize?"

"Yup. The storm's dying down already. The thunder isn't as close."

"Then why do I feel like I'm still on a rollercoaster?"

"The water will take some time to settle yet." He slid his fingers through her long hair. "We just have to wait it out."

Her heart rate started to pound even faster, but it was no longer from fear. She licked her lips, suddenly nervous as she recognized the hungry look in Jack's eyes. "I should probably see what broke."

He tightened his grip around her, and her breasts pressed more firmly to his chest. "I think you should stay right here. The mess isn't going anywhere."

"But it was glass."

"Mmhm." He cupped her face. "We don't want to add stitches to your list of today's traumatic events. We're safer staying put."

Why was she unsure about that? Her fingers

285

clutched against the smooth, firm skin of his shoulders as desire churned in her belly. Here they were, out in the depths of the bay, alone, in a storm. The man she loved lay under her, gorgeous and waiting for her to decide how the next few minutes were going to play out. She wouldn't make the same mistake she did earlier when she denied them both what they wanted. Alexa traced his lips with her fingertip. "What should we do while we wait?" Her voice thickened with desire. "There must be a game around here somewhere."

"I think we could come up with something."

"Like what? Uno? Cribbage?" She nipped his bottom lip and skimmed her tongue across his tensed jaw.

He trailed his palms along her waist. "This works." He lifted his head from the pillow and captured her mouth. What started off playful turned desperate in an instant.

Alexa moved her legs, straddling him and he cupped her ass, bringing her against him. He was already hard. Whimpering, she sat up and ground them heat to heat, making him moan.

His fingers clutched her hips as she continued to move in her teasing rhythm, torturing them both. It had been so long since she'd felt the heady power of taking Jack to the brink. The last time they were together, he had been in charge.

Jack reached for the ties of her bikini and she took his hands in hers. If he touched her, she would lose her advantage. She leaned forward and pressed his hands above his head. "Stay." She followed her demand with a deep kiss. Within seconds, Jack's fingers were in her hair.

She tore her mouth from his and went to work on his ear, his neck, his muscled shoulder. Jack started a teasing journey of his own and she stopped on a ragged breath, taking his hands and putting them back where she'd pressed them before.

"Stay," she repeated as her eyes burned into his. "It's my turn."

"Bossy."

She smiled. "That's right. Make sure you listen."

He smiled back. "You have my full attention."

"I noticed." She wiggled her hips, and he hissed out a breath. Grinning her triumph, she went back to his shoulder where she'd left off and wandered to his pecs, savoring the flavor of salt mixed with Jack. She nipped at mounds of muscle and left open-mouthed kisses in their wake, reveling in Jack's deep breaths and sharp exhales.

She glanced up and met his eyes as she continued her work. Her tongue left a damp trail, stopping at his chiseled abs. She let the anticipation build for both of them as she traced blocks of taut muscle and smooth skin to the waistband of his swim trunks, watching his stomach jump with her caressing touch. Then she pressed her palm against him through his shorts and rubbed teasingly until he moaned and his thighs flexed.

"Alex."

She tugged his trunks down and off before her fingers skimmed him—just barely.

Jack clutched at the pillows, and his head tipped back as he expelled each unsteady breath. It had been a long time since she'd pleasured a man. She clearly hadn't lost her touch.

"Alex, come on."

She continued her feathered caresses and leaned in to tease him further with the heat of her breath.

Jack let loose another grumble in his throat as he looked down at her and twisted his fingers in her hair. "Come *on*, Alex."

She increased the pressure of her grip and started a rhythm, only drawing out her torturous teasing further. "How's that?" she asked, full well knowing this wasn't what he wanted.

"Alex." His hips jerked, rocking on their own accord. Her tongue flicked out, and his head fell back.

"God."

She finally gave in, going deep, giving him what he needed. His fingers tensed and flexed in her hair with her movements as they had a hundred times before. The years had passed, but so much stayed the same. She continued to work him, remembering the little things she knew made him crazy—lips here, fingers there. She wrapped her hand tighter, and he gasped as his toes curled and his leg muscles tensed. "Enough," he said as he tried to sit up.

"But I'm not finished."

"You are for now." Tugging her up, he brought them face to face. He took her mouth almost violently as he yanked at the tie on her bikini top. He grabbed the red fabric and tossed it away, pressing his palms to her breasts, moving in gentle, teasing circles until her whimpers turned into one long moan. His hungry mouth and tender hands were a lethal combination that left her reeling.

He jerked her up to her knees and suckled her sensitive nipples. "God, Jack," she groaned as his tongue lapped until the light throb in her center grew to a heavy pulsing. She clenched his shoulders, and he wrapped an arm around her waist as the boat dipped low again and thunder rumbled in the distance. The boat steadied from its dip, rocking more gently as the rain continued to pound.

Jack snagged her bikini bottom with his thumbs and tugged. Her bathing suit fell to her knees and he ran his hands up her waist, bringing her chest colliding against the hot, damp skin of his. She was ready. She wanted him now. "Lay back, Jack. Let me have you." She pushed at his shoulder.

"There's no rush." He trailed his knuckles down her spine, and she shivered.

But there was. Her body craved to be fulfilled. She pressed on his shoulder again, but he lay her back instead and moved his mouth to her collarbone, nibbling and nipping his way to the valley of her breasts, prolonging the delicious agony of her wait. He traveled further down her waist and hips, bathing her in open-mouthed kisses.

"Mmm," was her response as he spurned her churning desire and moved between her legs, caressing her knees, and then making his way up. His mouth heated her inner thighs with his breath, and she whimpered with the anticipation of what came next. "Jack," she whispered as moist heat slid over delicate, tender flesh. "Jack." She arched, gasping as her fingers flexed and kneaded in his hair, urging him to continue as his tongue stroked again and again. "Keep going. Keep going," she begged as she pressed his face closer with a jerk of her hands. "My God, don't stop. Don't stop."

His rhythmic caresses turned to gentle suckles, changing the pace, the pressure, the intense sensations, sending her soaring. "Oh, my..." The rest was lost on a rush of breath when he added his fingers. Sparks of heat radiated through her core as he increased his sinful rhythm. She reached above her, clutching at the pillows as she gasped his name mindlessly.

When she was sure she couldn't take anymore, he journeyed up, met her lips, and crushed down with bruising heat.

She wrapped her arms around him and clung, utterly

spent as they rolled and she lay on top of him. "The bag," he said against her skin. "Can you grab the bag?"

"Huh?"

"The bag. I bought rubbers." He snagged her ear, and she shuddered.

She looked over her shoulder at the bag still hanging and crawled forward on trembling legs as she grabbed the almost-empty canvas.

Jack yanked it from her hand and reached in. She watched him, struggling to stay on the bed as another tumultuous wave sent the boat in a deep dip. He pulled a wrapper free and sheathed himself before she had time to get her balance.

"Come here." He hooked her around the waist, lifting her until her back collided with his chest, and she straddled him. His lips heated her skin, and she locked her arms around the back of his neck, resting her head on his shoulder as he reached around and sent her flying with a rub of fingers. She bowed up and cried out as the pulsing sensations of Jack and her orgasm overtook her. "Jack. Jack," she repeated as she sagged against his sweaty skin. Before she fully recovered from the first onslaught, Jack gripped her hips and eased her down, leaving her no choice but to take him deep. Stunned, frozen in ecstasy, her arms gripped him tightly as another round of heat engulfed her, bringing her to flashpoint. "Oh my God." Her loud moan filled the cabin as Jack tensed and sucked in a gasp. Her muscles uncoiled from their involuntary spasms, and she began to move, wanting more. Jack reached around, molding her breasts, playing as she set her rhythm. She moved slowly, teasing them both, enjoying the sounds of Jack's staggered breathing close to her ear.

"Turn around, Alex. I want to see you."

She stood on her knees and turned as Jack lay among the pillows scattered about the small bed. Straddling him once more, she sat back, and they both groaned. She rested her palms on his chest and began her easy pace once more. Leaning forward, she kissed him. The sweet, lazy moment spun out until the kiss grew urgent and his hands were everywhere, starting new fires. Alexa quickened her pace as the deep ache for fulfillment consumed her.

Jack clutched at her waist as his breath tore from his chest. His hips moved with her, pumping up, thrusting hard. She grabbed his powerful forearms and squeezed as she went soaring for the fourth time.

Jack's head tipped back, and he tensed, exploding along with her.

Gasping, spent, Alexa sagged against him. She listened to the violent pounding of his heart over the rain still pouring outside. He wrapped his arms around her and held on. She closed her eyes, safe, content while the boat rocked much less violently than it had minutes before.

"This was so much better than Uno," he said against the top of her head.

She smiled.

He wiggled his shoulder gently. "You pass out on me?"

She lifted her head. "No, just recovering."

He reversed their positions, and she lay on her back. "What are you doing?"

"Getting comfortable. I can't have you recovering too soon. It's still raining too hard to head home."

She chuckled, and her heart kicked into high gear as his smile turned sly. "We just finished, Jack."

"If I can do it so can you." He pulled himself free of his condom and within seconds protected them both again before he pushed deep inside her. She whimpered, still sensitive from her last orgasm.

"I don't think I'll ever get enough of you." He kissed her and looked in her eyes. "I used to dream about being with you like this. I would wake up and realize you were gone, had been gone for some time, and I wanted to die."

His words touched her. How many times had she woken the same way? She brushed at the damp hair along his temple. "I love you."

His fingers froze against her cheek. "What?"

She hadn't meant to tell him, but she'd been powerless to stop herself while they lay together in a place they'd made their own so long ago. "I love you, Handsome Jack."

He stared at her for several seconds, and then caressed her cheek again. "I've been waiting... I wasn't sure..." He pressed his forehead to hers and she held on, treasuring this moment that was for the two of them alone.

"I never thought I would hear those words from you again."

As he smiled at her with hope shining bright, it was suddenly vital to give him more of her heart. "I never stopped loving you. A day hasn't passed that I haven't thought of you and wanted you."

"Alex," he whispered as he touched his lips to hers. The kiss drew out with tenderness before he eased back. "I'm so glad we're here again. I'm so glad we've been given this chance."

She smiled. "Me too."

"I love you." He captured her mouth and began to thrust slowly. They clung together, stroking, touching, enjoying the simple pleasure of having each other back. The rain stopped as suddenly as it started, but she didn't notice as sighs intermingled and breathy moans filled the disheveled cabin. He took her up and over and held her close as he followed.

CHAPTER 17

J ACKSON GUIDED THE CRUISER TO the dock as Alex hung up with his mother. "You ready to tie us off?"

"Yes."

"Careful. The dock'll be slippery."

Alex jumped from the back of the boat to the wooden planks with ease.

"You good?"

"Sure."

He hurried to the bow and sent the sturdy rope sailing in her direction, smiling as she caught it. "Nice hands."

"Just one of my many talents." Tugging, she crouched and twisted the rope around the tie-down the way he'd shown her long ago.

"Great memory." He walked to the stern as she secured the next tie in place.

"What can I say?" She shrugged and grinned, then held out her hand to him.

Delighted with the world in general, he helped her back on the boat and pulled her close, staring into her deep blue eyes. Alex loved him. He'd been waiting, hoping, but now that she'd told him... "How's Olivia?"

"She's fine. Grammy said they barely heard the thunder. The aquarium was pretty loud. Livy didn't even know there was a storm. If she did, she didn't say anything to your parents."

"See? All that worrying for nothing."

"Worrying's a mother's prerogative." She kissed his

cheek. "I'm going to get started on the mess down in the cabin."

He ran his fingers through her soft hair, stalling, not wanting the afternoon to end. The time away with Alex had been everything he'd wanted it to be. Her eyes were bright again and her shoulders relaxed. They'd laughed and had fun. "I'll give you a hand."

"Good. It'll go faster." She stepped from his easy embrace. "I think *everything* spilled from the drawers and cupboards."

He pulled her back, locking his hands around her waist, effectively trapping her in place. "What's the hurry?"

She pushed at his shoulders. "Jack, your parents will be home with Livy in another hour or so. I want to get the mess cleaned up and dinner on the stove. Poor Grammy and Grampy are probably exhausted."

"I had fun with you. I don't want today to be over yet."

Her eyes instantly softened, and her hands moved to frame his face. "That's very sweet."

He kissed her brow.

"I love you, Jack."

Would he ever get used to hearing her say that? He'd taken her feelings for granted all those years ago, but never again. "I love you too. I want more days like this. I want us to laugh again. I love watching your eyes light up when you smile. You're so beautiful."

"Do you want a tear or two as well? Because you're about to get a few."

He smiled as she did. "No. I didn't tell you enough before. There are so many things I didn't do right the first time around. I don't want to make the same mistakes."

"Things ended badly. What breakup doesn't? You've never been anything but wonderful to me."

"Not always."

"Yes, always." She kissed his chin. "I've made my own mistakes and have my own regrets." As she spoke, her fingers tensed against his skin and the bright light left her eyes. "I never want to hurt you, Jack. Ever. I want you to remember that."

He frowned at her serious tone. "Okay. I didn't mean to bum either of us out here. I just wanted to tell you I love you." He pressed his lips to hers. "And maybe take advantage of our alone time," he added with a wiggle of his brows, wanting the easy moment back.

She gave him a small smile, and then looked down.

"Hey." He nudged her gently. "Hey."

She met his gaze.

"Third times a charm you know," he whispered next to her ear.

"So I've heard, but I'm pretty well satisfied with the first and second time." She smiled fully.

He chuckled, relieved that she could still find the light mood they'd traveled home with. "Let's go to my room, then we'll come back and clean. Promise. I'll even help with dinner, because I think magical number three might take a while. I didn't have a chance to do nearly half the things I wanted to. I have a lot of time to make up for." His hormones were already raging as his imagination got to work on all the ways he planned to send Alex over the edge. Maybe it was caveman-like but there were few things—if any—that brought him the satisfaction he felt when he sent Alex over the brink. Watching her eyes go wide and hearing her call his name as she lost control was freaking *amazing.* He picked her up, and she gasped.

"Jack."

"Let's hurry." He stepped from the boat with a wobbly hop, only stopping long enough to steady himself. "In about thirty seconds, I'm going to take you." He pressed his lips to hers in a demanding promise as he walked up the small, grassy hill to his parent's home. "If we don't make it to my room, that'll be too damn bad."

She made a purring sound in her throat and attacked his mouth with teeth and tongue.

"Goddamn," he puffed out as he rushed up the steps. "Screw the bedroom. I'm taking you in the entryway. We'll get to all those things I plan to do in a few minutes. Looks like four is your lucky number today." He set her down and leaned her against the door, kissing her, palming her small, firm breast with one hand as he reached in his pocket for the house key.

"Hurry up, Jack," she urged as her hand snaked into his shorts, torturing them both.

He struggled to put the key in the lock as Alex revved him higher. "Oh my God, I'm going to—"

Without warning, Alex yanked her hand away as if he'd grown thorns. Their breath heaved out, mingling, and she clutched at his t-shirt. "Tucker's home."

Jackson glanced over his shoulder as Tucker pulled in the drive. "Fucking-A. I'm going to kick his *ass*."

Tucker got out and shut the door. "Sorry for interrupting."

"Is this payback for waking you up the other night? Go drive around the block a few times." Jackson snapped out of his haze when Tucker didn't smile or give some sort of crude comeback. "What's up, man?"

"There's been another kidnapping."

Alex's rosy cheeks paled, and her swollen lips trembled. "Livy? They took Livy?"

"Not Livy, Alexa. She's with George and Carol."

Alex sagged against him, and he wrapped his arm around her. "Where?"

"On the outskirts of Servena Park."

Alex straightened. "Servena Park's not that far

from here."

"There was a van involved. The victim was visiting with a friend. The friend ran in to her house to tell her mother they were heading to the mall. When the friend came out, two men were yanking the victim into the back. Just like that, they were gone."

"Not again," Alex whispered as her body tensed and her hands clutched together at her waist.

"Come on. Let's get inside." Jackson had no trouble sticking the key in the lock this time. He twisted the knob and let Alex and Tucker in.

"The media's all over this one. Amber Alerts were blaring over every station on the way back from DC. I put in a call to Canon, but we won't be hearing from him for awhile." They hurried to the living room, and Tucker picked up the remote. "What's the local news station?"

"Channel 12." Jackson walked up behind Alex and settled his arms around her waist.

Her clammy hands clung to his forearms as Suzette Martin, Baltimore's friendly anchorwoman, filled the screen. "—we follow this developing story. Again, fifteen-year-old Margaret Stowers was pulled into the back of a white Chevy work van by two unknown assailants at 3:09 p.m. today in the upscale suburb of Servena Park." A picture of Margaret Stowers replaced Suzette Martin's pretty face, and Alex gasped as Jackson's stomach turned.

"Goddamn," he muttered as he stared.

"No. *No.*" Alex tore herself from his arms. "This isn't happening."

"The girl from Club Jerhico... The picture you took," Tucker chimed in.

Helpless rage iced Jackson's veins as he nodded, unable to believe it. "I think we can officially connect Timothy Monroe to the sex ring. It's a pretty big coincidence he spotted this girl, talked to her, gave her a card, and now she's missing. I want to get Ethan in on this. Let's play this out and see if we can find a profile on Baltimore Dates—see if there might be a link. Kristen Moore snuck into clubs, had a profile, and disappeared. Let's see if Margret did too."

Tucker glanced at Alex as she stared at the floor. "I'll get on it. Come up when you can. I need to talk to you."

"I'll be right there."

Jackson struggled to relax his jaw as Tucker disappeared up the stairs. How many more young women's lives were going to be destroyed before the taskforce found their connection?

He curled his fist, wanting to punch something, then flexed his hand. Destroying his parents' wall wouldn't fix the situation. He glanced at Alex and sighed. "Are you okay?"

"No, I'm not." She looked up from the floor with tears pooling. "Why aren't the police taking this seriously? How many more girls have to disappear?"

"They're taking this seriously, Alex."

"How can you stand here and say that when we both know their only interest is in nailing Zachary Hartwell? There's so much more to this than the damn CEO of Starlight Entertainment." She turned away, took two steps, and whirled back around. "Margret's just a *baby*."

He jammed a hand through his hair, unable to deny anything Alex said. "We've got Ethan on this. If he finds something, we'll go with it and get Miranda in on it as well."

Alex scoffed and rolled her eyes.

Surprised, Jackson stared at her. "What's that supposed to mean?"

She shook her head and went to the stairs. "Nothing."

He followed and pulled her around. "Alex."

"I'm sorry. I'm just tired, frustrated, and very, very sad for Margret and her family. They have no idea what they're in for."

He skimmed her jaw with the pad of his thumb, knowing this was eating her up. "Why don't you lie down for a few minutes before Olivia gets home?"

A spark of heat snapped into her eyes but quickly died away. "That's a good idea."

Puzzled, he held her gaze.

"I'll catch a nap, Jack. Go ahead and talk to Tucker." She walked up the steps, and he stared after her. What the hell was that? Seconds later, he headed upstairs, glanced at Alex's closed door, and went into the office as Tucker hung up the phone.

"Ethan's on it."

"Good." Jackson leaned against the desk and rubbed his fingers over the sudden throbbing in his temple. With a sigh, he dropped his hand. "Fucking-A, man."

Tucker leaned back in the chair and crossed his feet. "He said he'll call us back in an hour. He was scanning Margret's photo into his computer."

"Hopefully he'll find something. The club is officially one of their avenues for luring these girls in, so is the website, but does one have anything to do with the other?"

"Good question. Maybe we'll have a better idea when Ethan gets back to us." Tucker eased back further until the chair squeaked. "So, what does Alexa think about all this?"

Something in Tucker's tone had Jackson on alert. "She thinks it sucks. Why?"

He shrugged.

Jackson's eyes narrowed a fraction. "What's up?"

Tucker shrugged again. "I met with Miranda's old partner today—lead sex crimes detective down in DC.

Seemed to know a lot about Abby's case and the ring. I toyed around with a few theories. Brought up the other victims and our thoughts on Baltimore Dates. He was intrigued."

"Okay."

"He and I spent a good hour doing some perusing of our own, trying to get things moving again. We found something." Tucker sat up in front of his laptop and started typing. "Does JennyLove ring any bells?"

"Jenny Love? No. Who the hell's Jenny Love?"

Tucker turned the screen. "Take a look for yourself."

Jackson stared at the gorgeous blonde with Alex's face. "What the fuck?" He spaced out each word, unable to believe what he was looking at. "I told her no."

"Yeah, well, apparently she didn't listen."

His pulse throbbed as he read Jennifer's profile— just turned 18 and graduated high school. Wants to model or be a fashion photographer. Loves to party and hang out with friends. "I can't fucking believe this." He shot off the desk and whirled to face Tucker again. If he'd ever been angrier, he couldn't think of a time. "I can't *believe* this. She went behind my back. When did she…" He trailed off, trying to get a grip on his breathing. "Does she have any idea how dangerous this is?"

"I had a feeling this was going to be a shocker. I called Ethan while I was still in DC and had him get started on this." Tucker pulled a short stack of papers from his laptop case. "She's gotten a hell of a lot of hits. Two of them are definitely promising."

"Give me those." Jackson yanked the sheets out of Tucker's hand and scanned the numerous correspondences she'd made over the past three days— well over fifty hits, and she was stringing them all along.

"She just went online."

He tore his gaze from her flirty replies. "Huh?"

"She's online right now."

Jackson glanced at the small, green dot by her picture, alerting potential daters that she was available to chat. So much for Alex's nap. He tossed the papers to the desk and started for the door.

"Where you going, man?"

"Where do you think?" He rubbed at the slow burn of anger scorching his stomach.

"She's made more contacts than Melinda. Ethan's running two of the profiles as we speak."

He stopped and faced Tucker. "What's your point?"

"My point is I think you should take a couple of deep breaths before you go storming in that room."

"She lied to me. For three fucking days she's looked me in the eye and lied."

❦

Alexa closed herself in her room and hurried to the couch, replaying the last of her conversation with Jack. "Go take a nap?" she seethed as she sat and pulled her laptop on her legs. Did he have any idea how insulting that was? "I'll go sleep while Abby suffers and another girl disappears." She glared. "I don't think so."

Fuming, she stared out at the restless waters, attempting to gather herself, thankful that Livy wasn't home just yet. Her little girl would be bursting with excitement over her aquarium adventures, and Alexa wasn't in a place to enjoy her baby's lively stories. She couldn't get Margret Stowers' pretty young face out of her mind or the echoing screams of her sister when the two men pulled her into the back of the van, just the way they had their latest victim.

Determined to do what she could, Alexa settled the laptop more truly on her legs and typed in the address for Baltimore Dates. She tapped her finger against the mouse in a rapid, restless rhythm, waiting, while the small circular rainbow spun in the center of her screen. "Come on." The connection was taking *forever*. Finally the site popped up, and she logged in and immediately scanned her messages for a return correspondence from either of the two profile names that made the hair stand up on the back of her neck every time she interacted with them. "Yes." She clicked on Steve-O and read:

> *Hey beautiful,*
> *I'm sitting here staring at your picture. When are you going to say yes and have dinner with me? I'll bring my camera. We can go to the park after and snap some pictures. I'll pass them on to my friend at the modeling agency.*
> *— S*

Alexa's pulse kicked into high gear as she shot to standing. This was their lure. This was Crazy80. She could *feel* it. She rushed to the door and opened it, ready to confess all to Jack, but stopped. How was he going to react? Not well. Not well at all. What if he didn't want her to answer? What if he put a stop to the whole thing? She chewed her bottom lip as she stared at George's office down the hall, listening to the deep murmurs of Jack and Tucker's voices through the partially open door.

Not yet. She couldn't tell him yet. Alexa closed herself back in the room and pressed her forehead to the wood. This was another giant leap down a road that could ruin her and Jack, but she had to think of Abby. Her sister was depending on her. She would make Jack understand.

With her mind made up, Alexa took a deep breath

and hurried back to the computer. If she secured a date with Steve-O first, then went to Jack and Tucker, they would be more likely to let her meet the guy, especially after she showed them the chats she'd been printing and hiding in her suitcase for the past two days. They were so similar to the conversations between Crazy80 and Kristen Moore. Alexa wiggled her butt more firmly in the seat and placed her hands on the keyboard. "Okay." She wiggled again. "Here goes nothing."

> Steve,
> *This must be fate. I've been thinking of you all day.*
> *I would love to have dinner.*
> — Jenny

She read the three lines several times, scrutinizing every word. Was her message too much, or too little? Did she sound young enough, or perhaps too old? She was wasting time. If Steve-O was part of the trafficking ring—and he almost certainly was—he wasn't interested in anything but an agreement to meet. Her hand hovered over 'send' as her heart thundered. This was it. She crossed her fingers and clicked the button.

She moved the arrow to the corner of the screen, intending to ex out, but stopped when the computer alerted her to a new message. "Holy Cow." Steve-O had responded already. She clicked on the latest reply as the bedroom door crashed open. Alexa's hand flew to her chest as she gasped and looked at Jack. "You scared me half to death."

He walked to where she sat, looming over her, staring down, his eyes unreadable.

She quickly closed her laptop. "What is it? What's wrong?"

He didn't move, didn't speak.

Why was he looking at her like that? Swallowing, she got to her feet. "You're scaring me. Is Livy okay?"

"Quick nap." His voice was dangerously quiet.

"I wasn't—I wasn't tired." She curled her fingers around the charm on her necklace, and her gaze darted to the laptop, following his steady stare. Did he know? How could he? "I—"

"You lied to me."

She closed her eyes, absorbing the venomous slap of his words.

"I said you lied to me."

"Yes." She nodded and tried to remain calm, hoping she could find a way to make him understand. Her stomach sank as she opened her eyes and met his. "I lied to you."

"I've been honest with you from the start, and you went behind my back."

What would they have left after they finished here? "Yes. I didn't feel like I had any other option."

He let loose a humorless laugh. "Give me a fucking break."

"I'm sorry." She brushed a hand over his arm, and he stepped back. "I never wanted to hurt you."

"You're sorry?"

"Yes, very. I didn't want to do this. I tried to think of another way, but you tied my hands."

His brow shot up. "I tied your hands?"

"You wouldn't hear me out when I suggested you use me as a decoy."

He rocked back on his heels. "I wouldn't hear you out?"

"Stop that," she snapped and turned away from his ruthless gaze. "Stop repeating everything I say."

He whirled her back around. "I didn't hear you out because there was no reason to continue with the conversation. This is *dangerous*, Alex." He scrubbed his hands over his face. "Goddamn, I'm so fucking pissed I don't even know what to do with myself. Of all the stupid things..."

Her shoulders snapped straight. "I'm not stupid."

"No, you're not. That's why I can't figure this out."

"Why is this so hard to comprehend? Why can't you see that I have to do this for Abby? Of all people—"

"I do understand, Alex. No one gets you better than I do, but I get *them* too."

With her own temper straining, she began to pace. "You act as if I've walked into this blindly. I've done my research. I've done nothing *but* research."

"Yeah, well so have they. They know who you are."

"No." He was trying to scare her.

"Yes." He pulled her back in front of him and held her shoulders. "They know your face. You've been on the news. You were their *ransom* target, for Christ's sake. If they make that connection and realize you're trying to bring them down... I don't even want to think about what they'll do to you."

She yanked away from him. "That's what the wig is for. I look nothing like the Alexa Harris they know— nothing like Abby."

"You're counting on a wig to save your life?" He pressed a hand to his forehead. "You were safe here. You and Olivia were *safe*."

The words 'were safe' made her instantly ill. "We still are, right?"

"Hell if I know." He threw his hand out to the sides. "Why couldn't you leave it alone?"

"They can't find me," she said frantically, reassuring herself, since Jack wouldn't. "I've used a fake name. I set up a dummy e-mail account on Yahoo. I've covered my tracks."

"And how long do you think it took Ethan to figure you out? Tucker recognized you immediately."

She was starting to see. "But—"

"You better start praying they don't have someone even half as brilliant as Ethan checking in to you. Fucking-A." He seethed as he started toward her computer. "We need to close your accounts. Now."

"No." She rushed up to block his way. "We can't. I have a date."

"What?" He stopped dead and stared at her. "You what?"

"One of the men contacted me. I'm positive he's a trafficker—Steve-O. He asked me to dinner."

"Did you hear what I just *said*?"

"Yes." Even after everything, she couldn't let this go. "How can you ask me to walk away? You and I both know this could be the beginning of the end. There has to be a way to make this work. "

"Forget it. We're finished with this." He skirted around her, and she clung to his arm, terrified he would erase her only chance at getting Abby back.

Tucker knocked on the doorframe. "Sorry to interrupt, but I need to talk to you both."

"What?" Jack snarled.

"Ethan just called."

"Give me a minute. I'm busy." He yanked up the laptop.

"Clear your schedule. This is important."

Jackson dropped the laptop to his side, and Alexa struggled not to give in to her need to grab hold and play tug of war over the computer.

"Ethan linked an account to Margret."

"Good. We can talk about that in a minute. Let me take care of this first." He held the computer up again.

"Jack. Don't you dare." She made a grab for it, and he pivoted. "Jack," she warned.

"The person who reeled Margret in has been talking to Alexa too."

Alexa's gaze flew to Tucker's. "Steve-O. Is it Steve-O?"

"Yes."

"I knew it. I *knew* it. He and I have a date."

"When?" Tucker stepped further into the room.

"I don't know. I haven't gotten that far. I was just about to read his reply when Jack barged in."

"What does it say?" Tucker asked Jack.

Jackson held Tucker's stare for a moment, then looked at the screen. "It says 'How about Bayside Café—Friday night, seven o' clock? We can walk to the park after and take those pictures.'"

"I have to do this." She glanced from Jack to Tucker with a growing sense of urgency while the two men looked at each other. "We have to make this happen. He's the lure."

Tucker nodded but said nothing.

"He knows where Abby is. He knows where my sister is. What do I need to do?"

"Agree to meet him," Tucker said, and Jack swore.

That was the green light she'd been waiting for. She reached for the computer. "Give me my laptop."

"No." He held it out of reach.

She swallowed as she looked into distant, angry eyes—so much like the night he dumped her. "I'm sorry it has to be this way, Jack. I wish there was another way, but I'll do this with or without your support. I need to help Abby." Grabbing hold of her laptop, she yanked it free of his grip. She held his gaze a moment, then turned to Tucker and sat. "What—what should I say?"

"Give him the okay, then I'll call Canon."

She glanced at Jack once more, but he was no longer facing her and Tucker. He had moved to the window, staring out at the water. "I'm sorry, Jack," she said again. Then she turned to her screen and typed.

Sounds great. How will I find you?
— Jenny

"How's that?" she asked Tucker.

"Good."

She pressed 'send' and glanced at Jack's rigid stance. Had they fought their way back only to lose again?

Her laptop beeped with a new message.

I'll find you, Beautiful.
— S

She shuddered as she read Steve-O's last response. "I guess it's all set. I can't believe this is really happening."

"I need to call Canon and set up a meeting with the taskforce. Forty-eight hours is cutting it close."

"Yes, of course. Whatever it takes. My sister's life is depending on this."

"What about your life?" Jack exploded, making Alexa jump. "The cops are going to wire you, Alex. Do you have half a clue what will happen if they figure out you're tapped? We're calling this off."

"No. That isn't an option. I won't get caught and I won't let them hurt me."

"Like you didn't let them hurt Abby?"

She flinched from the verbal blow, and tears instantly flooded her eyes. Was this what was left between them—harsh words and resentment? "I know I let my sister down. I'm doing what I can to fix that now. Tucker, if you can, let me know how we should proceed. I'm going down to make dinner." She stood and swiped at the tears trailing down her cheeks despite her best efforts to keep them at bay.

"Alex, wait a minute."

Ignoring Jack, she closed the door behind her.

308

CHAPTER 18

"**D**AMN IT!" JACKSON PUSHED PAST Tucker to follow Alex. If he could've screwed this up any worse, he wasn't sure how.

"Pretty smooth there, man. Way to keep a level head."

Out of patience, Jackson whirled and yanked Tucker forward by the collar of his polo. "Fuck off, Campbell," he said between clenched teeth.

"There are no free punches. FYI."

Jackson stared into Tucker's calm Hazel eyes, sighed, and stepped back. "*Goddamn.*" He jammed his fingers through his hair and turned, overwhelmed by torrents of emotion. The anger and gut-clenching fear alone... "What the hell *happened* here? Not even an hour ago I was having the time of my life on a boat, now we're dealing with this. I can't keep up."

"Things've gotten interesting."

"Interesting." He choked out a laugh and stared out the window. "Yeah, I guess." He still couldn't believe Alex lied to him. "So, how should we handle this?"

"Call Canon."

Jackson turned from his view of the choppy bay. "She's not doing this."

"Then what do you propose? We're drowning here, man. Our leads are dead. Miranda hasn't gotten jack shit. I have to get back to LA sooner or later. This is our in."

Everything Tucker said was the absolute truth, but he couldn't risk Alex. If something went wrong... "There has to be another way."

"Yeah, well, nothing's coming to mind."

"Give me a minute to think."

"A minute's about all we've got. Forty-eight hours isn't much time."

Jackson struggled to push past the fear and find another solution. The stirrings of dread grew stronger as each new idea brought him back to Alex as their only option. "I don't want her here anymore. We should head back to LA."

Tucker held his gaze, his eyes full of understanding. "You can cross that off the list. She's going to do this. You and I both know we can't stop her. The Feds will use her. This could be their big break, especially after we present them with all the evidence Ethan's dug up."

Jackson sat back on the arm of the couch as it sunk in that this was really happening.

"The way I see it, we have one option, and that's to get in on the sting from the beginning, or else they'll push us out. We both know we're at their mercy if that happens. If we establish ourselves as her personal security, they'll have to work with us more than they would otherwise."

"That's true." What else could he say?

"I'll call Ethan and get the ball rolling before we contact Canon."

He didn't want to think about this. For every step he and Tucker took, the taskforce and traffickers would be five steps ahead. "I need to talk to Alex." He had hurt her. They had hurt each other, but he couldn't stand knowing he made her cry.

"Come get the release forms before you do." Tucker opened the door and left the room.

Alexa grabbed another leaf of romaine and tore it from the heart, then tossed it into the large, wooden bowl. She picked up the same pieces she'd already shredded and ripped them some more, paying little attention to her dinner preparations. God, she'd made a mess of things. Her lower lip wobbled, and she sniffed. A tear tracked down her cheek, and she swiped it away with her forearm.

She should be celebrating, not crying. Her plan worked. She had a date. In less than forty-eight hours, the authorities would know who Steve-O was and would be one step closer to bringing Abby home—a *real* step closer. But she'd hurt Jack to make that happen. She shuddered out a deep sigh. Why did she have to lose to win?

Alexa grabbed more garden-fresh lettuce from the basket and absently ran the head under the cold spray. This whole situation was so complicated. By helping Abby, she was risking Jack. And Livy. Could the organization really trace her to Kent Island? A hot rush of fear buckled her knees as she thought of her beautiful little girl trapped in the clutches of sex traffickers. Margret's abduction had taken place less than thirty minutes from here—too close. Would she watch another member of her family be yanked into the back of a van? She leaned forward and rested her head on the solid wooden cupboard, trying to steady her stuttering heart. Why did she have to choose between the people she loved most?

"Alex." Fingers brushed her shoulder, and she whirled.

"Sorry." Jack dropped his hand. "I didn't mean to scare you."

She swiped at her damp cheeks. "You didn't. I'm fine."

Seconds passed in silence while Jack held her gaze.

What should she say? Unable to bear the scrutiny of his stare, she turned to the cutting board and began to chop the head of lettuce with an unsteady hand, but soon set the knife down, afraid she might cut herself.

"Alex—"

"I didn't want to—" They spoke at the same time, and she turned. "I didn't want to lie to you, Jack. I hated lying."

"But not enough not to do it."

"If there had been another way..."

He shook his head, dismissing her. "It's over. We've both done things, said things we regret."

She nodded, reading between the lines perfectly. He'd accepted the situation, but he wouldn't forget. Where did that leave them?

He held out a small stack of papers.

Frowning, she took them. "What's this?"

"A legal agreement."

She stared down at the bold black and red insignia of Ethan Cooke Security's letterhead. "I don't understand."

"By signing those, you'll be consenting to formal close protection services for yourself and Olivia. Tucker and I will be your bodyguards of record for the remainder of our stay in Maryland."

"Bodyguards? Is that—is that necessary? I can't afford—"

"Canon's going to be pissed when he finds out we've been holding back on him. He'll want to whisk you and Olivia off to a safe house until the conclusion of the sting. I'm not leaving my daughter's safety in someone else's hands."

"A safe house?" The gravity of the situation was becoming more apparent. What had she gotten them tangled up in?

"Once we bring Canon and the taskforce in on this,

you'll be considered a State's witness if this somehow links to the ring. Testifying on behalf of Immigrations and Customs Enforcement is federal."

"I don't want to testify. I just want my sister back."

He shrugged. "Arrests could be made from the information gathered while you're wired. It all goes together."

She leaned against the counter, attempting to take everything in. "I don't—I don't..."

"You'll be offered witness protection by the United States Marshal's service. We're going to make sure that isn't necessary. Their priority will be keeping tabs on you. They won't want anything happening to their prize witness."

He had to know she was terrified—for herself, for their daughter—but he didn't seem to care. There was no compassion while he spoke; Jack laid it out matter-of-factly. "Is this payback, Jack? Is this your attempt at scaring me?"

"Nope. Just telling you how it is. Having top-notch bodyguards from a world renowned firm will keep Canon off your back and guarantee he'll stay cooperative instead of shutting me and Tucker out—at least logistically."

"I want you to take Livy to LA."

"Fill out the papers." He spoke to her as if they were strangers.

"Why are you being like this?"

"I'm not being like anything. Risks were taken, now there are consequences. This is the way you wanted it."

She stared at the aloof man who claimed to understand her better than anyone. Did he realize he was ripping her heart in half with his cold indifference? "I never *wanted* any of this. I have to do this for Abby."

"And take Olivia along for the ride."

She gasped from the shock of his well-aimed blow.

"How dare you. How dare you stand there and say that to me in your smug tone. You have no idea what this is like. They're killing my *sister*. They're killing her by inches. Every day that she's trapped in a life she never asked for, she's dying. How can you ask me to turn my back on that?"

Undone by Jack's callousness, she yanked up the pen by the phone and scribbled her name on the highlighted spaces requiring her signature. "There." She tossed the papers at him, and they sailed to the floor as she walked off, leaving him staring after her.

Jackson sat beside Olivia at the dining room table. She hadn't stopped talking since she came clamoring through the door half an hour before, loaded down with souvenirs and dragging his tired parents behind her.

"The sharks were very big. I didn't like them. But they can't hurt me, right Grampy?"

"That's right, honey." He gave Olivia a wink and a smile. "The glass is thick and strong."

"The glass is strong," Livy repeated as she shoveled up a bite of grilled chicken slathered in barbeque sauce.

"Sounds like you had a great time, Liv." Jackson tried to muster up some enthusiasm for his little girl, but it was a struggle. He slid a glance to the right, in Alex's direction on the other side of their daughter. She hadn't looked at him since their conversation in the kitchen. He couldn't blame her.

He remembered his cool, self-righteous tone and winced. It hadn't been his intention to scare her shitless. He set his fork down and sighed. Yeah it had, but the extra dollop of asshole he'd thrown into the mix had been unplanned. He screwed up—plain and simple—

and ended up hurting her even more.

Everything he'd said to Alex was true. The stakes were high and incredibly dangerous. He was terrified—for Alex, for Olivia—and was handling it like a moron. It was knee-jerk to want to keep her safe and whisk her and their daughter away. If he could get away with it, he probably would—State's witness or no State's witness. *They're killing my sister. They're killing her by inches.* Her wrenching eyes had simply undone him when she'd tossed those words at him.

He glanced her way again, noting the misery in her eyes despite her attempt at cheerful conversation. He clenched his jaw, yearning to give comfort, and realized he couldn't take her back to LA, or anywhere for that matter. Alex had to do this. She had to keep her 'date.' Abby wasn't the only one dying inside. Alex died a little each day too. He and Tucker would get her through Friday night's operation—two or three hours of pure hell. They'd handled worse situations. Detective Canon would have his chance to gather new leads, but all bets were off once the sting was over. Saturday he was taking Alex and Olivia home. They were going back to LA.

"...and the crab. He was *so* pinchy." Olivia's fingers turned into enthusiastic little pinchers as she demonstrated for the table. "Huh, Grammy?"

"That's right, my brilliant girl."

Alex made a grab to save Olivia's cup of milk before the glass toppled. "I'm glad you're excited, Livy, but I want you to eat some of your dinner."

"Sorry, mommy."

"That's okay." Alex touched the tip of Livy's nose and smiled, but it didn't reach her eyes.

Livy quieted as she attempted to fork up a bite of confetti-sized salad. "I can't—I can't get any lettuce, Mommy."

"Use your spoon, sweetie."

"Guess your mom didn't want anyone choking tonight." Grampy winked at Olivia, then at Alex.

"I'm sorry, George. I guess I got a little carried away with the chopping." Alex toyed with her chicken, then set her fork down.

"I'm just teasing. It all goes down the same whether you have to chew or not." Dad chuckled at his own joke, and Jackson shook his head as his mother muttered something. "Is this thing on?" His father tapped his imaginary microphone. "Rough crowd tonight."

Livy giggled. "Rough crowd, Grampy."

"So," Mom interjected when the room fell silent, "how was *your* day, Jackson and Alexa?"

"Fine," the two of them said in unison. They glanced at each other, but Alexa quickly broke their stare. Had they truly laughed and had fun just hours before?

"When I spoke with Alexa on the phone, she mentioned you got stuck in the storm."

Jackson flashed back to the thunder and lightning and Alex's gorgeous naked body moving with his. "Yeah. It was a doozy." He stabbed up a large piece of chicken and popped the bite in his mouth, wanting to drop the subject.

"And what about you, Tucker? Did you have a nice time on your adventure to DC?"

"It was stellar, Mrs. Mathews. I can't remember the last time I enjoyed a meeting so much." Tucker grinned.

"You're a handsome devil, Tucker. A handsome devil with a wily smile. Do you have a beautiful woman waiting for you in California?"

"I thought you were my beautiful woman."

Mom laughed. "You need someone with spice. There's too much mischief behind those eyes. Isn't that right, Jackson?"

"You call it mischief; I call it bullshi—" he cut himself off when he caught his daughter's eye.

"Daddy, did you use the fishing pole today? Did you bring me any pink fishies?"

"No. No pink fishies, Liv." He smiled and tugged gently at her ponytail.

She grinned. "I saw pink fishies at the shark place. They were mommies and daddies."

"Oh yeah?" He reached for his glass of milk and took a big swallow.

"Yes. They gave each other kisses like you and mommy do. Kissy. Kissy. Kissy." Livy slapped a hand over her barbeque-mess mouth, trying to suppress her giggles.

Alex pushed away from the table. "Livy, are you finished with your meal?"

"Yes, I'm full."

"You need a bath." Alex scooted Olivia's chair back and pulled their daughter into her arms, transferring Olivia's mess to her own clothes and arms. "If you'll excuse us. Oh, and don't worry about the dishes, Mom. I'll take care of them after I have Livy settled in for the night."

"Come on, Daddy." Livy held out her hand.

"Daddy's busy, sweetie. We'll see him later," Alex chimed in.

Livy's tired eyes filled with tears. "But I want Daddy too."

He wanted to give Alex the space she clearly sought, but Livy's needs came first. "I'm coming, Liv." He stood.

Alex turned and headed for the stairs.

"Wait for Daddy, Mommy."

"He's right behind us, honey." She kept going.

"*Wait*, Mommy. Waiting is polite, right?"

Trapped by manners, Alex stopped on the first stair.

"Yes it is." Alex was forced to look in his eyes when he stayed at the foot of the steps.

"I'm right here, Liv."

Olivia glanced from him to Alex.

"Kiss Mommy, Daddy. Like a kissy fishy."

"We need to get you in the tub. You're covered in sauce."

"Kiss like a kissy fishy!" their daughter demanded louder, and her lip trembled.

"Olivia, that's enough now," Alex scolded.

"She's probably picking up on the tension."

"I imagine you're right." Alex rubbed Livy's back and pressed her cheek to her hair.

"Kissy fishy, Mommy," Livy whispered.

"Okay, kissy fish." She smiled at their daughter, and then looked to Jackson.

They leaned in toward each other. Their lips met briefly, then Alex pulled away. She turned to take the next step, and he snagged her arm. "I'm sorry, Alex."

She attempted to free herself, but he held her still. "I'm sorry for...everything." How could he say what he needed to, the way he wanted to, with their little girl blinking at him with curious eyes?

"Daddy said sorry. Isn't that nice? Do you feel better, Mommy?"

"Yes, much better." She turned and walked up the stair with hurt and anger still clouding her eyes.

CHAPTER 19

A LEXA TOOK ANOTHER DEEP BREATH in an attempt to settle her fraying nerves as she scrutinized herself in the mirror. When that didn't work, she pressed a hand to her queasy stomach and sighed. It was no use. No amount of breathing or silent pep talks was going to banish the weight settled on her shoulders. Tonight was the night, and she was a wreck. She had only one 'date' to accomplish so much. Tomorrow they were going back to LA—with or without answers for Abby.

In less than two hours, she would stand face to face with the man who played a part in her sister's abduction—she was sure of it, despite Tucker's warnings to keep an open mind. Would Steve-O recognize her from the short news clip all those weeks ago when she'd tried to flee from the cameras? Did she still look too old, despite the endless preparations, or too much like Abby? Unsure, she leaned closer to the mirror. She'd kept her makeup light and natural. She'd made her eyes enormous with a slide of navy blue eyeliner and several quick sweeps of mascara. Her lips were shiny with clear gloss. She appeared as she did in the photo Steve-O found appealing, but would it be enough? It had to be.

She stepped back, judging her young, flirty outfit. The pretty, white, button-down, sleeveless blouse and mid-thigh navy blue skirt covered with tiny flowers hugged her curves. The snug, yellow shirt below her blouse showed a hint of cleavage. The two side-braids she'd twisted into the blond wig added to her sexy schoolgirl appeal—she hoped.

This had to work. But what if it didn't? "Oh *enough.*" Tired of her endless racing thoughts, she turned off the light and stepped from the bathroom. She slipped on her strappy white sandals, grabbed her purse, and walked into the hall. She stopped short when Jack came out of the office.

They'd barely spoken over the last two days. They'd cared for Livy together with the most basic of conversations and a solid wall of tension between them. Jack had apologized late Wednesday night after Livy had gone to bed, and she'd accepted, but there was no peace. Everything was different now. Jack's sense of humor had vanished, and her guard was up, waiting for him to walk away after he met his obligations set forth by Ethan Cooke Security's legal contracts. She'd hurt him, and he her, but that was only half their problem. The enormity of their situation loomed like a black cloud, smothering any dredges of happiness.

Jack had changed. He no longer laughed and joked when they took Livy to the park, grocery store, or any of the other places they visited; instead, he kept her and Livy close, scrutinizing everyone, analyzing, looking for potential danger. Danger *she* had put them in.

By day, they sat next to each other at the breakfast table or on the couch when Livy insisted they watch movies snuggled together, but he no longer slept in their bed. The nights were endless while she lay alone with their daughter, worrying about Abby and her little girl's safety and the uncertain future she had with Jack. Any progress they made at rebuilding a life together had come to a screeching halt. Any hope she'd allowed herself to feel was unraveling. They had come so far only to lose it all again. It crushed her heart to stare at the man she loved while he looked at her as a client. For surely that's what she was now—a 'principal' under his protection. She lifted her chin against the pain and started past him to the stairs.

He snagged hold of her arm. "How you holding up?"

"Fine. I'm fine." She reached for the charm on her necklace and immediately dropped her hand.

Jack held her gaze, studying, and nodded. "Good. Tucker should be ready in a couple minutes."

"Good. Great." God this was painful.

"Our flight is booked for tomorrow—ten AM."

"We're all packed."

"LA or bust."

She gave him a stiff smile, then nibbled her lip, drowning in discomfort. "I, uh... I should say goodnight to Livy."

"Yeah, sure. Be careful tonight. Listen to Tucker."

She didn't want Tucker; she wanted him. More than anything, she needed Jack to wrap her in a hug and tell her everything was going to be okay, but he didn't. "Thanks. I will." She turned for the stairs, struggling to hold back her tears. Crying was a useless indulgence that would change nothing. She stepped over the threshold into the kitchen, and her despair instantly vanished into delight as she watched her little girl chattering away with Grammy while they worked on a twenty-four-piece puzzle of the Disney princesses. "Look how well you're doing, Ms. Smarty. You almost have all the edges together."

Livy glanced up and gasped. "Mommy."

She smiled at Livy's sheer astonishment. "Kinda silly, huh?"

"I want to play dress up too!" Livy got out of her chair. "Grammy, let's have a tea party. I want my princess dress."

"Wait, sweetie." Alexa crouched in front of her eager daughter. "I can't play dress up with you right now."

Livy's face fell.

"I'm sorry, honey. I want to stay home and play. You have no idea how much, but I have to help someone very special to us."

"Who?"

"Auntie Ab needs me."

"Auntie Ab." Livy brightened. "Bring her here. I miss her very, very much. Where did she go?"

"She had to leave for a while." Alexa hugged Livy tight, relieved that her little girl didn't seem to remember the traumatic moment at the rest stop. "I miss her too—very, very much. She can't come here right now, but hopefully soon. Will you stay here and be a good girl for Daddy and Grammy?"

"Yes."

"I want you in bed on time. We have a busy day tomorrow."

"We're going on a plane to see my puppy. I miss Mutt, and Kylee too."

"You'll see them both in the afternoon." She kissed her finger and touched Livy's nose. "Have fun, sweetie."

"You know," Carol said as she stood, "I think Livy and I are going to be princesses and have a little party after all—a going away party."

Livy jumped up and down. "A party! I *have* to be a princess now, Mommy."

Alexa gave her sweet girl another hug. "Okay. I love you. I'll be home not long after you've gone to sleep."

"Okay. Daddy will leave my light on. He doesn't sleep with us anymore."

Alexa winced inwardly and met Carol's knowing eyes. "Daddy will leave your light on. I need to go." She stood.

"You be careful tonight, honey." Carol hugged her.

"I will. I wish there was another way." She shrugged helplessly, hoping for Carol's understanding. "I have to do this for Abby."

"I know you do, and so does he." She gestured to the ceiling. "He's afraid for you. He loves you."

Alexa nodded, not so sure anymore.

"He loves you to the moon and back. His eyes have their sparkle back—or they did. And they will again when you get home to California and put this business behind you." She gave her another hug. "Go on now. Livy and I have a date."

She nodded, met Tucker in the hallway, and they left.

"We'll be in the vans recording everything. The surveillance vehicles are already in place," Detective Canon said on the other side of the divider while a female officer secured a wire on Alexa.

"I think you're all set." The pretty, brown-eyed blonde smiled at her. "Go ahead and put your shirt back on and we'll make sure."

Alexa pulled the snug yellow top on, then buttoned her sleeveless blouse, stopping just below her breasts. She smoothed her shirt down with cold, clammy hands and shuddered out a long breath as she met Tucker's eyes over the privacy screen.

"Placement's good, Detective." Officer Detrick said as she scrutinized Alexa's chest, turning her from side to side. "Can't tell it's there." She surprised Alexa when she pulled her into a hug and patted her down. "Can't feel it, either."

"Good. Is the mic picking this up?"

A man across the small room gave Detective Canon

a thumbs up. "Crystal clear."

"Alexa, come on over and we'll review this one more time."

She nodded and pressed a hand to her unsteady stomach. If she made it through the evening without losing her dinner, she would be amazed. The anticipation was becoming *unbearable.* If only Jack were here to make her laugh. He always knew just what to say.

"Excuse us for a second." Tucker took her hand and pulled her aside. "How you holding up, champ?"

"My stomach's a mess." She sighed and rolled her eyes.

He gave her fingers a gentle squeeze. "I'll be close by tonight, along with several other officers. They'll be eating and drinking among the patrons and strolling through the park. You won't take a breath we don't know about."

"I know. I'm just..." She glanced down. "I just wish..." She shook her head, then she met Tucker's calm eyes. "It doesn't matter."

"It's better that he isn't here. You need to focus on staying safe and playing this out with Steve-O. You have to push everything else to the back of your mind."

"You're right." But vanishing Jack from her thoughts was easier said than done. He'd been her rock through this entire ordeal. She had never needed him more than now, and he was nowhere to be found. "I'm worried—really worried. I have to get this right. We're leaving in the morning. What if I don't get enough to help Abby?"

"You'll get what you can, then it's time to get you and Olivia out of here and back to California. This situation has the potential to get dangerous the longer it goes on."

"I know." She hated that she was abandoning her sister for the second time. Abby was supposed to be with them when they went back to LA.

324

"Let's finish this so we can get home."

"The coward in me wants to turn tail and leave right now."

"We can. You say the word and this is over."

"No." She shook her head vehemently. "No. This isn't about me. Tonight is for Abby. Someone set this nightmare in motion for my sister. If I can end it..." She huffed out a determined breath. "I'm ready."

Tucker's eyes narrowed as he studied her. "You're one hell of a woman, Alexa Harris."

Despite her nerves, she smiled.

"Let's do this."

Bolstered by Tucker's confidence, she gripped his fingers tighter and nodded. "Okay."

Hand-in-hand, she and Tucker joined Detective Canon, along with Officer Detrick and a buff, bald man Alexa had never seen before.

"Alexa, this is Special Agent Jerrod Terron from the FBI. He's one of our taskforce members. He'll be working with us tonight."

The agent held out his hand. "Ms. Harris, we appreciate your willingness to help."

Alexa returned his handshake. "I'm doing this for my sister."

"I'm familiar with your sister's case. We're doing everything we can to bring her home."

Alexa's brow winged up as she digested the agent's load of bull crap. "Are you sure about that? It seems to me everyone's more interested in arresting Zachary Hartwell than they are in helping the victims in this ordeal."

Detective Canon choked on his coffee.

Tucker winked at her and glanced down in his attempt to hide his grin.

Detective Canon put his cup down. "Alexa, we should

run through the safety precautions one last time before you head over to the restaurant."

"Yes. Okay."

"There will be several undercovers planted around the restaurant, the parking lot, and the park. We'll be monitoring your entire conversation from the vans. Make sure you leave the wire alone. Don't fidget or call attention to the device. If for any reason you feel like something's off, use your phrase—'Is it hot in here?'—and Officer Detrick will interrupt the date. She's your long-lost friend, Christina, from school. She moved away your sophomore year."

That wasn't so much to remember. "Got it."

"It's six-forty. You should head over."

After weeks of waiting for a moment like this, it was here. Alexa took another deep breath. "All right."

"You'll do great," Officer Detrick patted her shoulder. "Having a few nerves actually works in this situation. It's a first date."

This was her *only* 'date.' Alexa gave the officer a small smile. "That's true."

"Here you go." Agent Terron handed her a set of car keys. "It's the red Kia just outside. When the evening's over, drive back, and we'll debrief and send you on your way with Mr. Campbell. Remember, do *not* make further plans with this man tonight. Tell him you have to check your calendar and you'll get back to him should he try to pursue a second meeting."

She nodded and looked at Tucker before heading for the door. It was show time, and she was as eager as she was terrified to begin. Under the layers of nerves was a burning desire for justice. She wouldn't screw this up; she couldn't afford to. Alexa stepped from the small, empty apartment two blocks from the restaurant, walked to the government-issued vehicle she would borrow for the next couple of hours, and got in. Pulling down the visor, she checked her hair and makeup. "Here goes nothing," she murmured to herself as she started the car. "I'm going to kick ass for you tonight, Ab." She flipped the visor back up with a snap, reversed out of the parking spot, and turned right on Boston Street. Within minutes she pulled into the large communal parking lot close to the Bayside Café and parked just a short walk away.

She got out and scanned the cars around her as her anxiety built. Where were the surveillance vehicles? Where was Tucker? Who were the cops among the busy crowds of people milling about? Beads of sweat dripped down her back, and her hands trembled. "Stop," she whispered as she looked down and closed her eyes. "Stop," she repeated. This wouldn't work if she couldn't keep it together. She couldn't worry about who was whom and who was where. She needed to focus on finding Steve-O and gathering information that would help Abby—period.

Steadier and ready to begin again, she smoothed her skirt, straightened her shoulders, and headed for the beautiful old mill building that was the Bayside Café. Two men waited close to the door. One had to be in his early fifties. Surely that wasn't Steve-O. The tall, thirty-something in khakis and olive green top with light brown hair and a handsome face glanced at his watch.

Was that him? Was that Steve-O? The profile picture he'd used was so...vague; it was no help right now—and certainly that was the plan. Should she call out to him? What *did* she call him? Steve-O? What had she been *thinking*?

The man in the kakis looked up. "Jenny?"

Oh God. Oh *God*—this was it. She forced a smile through the fear. "Yes."

Grinning, he walked forward, took her hand, and kissed her knuckles. "You're even more beautiful in person."

Her smile widened as her pulse continued to hammer. "Thank you."

"Should we get a table?"

"Yes. Definitely."

He opened the door and pressed his fingers to the small of her back as she went in before him. She stepped with him to the hostess stand, her legs trembling. What had she gotten herself into? Why did she think she could pull this off? She'd never dated. Jack had been her first and last everything. They'd hit it off so naturally. He'd always made the moves, at least until she stopped being shy. She didn't know how to do this. She wasn't an eighteen-year-old free spirit; she was twenty-seven with a beautiful three-year-old waiting for her at home.

"Stevens," Steve-O said to the attractive, raven-haired beauty behind the small table. "Party of two." He stroked his finger down Alexa's arm and sent their hostess a wolfish grin.

Stevens? Was that his last name? What was his first?

"Inside or outside dining tonight?" The woman smiled back, ignoring Alexa.

Steve-O returned his attention to Alexa, as if she was the only person in the room. "Inside or out?"

"Out is fine." The cooling breeze off the water would be refreshing. She was burning up.

"Out it is."

The hostess in her short black skirt and revealing red top showed them to the deck overlooking the harbor. "How's this?"

"Does this work, Jenny?" He smiled.

The lights around the city were starting to wink on. Boats floated by on the bay. "It's perfect."

"This'll do. Thank you," Steve-O said with a flirty grin for their hostess.

"Enjoy your evening." She set down two menus and winked. "Rachel will be your server." She walked away with a little extra sway in her hips.

Alexa barely suppressed an eye roll. Their hostess wouldn't be so quick to sashay about if she had half a clue that a nasty snake slithered below the charming smile, neat khakis, and expensive polo of Mr. Stevens.

"Are you sure this is okay?" He pulled out her chair. "The breeze is kind of brisk. I think it might rain later."

"Really, it's lovely." She pressed her lips together as she admonished herself. Eighteen-year-olds did *not* say 'lovely.' They said 'cool' or 'awesome'—anything but 'lovely.' "It's great," she added. "Really great."

"Have a seat."

She smiled under her lashes and sat. "Thanks."

"No problem."

He settled on his side, and Alexa set the strap of her purse around the back of her chair. She scanned the tables around her and the brick walking path just feet from the deck. Her eyes locked on Tucker's among the busy pedestrians rambling about.

"—drink?"

"Huh?" Alexa's gaze shot to Steve-O's.

He smiled. "I said would you like something to drink?"

"Sorry. Water. Water's fine." She needed to get his name. The police would be able to track him down if they knew his full name. "So, I don't know... This is really embarrassing. I don't know your name. I thought it was Steve or Steven, but that's your last name."

He chuckled. "I'm Eric. Eric Stevens."

She smiled. "Eric." Hopefully Detective Canon heard that loud and clear. They now had a face and a name. Despite her nerves and doubts, Alexa was more determined than ever to pull the night off.

Their waitress wandered over to the table. "Welcome to Bayside Cafe. I'm Rachel. Can I start you with a drink?"

"The lady will have a water, and I'll have a Bud draught." He smiled at Alexa and took her hand as the waitress walked away. "I'm glad we could do this. When I saw your picture and read your profile, I knew we were going to hit it off."

And the curtain was officially up. It was time to get down to business. There would be few distractions now that their drinks were on the way. She consciously relaxed her shoulders and leaned her forearms on the table. "I was a little nervous. This is my first time doing the web-dating thing. One of my girlfriends had some luck, so I thought, why not?"

"I've met a lot of really cool people online."

"I bet. I guess I was a bit hesitant to dive in though, because of the whole creep factor."

His brow shot up. "Creep factor?"

"Yeah, you know, those creeps you read about in the newspaper that like to take advantage of women. It leaves a girl wary."

He held up his hands. "You're in luck. I'm one-hundred percent creep-free."

She chuckled as her brain screamed 'liar.'

"So, you're into photography?"

"I am. I love it. I took a course in high school—my junior year. I've been obsessed ever since."

"I'm a fashion photographer."

"That's what you're profile says—pretty sweet."

The waitress was back with their drinks. Eric murmured his thanks as Rachel walked away. "Do you want to order anything?"

She shook her head. "I'm good for now. Tell me more

about yourself, especially your job. It sounds exciting."

"It really is. I enjoy the travel, the art, the beautiful women—pretty much every part of it."

Alexa fiddled with her straw, stirring the clear plastic among the ice cubes with her free hand, happy to have somewhere to direct her nervous energy. "I would love to have a career like yours, but I still have so much to learn. I need to go to college. My parents are totally on my butt about the whole thing, but I don't want to right now. I want to travel and see the world for a while, ya know?"

"I wouldn't waste my time *behind* a camera if I were you." He took her chin between his thumb and index finger and turned her face slightly. "You're bone structure is amazing. I'm itching for my camera right now. You could make millions."

She struggled not to pull back as he continued to touch her. Was this how he did it? Did they fall so easily for the positive strokes and promises of a profitable career? "Millions? I would *love* that." Giggling, she leaned in closer and felt the wire against her chest connect with the table. She sat up quickly and fought not to touch her shirt and give herself away. "You know, that's my dream. To be every man's fantasy and make money while I do it. Maybe that sounds demeaning or like I don't have much of a self-esteem—wanting every man to want me."

"Every man *does* want you, Jenny. Trust me." He smiled. "And I can make your dreams come true, especially with that face and body of yours. They're going to take you a long way. I can probably get you some hours at my next shoot. It's underwear. Your legs are screaming to show off a beautiful pair of silky panties."

She shook her head and looked down as she swallowed her disgust. This guy was a pig. "I can't believe this might happen. I can't believe my dreams might come true."

"You're gorgeous."

She almost said, 'Thank you,' but she remembered the girl he wanted would have a shaky self-esteem at best. "No, I'm—I'm not. But I want to be."

"You're gorgeous," he whispered and kissed each of her fingers. "Let me photograph you."

"At the park?"

He shook his head. "Not with the rain coming in. Come to my place. Monday night. I'll cook you dinner."

"Oh, I don't know." She feigned reluctance as she gained confidence in her ability to pull this off. Eric was eating it up. "I have to check with my mom first."

He frowned. "Your mom?"

She looked down. "Yeah, we have plans Monday. I've been trying to do stuff with her now and again since my dad left. I'm sure I can break them and make it up to her another night, though. Let me check."

"Sounds good." He played his thumb over her bottom lip. "I'm looking forward to showing you what everyone else sees. Bring your camera. We'll trade techniques."

She suppressed a shudder, wishing desperately that he would stop touching her. "Trade? But you're a professional."

"Gotta start somewhere, right?"

She smiled. "That's true."

A tray full of entrees crashed to the floor, and Alexa jumped. She glanced over and gasped as the waitress scrambled to clean up her mess. There he was, sitting at a table with a stunning blonde. Renzo met her eyes across the room and smiled. She turned back to Eric and yanked up her glass, desperate for a sip of cool water.

"Are you okay?"

She nodded. "Yes, I'm fine." Why was he here? Why

was Renzo here at this restaurant? The coincidence was too huge.

"You sure?"

"Mm, definitely."

"Are you ready to order some food?"

"Absolutely." They'd been here for almost an hour, but she didn't plan to go anywhere until she had plenty of time to study her sister's worst nightmare sitting across the room. There had to be a connection between Lorenzo Cruz and Eric Stevens. There simply *had* to be.

Jackson sat in the surveillance vehicle, hanging on Alex's every word as they transmitted from her wire into his headphones. He hadn't moved from his uncomfortable corner on the small cramped bench in more than an hour and a half. He rubbed at the burning ache in his shoulders while he scrutinized the live video feed on the laptop, trying to interpret every gesture crossing her face. The discomfort squeezing the base of his neck was almost as brutal as the agony of having to sit back in the safety of the van while Alex risked it all. But she was doing a hell of a job. She could safely add acting to her list of numerous talents. If he didn't know Alex as well as he did, he would believe she was enjoying herself. She'd gone from tense and shy to relaxed and flirty as the evening dragged on.

Her laughter flooded his ears, and he ground his teeth when Eric Stevens made another bad joke. Damn, he was ready for this to be over. He'd been ready to end this since the word 'go.' Getting Alex back to California and out of harm's way couldn't happen soon enough. He glanced at his watch. A little more than twelve hours and they were out of here.

He wanted things back the way they had been just two days ago, when she laughed and smiled for him. He wanted Alex in his home—in his bed, with their daughter sleeping in the room across the hall. But that would take some time. They had a lot to come back from. Deception and harsh words left their relationship in tatters. They lost more ground still when they'd stumbled through the awkward conversation by his parents' stairwell hours before. Alex's eyes had pleaded for comfort and reassurances, but he hadn't been able to give them. He'd wanted to pull her against him and tell her he would be with her every step of the way, but he'd stayed silent and let her walk away.

Growing restless, Jackson stretched his cramping legs and sat back as the waitress came to check on Alex and Eric's progress with their appetizer platter. How long could they drag out an evening when the mozzarella sticks and loaded potato skins were almost gone? It couldn't be much longer. Hopefully Alex would make her way back to the apartment building within the hour. He would meet her there and take her home while Tucker dealt with the bullshit. They needed to talk. Maybe they could sit on the dock and figure things out. He wanted to lay with her tonight. He missed falling asleep with her. Hell, the past few nights he hadn't done anything but toss and turn in his own bed.

"You know," Eric said, "I'm having a really good time."

Alex swallowed her bite of fried mozzarella and smiled. "Me too."

"I want to do this again."

"We are on Monday." She sipped her water.

"Before then. My friend Zack is having a huge birthday bash tomorrow night. Why don't you come with me?"

"Tomorrow? I'm not sure—"

"It's at his place in DC." Eric took her hand. "We'll have fun."

"Son of a bitch," Detective Canon said. "Is he talking about fucking Zachary Hartwell? Get me a DOB on Zachary Hartwell," Canon demanded into his microphone.

Jackson struggled to listen to Alex's conversation as he wondered the same thing. This was huge. This was beyond dangerous, and he wanted Alex out—now.

"I don't know, Eric."

"Aw, come on, Jenny. There will be a live band and great food. He knows how to do it up right. A couple of modeling contacts might be there."

"It sounds fun."

"Fucking unbelievable," Cannon shouted. "It *is* Hartwell. DOB matches."

"Please come with me. I want to show you off," Eric coaxed.

Jackson's jaw clenched when he recognize the determined gleam in Alex's eyes, and she smiled. "Don't you do it, Alex," he muttered. "Don't you—"

"Okay. I'll come."

Jackson rushed to his feet, unable to believe his own ears, and smacked his head on the roof of the van. "What the fuck is she doing?"

"Take it easy, Mr. Matthews," Agent Terron warned.

Jackson's gaze flew to the Agent's as he rubbed the sore spot on his skull. "Take it easy?"

"This could be our big break. She's in."

"Forget it." Dread curled in his belly as he stared at Terron and Cannon. They were practically rubbing their hands together with excited anticipation. They were going to allow Alex—hell, they were going to *encourage* her to take this next step. "We didn't agree to this. We're leaving for Los Angeles tomorrow morning. You can

335

forget the whole thing."

"If our informant is a willing participant... We'll proceed forward if Ms. Harris gives us the green light." Canon tilted his head to speak into the microphone and said, "Let's get some preliminaries going on this. We need a confirmed address for the party and a new staging location in DC."

He was already losing control of the situation. Helpless rage sent his pulse pounding. He could barely hear the fucker speaking over the rapid beat throbbing in his skull. "I'm telling you *no*. As head of her security, I'm pulling the plug on this. You're not worried about Alex's safety anymore than you are about bringing Abby Harris home. You see a way to get to Zachary Hartwell, and that's it."

"As I said—"

"I heard what you said. Now you listen to me," Jackson spat. "Alex isn't thinking of the danger she'll be in. The only thing she sees is a possibility of getting to her sister. You and I both know the odds are slim to none on that happening."

"The probability is zero if she does nothing."

"There won't be anyone on the inside to keep her safe. They could take her right then and there, and we wouldn't have a clue. We're done with this." Jackson stepped from the van and slammed the door, afraid he would punch the bastards. It was tempting, more than tempting, to walk into the restaurant and ruin the sting by posing as a jealous boyfriend, but that could be dangerous for Alex and Abby, so he walked to his car instead. Seconds later, his cellphone rang.

"Things are getting interesting," Tucker said.

Jackson scoffed. "Yeah, that's a word for it."

"She's going to do this."

"Not if I have anything to say—"

"You don't."

"Like hell I don't. She signed a legally binding agreement with Ethan Cooke Security." Even as he spewed the words, he recognized how ludicrous they sounded. "We're boarding a plane for Los Angeles in less than twelve hours."

"So, what, are you going to have Ethan sue her for breach of contract, or let the feds talk her into witness protection? We've got the same scenario as two days ago, but the stakes are a lot higher."

"Tell me something I don't know." He smacked his hand on the top of the rental. "Goddamn. How are they going to guarantee Alex's safety while she's on the inside? You know as well as I do that Steve-O or Eric or whatever the hell his name is has every intention of adding her to Hartwell's collection of prizes." He scrubbed his hand over his face, struggling not to yell out his helpless frustration.

"We'll have to make sure that doesn't happen."

"Yeah, well, you get me a guarantee, and we'll move forward."

"I'll call Ethan and have new paperwork waiting for Alexa to sign when we get back to the staging area. We have to keep ourselves in this. You going back to your parents?"

It was tempting to head out and let Tucker handle the rest, but he couldn't go until Alex was in her car heading back to the apartment,with the police tail following behind her. "In a couple minutes. I need to pull my head together first. Doug said he could stay with Olivia and my parents until midnight. Looks like I'll be asking him to help us out tomorrow night, too. Luckily, he's off duty. I owe him big time for this." Jackson unlocked the car and sat down in the driver's seat. He turned over the ignition and rolled down the window in an attempt to escape the stifling heat.

"I need to go. Looks like the date's wrapping up. They're walking out your way."

"Okay. I'll see you back at the house."

"Later."

On a steaming breath, Jackson rested his head against the seat, trying to find a grip on his anger. Flying off half-cocked wasn't going to help Alex. He needed to do his job and move in steps. The first was to make sure Alex got back safely, then call Ethan and have him pull up every scrap of information he could find on Zachary Hartwell's residence—blueprints, his security measures, everything. By tomorrow night, he and Tucker would know every room Alex would step in and all possible exits as well as Hartwell did himself.

Jackson came to attention when Eric and Alex stepped from the restaurant, hand in hand. They made their way to the little red KIA parked two rows in front of him and stopped at her door. Although the night was a farce, Alex and Eric appeared like any man and woman out for an evening of fun. There was no denying they made a striking couple.

Eric's deep voice drifted in Jackson's direction, along with Alex's gentle laughter. Jackson clenched his hands against the wheel as Eric wrapped his arms around her waist and continued with his yammering. Moments later, he reached in his back pocket and handed her a card. She smiled and slipped it in her purse.

Alex's smile disappeared when Eric touched her chin with his thumb and moved in, brushing his lips against hers.

Jackson ground his teeth and his foot began to bop up and down when Eric deepened the kiss and Alex's arms came up to rest on his shoulders. "Goddamn." This was a stab to the fucking heart. She wasn't exactly fending him off. After what felt like an eternity, Eric finally eased back.

"You taste good."

Jackson rolled his eyes and steamed a breath out his nose. He hadn't been able to catch one fucking word of their conversation since they stepped outside, but he heard that loud and clear. Alex tasted good—damn good; he hated that someone else had gotten a sample.

Eric opened Alex's door, and she got in. Her headlights came on and she backed up, waved, and drove off. The police tail followed behind seconds later, but so did a black Escalade.

Jackson dialed Tucker's number and kept an eye on Eric Stevens.

"Yeah."

"Where are you?"

"Right behind Alexa."

"Good." He relaxed a fraction. "I think you've got a tail, or Alex does, anyway—black Escalade."

"Yeah, I see it. Hold on." Tucker mumbled something to the officer driving him back to the apartment. "It's been radioed in. The cops'll pull them over and give us a little time."

Jackson watched as Eric talked on his cellphone and headed back in the restaurant. One of the cops from the surveillance van followed behind discreetly. Eric was officially on the taskforce's radar.

"They just pulled the Escalade over," Tucker said into his ear. "They'll keep them that way until we radio that Alexa is secure at the apartment. We're pulling in the parking lot now."

"Okay, good. I'll see you at the house." It was over—for tonight. Alex would come home safe—this time. Jackson clicked his seatbelt in place and shifted into first. He eased off the clutch and stopped when Eric came out with Lorenzo Cruz at his side. "Son of a bitch."

The two men piled into a pretty, laser-blue Porsche and peeled out of the parking lot. A vehicle followed behind. This wasn't even close to over. This whole nightmare had just begun.

CHAPTER 20

J ACKSON STARED OUT HIS BEDROOM window, watching the trees sway in the misting rain. Despite his hour-long stint sitting on his parent's dock, breathing in the humid bay air, and a sweaty bout with the punching bag in the garage, he couldn't settle. His heart still pounded an angry beat while his stomach churned from a level of anxiety he'd never felt before.

Alex was in more danger than she could possibly realize, and there wasn't a damn thing he could do about it. She was bound and determined to help Detective Canon and Agent Terron with the second stage of their sting, and his hands were tied. Short of kidnapping her himself, there was nothing he could do to stop her from entering Zachary Hartwell's estate—alone and unprotected—in less than twenty-four hours.

Jackson pressed his forehead to the cool glass and steamed out a breath as another bout of helpless frustration consumed him. Tomorrow night wouldn't be a medium-risk operation like the dinner date had been. This was a 'code red,' and he could do nothing more than sit back and let the authorities handle the bulk of the preparations.

Ethan had faxed and e-mailed every last document he was able get his hands on pertaining to Hartwell's mansion in the wealthy northwest section of DC. The blueprint had been a maze of twists and turns, with several dozen rooms spread over two enormous wings. Even if he had every member of Ethan Cooke Security's

Los Angeles branch on hand and a month to study the layout, the job would still be a challenge. It simply wasn't possible to watch every door and window on a home that size. The odds were definitely in the traffickers' favor, and he was becoming more worried by the second.

Why couldn't Alex have just stuck to the damn plan? She'd done her part. The authorities had new leads to work with, but it would never be enough. Alex would continue to risk everything in her attempt to save Abby, and Canon and Terron were taking advantage, thinking little of the life they were risking to build their case against a man who would lawyer himself up so deep it would be all but impossible to make anything stick.

"*Fuck.*" Jackson pounded the side of his fist on the window frame and turned away. He moved to his bed, sat on the edge, and rested his face in his hands. Where was Alex, anyway? It had been *hours* since he watched her make a left out of Bayside Café's parking lot. She and Tucker should've been back by now. He wouldn't be able to rest until she was home. Hell, he wouldn't be able to *breathe* again until she was finished with this entire mess. A light knock sounded at the door, and his head shot up from the cradle of his palms. "Yeah, come in."

Alex peeked in. "I wasn't sure if you would still be up. How did Livy do tonight?"

"Fine. My mother said they went out for ice cream, fed some ducks, read a few stories." He studied her stunning face. She'd taken off her wig and left her hair tied back. She still wore her sexy schoolgirl outfit. It was impossible not to *want* her with that tiny skirt showing off a sinful amount of leg and that tight yellow shirt accentuating hints of spectacular cleavage beneath the proper white blouse.

She frowned. "You didn't go with them?"

342

"No, but Dougie Masterson did. He kept an eye on things around here."

Her frown deepened. "Where were you?"

"In a surveillance van."

"You..." She shook her head. "I thought..."

"I was there the whole time—heard everything, saw everything. Did you really think I would let you go through this alone?"

"No. Yes. I don't know. No." She gave him a jerky shrug and sighed. "No. But you don't approve of what I'm doing."

"Damn straight I don't." He pushed off the bed to stand. "I'm worried, Alex. This is incredibly dangerous."

Her eyes filled. "I know."

"Do you? Do you really understand what you're getting yourself into?"

"I know we've found two of the key players in the Mid-Atlantic sex ring, and they have no intention of letting me walk out of that house tomorrow night. I saw Renzo at the restaurant. He was sitting a few tables away."

"And you're still planning to go." He shoved his hands through his hair. "You're walking into a losing situation. How am I supposed to be okay with that? I *love* you, Alex. You're asking me to sit back and watch a disaster unfold."

"I imagine it seems that way, but Agent Terron assures me the house will be well monitored."

"Fuck Agent Terron." He rushed to her and grabbed her arms. "He'll tell you whatever you want to hear as long as you'll risk your life to give him what he wants. Have you seen the size of Zachary Hartwell's estate?"

"No."

"It's fucking enormous. This is no good, Alex. Ethan pays me big bucks to assess risks just like this one, and I'm telling you this is no good."

She sighed again, her eyes weary. "This is an opportunity to get closer to Abby. I have to take it."

He turned away as embers of anger burned bright in his chest. Her calmness was infuriating. "Are you listening to what I'm saying? You're playing a deadly game here. Why can't I make you *see* that?" He whirled back as the flames grew hotter. "There's a huge chance none of this will lead to Abby. What if all of this is for nothing but now they have you both? You're not thinking this through. This is madness." He began to pace as fear overtook him. "This is *stupid*."

"This is not stupid." She took a step toward the door. "I'm trying to save my sister's *life*."

"And I'm trying to save yours. Fucking-A, Alex."

"Don't speak to me that way. This conversation is over if you're going to be unkind."

"*Unkind*," he laughed as he advanced on her. "You think I'm being *unkind*? You have no idea what *unkind* is. I'm just fucking pissed, but I'm not cruel." He took her arms again and backed her against the door, wanting to send his point home. "But Eric is—and Renzo. They don't give two shits about you. Do you know what you'll be doing tomorrow night when you walk through that door?" He pressed himself against her and yanked her white sleeveless blouse open, sending buttons flying.

"Stop," she shuddered.

"Stop? Do you think they respect that word, Alex? Do you think they'll back off and walk away just because you want them too?"

"Why are you doing this?" She pushed at his chest. "Why are you acting like this?"

"Because I'm giving you a little taste of what you're in for. Do you think tomorrow will be anything like tonight? There won't be cops just steps away ready to jump in and save you." A tear trailed down her cheek,

344

but he kept going. "What, can't you handle it? It'll be so much worse," he fired at her. "Eric won't be so gentle with his kisses if and when he decides he'll have a few."

She stopped struggling against him. "You saw that? You saw him kiss me?"

"I told you I saw everything." The jealousy bubbled up, despite his best intentions to dismiss the whole thing, knowing that was the least of their troubles.

"I'm sorry, Jack." She took his face in her hands. "It didn't mean anything."

"Just part of the gig, right?" He sent her a humorless smile.

"Yes. Kissing Eric made me sick. I only want you."

"Lies. Kisses. Broken deals. But the end justifies the means, right?" He pressed himself closer. "What else will you do to get to your sister?"

"Not what you think. I only want you, Jack." Instead of pushing him away, she pulled him closer, and something changed. The urgency humming in the air no longer had anything to do with Eric Stevens or the sex ring. "I only want you," she repeated.

His breath heaved out, mingling with hers as they eyed each other.

"Only you, Jack."

He nipped her lip as he glided his palms over the back of her thighs and under her skirt. "Show me." He grabbed her ass and brought her against him.

"Not like this," she panted. "Not when you're angry." Despite her words, her fingers curled at the nape of his neck.

"Does it really matter?" He crushed his mouth to hers, and tongue met tongue.

"Jack—" her word ended on a strangled gasp when he pushed her panties aside and shoved his fingers in deep. Wanting to dominate, he worked her to a violent

345

peak as he held her gaze.

Moaning, breathless, she sagged against the door, but he wasn't finished. Sex seemed to be their only connection these days, the only place where they made any sense. He sent his fingers to work again, and her eyes widened as she let loose a strangled cry. "I hated him touching you. I hated him tasting you. I hate that you won't listen to me," he said, then he took her mouth again.

Tongues danced to the rhythm of his plunging fingers and she clutched at his shoulders and groaned loud and long. "Jack. Jack, come lie down with me. I want you to lie down with me."

"No." He didn't want tenderness right now, or to be soothed. He wanted to show her he was the only one. He tossed her blouse aside and yanked her clinging yellow top up over her head. Her bra followed with a flick of the wrist. He played his palms over her hardened nipples and nibbled her lips until she whimpered and her hands started a frantic journey of their own.

She threw his shirt aside and her long, cool fingers moved over his chest, his stomach, sending him into overdrive as he sent her flossy panties to the rug.

"Jack, come to the bed," she muffled against his neck in between gasps.

"Right here." He freed himself, lifted her skirt, and rammed into her hot wetness. Frozen, stunned from the indescribable pleasure, he groaned when her muscles pulsed around him.

"Oh, God, God..." She clutched at his shoulders as her body went rigid.

He swallowed her cries and gripped her hips, desperate to bring her even higher. Holding on, he shoved himself deeper with each violent thrust, never letting up when she bowed back, tensing, and came yet again. He followed seconds later on a primal grunt as he emptied himself inside her.

They stared at each other as their breath heaved. Alex's face was damp and flushed, her eyes glassy, her lips swollen. "What—what was *that*?"

They had never been like that before and never would be again. There had been no kindness, no affection. He shrugged, trying to dismiss the shame swamping him as Alex's confused gaze continued to hold his. "I don't know." He freed himself from her, stepped back, and pulled up his pants.

"Are you punishing me? Are you showing us both that I'm still yours?"

He clenched his jaw, saying nothing as she hit the mark.

"I won't let you use us like this. Don't ever do that again." She reached down for his t-shirt and yanked it over her head.

"You didn't exactly stop me, but you didn't exactly stop *him* either." What the hell was he *doing*?

Her rosy cheeks paled, and her eyes widened as she whirled and twisted the doorknob.

He reached out and took her arm. "I'm sorry." He pulled her back against him and wrapped his arms around her waist. "I'm sorry."

She sniffled.

He nuzzled his face in her hair. "That was below the belt, and I didn't mean it. I'm sorry," he repeated.

"I don't want it to be like this, Jack. I don't want us to be like this."

"I don't either." He turned her to face him. "Cancel tomorrow night," he pleaded. "Let me take you and Olivia back to LA where it's safe. We need to fix us before it's too late."

"I want to, but it's not that easy."

347

"Yes, it *is*. You're the only one who can stop this now."

"And what about Abby?"

"We'll find another way."

"No, we won't."

"Alex, please." He pressed his hands against her skin.

"I don't want to go tomorrow night. I'm scared—terrified—but there's no other way. Do you think I needed your...demonstration to understand what might happen to me?"

He clenched his jaw as he absorbed her verbal sucker punch. "Low blow, and I deserve it." He closed his eyes. "You're desperate to get Abby back. I know that, but this isn't the *way*. Sending you into a no-win situation isn't the solution."

"From any angle you look at this, it's a no-win situation. It has been all along. I have to do this, Jack. Why can't you understand?"

"Because every instinct in my body is telling me this is wrong. My gut is screaming that something bad is going to happen. You're their next target."

"That doesn't help me."

"I don't know what else you want me to say." He tossed his hands up in the air and let them fall. "The woman I love is walking in to a trap, and I'm just supposed to pat you on the head and say, 'Go get 'em tiger'? What do you want from me?"

"To be here. To support me."

"I am. I'm right here." He pulled her to him and rested his forehead against hers. "I'm right here, Alex, but I can't tell you what you want to hear. I don't think this is the right approach. I don't think this is what's best for you or Olivia *or* Abby."

"Then what is?" she snapped and pulled away. "What is, Jack?"

"I don't know. I really don't."

348

"That's so helpful." She burst into tears. "God." She swiped her wet cheeks. "We've exhausted every other effort. This is the only one getting us results."

"And when does it stop?"

"When Abby's home. I can do this, Jack. I believe I can do this. Why don't you?"

"This has nothing to do with a lack of faith in you; it's a matter of not being able to ensure your safety. That's all I care about. I want you safe."

"What about my sister?"

"What about Olivia? What about your daughter, Alex? What if they take you tomorrow night? What if I can't get you back? What do I tell our little girl?"

Alex sat on the edge of the bed and covered her face as her tears streamed faster. "Don't use Livy that way, Jack."

He crouched in front of her. "I'll use anything I can to put a stop to this. I can't lose you again, Alex. I love you. I need you."

She dropped her hands and looked at him. "That's what this is about: you. Somehow it always comes back to what *you* need. *You* can't lose me. *You* need me." She rushed to her feet. "This isn't about Livy or my sister rotting in hell. You're afraid."

"Damn right I'm afraid." He stood, growing more pissed by the second.

"You're selfish." She pushed at him.

"What?" He captured her wrists. "How is worrying about you selfish?"

"Because you're more concerned with how this affects you than anyone else."

"Bullshit." Her accusation hurt him as much as it angered. "You're the one with a one-track mind. It's Abby or nothing and damn the rest."

"How *dare* you." She yanked free of his hold.

"*You've* put our daughter and my parents in danger. *You've* been advised to leave by not one but three security experts, yet you choose to stay. I think *you* should take a second and reevaluate who the selfish one is in this scenario."

"Bastard," she hissed. "How can you look at me and say that? Abby and Livy are all I have."

"They're all you have? Do I enter the equation here, or is that too selfish a question?"

"I promised I would always take care of her. She has stood by me through everything. She's never left me, Jack, and I refuse to leave her."

"So, it's going to keep coming around to the past? I left you, Alex. I sure as hell did and regretted it every day after. I made the biggest mistake of my life when I walked away from you. How many ways do I have to apologize?"

"This has nothing to do with the past and everything to do with giving my sister her life back."

"Sister Alexa to the rescue, no matter what." He laughed and turned away.

"That's it. That's enough." She rushed to the door and grabbed the knob.

He whirled and stopped her with a hand against the wood. "We're not finished here."

"Oh, we're long past finished. All this time. I've wasted so much time on you."

His heart stuttered as he measured the ice-cold blue of her eyes. "What's that supposed to mean?"

"Whatever you want it to." She reached up and yanked hard on the charm of her necklace, snapping the chain in two. She threw the gold to the floor, elbowed him in the stomach, and rushed from the room when he lost his breath.

Fighting for air, Jackson stared at the ruined piece

of glimmering gold as he tried to absorb the shock of Alex's actions and words. With a gasping cough, he scooped down and picked up the jewelry; it was still warm from her skin. She'd worn it for years, and now she was done. Even when he'd broken her heart, she'd kept it. Dread slammed into his gut as he digested what this meant. He'd just lost Alex, and it had nothing to do with the traffickers. He rushed to the hall as her door closed and the lock clicked into place.

He stared at the wood for several minutes, then raised his hand to knock but dropped it. His first instinct was to barge in and demand they talk until they'd fixed everything, but instead he walked away. They were at an impasse. She wanted him to sit back and tell her that tomorrow night was going to be okay, but he couldn't. Every fiber of his being warned him that Zachary Hartwell's birthday bash was going to end in doom.

Alexa pressed her back to the door and closed her eyes as Jack's footsteps faded down the hall. She swiped at her cheeks as unstoppable tears rained down from her eyes. What were they *doing* to each other? She walked to Livy, sniffling back her sobs, and stared at her beautiful girl. She pressed a finger to her lips and touched Livy's nose, then she smoothed the covers over her restless sleeper.

She lowered herself to the edge of the bed and picked up Livy's stuffed frog from the floor. The laughter from a night long ago echoed through her mind as she remembered Jack winning the mournful looking creature for her. She wanted that moment back, or any of the other thousand times they had made each other smile.

It had never been like this between them—the harsh words, the cruelty. The angry sex of moments before had been a shock. Jack's eyes had been so cold while he rammed himself inside of her. They'd had urgent sex, hungry sex, many times before, but what they just shared was dramatically different and nothing she ever wanted to repeat.

Alexa rested her forehead in her hands and closed her eyes, wishing she could take the last few minutes back. She didn't mean to call Jack selfish. Jack was many things, but selfish wasn't one of them. He'd put his life on hold to help her. He loved her, of that she had no doubt, and she him, but maybe love wasn't enough when the complications were so *big*.

So where did that leave them? Was this it? Was this really the end? They had come so far over the last month and a half. She had finally lowered her guard enough to let herself believe in the possibility of them being together forever. Everything she ever wanted was at her fingertips and quickly slipping away—and it was all her doing this time. Her obsession with Abby's case and seeing her sister again was destroying other facets of her life. Jack was so mad—as furious as she'd ever seen him. A huge part of her couldn't blame him. She'd lied, broken their agreement, kissed another man, and was taking major risks, despite his pleadings.

Tomorrow night was it—the last time she would help the authorities. It had to be. The wiretaps couldn't go on indefinitely. Jack's warnings weren't going unheeded. She understood the danger, but she had to give this one last shot. Saturday night was for Abby—her final attempt to bring her sister home. She couldn't turn her back when they were so close; she wouldn't be able to live with herself if she did.

She hated that she had to choose. It didn't seem fair that she had to pick between two of the people she loved most in the world. But since when had life been fair? She wanted it all—her sister safe and thriving, the family she'd stopped believing in so many years before, the man she loved desperately—but to have one she lost the others.

It was time to take a step back and reevaluate the direction she was taking—no more job-hunting, no more conversations with the realtor in Hagerstown about putting the house on the market, no more dreaming of a future with Jack—not when they kept ripping each other apart. She and Jack had their daughter to think of. Having parents who got along was more vital than having parents who lived under the same roof. They could give Livy a wonderful, loving childhood from two homes, even though one would be better. Perhaps she and Jack simply weren't meant to be together. Maybe the past was meant to stay the past...but she wanted a future with Jack no matter how she tried to dismiss her dreams. She wanted what they should've had all along.

In utter defeat, she lay back on her pillow, breathing in the scent of Jack, clinging to his t-shirt she still wore, and reached for her necklace no longer there. Sighing, she dropped her hand, snuggled up next to her baby girl, and held on to the only part of her life that made sense anymore.

CHAPTER 21

J ACKSON SAT ON THE BLANKET, legs crossed, leaning his weight against his hands, while Alex gave Olivia another push on the swing. Despite the clouds hanging low in the sky, he wore his sunglasses. The headache squeezing his skull was killer.

"Look at me, Daddy. I'm flying."

He smiled. "I can see. Hold on tight."

"I am." Livy beamed at him and went back to making her zooming noises.

Jackson looked to Alex, slim and pretty in her thigh-length shorts and pale blue t-shirt. She appeared young and carefree like the other mothers playing with their children, but the dark circles under her eyes and rigid stance told a different story.

"Mommy, I'm a plane."

Alex's smile didn't reach her eyes. "Where are you flying to today, Lovely Livy?"

"To Daddy's house far, far away. I want to play with Kylee and Mutt. I miss my puppy."

Alex glanced in his direction, then looked down. They'd barely spoken throughout the morning. She had skipped out on their daily routine of eating breakfast as a family. By the time he finished his seven AM meeting with Ethan and Tucker and raced to the kitchen to join them, Olivia had already been fed and was in the living room listening to Alex read a story.

It was probably for the best. There was already so much tension between them, and after his conversation with Terron and Cannon, it would've been worse. The bastards were being tight-lipped with their plans for the party, only sharing that 'Ms. Harris's safety needs were being seen to.' When Jackson had pushed for more, he and Tucker had been informed they would be filled in later. That wasn't good enough.

Jackson stifled a yawn and resisted the urge to lay back and catch a nap. He'd stayed up all night studying the Hartwell estate, attempting to memorize every possible route the traffickers might use to bring girls in and out of the house. He had no doubt there would be live entertainment, and he intended to plant himself at the most probable location they would utilize to whisk Alex away—for certainly that was the intention.

He pulled his phone from its holder and punched Tucker's number in, frustrated that they were eight hours from show time and still in the dark. Hopefully, Tucker's DC informant would have something useful. For two thousand bucks he'd better. If the authorities weren't willing to play nice, they'd go around them.

The phone was on its second ring when the black Escalade with blacked out windows turned in the park entrance. Jackson shoved his cell in his pocket and rushed to his feet when the vehicle slowed as it approached the bend in the long drive close to the swings. On high alert, Jackson walked closer to Alex and Livy, waiting for the SUV to pull into a parking spot and for a mother or father to take their kids from the backseat, but the vehicle continued along at a crawl with its windows up, making it impossible to identify who was inside.

Jackson hurried to the bright blue swing and brought it to a stop. "We need to go." He scooped Olivia up despite her protests.

"Jack, what are you doing?"

"Let's go." He wrapped his arm around Alex's waist and tightened his grip on Olivia as she pushed at his chest, wild with tears.

"What is it?" Alex looked around.

He continued to study the Escalade, memorizing the plate number as it circled the loop and started toward the exit. "It's time to get home."

Her eyes darted about. "Did they find me?"

"I don't know. I can't be sure, so we're leaving."

She nodded as her hand came up to clutch at the hip of his jeans.

"I want to fly in my plane, Daddy," Livy screamed and kicked. "I want to play with Kylee."

"Later, Liv. We have to leave." He waited for the SUV to turn onto the main road before he walked them the rest of the way to the car. "Go ahead and get in."

"I'll help with Livy. She's hard to manage when she's out of sorts."

"I've got it," his voice sharpened, and he winced. "Sorry. Get in. I want to get out of here."

Alex nodded again and said nothing as she opened her door and took her seat.

"No, Daddy, no!" Olivia fought and squirmed as he struggled to secure the belt around her booster seat. " I want to *play*." She bowed her chest out so he couldn't lock the latch.

"Olivia, that's enough."

His terse tone made his little girl freeze. He sent the belt home when Olivia sat back, her lip trembling on a fresh wave of tears. Goddamn, her sad eyes were breaking his heart. This was the first time he'd had to pull the 'authoritative dad' card. He would have to make it up to her when he was certain they were safe. Closing her door, he studied the area again.

The coast was clear.

Jackson got in on his side and started the car. They drove through the parking lot while Livy sucked in trembling breaths. He scanned the main road, keeping an eye out for the vehicle, and turned in the opposite direction of his parents' residence.

"Why are we going this way?"

"I want to be sure no one's following us before I head home. The last thing I want to do is lead them straight to the house." He checked the rearview mirror, the side mirrors, forever watching. The Escalade was nowhere in sight.

"I'm sorry, Jack. I just needed one more night," Alex said quietly.

He raised his brow in her direction.

"Tonight's it. I mean it. I want Livy safe. I want everyone safe." Her voice trembled, and a tear trailed down her cheek. "I don't know what else to do. She's my sister," she choked out and turned to the window.

Jackson glanced from Alex's hands clenched tight in her lap to Olivia's red-rimmed eyes staring at him form the backseat. The two people he adored most were in tears. Sighing, he took a back road to his parent's neighborhood, turning down several streets to make sure he was tail-free before finally they arrived home. He pressed the button on the remote, opening the garage, and pulled in to the empty spot. As soon as the car came to a stop, Alex got out and hurried to Olivia. Before Jackson could close the garage door and circle around, Alex had their daughter clutched in her arms and was heading for the kitchen entrance.

"Wait."

Alex stepped inside and closed the door behind her.

"Fucking-*A*." Leaning against the hood of the rental, Jackson scrubbed his hands over his face. "Now what?" He'd never been in this situation before. He wasn't in the habit of upsetting little girls and making women cry. Hell, he usually made people laugh, and that was the way he preferred it. Weary to the bone, he pulled his phone from his pocket, went into the kitchen, and watched out the window, waiting for an Escalade to drive by. He dialed Tucker again.

"Campbell."

"It's Matthews."

"I have a couple of stops to make, and I'll be on my way back."

"Are you sure you weren't followed last night?"

"As sure as I can be. Why?"

"I took Olivia and Alex to the park. An Escalade pulled in about half an hour after we got there—black body with blacked out windows. It was impossible to tell who was driving. The vehicle never stopped—just cased and kept going. I got a plate number. I'll have Ethan run it and see what he comes up with."

"Let me know what you get."

"I will." He rubbed his throbbing temple. "Tonight's it."

The line stayed silent.

He sighed. "Alex said she's done after tonight. I think she means it. This little incident scared the shit out of her. We're going back to LA tomorrow."

"Terron and Canon will be pissed. Alex is their new way in."

"Fuck 'em. Tonight's all they get. Even that's too much as far as I'm concerned." He opened the cabinet and found the bottle of Tylenol his mother kept on hand. He shook two capsules into his palm and swallowed them dry. "Did your informant have anything useful?" The pills stuck in his throat. He coughed and snapped on the tap, gulping down water.

"Could be. There's a house about five miles from Hartwell's. It's smaller, a bit rundown for the area.

There's been some speculation that it's a stash house. The cops ran a raid on the residence a couple years back after neighbors complained about the sketchy characters coming and going, but they didn't find anything. I'll do a drive by and get my own impressions. We'll map it out when I get back."

"Sounds good." His phone beeped, alerting him to another call. "I've got another call coming in."

"I'll be back in a couple hours."

"See you then." Jackson clicked to the waiting call. "Matthews."

"Mr. Matthews, it's Agent Terron."

"What's the plan for tonight?"

"We're still hammering out all of the logistics, but—"

"Not good enough. You give me something right now, or Alex will be a no show."

"Ms. Harris has agreed to—"

"Don't push me on this, Terron. If you want Alex, you'll give me something her security team can work with. I want to know how you're going to monitor her. There's no way you're sending her in with a wire strapped to her chest." Jackson climbed the stairs and walked into his father's office.

"We have our boys in the lab playing with a couple pieces of jewelry. She'll be wired and wearing a GPS. Ms. Harris won't be taking a step we don't know about."

As he listened, Jackson opened his laptop and shot Ethan an e-mail with the Escalade's license number. "And what's the procedure if the shit hits the fan?"

"We'll give her a phrase."

"So, you're telling me you're going to raid the place if things start to go bad for Alex?" He leaned back in the chair. "Won't you be blowing your whole case?"

"We're working on a tiered plan based on the level of threat to Ms. Harris. If she wants out, we'll get her out."

359

"And where do Tucker and I fall into the mix?"

"You don't."

He shot up straight. "Like hell we don't. We've signed paperwork that makes us legally and ethically responsible for our client's well-being."

"And my authority trumps your legal contracts, Mr. Matthews. This is a federal investigation. It's obvious you're personally involved in this case. I won't have you screwing this sting up."

He pulled the phone away, hardly able to believe what he was hearing, then set it against his ear again. "Are you *serious*? You wouldn't even *have* a case without the man hours Ethan Cooke Security has put into it."

"Nevertheless, we won't have you distracting Ms. Harris or using your emotional pull to sway her in any certain direction."

"You mean like convincing her to scrap the whole thing for her safety."

"Mr. Matthews," Terron warned.

"So, I'll back off." Like hell he would. "Tucker's in or Alex is out."

"That's not your decision."

"I just made it my decision. I want something faxed over in writing in the next five minutes that says Tucker Campbell is in on this operation, or I can promise you Alex and our daughter will be on the next flight back to LA. I better hear my fax line beep, or we're done." He hung up and faced the window. "*Damn* it." He should've known something was up. Canon and Terron had been their new best friends when he and Tucker gave them several leads to follow—funny how things changed.

"'Emotional pull to sway her in any certain direction,'" he muttered with a clenched jaw. "What the hell?" So, he was out. Tucker was in, of that he had no doubt. The authorities weren't about to blow their chance at taking down the Big Kahuna.

Jackson smiled when the fax line alerted him to an incoming transmission. He picked up the paper and scanned the documentation. His smile faded and he shook his head as he read one of the contingencies. *Mr. Jackson Matthews is to be at least 1,000 feet from the perimeter of the surveillance activity at all times.* "You fucker," he muttered.

He reread the same line several times, liking the idea more and more. He would be free to do a little surveillance of his own. As long as he and Tucker wore their earpieces, he would be kept fully apprised of Alex's situation. "Didn't mention anything about that. Nice try, bastard."

Jackson set the sheet on the desk and spotted Livy's stuffed frog in the corner of the couch. He sighed, knowing his next step was to make things right with his daughter—and hopefully Alex, too. He walked down the hall and knocked on their door. No one invited him in despite the murmurs he heard on the other side. He twisted the knob and peeked in. Alex and Livy sat on the bed, snuggled together with a book, both with blotchy cheeks and watery eyes as they looked up at him. He swallowed, suddenly nervous. "Can I come in?"

"Daddy made me cry," Livy said as her lip wobbled.

"Liv." He walked in and shut the door, unsure of what to do. "I'm sorry I made you cry. I didn't mean to."

"You made me so sad, Daddy." She wiped at her eyes.

He sat on the edge of the bed. "I hate that I made you cry, Liv. I never want to make you cry. He held out his hands and relaxed a fraction when she crawled from her mother's lap into his. "I love you."

She sniffed. "I'm a bad girl."

He kissed the top of her head and hugged her tight. "You're not a bad girl, but I needed you to listen to me

361

and let me buckle you in."

"I wanted to fly to Kylee and play." She burrowed her head against his chest.

"Liv." He looked to Alex for help, but she only stared at him. On his own, he eased Olivia away and dried her tears. "We'll go to the park again, but we had to go home. You can fly to Kylee's house another time."

"Okay." She nodded. "Do you want to read princesses with me?"

He blinked at her sudden change of mood. "Huh?"

"You can read princesses with me—the pink book."

"Okay. Sure." He crawled toward the head of the bed, realizing he'd just survived his first serious parenting situation. As he settled against the pillows and stared into Alex's miserable eyes, he knew it wouldn't be so easy to fix things with Olivia's mother. "We need to talk, Alex."

"Later."

"Here, Daddy." Olivia took the book from Alex's lap. "Read me the story."

Jackson lifted Livy up and plopped her in his lap, making her giggle. "I love you, Liv, so much."

"I love you too, Daddy. So much." She planted a sloppy kiss on his jaw.

He snuggled her closer and opened the book. "So, where are we?"

"This page."

Jackson picked up where Alex had left off.

Twenty minutes later Jack still sat against the pillows, watching Olivia prepare for the ball as the princesses had done on the final page of the story. Decked out in her favorite dress up gown, white gloves, and tiara, Livy ran the bright pink brush through the blond hair of her doll. "We're almost ready," she announced.

"You look beautiful." Alex gave Livy a smile, but it faded as she met his gaze. "I would like you to book our flights for LA. We can leave first thing tomorrow if that works for you and Tucker."

He nodded, relieved that she truly seemed ready to go. "Okay."

She traced her finger around the bold purple polka dots on Livy's blanket with small jerky movements. "I meant what I said. This is the last time. I know we can't stay here any longer."

He strained to hear her quiet voice over Livy's happy chatter. "I think it's a good idea, at least for a little while."

Her finger moved more frantically along the soft fleece as a tear rolled down her cheek.

"Alex—" He brought his hand to her arm, wanting to give comfort, but dropped it, unsure if she would accept his touch. He hated this—the uncertainty of where they stood.

She rushed from the bed as another tear fell, and her breathing shuddered out. "I should—I should get some laundry done and start packing things up." She turned away and went to the closet, grabbing the small basket of dirty clothes. She slid the pocket door shut and stood motionless while her hand gripped the oak handle.

He walked to her, recognizing her attempt to shore herself up and deal with her pain on her own—classic Alex. Hesitating, taking a chance, he rested his hands on her shoulders, refusing to back away when she stiffened. "Talk to me."

"I'm fine." Her breath heaved out in a helpless rush as she bent for the basket. "Really. I'm just fine."

He traced his thumbs in gentle circles along her rigid shoulders. "No you're not."

"I—I'm abandoning my sister." She pressed her hands to her face.

"You're not." Damn this entire situation. "You're not, Alex."

"Then why do I feel like I am?" She turned to him, her devastated blue eyes hopeless and brimming with more unshed tears.

Enough was enough. She could be angry with him later. "Come here." He pulled her against him and wrapped her up tight in a hug. Her fingers clutched at the waist of his t-shirt, and it no longer mattered that they were both walking on eggshells. She needed him. He pressed a kiss to her forehead. "We're not giving up on Abby." He eased her back until they looked at each other. "We're just taking a step back to make sure you and Olivia are safe."

"She might not come home." She pressed her face to his chest. "We may never find her. I'm trying to deal with that."

He could only imagine the depths of her despair. How could he make this okay when she was exactly right? Abby hadn't been seen since the night at the strip club. There was no telling where the ring had shipped her. "We'll never stop looking. I promise." He tilted her chin up and met her gaze. "I promise, Alex. We will never stop looking." He emphasized the last three words.

Her lower lip trembled, and she nodded.

He curled a lock of her soft hair around his finger. "We're not giving up."

"But we'll be so far away."

For all they knew, Abby was lost somewhere in the Orient or Europe or a million other places he couldn't even begin to imagine, but he kept that to himself. "Technology's pretty damn amazing, especially the stuff Ethan has on hand. It'll be like we're still here, but we can breathe a little easier knowing you and Liv aren't targets."

"I never meant to put our daughter in danger. I never, ever meant to do that, Jack. Ever."

"Of course you didn't, but I've certainly implied differently. I'm sorry." He wiped a tear from her cheek. "You're a great mom, Alex. There's no one else I want as the mother of my children."

She clutched at his fingers, which were still lingering at her jaw. Doubt clouded her eyes.

"Look what you've done all on your own. Look at that bright, beautiful little girl over there playing with her dolls. You did that."

"I don't know what I would do if anything happened to her."

He pulled her close again. "Nothing's going to happen to her. We're leaving first thing tomorrow."

"But what about the black truck?"

His cellphone vibrated against his hip, alerting him to a text. He wanted to ignore it, but there was too much going on to carelessly disregard messages. "Hold that thought." He pulled the phone free and read Ethan's note. *Escalade registered to a Christian and Chloe Ridgeway. No criminal background. Christian is an investment banker and Chloe a stay-at-home mom. Not seeing a connection here.*

"What is it? What does it say?" Alex leaned in.

Jackson read the message again. "Hold on," he said to Alex as he typed back. *Are you sure?*

The phone vibrated in his hand. *Ran it three times. Think you're good.*

Well thank God, but it still left him uneasy. Why was the Escalade moving so slowly through the parking lot?

"What's going on?"

He shoved the phone back in its holder. "Ethan

ran the license number from the vehicle at the park. Apparently it was just a really big coincidence. The owners have no criminal record and appear to be upstanding citizens."

She frowned. "Are you sure? Is Ethan sure?"

"He ran the plate and their records three times." He shrugged. "If Ethan's not concerned, I guess I won't be either."

"What about tonight?"

"What about it?"

"What about Livy and your parents?"

"Dougie's coming to stay again. Tucker's going to let Dougie and his wife use his family's vacation home in Utah for a week as thanks."

She pulled away from his arm still wrapped around her waist. "I just figured you would stay home."

"Doug can handle stuff here. I wouldn't leave my daughter and parents in his hands if I didn't think so."

"It's not that. I trust your judgment completely. You don't—you don't approve of what I'm doing."

"I'm worried the risks won't be worth the end result." He took a step back, concerned that they were about to head down the ugly path this same conversation had taken them down last night.

"I have to believe something good is going to come from this."

"I hope it does." He sighed as unease started to creep up his shoulders again.

She reached for her necklace and dropped her hand immediately, but not before she darted a glance at him. Despite their civil conversation of the last few minutes, her gesture brought the major obstacles of their relationship back to the forefront.

"I should get this laundry sorted and in the wash." She yanked up the basket, all nerves again, and headed for the door. "Go ahead and grab your stuff, and I'll wash it too."

"We need to talk about last night."

She stopped. "Not now."

"Why wait?" He wanted the air clear and to be on the right track again.

She turned to face him. "Because this is complicated. Because I don't know where we're going."

"The way we should've gone all along."

"I'm not so sure anymore. I have no idea what's left between us. What if—what if we're trying to relive the past?"

Shocked, speechless, he could only stare. They'd had a hell of an argument last night, but he'd chalked it up to a major difference of opinion and raw emotion; never did he doubt their relationship the way she did right now. "I don't—I don't even know what to say. We've had some problems over the past few days..." Completely deflated, he shoved his hand through his hair and sat on the edge of the bed. "I love the past we had. I regret walking away, but I'm not trapped in some time warp trying to recreate our glory days. I thought we were building a future. We have Olivia. I love you right now for who you are right this minute."

"I love you too, Jack. More than you'll ever know, but I'm not so sure that's enough. I just don't know anymore—about anything."

A kick to the balls had never hurt this bad. "I am. I'm sorry you're not." He stood and glanced at his daughter still playing with her dolls, then at the woman he didn't want to live without. His future was slipping through his fingers, but the guarded look in Alex's eyes told him he would only push them further backward if he didn't give her space. "I'm going to go make some phone calls." Shaken to the core, he opened the door and stepped into the hall.

"I don't want to hurt you, Jack."

But she had. She'd crushed him. "I'll see you when it's time to go." He walked downstairs without looking back.

The treadmill belt whipped around so fast Jackson had to sprint. Sweat flew from his arm as he punched the button and kicked the machine up another notch. He'd been hurtling his way to nowhere for several minutes, but it wasn't fast enough to outdistance the pain. Even though Alex had tossed his necklace aside last night, nothing could have prepared him for her major step back—all the way back.

They'd fought—big time. They'd hurt each other even more, but that didn't mean their relationship had to be over. Despite the odds, he and Alex had found each other again. They couldn't just walk away. Did she really think he was living in the past? How could she not *feel* how much he loved her?

He'd let himself believe they had moved beyond the biggest mistake he'd ever made. He'd fully expected to bring Alex and Olivia to California and move on with a marriage and more babies. If it was possible for a man to have a biological clock, he did, and it was ticking loudly. He wanted to fill Alex with another child and watch him or her grow, to be a part of everything from the beginning. But it was time to start preparing himself for a different ending.

What would happen now? Was Alex going to get her own place in LA? Would he have to schedule appointments to visits his daughter? How would he live without waking up to Olivia's voice every morning, or her smiles and hugs? He punched the motor up to the maximum as the thought tore at his heart. How could he not be there for every moment of Olivia's life? Alex and Olivia *were* his life. After several panting breaths in the silent room, he knew he couldn't be without his little girl. It would be like abandoning her all over again.

Completely spent, he hit the power button and stepped off the black tread. He paced the length of the room with his arms bent and his hands behind his head, sucking in gulp after gulp of air. Beads of perspiration dribbled down his face in torrents and fell from his chin.

Tucker stopped in the doorway of the small gym. "Jesus Christ, man, you're going to sweat yourself to death."

Jackson settled his hands at his naked waist as his pulse began to steady. "Just blowing off some steam."

"Come blow off some steam in the office. I want you to show you something. I got a decent look at the house our informant thought we would find interesting."

"Give me a second." He picked up the liter of Gatorade and took several small sips; he'd overdone his workout. "Let me shower off."

"I'm going to make a sandwich." Tucker turned to leave.

"I think Alex and I are finished." He had to say it out loud so he could start to believe it.

Tucker stopped and faced Jackson.

"Alex isn't sure where things are going between us. I thought she was coming home with me for good, but that may not be happening after all."

"I thought you two were okay."

"We were until this week. We had a hell of an argument last night. We both said things... What if she decides to come back to Maryland after all of this blows over? I can't leave Olivia. I'll have to quit my job and

369

move out here. I don't see any other way."

"This is coming out of nowhere, man. Think on it for a while. See where the cards fall in a few days. You're too damn good at what you do to throw your career away."

He laughed without humor. "I'm not doing a very good job right now. I've been tossed from tonight's operation."

"You're too involved."

He nodded. "Yeah, I am."

"Let's get through the sting and get everybody back to LA."

He sighed and stared out the window. The emptiness that had consumed him for four years was back with a vengeance. "I thought we were going to make it work this time."

"There's nothing saying you can't. Stress isn't good for any relationship, and it doesn't get any more stressful than this."

He ran a hand through his sweat-soaked hair, desperately hoping Tucker was right. "I guess."

The alarm beeped on Tucker's watch.

"How much time do we have?"

"Couple hours."

It was time to bury the ache of disillusionment for a while and deal with tonight. "Give me ten." He passed Tucker on his way to the stairs.

"Oh, hey."

Jackson stopped on the third step and turned.

"The Escalade was a false alarm. I spotted the vehicle at the bank on my way back through town. I stopped to check it out. The owner, a young woman with a toddler in a stroller and baby strapped to her front, was stapling lost dog flyers to telephone poles. I asked her if she'd been through the park earlier today. She said she had—several times."

"Yeah. Ethan ran the plate. Guess I got a

little paranoid."

Tucker shrugged. "Can never be too careful. Would've done the same thing myself."

"But now we know for sure we have one less thing to worry about." He relaxed a fraction knowing everything would be all right here tonight. "Meet you in the office. We'll look at some maps and you can fill me in on whatever you got today." It felt good to have something to keep him busy. Studying details and formulating strategies were great methods of distraction. He didn't want to think about the fact that he was on the verge of losing it all.

CHAPTER 22

J ACKSON SLOWED AGAIN IN THE stop-and-go traffic heading toward the city on Fifty West. Weekend rush hour was madness as usual; the accident up ahead and the setting sun blinding him despite his sunglasses didn't help. If they made it to the hotel on time, he would be shocked. He leaned back more comfortably in his seat and prepared himself for a very long ride in the tension-choked car.

Tucker's phone rang in the heavy silence. "Campbell."

Jackson tapped his breaks when the pickup in the left hand lane squeezed in front of him and cut him off. "Jackass," he muttered.

"Sounds like we have a problem then."

Jackson flicked Tucker a glance as Tucker looked at him. The muscles in his neck and back instantly tensed, and he gripped the wheel tighter. This wasn't going to be good. If Tucker said there was a problem, it was usually bad.

"No GPS means no Alexa."

"Wait a minute—what?" Alex moved forward in her seat. Her eyes met Jackson's in the rearview mirror, but he quickly returned his attention to the road. They'd barely spoken—their new pattern—since they hugged and kissed Olivia goodbye. Glancing back again, he studied her stunning face done up for the night ahead. He hated the damn wig she wore. The layers of soft black beneath the fake blond were so much better.

"Make something happen or we're turning around."

Tucker ended the call.

"What's up?" Jackson shifted over a lane as a stream of traffic merged in from the right.

"The GPS device doesn't want to cooperate tonight. The lab boys had wired up a pretty little piece of jewelry for Alexa to wear, but it's a no-go."

"Then so are we."

"Terron and Canon are working on plan B."

"They better work fast." Dread settled in his stomach like a lead ball. They weren't even there yet, and things were already going wrong.

"I have to go tonight," Alex piped up.

Tucker turned in his seat. "You aren't going in unless we know where you are at all times. We're already at a huge disadvantage being stuck on the outside. A GPS is the only way to keep you even remotely safe."

Jackson kept his mouth shut. He would let Tucker be the bad guy for a change.

"But my sister."

"You're safety comes first. This is a blind operation, and you're untrained. No GPS equals no sting." Tucker faced forward as if everything was settled. After a moment, his cell rang. "Campbell."

Alex scooted up as far as her seatbelt would allow and rested her arms on the front seats. Her vanilla and wildflower scent instantly invaded Jackson's senses, making him clench his jaw.

"That might work. I'll have Alexa call him. We'll let you know how we plan to proceed after she talks to him. I'll get back to you."

"What did he say?" Jackson and Alex said at the same time. Their eyes met in the mirror, but once again he quickly turned back to the traffic, trying to ignore her frown and pouty lips.

"The GPS is definitely out. They're thinking we could

send Officer Detrick in with Alexa."

"No. We can't."

Ignoring Alex's protest, Jackson stared at the endless break lights before him and digested the possible new plan, playing the angles through his mind. Alex would have an officer with her at all times. He nodded. "I like it. I like it a lot."

"I don't see how—"

"We could go with the same cover as last night." Tucker interrupted Alex. "Old friend from high school."

Jackson nodded again. "Perfect. She did say she had plans with a friend." Ideas were rolling now that he could think past the God-awful fear. "How about we play it that the day got away from them? It's getting late... She needs to bring Christina or cancel, because it doesn't make sense to go to Baltimore only to turn around and head back to DC. By the time she would get through the traffic, there wouldn't be much point in coming at all." Jackson held up his fist, and Tucker bumped his knuckles and grinned.

"That's fucking good stuff, man. Now we've got our person on the inside. If they stick together, which friends would do—"

"Do I get a say in this?" Temper heated Alex's voice.

"No," Jackson said, not bothering to take his eyes off the road. She was pissed, there was no doubt about that, but she would have to get over it. This was their opportunity to have a trained set of eyes on her. The odds of Alex coming home with him and Tucker were increasing with the prospects of Officer Detrick tagging along. "You should call Eric and let him know you're bringing a friend."

"This won't work," she huffed. "You don't bring a friend on a *date.*"

"Make the call, Alex. I'll let you decide if I take our

exit in two miles." He looked in the rearview mirror and held her gaze, daring her to call his bluff.

She yanked her phone from her purse, muttering.

"Don't use yours." Tucker handed her a prepaid cellphone.

"This is getting all messed up." She glanced from the card Eric had given her to the cell as she punched in the number. Her eyes narrowed as she put the phone to her ear. "Eric?" she smoothed the temper from her voice. "It's Jenny. Well, actually, I'm not sure I'm going to be able to make it."

Jackson moved over two lanes and took their exit.

"Christina and I are running behind," she went on. "By the time I drive her back to Baltimore and head to DC, it'll be really late. The traffic's... Maybe we should try to get together another time." She clenched her fingers against the phone.

Jackson caught the hints of desperation in her voice. If this ended the sting, she wouldn't forgive him. They would lose their only potential lead to Abby, but Alex would be safe.

"Are you sure?" Her voice brightened. "Okay, awesome. That sounds great. Thanks for understanding. We'll see you." She hung up, sighing as she sagged against her seat.

"So?"

"Eric invited Christina to join me."

Relief and anxiety battled inside Jackson. Christina would be with Alex, but if Eric was willing to put up with Alex's friend on their 'date,' he had little doubt the ring had any intention of letting her leave the party of her own free will. Christina was a beautiful woman. He could only speculate that the ring would be more than happy to take a two-for-one deal. Christina would have to watch her back as closely as Alex would have to watch her own. "See? It all worked out."

Her nostrils flared as she looked away.

⁓◦◦◦⁓

Alexa stared out her window as Jack took a left down another street lined with gorgeous, rambling homes. Zachary Hartwell was doing all right if this was his neighborhood.

"That's the house there." Tucker flicked his thumb at the enormous stone-and-glass structure beyond the beautiful iron security gates.

Alexa caught a glimpse of a spectacular fountain in the center of the circular drive. Water cascaded down several tiers and landed in the huge pool surrounded by lush shrubbery and vibrant purple flowers. Her spirits sank as she scrutinized the extravagant surroundings and the classy men and women stepping from their expensive vehicles along the well-manicured street. Surely the authorities made a mistake. How could a man who owned something so stunning have his hands in an establishment as trashy as Lady Pink? It didn't make sense.

She swallowed the lump in her throat and fought back tears. Jack had been certain strippers would be at this party, but as she watched a pretty older woman in a chic cocktail dress lock arms with her husband and make their way to the entrance, she knew that couldn't be true. Abby wouldn't be here in a barely-there bikini offering lap dances to DC's elite.

She glanced behind her as Jack continued past the residence on his way to the hotel. Minutes ticked by, and large, elegant homes gave way to dense trees as they approached the Northwest Parkway. Moments later, Jack turned into the EcoSuites parking lot and pulled up to their room on the first floor. The little red KIA she'd borrowed last night sat in the next spot over.

Officer Detrick opened the door with a bad-tempered yank and scowled, a hand on her hip. She looked miserable, yet stunning in her deep teal strappy top and short, black skirt. Her light blond hair was curled at the ends and clipped back with a barrette.

"Something's telling me Christina's not thrilled about this assignment." Tucker chuckled as he got out. "You clean up nice, hot stuff."

"Ah, bite me." Christina snarled.

Alexa got out as well and smiled at the woman who definitely didn't look like an on-duty police officer. "Hi. You look great."

"I feel ridiculous." She tugged at her vibrant shirt.

Alexa's smile widened. "I think Agent Terron and my bodyguards here should be more concerned with your safety tonight than mine."

"I don't know about that." Officer Detrick stepped to the pavement and rolled her ankle in her ice-pick heel. Gasping, she gripped the doorframe tight and caught herself before she fell. "I'm ready to get this over with."

"Me too." Alexa's stomach sank as she watched Christina stumble with her next step, and the one after. "Are you going to be able to walk in those?" They would hardly be able to pull this off if Christina sprained her ankle before they made it to the Hartwell Estate.

"You're a fucking mess, Detrick," Detective Canon said as he walked out behind her. "Ms. Harris, would you mind taking a couple minutes to show her how to be a woman."

"Uh, yeah. Come on, let's practice." She hurried over to Christina's side and took her arm. Their safety depended on them getting this right.

"You make it seem so *easy*," Christina complained.

"It is. You'll see." She met Jack's troubled gaze through his amber tinted lenses and turned away. She didn't want to see the doubt in his eyes; she was starting to have too many of her own. "The trick is heel toe, heel toe. Watch." Alexa demonstrated, taking a step on the spike of her pretty white heel and rolling effortlessly to the ball of her foot. "Heel, toe," she repeated with each step. "Now you try."

Christina took her first wobbly step, then the next, then caught herself on another ankle roll, making Alexa wince. Christina looked like Livy when she tried to walk around in her Mommy's work shoes, except somehow her three-year-old had more grace.

"How am I doing?" Christina glanced over her shoulder and managed to stop herself before she fell.

"Good Christ." Jack shook his head. "You're a shame to your gender. What's so hard about heel, toe?"

Alexa opened her mouth to defend Christina, but the officer cut her off. "Why don't you try it?"

"You got it." Jack raised himself on the toes of his sneakers and pulled off a decent 'heel to toe' walk. "Come on, Detrick, try again. But this time, don't forget a little *sashay*." He rolled his eyes and walked on his tiptoes, with plenty of sway in his hips.

Christina and Tucker burst out laughing, and Detective Canon swore under his breath. Alexa wanted to smile as Jack locked arms with the gorgeous female officer and they started heel-toeing it around the blacktop, but she couldn't. Instead, she blinked, utterly stunned, as a swift kick of jealousy washed through her.

"Move that *ass*, girlfriend. Shake it," Jack went on in an excellent diva imitation while he wiggled his butt. He glanced behind Officer Detrick as she added movement to her hips. "Yes. Yes, that's *it*." He and Christina grinned at each other and chuckled. "Now spin on those toes and turn that fine body of yours *around*." He licked his top lip and winked, making her laugh again. "You've got this. You *have*, darling. You definitely do."

Even Detective Canon snickered now.

Alexa reached for her necklace and dropped her hand as she struggled with bone-deep regret. There was the man she fell in love with, with his jokes and laughter and smiles. She *missed* him. She'd had him back not so long ago on their passion-filled day on the boat, but then she remembered the anger of last night and their almost violent sex. The man with the cold blue eyes and harsh words had been a stranger. She glanced up as Christina and Jack stopped. He gave the officer a graceful curtsy, then looked in Alexa's direction, and his grin vanished.

Alexa cleared her throat and made a reach for her necklace again, stopping halfway. She dropped her hand and balled it into a fist at her side. *Damn it! I have to stop doing that.* But the habit was engrained. Jack held her gaze for several seconds, then he walked over to Tucker and turned his back.

Looking down, Alexa sighed. She hated this, the icy indifference, yet she continued to push him away— another habit she couldn't break. With each angry word or frosty stare, she felt herself losing him and pulling further back. They were officially at a crossroads in their relationship. She didn't know how she would live without him this time, so she began the ritual of protecting herself by keeping him at an arm's length.

The phone Tucker had given her started to ring, startling her from her thoughts. She pulled the disposable cell from her purse, glanced at the number she vaguely recognized, and answered. "Hello?" She moved the phone an inch from her ear as electric guitar and a heavy drumbeat blared through the earpiece.

"Jenny, it's Eric," he shouted. "I just wanted to make sure you were still coming."

"Yeah." She put the phone back to her ear. "Yeah, we're on our way."

Detective Canon rushed over and shoved a piece of paper in her face. She scanned the scribbled notes he wrote telling her what to say. "Uh, we're about ten miles out, according to the GPS."

"Great. I'll keep my eye out for you. The band's awesome."

"Sounds like it."

"When you pull up, give your keys to the valet and let him know you're looking for me—if I don't find you first."

"A valet? I didn't..." Alexa closed her eyes as she realized she'd almost slipped and mentioned she didn't see a valet when Jack drove by earlier. She couldn't afford to make such foolish mistakes. Shaken, she walked further away from the group standing close by. "Okay." Was this the first step? The valet would take her keys; perhaps he wouldn't be willing to give them back. She didn't dare look at Jack as her stomach shuddered with anxiety. Turning, she met Christina's calm stare instead and tried to relax. She'd been hesitant to bring Christina along, but as the minutes loomed closer to Agent Terron handing over the keys to the little red KIA, she was glad she would have backup. "I better go. I don't want to get into an accident," she improvised. "I'll see you pretty soon."

"See ya."

She hung up.

"Picked that up loud and clear," Agent Terron hollered from the hotel room. "Sound is excellent. Detrick, you're mic is good. Ms. Harris," the large muscled man stood in the doorway. "Why don't you come in, and we'll get you mic'd up?"

Alexa studied the silver pendant hanging around Christina's neck and nodded before she walked to the small room with the single queen-size bed, still shaky from the adrenaline rush brought on by the brief phone call. She gave Agent Terron a small smile and swiped the curly strands of her wig to the side so he could fasten her new necklace in place. She fingered the pretty oval pendant, the size of the pad of her pinkie, trying to figure out how they fit a microphone beneath the fake pearl.

"Let's test it out."

Alexa nodded and walked to the other side of the room. "Test, test," she whispered.

"Sound is good. We need to get you ladies on the road. Eric will be looking for you."

Alexa pressed her hand to her stomach as her worries rushed back full-throttle. Everything came down to tonight. She would either discover something that would help her find her sister, or she would never see Abby again. Nausea left her lightheaded. "I need to use the restroom," she mumbled on her way to the bathroom.

She closed herself in the confines of the small room and braced her trembling hands on the edges of the sink. Closing her eyes, she took several deep breaths, but she couldn't settle as the gravity of the evening weighed heavy on her shoulders. What if nothing came of this? How could she tell Livy Auntie Ab was never coming home?

Sniffling, Alexa shook her head against her tears. Negative thinking wasn't going to get her through the next few hours. With a final deep breath, Alexa opened her eyes and scrutinized her appearance in the mirror. Despite the sweltering heat, her makeup was holding up. The loose curls in the wig and pale yellow, sleeveless sundress brightened the blue of her eyes. She appeared young, fresh, and innocent in contrast to Christina's chic and sexy outfit. "Time to go," she murmured, twisting the knob and stepping out, her gaze fixed on the charm of her temporary new necklace. She slammed into something solid and gasped as she tried to step back.

Jack's hand snaked out and caught her wrist, steadying her.

She licked her lips and pressed them together. "Sorry."

"Are you all right?"

"Yes, you startled me, that's all."

He stared at her, and she knew that wasn't what he was asking.

There was no use telling him she was fine; he knew her too well. "I'm a little nervous."

He continued to study her as closely as she'd studied herself in the mirror seconds before. "Make sure you stay with Christina." His finger came up to fiddle with the pendant at her neck before he dropped the silver against her skin. "Don't forget your code word. Use it if you need to."

She nodded. "I will." There was so much more she needed to say. "Jack, I'm sorry—"

"I'm working independently tonight," he interrupted. "I'll be wearing my earpiece. Tucker will keep me in the loop. I'll be close by."

"Ms. Harris, it's time to go," Agent Terron called. "You're running late."

"I'll be right there." She hesitantly took Jack's hand and pressed his palm to her cheek, hoping he could feel what he wouldn't allow her to say. "I have to go."

"I know." He skimmed his thumb along her cheek and rubbed his lips gently over hers while he stared into her eyes. "Be careful, Alex." He captured her mouth again, and she closed her eyes, absorbing the sensation of his lips and his familiar flavor. The clutch of fear in her stomach vanished as tingles of heat rushed through her core.

Jack eased her chin higher and changed the angle of the kiss, deepening their tender embrace. Tongue stroked tongue and she pulled him closer, clinging, treasuring his firm muscles pressed to her chest. This was the way it was supposed to be; this was the way it had always been. The moment dragged out before Jack eased away. "Be careful," he whispered again.

"I will." Alexa ached to tell him she loved him but stepped back instead. They'd left things so unsettled. She didn't want to keep hurting him or leave him with a sense of obligation to stay if that wasn't what he truly wanted. They'd damaged each other so much over the last few days—far more than the four years they'd been apart. When they were back in Los Angeles, they would talk about where they stood and what the future held, but she couldn't think about that right now. She had to concentrate on her meeting with Eric and getting home safely to Livy. "I'll see you soon."

He nodded and let her pass but grabbed her hand before she took two steps. Their gazes held before he let her go, and she walked from the room. Agent Terron followed her to the KIA where Christina waited. "Don't forget about your phrases. If you use them, make damn sure it's necessary. Your life better be hanging in the balance. We raid that place and our case is over."

Tucker walked up behind Alexa and opened the driver's-side door. "I think what Terron means to say is try to relax, because agents will be close by in vans and cars scattered around the neighborhood."

Alexa nodded as Jack gave them a wave and got

in the rental they'd been using since they arrived in Maryland. He started the engine, backed up, and left. "Where's he going?"

"He'll be around. Take care of yourself. Stay with Christina."

"I will."

"See what you can accomplish in two hours. Christina will develop a migraine right around then."

"Got it." They would have to see what they could do with the time they'd been given.

"Ready?" Christina asked as she opened the passenger-side door.

"I guess so."

"Let's go."

Alexa blew out a breath as she took her seat, started the car, and rolled down her window.

"They're on their way." Tucker spoke in to thin air, and Alexa frowned before she remembered Jack would be in on the whole thing from a distance. It settled her to know he would be close by. She wasn't sure where, but she had no doubt he would come if she needed him.

CHAPTER 23

J ACKSON WAITED FOR THE KIA to turn on the parkway with the police tail following before he pulled back on the road and trailed behind at a distance. He still hated that Alex was doing this, but there was no going back now. It eased his mind some to know Christina was with her and agents were scattered about the neighborhood in upscale vehicles monitoring the entire situation, but he wouldn't be leaving Alex's safety in their hands alone. He would be as close to the mansion as he could get without pissing off Hartwell's security or the FBI.

Canon and Terron said one thousand feet, but he was on his own—a civilian free to do as he chose. If he broke a few rules along the way, no one had to be the wiser; he just couldn't get caught.

Terron had briefed Tucker after their arrival at EcoSuites. Minutes later, Tucker turned around and filled Jackson in on the Feds' lame-ass plan. He shook his head as he remembered the glaring holes in their strategies that left Alex and Christina vulnerable. But that's where he came in. He and Tucker would be spending the next few hours patching up a mess bound to end in disaster if they left it as it was.

He adjusted his earpiece—his lifeline to Alex via Tucker via Christina. He still didn't like Alex and Christina's one-way communication with the agents, but they couldn't exactly wear an earpiece and not give themselves away. As long as they stayed together and he and Tucker did their part, the night had the potential to end as anticlimactically as yesterday's 'first date.' He tightened his grip on the wheel. No matter how many times he tried to reassure himself that everything would be fine, the shudder in his belly warned him that trouble lay ahead. He wouldn't be able to relax until he, Tucker, and Alex were cruising toward his parents' home.

Jackson came to attention when Alex rolled to a stop at the makeshift valet station. He kept going, peering in his rearview mirror for a last look at Alex in the bright lights of the enormous circular drive. "Take care of her," he muttered as Christina stepped from her side of the car. He clenched his jaw as the car keys changed hands. Alex and Christina were officially on their own.

A half-mile down the road, he spotted a black Audi Q5 with blacked out windows pulled to the curb. Two agents would be manning their post in the front seat, hanging on every word exchanged. Jackson turned right, making his way around the block toward the back of the estate.

"All agents are reporting excellent sound quality," Tucker said into his ear. "The last vehicle just rolled into place half a block from the residence."

"Good. I'm circling around. I'm almost back to where I want to be. Did you double-check with Ethan about the surveillance system along the perimeter?"

"Yeah. He hacked into Hartwell's security company's files. There's no record of a sensory light installation, and they don't use dogs."

"Idiots. Just think, some asshole could climb the wall in the dark, have themselves a seat, and stare in the windows for hours."

"Can't imagine what moron would want to do that. Got your rope?"

Jackson grinned. "Absolutely."

386

"Alexa and Christina just made contact with Eric." Tucker's voice went from joking to professional in an instant. "He's introducing them both to Hartwell and... hold on...son of a bitch, Lorenzo Cruz."

Dread surged through his veins as he thought of Alex standing face-to-face with the man who surely played a part in her sister's disappearance. "How does Alex sound?"

"Like a pro. Maybe she should give up her teaching gig and pick up a roll or two on the big screen. I barely hear her nerves. They work as well in this situation as they did last night."

"Thank God for that." Jackson turned on the parkway and slowed, catching glimpses of the twelve-foot wall through the dense tree cover. Who the hell was in charge of security? The pretty pillars with thick concrete mounts spread every thirty feet were aesthetically pleasing but completely impractical. "If Ethan could see this layout, he'd shit himself."

"Good stuff?"

"Hell no. I'll be up the wall in less than five minutes." He was looking forward to using Hartwell's security errors against him. Dick.

"No lights. No dogs. Some guys have all the luck."

"That's me. One lucky bastard." Jackson continued past the estate, taking advantage of the momentary ebb in traffic and flipped a u-turn. He idled on the shoulder and waited before backing closer to the shrubbery and trees. "Looks like I'm parked about an eighth of a mile from where I'll be."

"I have a decent idea of where you're at."

He reached for the door handle, ready to go, but stopped when he spotted the flashing yellow lights of a security vehicle turning into the doctor's office parking lot a hundred yards behind him. "A rent-a-cop's checking on the complex behind me. I'm going to wait a couple minutes." But he didn't want to. He was ready to be the asshole climbing the wall to stare in the windows for hours. The operation seemed to be going well, but he would feel better when he could verify that for himself. Glancing at his watch, he tapped his fingers against the steering wheel and blew out an impatient breath. What the hell was this guy *doing*? How long did it take to drive around a damn office building? He fidgeted in his seat and stabbed the power button on the radio. Crossfade blared through the speakers, and Jackson quickly turned it down. The gritty guitar and hard drumbeat fit his restless mood perfectly. He looked at his watch again, waiting for the security vehicle to move on. "Goddamn." It had been less than five minutes but it felt like an eternity. "Let's go, buddy." He grabbed his bag and settled it on his shoulder when the yellow lights reflected in his mirrors. "What's going on? How about an update?" he demanded in frustration.

"Nothing new. They're schmoozing in the foyer. The place is loud and jam-packed."

"You sure you're getting good copy?"

"Everything's fine. You do your climb yet?"

"I'm on my way." The security vehicle turned in the opposite direction and Jackson pulled his keys from the ignition, opened his door, and crossed the street. Vehicles whooshed by, their headlights blinding him as he walked along the shoulder waiting for another lull in the Saturday bustle. His moment came a minute later, and he dashed into the thick of trees. So far, so good. The pillar ahead was the one he wanted.

"Alexa and Christina are heading to the main living room. We can't hear much over the music."

"I'm about to secure the rope. I'll have a visual in less than five." He moved quickly, needing to get a glimpse of Alex. If the agents couldn't hear her, he wanted to see her. He made a loop in the heavy rope, lassoed it around the head of the pillar, and pulled leather gloves on his hands, ready to begin. Steaming out breath after breath, he fought against his own weight to reach the ledge. The rough texture of the wall wreaked havoc on his knees and forearms but made the climb easier. If the stone were smooth, he would've had a hell of a time. Thank God for Hartwell's dumbass security.

Jackson reached for the top. "Shit," he hissed as his knuckles connected with the unforgiving grit. He hitched his leg up and over. Finally on the ledge, he swiped at the sweat dripping in his eyes. "Damn." He pressed at his earpiece. "I'm up."

"Sound a little winded."

"Kiss ass," he said without heat. He wiped the blood running down his arms on his jeans and winced at the sting as he stared at the mansion lit up like glory. Every light on the first floor blazed bright through the windows. Where was Alex? He grabbed the binoculars from his bag and honed in on the triple set of French doors where the band played. Echoes of laughter and the bass from the drums blared all the way out here. "Has Christina updated their location?"

"They're still in the living room, as far as we can tell."

Jackson continued his search of the crowded space. "Where are you?" he whispered as he brushed at his forehead, wiping away the drenching perspiration. "Where are you, Alex?" He pressed his earpiece. "I can't establish a visual." Then he found her and he could breathe again—the relief was huge. There she was among the hordes of guests, talking to Renzo as she brought a flute of champagne to her lips but didn't actually sip. Jackson smiled. "That's my girl." He didn't have to worry about wine dulling her wits.

A balding, muscular man dressed in black came up behind Alex, and her smile vanished as Jackson's did. "Where's Christina?"

"She should be with Alexa. They're transmitting the same sounds. They're definitely in the room together."

"I don't see—" He spotted her talking to Hartwell not far from Alex. "There she is."

Christina smiled and edged closer to Alex. Alex took Christina's hand, and they followed Eric and the man in black out of the room. "What's going on?" Jackson clutched the binoculars tight. "What the hell's going on, man? I've lost sight of them."

"Hold up."

He scanned rooms frantically, waiting for Tucker's voice to come back.

"They're off to meet some big shot modeling agent."

"Where? What room? I can't find them."

"Audio transmission's coming through fine. They're together."

Tucker could hear her, but Jackson wanted his visual back. He peered at his watch. An hour and a half until Christina was scheduled to come down with a migraine. He didn't know if he could make it that long.

The noise was deafening and the room hot. Alexa glimpsed at the silver wristwatch her grandmother left her, feeling worried. Thirty minutes had already flown by, and they had nothing to report to the taskforce but a definite professional link between Zachary Hartwell, Lorenzo Cruz, and Eric Stevens. In her heart she knew they were all tied to the ring, but the justice system would require more than Alexa Harris's gut instincts to bring down a sex trafficking organization. She and

Christina needed to make something happen soon, or the night would end a complete bust. Sipping alcoholic beverages and making small talk wasn't getting them anywhere. The window to save Abby was closing with every minute passing. There had to be *something* incriminating among the maze of endless rooms she could bring to the authorities.

Alexa's gaze wandered to the beautiful curved staircase in the elegant entryway as she and Christina were lead to the ballroom. Maybe Mr. Hartwell had an office on the second floor. Surely there was information about his other 'business' in a filing cabinet or drawer. She just had to find it. After she met the modeling agent, she was *going* to find a way up those stairs. How she'd do that was another matter considering the swarms of people everywhere, but she would worry about that when the time came.

"I've never been in a house with 'wings,'" Christina gushed. "First the west wing, now the east. This is pretty cool."

"Definitely a little different than the parties we go to in Baltimore." Alexa played along while Christina gave Agent Terron, Detective Cannon, and Tucker their location. She glanced to the window and the summer dark beyond. Was Jack out there somewhere? He said he would be close by.

"In here." The large, serious man dressed in black gestured with his head.

Alexa looked over her shoulder, catching a second peek at the staircase, dreading that she would waste more time in yet another crowded room when she could be heading up those stairs. She turned back and bumped into someone. "Excuse me."

The buxom blonde in a clinging, black, sleeveless cocktail dress gave her a polite smile and continued

391

past. Alexa took two steps and froze as she remembered that face—Blondie. Whirling, she tried to catch site of the waitress from Lady Pink before she disappeared among the sea of guests. Craning her neck, frantically searching, Alexa spotted her down the long hall as she opened a door and closed it behind her.

Why was Blondie here? She looked so different with her hair done up in a twist and actual *clothes* on. Maybe she knew where Abby was. Alexa took a step, intending to follow and find out, but Christina's cool hand on her shoulder stopped her.

"Are you okay, Jenny?"

Shaken, yet eager to investigate, Alexa struggled to remember her role. "Um, yes. I thought I saw—I thought I saw Ms. LaTrain. You know, my mom's friend I used to cat sit for?"

"Oh, yeah."

"I'm pretty positive that was her. Let's go say hi. I haven't seen her in ages." She clutched Christina's hand and pulled her forward, wanting to tell her whom she just saw.

"Later." Eric stepped in front of them.

"Oh, but we'll lose her if we don't go now." She sent him a pleading look, hoping he would let them go.

"Let's do this first," he winked, smoothing the demand from his voice. "I'll help you find your friend after you meet Mr. Lee. He doesn't like to be kept waiting."

She and Christina exchanged glances. Without another option, Alexa nodded. "I guess we'll find her later."

She smiled at Eric and the big man in black as she and Christina continued behind them. Alexa moved closer to Christina and grabbed two flutes of champagne as a waiter passed, wanting to have something in her hand. "I saw Blondie," she said under her breath as she brought the glass to her lips. "A dancer from Lady Pink." She didn't dare say more.

Christina nodded.

As they continued through the crowd, Alexa scanned faces, looking for more people she might recognize from the strip club, but no luck. She turned her attention back to Eric as they stopped in front of a short, stocky Asian man in his late forties, early fifties.

"Ah, so you've come."

"Yes." Eric smiled. "It's nice to see you again, Mr. Lee." The men exchanged a handshake. "I want to introduce you to Jenny Carstens and her friend Christina Detrick, and of course you know Lenny."

"Lenny," Mr. Lee nodded. "And two very beautiful young women." Mr. Lee took their hands, one at a time, and kissed their knuckles.

"Jenny, Mr. Lee owns and operates Face, one of New York's top modeling agencies."

"Face." Her eyes widened and she pressed a hand to her heart, feigning her excitement. "I know what Face is." The sooner they got this over with, the faster she could get down the hall and find Blondie. "This is so *cool*."

"Have you modeled before, Ms. Carstens?"

"Uh, no, no—but I've always wanted to." She sent Eric a grin, trying hard to ignore her discomfort as Mr. Lee scrutinized her face.

"I've seen you before." He frowned. "Your eyes."

Alexa swallowed against the rush of fear clogging her throat. Was her cover blown? Did Mr. Lee recognize her eyes because they were identical to Abby's? A man in his profession would pay attention to such details. Was he part of the ring too, or did he meet her sister at one of the several fashion shows she'd attended? Alexa wanted to ask Mr. Lee if he'd been to the Fashion Fair here in DC when Abby had stolen the show with her clever designs, but she didn't dare.

"I know you," Mr. Lee insisted. "I recognize your voice." He reached for her hair, touching the curled ends of the wig.

She shook her head and glanced at Christina, knowing they were in trouble. "I'm afraid we've never met, Mr. Lee."

"This is so exciting." Christina stepped closer, bumping his arm further away from the wig. "I mean, I can't believe this. Jenny, do you *know* how many women would die to be in our spot right now?"

Mr. Lee flicked Christina a glance, dismissing her, and returned his attention to Alexa. "Ms. Carstens—"

The lights blinked, and the room fell silent. Then guests' voices rose to a dull roar. The chandelier above flickered again.

"Lenny," Eric said to the hulking man at his side, "go find out what's going on."

"We should head out to the patio before we get stampeded." Christina clutched Alexa's hand.

"Wait." Mr. Lee grabbed Alexa's wrist. Cold sweat dripped down her back. Mr. Lee had to know Abby somehow. She was going to be discovered, and all hell was going to break loose. "You look like—"

The room went black, and Alexa yanked away from Mr. Lee's grip. Christina kept hold of her hand, and they made their way to the glow of city lights well in the distance through the French doors.

"We need to get out of here." Christina tugged, moving faster. They bumped into several guests along the way.

"But the room down the hall—we have to get to the room down the hall."

"No. We're leaving."

394

Alexa pulled away. "I can't, Christina. Not yet."

"It's not an option. It's an order. You're cover's blown. Abort. We're heading out the back doors by the west wall." Christina was no longer speaking to her, but to Detective Canon, Agent Terron, and Tucker listening through their headsets.

This was it—the end of the road. The sting was over, but she couldn't go. Not without talking to Blondie first. Her heart jackhammered. They were almost to the doors. Once she stepped outside, she wouldn't be allowed to step back in, and Abby would be lost forever. *No.* This wasn't how it would end for her sister. Alexa took a deep, trembling breath and yanked her hand from Christina's. She ducked and pushed her way into the crowd, using the dark to her advantage.

"Jenny?"

Alexa moved away from the sound of Christina's voice. She had to get down the hall while she was still invisible to the people who would be searching for her. She just needed to find Blondie, then she would leave. Abby deserved this last-ditch effort. "I'm okay," she said into her necklace as she used her shoulder to not-so-politely rush through the crowds, bumping in to countless people in the shadows. Time was of the essence. "I saw Blondie, the dancer you flirted with the night we went to Lady Pink." Tucker would remember. How could he forget? "I have to find her and ask her about Abby."

Tucker, Detective Canon, and Agent Terron could not respond, but as long as they knew her plan, everything would work out. They were going to be pissed. Jack probably wouldn't talk to her for days, but this was the closest they'd come yet to tracking down her sister. Blondie had answers; she could *feel* it. Alexa's gut had warned her not to leave Abby and Livy that night at the rest stop, but she'd ignored it, listening to Abby's teasing about her overprotective streak. Tonight she would go with her hunch and deal with the consequences later.

Finally she made her way to the pocket doors where the ballroom met the hallway and turned the corner. Alexa stopped short when she caught site of Lenny and another large man, with a grizzled black beard and crew cut holding a flashlight, walking her way. She gasped as they moved closer. "I see the man who stood lording over my sister at Lady Pink when Jack and I were there. He's the same man from the bachelor party picture Detective Canon had me look at to identify Abby."

She faced the wall as they continued in her direction, desperately hoping Lenny would continue past. She slammed her eyes shut and barely breathed when he stopped next to her.

"Ladies and Gentlemen," he shouted. "The neighborhood is having trouble with power this evening. Crews are working on the problem now. The generators will be up and running in a minute or two. Please stay calm."

Calm? Stay calm? Alexa was anything but calm as she clenched her teeth and eased to the left, attempting to skirt by. If she could just move past him... She clutched her trembling fists, fearful her legs would collapse out from under her. The inches of progress she made didn't matter, because Lenny took a step back and bumped her shoulder.

"Sorry," he mumbled.

Nodding, she advanced forward, not daring to look back as she attempted to squeeze by an elderly couple blocking her way. "Excuse me," she muttered, but they didn't budge in the chaos of the dark. *Come on. Come on.* She pressed her lips together and gave the older man a shove. "I'm sorry." She took advantage of the small opening and fled another few inches.

She had to get away. The generators could kick on at any moment. If Lenny spotted her, she wouldn't be going anywhere. He'd watched her every move since she walked through the door. His scrutiny had been easier to deal with when she'd pretended to sip champagne in the light and had a cop standing next to her. Now she was on her own.

"Hey, Len, I'm going to check on a couple things."

Alexa risked a peek over her shoulder to glimpse the vile man with the beard speaking to Lenny.

"I'll go find out what the fuck's taking so long with the lights." They merged into the crowd and vanished as quickly as they'd appeared.

Alexa pressed an unsteady hand to the wall and struggled to stay upright as a rush of relief left her dizzy. "I'm okay. I'm okay," she repeated into her mic, reassuring herself as much as the men listening. With the coast clear, she pressed her body to the cool wall and slid her way around bent elbows and broad shoulders crammed into the tight space. "I'm almost there." She let loose a quiet laugh—part nerves, part relief. "A few more steps, maybe twenty, and I'll be to the door I saw Blondie go in. I need to see who's in there and talk to Blondie, then I'm coming out. I'll be ready to go. One more door. Jack's going to be mad." She knew she was babbling, but she couldn't stop. "I'm sure you are too, but I have to do this. I can get on the plane tomorrow after I do this."

The door Alexa stared at opened, and another muscular man stepped out with flashlights in both hands. He made himself at home leaning against the wall. "No. Damn it. How am I going to get in that room?" Struggling with tears of frustration she closed her eyes, attempting to think over the wrench in her plans. Walking through that doorway wasn't an option any longer, but what about a window? The room had to have a window. "I'm heading outside." She turned and slammed into a broad chest. The force of the blow knocked her back a step. Her hands automatically went to her wig, making certain it stayed in place. "Oh, excuse me."

"Sorry about that."

"It's okay." She gave the college-aged kid a smile and kept moving as quickly as the crowd would allow. "I'm almost to the ballroom. I'll go through the French doors facing the back. I just have to get there without Eric seeing me." Why had so many people stayed inside, standing around in the stifling air? She glanced behind her, paranoid that Renzo, Mr. Lee, or Lenny was just a step away, and did a double-take. "Abby," she whispered. "Oh, my God, I see Abby." Alexa pressed a hand to her trembling lips, hardly able to believe it. "She's here. She's in the hall with Blondie, two other girls, and a bouncer."

Staring, unable to move, Alexa studied her sister. Pretty, vibrant Abby looked so different. The clinging, sleeveless black cocktail dress—identical to Blondie's and the other young women's—accentuated a drastic weight loss—weight her sister's willowy frame couldn't afford to lose. Her once bright eyes were dull, and her lashes caked with too much mascara. Her long, black hair was pulled up in a ponytail, the luster gone from her typically gorgeous locks. What had they done to her sister?

Without thinking, Alexa rushed forward, back from the way she'd just come. She had to get Abby. She had to get her away before they damaged her more. "I'm getting my sister. Be ready to come in guns blazing because I'm not leaving without her." She glanced toward the stairwell cast in shadows. "We'll be waiting for you upstairs if I can get us there." It was better to find a hiding spot and hold tight than risk being stopped by Eric or one of the others.

It was over. Abby's nightmare was finally over. Alexa's eyes locked on her baby sister, determined not to lose her in the crowd. The bouncer said something close to Blondie's ear as the group of five walked closer.

"Just a few more steps." Alexa wiggled her fingers and licked her lips, gearing herself up for the fight of her life. Heart hammering, Alexa pushed forward through the crowd and locked her hand around Abby's thin arm as she passed. Abby's surprised gasp barely registered as Alexa stuck her foot out in front of the bouncer.

"What the fuck?" He stumbled forward, dropping both of his flashlights as he tried to catch himself but fell to the floor, bringing Blondie with him.

Alexa capitalized on the moment of confusion. "Come on, Abby. Let's go." She yanked on Abby, propelling them back into the mob of guests. "Duck. Duck down and walk," she said as she shoved at the people in front of them. "It's hot in here," Alexa said into her mic. "It's really damn hot in here. Come get us."

"Fawn!" the bouncer shouted, and Abby stiffened, her sweat-slicked skin trembling beneath Alexa's fingers.

"It's okay. Keep going, Abby. Keep walking with me. We're almost there." They were getting closer to the stairs.

Where were the agents? Where were Tucker and Jack? "It's *hot* in here. I have her. I have Abby." She glanced to her left. "Oh, God." Lenny and the bearded man were coming their way. Surely the authorities were going to storm through the door at any second and end this hell. But ten seconds turned into twenty, then thirty, and they still hadn't come.

Alexa held her breath and skirted around more people, pulling her sister with her to the stairwell just steps ahead of Lenny. She hovered behind the thick post, struggling to catch her breath as she followed the beam of the flashlight along the walls, watching it move further away. She wiped at her sweaty forehead. The lack of air conditioning and sheer terror left her drenched. "We have to get upstairs."

"I'm afraid," Abby whispered.

"Jack's going to save us. He's coming. So are the police."

Tears streamed down Abby's cheeks. "I can't go."

Alexa clutched her sister's arm, afraid Abby might run back to the danger she was trying to save her from.

"They'll hurt Livy if I get away."

Fear flooded her system and sickened her stomach as she thought of her beautiful little girl. "They won't hurt Livy. Livy's safe with Jack's parents and Doug Masterson, Jack's old roommate. He's a cop, remember? They're taking good care of her." She had to believe that was true. Jack wouldn't have left Livy if he'd thought differently. He'd said so himself. "Livy's safe. Come on, let's get upstairs. We have to hurry."

They crouched and moved quickly up the carpeted steps. Alexa sighed her relief as Abby kept up with her of her own accord, but the moment was short lived as she spotted two beams of light bobbing closer to the stairs. By now, they must have figured out Abby had fled. It would only be a matter of time before men started combing the second floor. "It's hot in here. Swarm the damn house already," she hissed into the necklace. "Tucker, what are you doing?"

Exhausted and running on adrenaline, Alexa grabbed Abby's hand as they hit the threshold of the second story. "Let's go." They ran passed several closed doors, stopped at a random room, and stepped inside. Alexa shut the solid wood behind them and flipped the lock, but then quickly twisted it back. A locked door would give them away. Still clutching her sister's fingers, she leaned against the wall and took several deep breaths. She couldn't think over the pounding of her heart and the outright fear. "We have to get out of here."

"How?"

"I'm not sure yet." Steadier, Alexa moved closer to the large picture window overlooking the summer gardens, greedy for the bright glow of DC's distant lights against the sky. It seemed as if they'd been in the dark for ages. She glanced down at her necklace, ready to give the agents her phrase again, but yanked the pendant up instead. "Oh my God." The fake pearl was missing along with the microphone. How long had she been on her own? Had they realized she wasn't transmitting?

"What's the matter?"

Alexa looked into her sister's defeated, nervous eyes, wanting to shield her from their latest problem. "We have to call nine-one-one and get help. We need to hide until the authorities come get us."

"I don't think I can keep going." Abby's lips trembled. "I'm so tired, Lex."

Alexa wanted nothing more than to comfort the quiet stranger before her, but there wasn't time. "It's going to be okay." She rested a hand on Abby's shoulder, and her sister started to cry. "Oh, Ab." Unable to stand the soft, helpless weeping, Alexa pulled her into a hug for the first time in weeks and held on, struggling to concentrate on the relief of having her sister close, instead of Abby's bony ribcage pressed against hers through the thin fabric of their dresses. She must have lost ten pounds. "We're going to get out of here together. Jack's taking us to LA for a while. He lives there now.

We're going to get you back on your feet. I promise."

"What if I can't?" she choked out. "What if I can't do it? I feel so...broken. I'm so broken, Lex."

"You can." Alexa eased back and took Abby's cheeks in her hands, staring into her eyes, willing her sister to absorb some of her strength. "I *know* you can. You're Abigail Harris, one of the strongest women I've ever met. Livy's been waiting for you. She wants her Auntie Ab back."

Abby gave her a watery smile, and Alexa fought against her own tears; a good cry would have to wait until later. "Let's go home, Ab." She needed Abby to hold on for just a little longer.

"Okay." She shuddered out a sigh and fingered Alexa's wig. "This thing's awful. It's so not you."

Alexa pulled Abby back for another quick hug. Despite her best efforts, a tear escaped as she grinned. The small glimpse of the Abby she knew gave her hope. "It's not my favorite either." She freed herself from her sister's grip and hurried to the phone on the nightstand. She yanked the receiver up and dialed nine-one-one, but there was no dial tone. "Hello? Hello? The line's dead. We have to—"

Footsteps crept down the hall, stopping outside the room next door.

Abby's eyes widened and her breath began to heave as she backed up. Alexa grabbed her hand as her gaze darted around the spacious bedroom. They had to hide, and now, but *where*? She tugged Abby to the closet but stopped by the gargantuan wardrobe instead and yanked the door open. The space was crowded with men's shirts and slacks. "Get in," Alexa whispered.

"What about you?"

"I'll hide in the next spot over."

Abby pushed herself in among the clothes.

Alexa closed the door and opened the next—suit coats, more slacks, and two large containers filled to the brim with socks. "Crap." She wouldn't be able to fit. Frantic now, she hurried for the closet but changed her mind at the last moment and dove for the bed. She shimmied her way under the tight fit of the frame, forced to keep her head turned to one side. Her back pressed against the mattress with each breath, and she fought not to panic in the tight space.

The bedroom door opened a crack, and Alexa nibbled her lip, praying it would close just as quickly.

"Fawn, it's Blondie." Blondie stepped in the room. "Are you in here?"

Alexa balled her hands into fists and willed her sister to stay where she was.

"If you come out now, I'll make sure they don't punish you." Blondie walked by the bed, her black heels sinking into the plush, oatmeal-colored carpet. "Fawn?" She opened the closet door, and Alexa held her breath, desperately hoping it wouldn't occur to the buxom blonde to focus on the wardrobe at her back.

"You find her yet?"

Alexa recognized Renzo's voice. It was harsher without the fake charm he'd oozed throughout the evening.

"No."

"Hartwell's going crazy." Renzo's leather dress shoes stopped inches from Alexa's face. "Make sure you check all the rooms. Don't stop until you find her. She knows too goddamn much. *Fuck.* She's gonna pay for this. She'll be on the first flight to the Orient. We'll see how she likes living over there. Ungrateful bitch." Renzo turned and disappeared from the room.

The light flicked on and Alexa blinked against the sudden brightness.

"Power's back on," Eric said. "You see the blond I

403

invited here tonight or her pain-in-the-ass friend?"

"We got bigger problems," Blondie said as her heels passed Alexa again. "We can't find Fawn. If she gets her skinny ass to the police, we're all going down. I knew Renzo shouldn't have trusted her with the files," Blondie spat.

Alexa stared at the ornately carved base of the wardrobe as she digested the conversations she was hearing. Blondie was part of the ring. All this time she'd thought her a victim too. She remembered the way Renzo grabbed her at Lady Pink.

"I'll help you look. Keep your eyes open for the blond. Her name's Jenny. Hartwell wants her."

"And what about Jenny's friend?"

"We'll have to take care of her. No witnesses. Let's go." The light went off, throwing the room into shadows again.

"Christina," Alexa whispered. Christina was in trouble. She and Abby had to get out of here and alert Detective Canon and Agent Terron right away. Straining her ears, she listened for voices and footsteps while she wiggled her way out from under the bed. She crawled to the edge of the mattress and cautiously peeked around the corner, half expecting Renzo or Eric to be standing there waiting to grab her or Abby. They were both sought after now. She eyed the open door wearily and hurried to the wardrobe. It would only be a matter of time before someone came back. She pulled the heavy wardrobe door open. "Okay, Ab."

Her sister sat huddled among the clothes, her teeth chattering as she trembled. Tears rained down in black streaks of thick mascara. Here was the frail stranger again, defenseless and completely broken. "Come on, Ab. We have to go."

"I can't."

Alexa held out her hand. "Yes, you can. Livy's waiting for you. We're so close. Please come with me."

"They're going to send me away."

"No, they're not." She crouched down, holding her sister's gaze. "I won't let them. You're mine. Mine and Livy's. They don't get to have you." She reached further in, waiting for Abby to take her hand, meaning every word she said. No one was taking her sister from her. "Please, Ab. Please." She glanced behind her, terrified that they would be discovered at any moment.

Abby reached out and clutched Alexa's hand. "Get me out of her, Lex. I think I'm going crazy."

"You're not going crazy. You've been through a lot." She wrapped her arm around her sister's bony shoulders and helped Abby free herself from the slacks.

"Not as much as the others. Not nearly as much. Business kept me from the worst of it."

What did that mean? The files Blondie was talking about? She wished she had time to ask. She yearned to let her sister talk it out, no matter how disturbing her experiences. "Hold on a little longer."

"Did you hear that?" a man's deep voice asked.

"Sure as hell did," Blondie said.

Abby's breathing accelerated. "They're going to get me," she whispered. "They're coming to take me away."

"Shh. Shh, Ab." Alexa pulled them into the bathroom and prayed that whoever was in the hall would keep moving.

"Fawn?" Blondie called, now lacking the kindness she'd tried before. "Fawn? Where the fuck are you, little cunt?" The bedroom door slammed shut, making Abby jump. Alexa sagged against the cool white tiles lining the wall and closed her eyes. How the heck were they going to get out of here?

"They're going to take me." Abby slid to the floor

and tucked her arms around her knees, consumed by a full-fledged panic attack. "She's worse than the men. I tried to protect the girls. I tried, but most of the time I couldn't. She hates me. She'll punish them. She'll hurt them to hurt me."

Alexa risked their safety as she closed the bathroom door and twisted the lock, then she knelt down next to Abby. She stared into her sister's tortured eyes and memories of their mother came flooding back. How many times had mom looked at her with the same hopeless expression before she gave up and took her own life? She couldn't let that happen to Abby. She couldn't bare the thought of walking into a bathroom and finding her sister's pale, lifeless body sitting in a sea of blood.

Abby dropped her face in her hands and wept.

"Abigail." Burying her own fears, Alexa squeezed her sister's arm and used the same scolding tone that always got Livy's immediate attention. "Abigail, look at me right this minute."

Abby's eyes met hers.

"I'm sorry for what you've been through. So sorry," her voice gentled. "You have no idea how much I wish I could make all this go away. I need you to take a few deep breaths and help me. I need you to help me get us out of here. We have to go to the police. They're right outside. Right outside, Abby, waiting for us. Please get up. *Please.*"

Abby sat where she was, still shuddering and crying—a mess. She was so damaged. Somehow Alexa had let herself believe that Abby, her strong, sweet, vibrant Abby, would make it through her ordeal with fewer scars.

"Please help me, Abby," she whispered. *So I can help you.*

"The police are waiting for us?"

"Yes, Jack and his friend Tucker, and an FBI agent, the Baltimore and DC police. We've been searching for you, Ab. Not one day has passed that we didn't spend looking for you."

"Jackson's back."

They didn't have time for this, but she couldn't afford to move forward until Abby was in control of herself. "Yes, Jack's back."

"You love him."

She nodded. "I always have."

"He's still hot."

Blinking her surprise, Alexa grinned. "He's not ugly. Wait 'til you get a look at his friend Tucker." For a moment everything felt normal—just sisterly boy-talk, but it wasn't. Abby was an emotional disaster. They were trapped in a second-story bathroom in the mansion of the man who'd profited from abducting her sister. "Come see Jack. He's been as worried as I have. Come meet Tucker. He's been amazing. Let's go home to Livy."

"Okay. I'm ready." She wiped at her face with her arm, smudging more mascara over her cheeks and temples. "I'm sorry. I know I'm a mess. I had to keep myself together for the girls. I did a pretty good job, but now you're here and I'm..." she shook her head. "You seem to bring out the cuckoo in me, Lex."

These small glimpses of Abby were wrenching. Alexa wanted her sister back.

"How are we going to get out of here?"

Alexa got to her feet and cautiously walked to the edge of the window. The stone porch rooftop overlooking the gardens was six or seven feet below the bathroom. "Out the window."

Abby rushed to her feet. "Out the window?"

"We don't have a choice." Alexa unlocked the window,

ready to begin. Their luck would run out sooner or later. "It's now or never, Ab. We can do this. We have to." She slid the glass up, and warm muggy air rushed in, along with the clatter of a busy kitchen below. They had to be in the east wing. She pushed at the screen and cringed when the frame fell to the porch roof with a clatter. "Ready?"

"Not really."

"Don't be a wimp. I thought you were the adventurous one."

Abby eyed the window hesitantly.

"Freedom's right outside. You can do this."

Abby sighed and took off her shoes. "Okay." She slid a leg over the sill and awkwardly sat half in, half out as she handed her heels to Alexa. Moving swiftly, her foot left the bathroom floor, and she lowered herself down.

"Good," Alexa encouraged in a whisper as Abby dangled from the baseboards and jumped to the roof.

It was her turn. Alexa got up off her knees and tossed Abby's shoes down one at a time. She walked to the bathroom door and cautiously opened it, then hurried back, eager to make her escape. She scrambled over the sill as Abby had and reached for the window's rail as she hung by one arm. Her muscles trembled with her effort to hold her bodyweight while she attempted to close the window behind them. Her fingers made contact with the wood, and she pulled down. The glass slid several inches, but she lost her grip and tumbled, landing on the rough grit of the rooftop in a crouched position. She groaned as rock bit into her palms and a sharp, hot ache radiated through her right ankle. Unable to bear the pain, she immediately and awkwardly fell back on her butt, skinning her elbows in the process. "Damn. Damn. Damn."

"Oh my God, Lex. Lex, are you okay?" Abby crawled

to her.

She struggled for her breath as her ankle tingled and swelled. "I'm fine. I'm okay," she tried to convince herself. "The fall scared me more than anything else." She pulled off the stupid blonde wig dangling half off her head and threw it behind her.

Abby scrutinized Alexa's foot and pressed gently at the tender skin. "Holy crap, Lex. I think it's broken. If not, it's definitely sprained.

"No, it can't be." She eased forward for a closer inspection and closed her eyes as the deeply bruised skin of her foot puffed around the thin strap of her high-heeled sandal. "I can't *believe* this."

"We have to get help." Abby slid her finger over the worst of the swelling, and Alexa sucked in a gasp, fighting the sudden urge to vomit from the excruciating pain.

"Ow. *Please* stop touching."

"Sorry but I have to get your sandal off."

"Let's leave it alone." She tried to move away from her sister's probing fingers, but it felt better to remain perfectly still.

"You'll lose circulation if your foot gets any bigger. I'll be gentle." Abby slid the strap free of the small buckle, and Alexa ground her teeth, trying not to cry out.

"There. That's done. We're almost finished."

"Thank God."

"I just have to take it off." Abby bit her lip as Alexa glared.

"Go ahead and shoot me instead."

"I don't have a gun, but I can slap you if it'll make you feel better."

"Take it off," she snapped, not in the mood to appreciate her sister's smartass sense of humor.

"Okay. Geez." She huffed out and flexed her fingers. "Okay. We need to prop your leg up just a bit. I think it'll hurt less. Can you lift it?"

Alexa leaned back on her elbows and hissed from the bite of rough gravel against raw wounds. She raised her leg and pressed her lips together with a wrenching moan. The lack of support for her ankle was excruciating.

"Close your eyes. I'll be quick and careful." Abby's cool hand braced Alexa's calf as she grabbed the heel of the shoe with the other.

Alexa slammed her eyes shut and grit her teeth as Abby tried to ease the sandal off. "Oh, Lex, it's stuck. I'm going to have to pull harder."

"Just do it," she choked out.

Abby tugged; Alexa whimpered.

"It's off. It's off."

She opened one eye, looked down, and winced. Her foot was easily triple its normal size. "I think—I think it's going to split open."

"I need to get us help." Abby peered over the edge of the small rooftop. "You need a doctor, big time."

"No." She grabbed Abby's wrist. "We stay together."

"Lex, you can't jump down. It's like eight, maybe ten feet to the bottom."

"We stay together. I won't lose you again. If you go, I go too." Alexa struggled to rip the hem of her thigh-length dress. "Help me wrap my ankle first."

"Lex..."Abby's brow rose with her 'give me a break' sneer.

"Some support is better than none. I'll try to land with most of my weight on my good leg." She yanked on the summery yellow cotton again, and the fabric finally gave way. "Help me rip some more."

"Fine, but this is a really dumb idea." Abby yanked, and another few feet pulled free.

"If you have a better idea..." Alexa glanced at her watch. Another thirty minutes before her original two hours was up. Was Christina still searching for her among the crowded rooms? She had to be okay, or the agents would've raided the house.

Abby yanked at her own dress and freed a long piece of black satin. "Between your dress and mine I think this will be enough. Prop it up again. Rest your leg on my lap this time."

Alexa breathed in and expelled a whoosh of air when Abby jostled her ankle. "I didn't think there was anything that hurt as much as childbirth. I was wrong." She wiped at the tears streaming down her cheeks.

"I'm almost finished. I don't want the wrap it too tight or too loose." Abby tucked the ends of tattered yellow and black fabric among the strips she'd circled around the arch of Alexa's foot and ankle. "There."

Alexa studied the makeshift splint and smiled, despite the discomfort. Her foot looked like a bloated bumblebee. "Thank goodness you didn't choose medicine as your profession."

"I think I'll stick with mannequins and sketch pads. Consider this the first and last design from my 'Escape' line."

Alexa lifted her foot an inch off Abby's thigh and winced. The flimsy support of two torn summer dresses would have to do. Sighing, she braced herself for more pain and moved to the edge of the roof. "You ready?"

"I'm ready to get you to a hospital."

Alexa nodded her agreement and scooted forward gingerly. She bumped her injury on the rough surface and tried to ignore the nausea roiling her belly as she stared down at the well-manicured bushes and lush green grass. They were a long way up. It would be a good four to five feet to the ground after they let themselves hang off the side. Then what? She glanced at the pretty stone path lit by candles in decorative glass, leading to the front edge of the house. If they could make it to the shrubs along the security wall, they would be able to sneak out to the street from there. A surveillance vehicle wouldn't be too hard to track down after that. She could do this; she had to. "After we jump, we have to hurry to the bushes."

"Are you sure this is a good idea with your ankle?"

"What choice do we have?" She glanced up at the window still partially open. "If someone notices that, we're in trouble."

Abby nodded. "I'll go first." She moved to the edge of the roof, rolled to her stomach, and wiggled her body until her legs dangled. "The stones on the house stick out a bit. I can rest my feet on them."

Alexa turned on her belly and eased her legs over the side, slamming her eyes shut when gravity pushed more blood to her foot. The throbbing pressure was almost more than she could bear.

"Here I go." Abby let herself hang by her fingertips and counted to three, then let go.

Alexa's heart stopped when she heard the thud of her sister's landing. "Are you okay?"

"Yeah. I'm all right. Come on down. I'll help you."

Alexa pushed herself further over the edge until she hung like her sister had. The rough shingles bit into her fingers and she pressed her lips firm as she released her grip. Gasping, falling, she tried to maneuver her body to land on her good leg. Her foot met ground and she lost her balance. She rolled once, and her wrapped ankle slammed against the stone on the pretty walking path. The shocking pain stole her breath, and she whimpered, fighting her tears, as she clutched the cool grass.

"Lex. Oh, Lex." Abby rushed forward, crawling, and cupped Alexa's sweaty face in her hands.

Alexa struggled to clear the gray haze of

unconsciousness from her vision as Abby stroked loose strands of hair from her damp forehead. She could *not* pass out.

"You're so pale. We have to get away from the path. Someone might see us."

She blinked, relieved when the tiny dancing spots vanished from her vision. "I need—I need a minute."

"We don't have a minute. If someone happens by the window, they'll take us away. Come on, Lex." Abby hooked her arms under Alexa's armpits and dragged her to the shadows.

Alexa groaned as the jerking movements caused her more unspeakable agony.

"I'm sorry. We're almost there." Abby gave her another tug and sagged to the ground out of breath. "Let's rest for a few minutes. It doesn't seem like too many people are on this side of the house."

Alexa nodded and leaned her head on the rough rock of the house. "Most of the party's in the back half of the east and west wings." She closed her eyes, attempting to summon up any remaining dredges of strength. The last few minutes had drained her dry.

"I knew this was a bad idea. You should've stayed on the roof. Why didn't I make you?"

"Because there's no way you could've. I'm not leaving you." She reached for her sister's hand.

Abby grabbed her fingers and held tight. "I'm sorry you had to do this. I'm sorry I didn't escape."

She opened her eyes and looked at her sister. "Ab—"

"I wanted to. It was all I thought about at first."

"We're together and you're safe. That's what matters."

"I tried once." Abby continued on, despite Alexa's reassurances. "I saw an opportunity and went for it. One of the guards went to the bathroom, and I snuck away from the basement they kept us in and ran right out the front door, but they grabbed me and told me they would make you and Livy suffer." Her eyes watered and her lip trembled. "They called you and made me listen. I could hear the fear in your voice when they told you I was going to die." She clutched Alexa's fingers tighter. "They held me down while Eric talked to you and came at me with a syringe full of clear liquid. He told me to say goodbye. Then they shoved the needle in my arm and I didn't wake up 'til the next day."

"Ab, I'm so sorry."

"I didn't try to run again, but I tried to call."

"I remember."

"I wanted to tell you where I was, but I didn't know. They cover our heads when they put us in the vans. Sometimes we're in there for minutes, other times hours. The phone idea was just as bad as trying to run. They realized a phone was missing and started beating one of the girls…"

Alexa rested her head on Abby's shoulder. What could she possibly say to lessen such a trauma?

"After that, I lost hope that I was ever going home. They reminded us daily that we were theirs and escape meant death to our families."

"I left." Alexa blinked away her own tears. "I put Livy and myself on a plane and fled to Los Angeles. I didn't want to—"

"I'm glad you did. I was constantly terrified they would take you and Livy. They're evil. The things they make the girls do… They're so young, and I couldn't stop it."

"It's not your fault."

"No, but it doesn't change what I saw or what I listened to. They made me—they made me keep the books. All the questions Renzo asked about my business background…" She shook her head. "I thought he was interested in me... It was my job to handle the organizations books as well as dole out the girls—ten to twenty times a day." She sniffed. "God. I can barely stand the guilt. There were so many nights I wanted to die, but then I saw you with Jackson at Lady Pink."

"I wanted to take you with us, Abby. You have no idea how much."

"Probably as much as I wanted to go. But I knew I couldn't." She leaned her head against the wall. "I was never more surprised than when I opened the door to that disgusting room and saw Jackson Matthews grinning at me. He looked at me with his kind eyes and told me he would be back...and I started to believe again."

She pulled her sister against her. "I hate that you went through this. I hate it so much."

Abby clung. "I just want it to be over."

"It is. They're waiting for us on the other side of that wall—or down the next block, at least."

"Whenever you're ready, I want to leave and never look back."

"Then let's go."

Abby frowned as she studied Alexa's face. "You're still pale."

"My ankle hurts a bit." 'A bit' was an understatement. Her foot begged her to be still as the swollen skin bulged around the yellow and black wrap. The second fall had injured her further but they couldn't afford to stay here any longer. "I'm okay." She swiped at the sweat beading along her forehead. "I need you to help me up."

"Of course." Abby crouched and wrapped an arm around Alexa's shoulders. "I'll lift on the count of three."

Alexa nodded.

"One...two...three."

Alexa kept her right leg extended and used her left to help propel herself up with Abby's tug. The stabbing throb almost sent her back to the ground.

"Lex, this isn't going to work."

"It's fine," she said, her voice strained. "Let's just go."

Abby hesitated.

"Please, Ab. I can sit down again when we get to the bushes."

"Okay." Abby wrapped her arm tight around Alexa's shoulders.

Alexa leaned in to the support her sister offered and hooked her arm around Abby's waist. They hobbled forward with little grace. Putting weight on her right foot was impossible. They paused as they came to the first large window of the formal dining area.

Abby peeked in the edge of the glass. "There're only a couple people mingling about. If we duck, I think we'll be okay."

"This should be interesting."

"Never a dull moment when the Harris sisters are together."

They both smiled.

"Here goes nothing," Alexa said as they leaned forward and moved slowly with Alexa's awkward hop.

"One more window to go." Slightly out of breath, Alexa pressed a hand to the house and eyed the bushes ahead. She needed to sit down. "I'm ready if you are."

They were faster this time, as Alexa found the rhythm of her one-legged gait. "We're almost there."

They stopped as they came to the edge of the house. There were fewer shadows to hide in as the walking path widened and twisted toward the bright lights of the party a few windows away.

"Take a rest, Lex."

"Let's keep going." Alexa pushed off the side of the house and stumbled with Abby as they crossed the path.

"No, man, I'm outta here."

Abby and Alexa froze when they heard the man's voice heading in their direction.

"Something isn't right. They're going to bust us; I can feel it. The valet drove my car to the side gate."

"Back up," Alexa mouthed, but it was too late. Renzo turned the corner and stopped short of running into them. Shock registered on his face, but then his eyes changed, and a harsh smile crept across his mouth. "I've gotta go." He slid his phone in his pocket. "Well, well, well what do we have here?" He studied Alexa and shook his head. "I *knew* you looked familiar. What happened to your blonde hair, Jenny—or should I say Sister Alexa?" He advanced.

Alexa struggled to stand upright as Abby took two steps in retreat. What were they going to do? She fought to think over the kick of panic. "I've—I've been working with the FBI. They're coming. They're coming for you. The cops have been watching you all night." She expected him to run, but he didn't.

"Good thing I won't be here, and neither will you. Let's go." Renzo grabbed Abby's arm, and she gasped.

"Leave her alone. Help!" Alexa screamed as loud as she could.

Renzo shoved Abby down and yanked Alexa against him, slapping a hand over her mouth, and squeezed. "Shut up," he said between his teeth. "You shut the fuck up." He jerked her closer, and she whimpered as pain shot through her foot. "Try that again and your sister's dead. Fawn, get your ass up and let's *go*."

Abby stood on visibly shaking legs and did as she was told.

Renzo clutched Alexa's arm and yanked her forward. She had no choice but to put weight on the foot that wouldn't hold her. Crying out, she lost her balance and fell.

"I don't have time for stall tactics. Get your ass up." He squeezed and jerked on her arm, sending a hot wave of pain through her shoulder.

"I can't." Tears coursed down her cheeks. "My ankle."

"Fine." He smirked and pulled her by the wrist, dragging her along.

Rocks, twigs, and other sharp items bit into her skin as she tried to gain her balance and get to her knees, but Renzo moved too quickly, and she fell back to her butt.

He stopped at a wrought iron gate hidden among the bushes, lifted a small utility-type box several inches to the side, and pressed a button. A hum filled the area as the latch released.

Alexa tried to gain her feet once more with Abby's help. Her sister's teeth chattered and her hands shook as she eased her up. She stared into Abby's terrified eyes as she clutched her arm around her waist. "It's going to be all right, Abby," she murmured close to her ear.

"No it's not. You're a witness," he pointed at Abby, "and you're a snitch." He rammed a finger into Alexa's tender shoulder. "Nothing good's going to happen to either of you." Renzo chuckled and shoved them out to the sidewalk. Alexa tried to catch her fall with her injured foot and tumbled. Concrete ripped at her already shredded palms and elbows, and her knees screamed. The pain in her ankle had her seeing stars. She whimpered and bit her lip, attempting to fight back her need to weep.

"Lex. Oh, Lex," Abby sobbed as she crouched next to her.

"Quit your fucking blubbering and get in." Renzo yanked Abby up and pushed her toward the car.

Terror coursed through Alexa, quickly followed by adrenaline as Renzo opened the door and shoved her sister. If he took off with Abby this time, she would never find her. Unable to run as she wanted to, Alexa crawled forward and clung to Renzo's pants as she fought her way to standing. "Don't you touch her." She sunk her teeth in his bicep, and he let go of her sister with a string of curses. "Run, Abby! Run away!"

But Abby stood where she was, quaking and crying.

"You bitch." He whirled, swung, and caught Alexa on the chin.

The force of the blow sent her back to the ground, but she got to her knees just as quickly when Renzo opened the car door.

"Get in, Fawn. Now." He pushed her in.

"Abby, fight, damn it!"

Alexa wedged herself in the opening, afraid he would leave her behind. "We can take him."

Renzo let out an amused chuckle. "Oh, I'm shaking. Pansy-ass and gimpy here are going to take me down. He stooped low and tossed Alexa in with a nasty shove, then slammed the door.

"Honk, Abby!" She struggled to open the door, pulling frantically on the handle, but the door held firm. "Honk, Abigail!"

Abby pressed her shaking hand to the steering wheel, and the horn echoed through the street.

"Again."

Renzo hurried around to his side. "Stop." He backhanded Abby and turned the key in the ignition. He pulled away, made a u-turn, and sped down the street.

Alexa's breath heaved out as Abby cried uncontrollably in the cramped seat next to her. They lurched forward when Renzo slammed on his brakes at the four-way stop, then accelerated, burning rubber on the empty parkway. Alexa stared at the trees rushing by, desperately thinking of a way out of this, but there wasn't one. They were trapped.

CHAPTER 24

"KILL THE POWER," TERRON SHOUTED, loud enough for Jackson to hear.

"What's going on? What the hell just happened?" Jackson stared through his binoculars at the dark house.

"An agent—hold on. Christina just called an abort. Lee keeps making reference to Alexa's eyes. He's insisting he knows her. They're getting out. They're moving to the French doors in the west wing."

"Son of a bitch!" Jackson bit off as he reached in his bag for his night-vision goggles with unsteady hands. "I knew something like this was going to happen. I fucking knew it." He peered through the green-hued lenses, waiting for Alex and Christina to step through the open French doors. Several seconds passed as guests stepped into the warm, muggy air; Christina and Alex weren't among them. "I don't see them." He felt around for his leather gloves as he continued to stare ahead. They had one minutes, then he was jumping the wall.

"It's crowded. Give them a—Goddamnit."

Jackson's flexed his fingers on the hard plastic as his stomach sank. "What?" He ground his teeth when Tucker didn't answer. "What the fuck's going on, man?"

"Alexa got away from Christina."

"What do you mean 'Alex got away from Christina?'"

"Wait a minute. Hold on. Alexa's talking. She says she's okay. She's going after Blondie. She wants to ask her about Abby, then she'll leave."

Fear and anger raged through his system as he thought of Alex alone among a house of monsters. "Fuck that. I'm going in."

"Wait, Jackson. Wait. She's fine. Christina's going to find her. She's still talking to us. Her breathing's shallow. She's babbling. She's afraid. She knows her phrase. If she needs to use it, she will. As long as we have audio, we're good."

Jackson glanced at his watch. "Twenty minutes."

"Alexa knows there'll be hell to pay. She's already guessed we're all pissed. She's almost to the room..."

Jackson clenched his jaw as Tucker sighed. "What?"

"A bouncer just came from the door. She's convinced Blondie knows where Abby is. She wants to go outside and get a look through the window."

"She's coming out?"

"Yeah, she's turning around. She should pass Christina. I think she bumped into someone. Yup, she excused herself."

Jackson struggled to uncoil the tension in his shoulders. Christina would catch up with her any second now and drag Alex's ass outside. "What's going on?"

"She's not talking, but we can hear the party. There's some sort of commotion, but it doesn't seem to be affecting Alexa. Christina's still heading her way—rip-roaring, by the way, muttering stuff. I don't think we'll have to rip Alexa a new one; Christina's going to take care of it."

"I'll take a turn anyway. Of all the stupid-ass things to do." Jackson zoomed in, growing impatient, waiting for Alex to appear or for confirmation that Christina had her again.

"Christina doesn't see her yet, but we're good, man."

Jackson glanced at his watch as eighteen minutes turned into nineteen, and still he didn't hear anything from Tucker. "Something's wrong."

"It just got quiet. A man's talking to Christina. I think it's Eric. He wants to know where Jenny is."

"Christina's telling him she's not sure. She's looking for her too. He says they can look together. He's grabbing her arm. He's pulling her into a room."

"That's it. I'm going over." Jackson scrambled to his knees.

"Whoa, whoa, hold up."

Jackson cringed at the alarm in Tucker's voice. "What—"

"Call it! Call it!" Tucker shouted. "They have a needle on her! Christina's in trouble. Call it!"

"Not yet," Cannon hollered back.

"They just stuck her, you prick. They're taking her. Call it, Goddamnit or I'll do it and have your fucking badge."

"All agents go! Go!"

Jackson yanked at the rope and paused when a bloodcurdling scream for help echoed over the chaos in his left ear. He scanned the dark lawn frantically, searching for the source. "Someone's screaming. It sounds like it came from the east side of the estate." His earpiece stayed silent as the commotion of the raid began. Moments later, a horn honked and tires screeched as a car accelerated in his direction. Jackson made a split second decision and hustled down the wall, street side, burning his hands on the thick nylon.

"Someone got away," Jackson shouted as he sprinted toward his car. "He's coming my way." The laser blue Porsche screeched to a stop, then peeled around the corner and took off like a shot down the street. Jackson caught sight of a woman's hand pounding against the glass as the vehicle passed a streetlight and disappeared around the corner. "Renzo made a right on the parkway.

He has a woman with him. Do you copy?"

"I copy. We can't find Christina. All agents have arrived and are searching for her and Alexa."

"I'm following Renzo. I think he's going to the stash house."

⚜

Alexa's palm was numb from her ceaseless pounding on the glass. She kept up her unstoppable rhythm, hoping someone would notice she had been taken against her will, but it was late, and the streets of the wealthy neighborhood were quiet.

Abby sat next to her, still trembling but silent now as she clutched her hands together and stared at the floor. All traces of the vibrant woman she recognized had vanished. Renzo's presence had stolen her sister away and replaced her with the terrified, emotionally fragile stranger that reminded her too much of their mother.

Renzo dialed his cell again as he careened down another street. With each turn he took, the homes lost their charm and square footage. He'd backtracked and taken so many side roads, she no longer knew where they were.

"It's Renzo. Send word to clear all the houses, now. There was a raid at Hartwell's. Lenny got a call off before they took him down. Destroy the paperwork; take care of the computers. The local house is empty. I'm going to deal with any remaining evidence." He jerked the wheel and skidded around another turn. "I'll meet you in Paris tomorrow. I'm bringing some additional product." He glanced at Alexa and smiled.

She turned away, barely suppressing a shudder as she pounded the glass harder with the side of her fist, trying to keep calm over her rising terror. Renzo was taking them overseas. He would book a private charter, and there would be no record of an Abigail or Alexa Harris ever boarding a flight. Jack wouldn't be able to track them down. They would be lost forever, and Livy...

Alexa took a deep shuddering breath and swallowed the lump in her throat as she thought of her little girl. Her poor Livy would wake in a few hours expecting her to be there. Jack had been right. He'd been spot on all along, and she hadn't listened.

Renzo braked hard and turned into a short drive densely lined with trees. He stopped in front of a charming older house in need of numerous repairs. Branches on several of the maples needed to be trimmed back. The home begged for fresh paint, pretty flowers, and updated windows. It had the potential to be beautiful, but no amount of improvements would wash away the horror that went on behind the walls.

Renzo opened his door. "Get out."

"We—"

He grabbed Abby's hair and yanked, cutting Alexa off when her sister yelped.

"Don't talk. Just do what I say." He dragged Abby out his side and pressed a button by his seat. Something clicked, releasing the lock on the passenger door.

Alexa pulled the handle, and her door opened. She scooted to the edge of the soft leather bucket seat and jolted from the shock of pain to her ankle. Closing her eyes against the flood of tears, she lifted her injured foot from the car and used the frame of the vehicle to boost herself up, refusing to acknowledge the need to sink to the cracked pavement and sob in utter defeat. How would she make it to the house a good twenty yards away? Better yet, how was she going to escape? Her foot simply wasn't going to hold her, and she couldn't crawl; her knees and palms were completely shredded.

"Jesus H. Christ. Would you hurry the fuck up? Get in the house."

"I—I can't walk."

"Don't fuck with me, Sister Alexa. I don't have time for your shit."

She braced her weight on the hood and hobbled around, each jostling movement a misery. "If you help me, I'll be able to move faster." She could only hope he would assist her with more compassion than he had back at the mansion.

"Fawn, you're sister's a pain in my ass. Go wait inside."

Abby held Alexa's gaze for a moment, then started toward the house. Where was Abby's *fight*? Where was the feisty woman that didn't take crap from anyone? She wanted to rage at her sister to snap out of it, but her frustrations wouldn't help them.

Renzo huffed out a breath as he wrapped an arm around her waist. "Move it." He yanked her forward, bumping her foot as he dragged her, and she gritted her teeth against the waves of dizziness his quick steps caused. Alexa whimpered, despite her best attempts to stay quiet.

"You think this hurts? Wait 'til you see what I have in store for you when we get to Europe. I know some guys that like it rough—whips, chains, domination. They'll love you."

She wanted to be afraid. The terror in her somewhere, but she couldn't think over each torturous jolt and her need to get back to her daughter.

They made it to the crumbling stairs, and Alexa grabbed for the railing. "I can do it now."

Renzo didn't listen. Instead, he reached his hand under her dress and cupped the thigh of her uninjured leg, raising it up, causing her to be unsteadier with each step he took. Alexa had no choice but to cling to his waist as she struggled to keep her ankle from connecting with the concrete, but her efforts proved useless. Her tender foot hit once, twice, three times. Tears coursed down her face, and she cried out as he stopped at the threshold.

Renzo chuckled. "Very theatrical. We'll have to get you on tape—maybe a little sister-on-sister. You can moan and groan then, too."

Alexa sucked in several ragged breaths, fighting the need to weep, but the unbearable pain was too much.

Abby rushed out the door and pushed at Renzo. "I'll do it. I'll help my sister."

He shoved Abby back in the house, sending her crashing to the solid wood floor. "Don't ruin my fun."

Abby righted herself as quickly as she'd fallen. Her pale, mascara-drenched cheeks grew rosy with temper. "Leave her *alone*."

Alexa cringed as something dangerous flashed in Renzo's eyes. He would hurt Abby if she continued to try to defend her. "I'm okay, Abby. I'm okay."

"No, you're not." She nudged herself between them. "Please, Renzo. Let me help."

"I should punish you. I *will* punish both of you, but it'll have to wait." He rammed Alexa with his shoulder as she balanced against Abby, sending the two sisters careening into the wall. "Bring her upstairs. I'm going to the office. If you two even think about trying anything funny, you're dead." Then he looked to Alexa. "Your daughter is too." He ran up the steps without a second glance.

Alexa looked over her shoulder at the open door and the freedom beyond. She untangled herself from Abby as Renzo hit the last stair and disappeared down the hall. "I want you to go. I want you to run and get help. There's a house across the street. I saw it when we pulled in. Their lights are still on."

"No," Abby hissed. "No, I can't. He'll kill us and Livy." She hooked an arm around Alexa's waist and started toward the stairs.

"He's not going to hurt Livy—he has no idea where she is. But he will hurt *us* if we don't try to get away." Something heavy crashed to the floor above them, and they both jumped. "I'll start up the steps. He'll never know you aren't with me."

"No, Lex." She shook her head vehemently.

"Damn it, Abby," her voice broke in her despair. "I'm never going to see Livy again if we don't get some help. I'd run right now if I could. What about my little girl?"

"What if he *does* see that I left and hurts you? He's a monster." Her fingers bit into Alexa's waist. "He beats the girls all the time."

"I'm willing to risk it. I'd rather die trying to do *something* than live without seeing my baby again." She dashed at her cheeks.

"Okay. I'll go. I'll go." She made it down two steps, but then Renzo walked from the office and chucked a computer over the balcony. The computer's tower broke in several pieces as it crashed to the floor.

"What's taking you two so damn long?"

"Uh, Lex needs a drink of water. Her injuries are making her sick to her stomach."

"Too bad. Get up here now." He stormed away.

They'd missed their opportunity. Alexa sunk to the step and held her face in her hands as tears fell. "My poor Livy."

"Please don't cry, Lex." Abby sat next to her and rubbed her back. "We'll think of something. Get up and come with me. We'll think of something," she repeated.

But what? They were a sorry pair, with her useless

foot and Abby's unwillingness to stand up to Renzo. She tried to pull herself together as hope withered. Crying wasn't going to get her anywhere. "You're so afraid of him. I'm trying so hard to understand. Why won't you fight to save your own life?"

"He's brutal. Renzo and Blondie are worse than everyone else combined." She clenched and unclenched her fists. "He—he raped me."

Alexa clutched her sister's wrist as her heart broke. "Oh, honey."

Abby shook her head. "He's a monster. I had no idea I was going out on dates with pure evil all those weeks ago."

"Of course you didn't. This isn't your fault. You aren't to blame for any of this."

"I know." Abby glanced over her shoulder. "We need to get upstairs before he gets mad."

Alexa studied her sister as they stood and started up the steps again. She wasn't so sure Abby truly believed she wasn't to blame. "This isn't your fault, Abigail," she repeated.

Her sister's lip trembled as her eyes filled. "Then why do I feel like it is?" She wiped at her damp cheek. "I can't stop thinking about the girls—young teenage girls, Lex. They had it so much worse than me. Renzo raped me once, but they were abused over and over again by so many different men."

"Even one time is too much."

"I didn't do enough to protect them."

"You did the best you could." Alexa lifted her foot up another stair and used the rail to support her bodyweight.

"I wasn't used the way the others were. I danced and stripped occasionally, but I did the books, made clothes, did the girls' makeup when they were going to be used for a party. I helped Renzo and Blondie prostitute innocent teens. How do I live with that?"

Alexa shook her head as she tried to imagine the depths of her sister's hell. What could she possibly say to make this better? "You didn't have a choice."

"I tried to protect them, but it hurt more than it helped." She sniffled and wiped at the streaming tears. "When they brought Jenna here—her real name's Margret—they sent her to a man right away. She was a virgin and terrified. After the guy left, I was helping her—cleaning her up and comforting her, trying to make it better—and Renzo came in. He went wild, absolutely crazy. He threw me down on the bed and raped me in front of her. He told her that was how things were done around here and to get used to it. Then he raped her and made me watch. She was sore after her first time, and he was extra mean. She bled so much afterwards. I was afraid I wouldn't be able to make it stop." She sobbed quietly as she relived her nightmare.

"Abby—"

"I don't want to be afraid of him. I know he wins, but every time I'm around him I can't seem to make myself remember that. It all comes back, and I feel like I shrink down to nothing."

Alexa fought her way up another stair and looked at her sister as Renzo smashed something in the next room. She hated Lorenzo Cruz. She loathed the man who ripped Abby's life apart. They had to find a way to stop him and give Abby her power back. "We're going to make it through this. We're not getting on a plane with him."

"What are we going to do?"

"I don't know yet, but when the opportunity presents itself, the Harris sisters are going to kick some ass." Her arms trembled as they approached the last step. She'd used all her energy to make it up the endless staircase.

"Good, just in time." Renzo walked from the room he trashed. "The flight's been arranged. Go sit your asses down until I say otherwise."

Alexa held Abby's gaze, willing her to be strong.

"Come on, Lex." Abby helped her hobble to the first bedroom on the right. The room had been destroyed. Dressers were toppled, pillows shredded, and another computer lay smashed in pieces. "Let's sit you down over here."

Alexa collapsed on the firm plastic milk crate next to an old-fashioned steam radiator. Her body was spent. She just needed a minute to regroup, then they were going to find a way...

"Time to go night-night." Renzo came back with two syringes.

"What are you doing?" Alexa stared in utter horror as she used the heater to help herself stand.

"Going to put you to sleep until we get where we need to go."

The thought of being drugged was somehow more terrifying than what would happen if he actually got them on the plane.

He flicked the syringe and squeezed a small stream of liquid from the needle as he continued his advance. "It'll only hurt for a second. Arm out."

"No." She scrambled back and rapped into the copper heater with no place else to go. "Get away from me."

"Stop it!" Abby charged forward and clawed at Renzo's face. He yelled out as blood bloomed across the gouges in his cheek, and he fought her off with a solid backhand. "You *bitch*!" He swiped at his face, and his brown eyes turned black with rage. "You little bitch!"

He dropped the needles and charged after Abby. Alexa lunged awkwardly, hopping on his back. She gripped her arm around his neck and squeezed as she pummeled at his temple with all her might. "Don't ever touch my sister!" Seconds passed before she realized he was yanking her hair through her blinding anger, but she refused to let go. He whirled and slammed her in to the tall radiator. The shocking impact stole her breath, and she fell to the milk crate.

"You're going to pay for that." Breathless himself, Renzo reached for the handcuffs in his pocket.

"No!" She didn't want to be chained and at his mercy. No!" She fought him but she was no match for his strength. Renzo shackled her wrist to the radiator and turned, grabbing for Abby. "You're next."

"Don't *touch* me." Abby struggled as he reached for another set of cuffs and tried to secure her next to Alexa.

"I'm going to do more than touch you, cunt, and your bitch sister's going to watch."

Alexa's breath heaved as a well of rage burst to life. She pushed her legs back as Renzo crouched in front of her and slammed her feet forward as hard as she could, tagging him in the balls. She screamed from the unbelievable agony radiating through her ankle as Renzo crumble to the floor. "Run! Run, Abigail! Go get help!"

Abby didn't hesitate this time. "Help! Help!" she screamed as she dashed down the stairs.

Renzo coughed and moaned as Alexa reached for his pocket and the key that would free her, but he was too far away.

He pushed himself up on all fours and looked her in the eye. "Forget Europe. You're going to die now." He coughed again and tried to get to his feet.

She had no doubt he meant what he said. Frantic, she grabbed the broken lamppost at her side as he looked down and swung, bashing him against the temple. Renzo fell forward, swearing, and rolled to his side—too far for Alexa to hit him again.

He would get up soon—any second, and she had nowhere to go. She yanked her arm, desperately trying to pull her wrist free of the metal trapping her in the room.

"You're going to pay." Renzo crawled to the door. Blood oozed from his temple and cheek as he slowly got up. "You're going to fucking burn." He pulled a lighter from his pocket and flicked the small red butane to life, touching it to the papers he picked up off the table. White sheets curled black as the flames grew. He dropped his phone, stomping it twice, and walked from the room, chuckling as he tossed the paper into the bedroom across the hall.

Alexa stared in horror as the whoosh of flames spread instantly among the mess.

"While your waiting to cook, I want you to think about how I'm going to torture your sister every day." He reached in his other pocket and pulled out the key for the handcuffs. "I bet you want this." He threw it into the room among the blaze. "Too bad for you." He grinned madly and slammed the door closed.

"He's coming! Run, Abby!" she screamed as she furiously yanked her arm. Wisps of smoke began to curl under the crack in the door. "Oh, God. Oh, God." She got to her knees and pulled again and again, fighting for her life. Her wrist turned an angry, raw pink and bloomed with bruises with each violent jerk. Something in the next room exploded and crashed to the floor. "Come on. Come *on*." There was no way she would be alive by the time police and fire department got here. She would either slip free or burn. Tears fell from her eyes as she thought of Livy and Jack. Sobbing desperately, she continued her war with the metal trapping her in place while she stared at the smoke slowly crowding the room. No matter how she tried to break free of the cuff, it was too tight against her skin.

Jackson jerked the wheel and skidded around another turn. The house hadn't seemed so damn far away when he and Tucker studied the map earlier that afternoon. "I think I'm almost there. I just turned on Drake Avenue."

"Take the next right—second driveway on the left. The cops should be right behind you. Terron and I are five, six minutes out at the most."

"Renzo has her. He has to." Hartwell's house had been searched from top to bottom. The man himself along with Eric Stevens, Blondie, Lenny, and Mr. Lee had been arrested and were on their way in for questioning. Christina had been found unconscious, shoved in a downstairs closet. Two young women, long since thought dead, had been recovered as well, but Alex was still missing. Had that been Alex's hand pounding against Renzo's window as his Porsche took off down the parkway?

Jackson barreled around the next right and screeched to a halt when a woman ran out in front of the vehicle. "*Fuck.*" He gripped the wheel and sucked in a tearing breath, trying hard to swallow as his heart lodged in his throat. Finally it registered that the woman screaming hysterically at his driver's-side window was Abby. "Holy shit. Abby."

Tears streamed down her dirty face as she pointed frantically at the house beyond the trees. "He has Alexa!" She clawed at the door handle. "He's hurting her! Help her!"

The relief of finding Abby quickly vanished. Jackson

433

grabbed his gun and cellphone that had fallen to the floor when he stopped violently and yanked his door open.

"He's hurting her! He's hurting her! Help her, Jackson. Please."

"Where is she?"

"Upstairs."

He glanced toward the house again and blinked. "Dear God. No. *No*." He took off at a sprint. "Get in the car and drive, Abby. Go. Get away from here." He called over his shoulder. "The house is on fire," he hollered into his phone. "She's inside. Alex is inside and Abigail Harris is in my rental car. We found Abigail Harris."

"Fire and rescue should be there soon. ETA's two and a half minutes."

"Tell them to fucking hurry. The upstairs is all lit up." He ripped the front door open and charged up the steps, coughing from the smoke choking the air. "Alex! Alex!" He slammed into something solid and fell back, fighting to keep his balance. Through the gray haze he made out Renzo's figure. "Where is she?"

Renzo smiled.

"You motherfucker." With a rage he didn't know he possessed, he threw his arm back and swung. Blood spurted from the bastard's nose and mouth as his head lolled back and his eyes rolled. He collapsed and toppled down the stairs with several sickening thuds.

Jackson kept moving. "Alex!" He coughed again as the smoke grew thicker with every step.

"In here. In here, Jack," came her dull voice over the roar of hot, hungry flames.

Eyes burning, overcome by the blinding smolder, he crawled toward the sounds of her violent coughing. Choking himself, he slid his nose and mouth into the neck of his t-shirt. "I'm coming, Alex!" His shoulder rammed into the wood of what could only be a door, and

434

he felt for the knob. He hurried in and slammed it shut behind him. "I'm here!" He crawled forward, stumbling over scatters of paper and overturned furnishings, until he stopped in front of her. Swamped with relief, he grabbed her cheeks in his hands and kissed her, despite the urgency of their situation. "You're okay." He pressed his mouth to hers again before he eased back and took in her swollen and badly bruised foot, her legs and arms raw and bloodied in a nasty road-rash pattern. "My God."

"Help me, Jack." Tears dripped from her bloodshot eyes, leaving tracks through the soot coating her face. "I'm stuck." She wiggled her equally swollen and black-and-blue wrist. "My arm." She coughed.

Jackson stared at her wrist cuffed to the radiator and digested a new wave of fear.

"The key... Renzo threw the key into the flames."

"Okay. We'll find another way." He had to get them out of here before they suffocated. He noticed the window behind her and the white paint sealing the track shut. "Cover your face. I'm going to break the window." He scanned the area for a solid object and spotted a footstool. Standing, he heaved the wood at the thick glass and it shattered around them. He stuck his head out, greedy for a breath of muggy summer air. "Your turn." He crouched next to her. "Let's get you some of this."

She scooted as close to the window as she could, but it wasn't enough to breathe pure, smokeless air. Her eyes were growing heavy. He was losing her. Jackson dashed into the bathroom, yanked off his shirt, and soaked the grimy cotton in tap water. He rushed back and tossed the sopping shirt at her. "Cover your face with this."

She stared at him, blinking.

"Cover your face, Alex." He shoved his top against her nose and mouth, struggling to think over the terror and wretched stench of the burning structure. "We've gotta go. Now." He took her trapped wrist in his hand and yanked hard.

She cried out.

"I'm sorry. I'm going to do it again. Hold your breath." He pulled even harder, and she screamed. It was no use. The swelling around her wrist was biting into her skin.

"Get out, Jack," she sobbed. "Get out for Livy."

"No."

"Please."

"I'm not leaving you!" His mind whirled, desperate for a solution. "Hold out your wrist. Move your body as far to the right as possible and pull on the cuff." He ripped his gun from the back of his waistband. "Don't move. Don't move, Alex." He squinted through the smoke, aimed, and fired.

Alex barely flinched from the deafening pop as her arm smacked against the wooden floor. "It worked. You're free. You're free," he repeated as he scooped her up. "Hang on, Alex." He shoved her face into the fresh air through the window and heard the sirens in the distance. "Big breaths."

She breathed deep and coughed.

"Couple more."

She did as she was told.

"Here we go." He settled his shirt over her face and hurried to the door, feeling for the knob. It was warm but worth the risk.

"Livy. My Livy," Alex mumbled. Then her head sagged against his shoulder.

"No. You stay with me, Alex. Don't you pass out on me." He opened the door into a plume of smoke and gasped as the toxic air stole his breath. He tripped and stumbled over objects as he made his way to the stairs. The building groaned and large pieces of ceiling crashed around them. He gripped the railing as he clutched Alex against him. The room began to whirl as it grew harder to draw each breath. He moved on instinct, following Abby's screams for her sister as it became impossible to think. They were almost there. The door... There it was...wide open... His arms shook as he reached the threshold and sucked in gasping puffs of fresh air again. Renzo was being loaded onto a stretcher. Tucker came rushing up the stairs before the police officer could stop him, shouting something, but Jackson wasn't sure what he said. His vision blurred, going gray. "Take her."

Jackson struggled to stay upright as Tucker reached out for Alex and grabbed hold. The weight of her body left his arms, and the black came up to swallow him whole.

CHAPTER 25

HE'D BEEN STARING AT THE ceiling for *hours,* while oxygen hissed into his nose and the EKG monitored his heart. The oxygen saturation thing clipped to his finger, and the blood pressure cuff squeezing his arm every twenty minutes was pissing him the hell off. His throat was on fire, and his eyes too. Each swallow and blink was pure torture. He'd had blood drawn, two chest x-rays, an IV that had since been removed, and a stream of physicians and nurses in and out of his room. Despite being given a clean bill of health, Jackson's mood sucked. How much longer did he have to *lie* here?

It was ten-thirty in the morning for God's sake. Was the doctor coming to release him or what? He needed to see Alex. Tucker had been by to assure him that she was expected to make a full recovery, but he wouldn't be able to settle until he saw her for himself.

Someone knocked on the door, and he grunted.

His mother peeked in. "Can we come in?"

"Yeah, sure." He winced as his scorched throat protested.

She stepped through the doorway, and he smiled.

"Daddy!" Olivia wiggled to get down.

"No, Livy. Stay with Grammy."

"I want Daddy." Her lip turned down.

Mom walked to the bed and clutched his hand.

He squeezed back, reassuring her he was okay. "You—" He coughed as he looked at Olivia. "You wanna sit with me?" he whispered and patted the spot at his side, desperately wanting his little girl.

Olivia's eyes grew wide. "You're a growly dog, Daddy."

He grinned. "My throat hurts."

"You're eyes are red and very blinky."

"They hurt too. Come sit with me, Liv. I need you." He flicked off the oxygen monitor, held out his arms, and pulled his daughter against him. Holding her tight, he closed his eyes, fighting back tears. He'd thought of Olivia as he struggled to get down the stairs of the burning house, terrified he wouldn't see her again. Now here she was in his arms. "I love you, Liv. I love you so much."

"I love you too, Daddy." She shoved her hands against his chest and pulled back. "You're very stinky. Grammy, Daddy stinks a lot. A lot," she emphasized as she plugged her nose.

Jackson chuckled, then coughed. He took the Styrofoam cup his mother offered and drank deep. The cold liquid was heaven on his parched throat. "They tried to clean me up, but I haven't had a chance to shower off the worst of the stench." He sipped again when he realized the water almost made his voice sound normal.

"I'm just glad you and Alexa are okay. We're going to visit her next, but I wanted to drop off some fresh clothes." She gestured to the bag she set at the foot of the bed. "I spoke to the doctor before we headed down. He said they're planning to release you within the hour."

"What about Alex?"

"They wouldn't tell me, but I talked to Abby. She said the doctor wants to keep Alexa until this evening at least."

He sat up. "Why? Tucker said she's going to be fine."

"She is, sweetie. They just want to keep an eye on her and give her a little more time to rest. She's pretty banged up. She was in the smoke a lot longer than you."

The machine monitoring his heart beeped faster as he thought of Alex trapped. It made him sick to remember. "Her wrist." Her screams of agony as he'd yanked on her echoed through his mind. "I hurt her."

"You saved her, honey." She patted his hand.

"I should've shot the cuff off as soon as I got there. I wasn't thinking." He pressed his hands to his face, bumping the oxygen line. He couldn't forget the way her body had gone limp in his arms. He'd replayed the terrifying moment over and over. "I thought she was—I thought she was... Damn it."

Olivia gasped and slapped a hand to her mouth. "Daddy said a bad word."

"Yes, he did." His mother pulled Olivia from the bed. "But we'll let it slide just this once. Will you be home later?"

"I'm going to stay with Alex if you don't mind keeping an eye on Liv for a while longer."

"Of course I don't." She kissed Olivia's cheek. "My beautiful grandbaby will be heading home with her Mommy and Daddy before too long."

They were going to Los Angeles, but that didn't mean he and Alex would be living together. He averted his gaze from his mother's questioning stare and quickly changed the subject. "How are things working out with Jerrod?"

"Fine. He's waiting right outside the door. So many handsome men in my house these days. You're father's getting jealous."

He grinned. "Jerrod's a hell of a guy." Ethan had sent another agent out to help keep an eye on things until they were ready to head back to California. Several of the major players in the Mid-Atlantic sex ring were now in custody, but they weren't taking any chances. Abby and Alex were key witnesses for the federal prosecution, which made his family a target. He was never more eager to get everyone back to LA, where Alex and Abby could lay low for a while and recover.

"Jerrod will take me and Livy home when we're ready—and Abby too. First thing I'm going to do is make that girl something good and fattening to eat. Poor thing is skin and bone and jittery too."

"She's been through hell."

"Yes she has, but she's strong. A little time and therapy's what she needs. She'll be a hot ticket again soon enough."

"I hope so."

"She will. Trust your mother." She took a step back before Olivia could press the call button on the bed. "We should go check on Alexa now. We'll see you soon." She leaned over and kissed his forehead. "Whew, you do stink."

He smiled. "Bye, mom. Bye, Liv. See you later." He kissed the pad of his finger the way he'd seen Alex do and pressed it to Olivia's nose. "I love you." He coughed again and sipped at his water.

"I love you too, daddy. I'm going to visit mommy and Auntie Ab. She went away but she came back. I'm so glad."

"Me too. Have fun."

His mother pulled the door open. "I put a couple of extra things in your bag for you—shampoo, your toothbrush and razor. Oh, and Livy packed you one of her princess books—just in case you get bored."

"You two are awesome." Grinning, he leaned back against the pillow.

"And don't you forget it." She winked, and she and Olivia were gone.

Chuckling, he reached for the duffel bag, and the door

opened again. The doctor stepped in. "Mr. Matthews, I have some good news."

"Tell me I can take a shower, and we'll be pals for life."

"How about a shower and a discharge?"

"Definitely friends for life." He held out his hand, and the doctor took it, returning the firm handshake.

"The nurse will be by shortly with your instructions for the next couple of days, but first I want to get a final listen to your lungs."

"Can I take this damn thing off my face?" He pointed to the oxygen.

"Go for it."

Jackson pulled the tubing from behind his ears and removed the piece from his nose.

The doctor adjusted his stethoscope and pressed the cool metal to Jackson's chest. "Deep breath. Good. Another. Excellent." He took a step back and settled the stethoscope around his neck. "Your lungs sound great, your oxygen saturation is perfect, your blood work is well within normal range—I'm expecting you to make a full recovery. You and Ms. Harris were incredibly lucky. If you hadn't broken the window, I can't be sure the results would've been as favorable. Smoke inhalation is very serious business. The fresh air saved you both."

"Yes." Tucker told him Renzo hadn't faired as well. He was ventilated in ICU, fighting for his life. "How's Christina Detrick doing?"

"She was sent home about an hour ago. We monitored her while she slept off the tranquilizer she was given. Lucky for her, the syringe used on her appeared to be sterile. The last thing she remembers was watching one of the suspects peel the syringe from a package and pull the cap from the needle before they prepared the dosage. Several boxes of disposable needles and three vials of GHB were found in a passenger van parked in the garage. Someone in the medical field was supplying them with syringes and the medical-grade sedative. She's a bit shaken up, but she's cleared to go back to work as soon as she's ready."

"I'm glad she's going to be okay." He held out his hand for another shake. "Thank you again for everything, Doc."

"It's been a pleasure. Go get that shower. I heard you stink."

Jackson chuckled. "That's the word around town, according to my mother and daughter."

"Your daughter informed me on my way in."

Jackson shook his head, laughed, and coughed. Would he ever get enough of his little girl?

"Take it easy for the next couple days, Mr. Matthews. Drink plenty of fluids."

"Check." He got up and grabbed the side of the bed, surprised to find himself weak and dizzy. "Well, shit."

"Your body has been through a lot. As I said, you'll need to rest."

"I guess I'm not used to being down for the count."

"You're strong and healthy. Give yourself about forty-eight hours. Are you comfortable if I leave?"

"Yeah. Sure." He took a deep breath, coughed again, grabbed his bag, and made his way to the bathroom, refusing to give in to his need to sit back down. He didn't have time to be shaky on his pins. He twisted on the shower and pulled off the pale blue hospital gown, then he unzipped his bag and took the shampoo from the small travel case. After testing the water temperature, he stepped under the warm spray and groaned. "God, this feels good." Not wasting any time, he peeled the paper from the bar of soap and began lathering up.

Several minutes later, Jackson sniffed at his arms, relieved that the smoky smell was finally gone from his skin. He'd scrubbed himself three times. Refreshed and feeling like a new person, he shut off the stream of hot water and took a final deep breath of the soothing steam. Then he stepped from the stall and toweled dry.

He glanced in the mirror and rubbed a hand over the rough stubble on his jaw and chin, debating whether or not to shave. His eyes were an angry red and his hair a mess of wild tufts sticking up here and there. He sure as hell did look like a growly dog. Grinning, shaking his head as he thought of Olivia, he reached in the travel case in search of his razor and shaving cream and felt a thin, rectangular box. "What the hell?" He frowned as he pulled the mystery item free, opened the lid, and stared at the shiny gold of Alex's repaired necklace. He sighed as he rubbed his thumb over the triangular pendant, fully understanding his mother's gesture. "It's not that easy, mom," he muttered. "I can't just hand it back."

His light mood faded, and depression loomed as he touched his thumb to the cool gold once more, then replaced the lid. Alex didn't want it; she'd made that perfectly clear. She loved him, and he her, but she wasn't sure about their future. He swore as he shoved the box back in the case and brushed his fingers across a folded piece of paper. "You've got to be kidding me." He opened the floral stationary and shook his head, recognizing his mother's pretty handwriting.

I saw this on your dresser and figured Alexa would want it back. I know you're too smart to make the same stupid mistake twice. It's been nice seeing that handsome smile of yours again. Don't let her get away this time, Jackson.
Love,
Your wise and meddling mother

Heaving out a weary breath, he folded the sheet and rubbed at his temple. He didn't *want* Alex to get away. Over the last two months, he'd done everything in his power to win her back—and it had worked...for a while. He and Alex had laughed again and held each other close. They'd flirted and made love. They'd spent the summer raising their daughter together, taking Olivia to the park, teaching her to fish, reading her endless stories. A glimpse of their future had been right there for them both to see—until Ethan discovered the profiles on Baltimore Dates. Everything had gone straight to hell after that.

They needed to get back to where they'd been not even a week before. He had to find a way to show Alex that what he felt for her at this moment had little to do with their college days and everything to do with the woman she was right now. But 'how' was the question? He reached for his deodorant and stopped as he spotted the light pink edge of Olivia's princess book. "That's it." He grabbed the prettily decorated hardback and held it in his hand knowing exactly what he had to do. He moved quickly now as he brushed, shaved, and dressed. He had to catch Olivia, Abby, and his mother before they left.

Someone knocked on the door, and Alexa set down her magazine. "Come in."

"Hey." Jack peeked in the guest room and smiled.

"Hi." She smiled back as a surge of butterflies took flight in her stomach. He was so handsome. "When did you get home?" She struggled to sit up with one wrist splinted and her casted foot elevated on a mound of pillows.

"Don't try to get up." He rushed to her side, adjusting the pillows back the way Abby had fixed them, and stared down, studying her as he stood straight again. "I've been here for a couple hours. I didn't want to bother you. I thought you might be sleeping."

"No, I'm wide awake."

"I'm sorry I missed your homecoming. I checked in on you before I left the hospital to run a few errands. The nurse said the doctor wasn't going to spring you until late tonight or early tomorrow."

That's what they'd told her too, but she'd insisted they release her. She hadn't been able to stand the thought of being away from Livy and her sister for another minute. "They changed their minds."

He grinned. "So I heard."

She shrugged. "There was no point in keeping me. I'm perfectly fine." She coughed as she'd done off and on since she came to in the ambulance several hours before.

"Here." He handed her the glass of water, and she sipped. "You should've stayed until they were ready to let you go, Alex."

She handed him back the glass. "I'm sore, and my throat hurts. It's no big deal. I wanted to be here. Every now and again I can hear Livy and Abby laughing. That's all the medicine I need to get better." She sniffed at the heavenly aroma hanging in the air. "And some of whatever your mother's cooking."

"Mom's preparing a summer feast."

"I should be helping." She tried to sit up again, but Jack pressed a firm hand to her shoulder.

"No, you shouldn't. You need to lay here and rest."

If one more person told her that... She huffed out a breath. "I'm not sick."

"True, but you're covered in road rash and bruises,

you're experiencing mild effects from smoke inhalation, and have a strained wrist and a grade-four sprain that might not require surgery if you do what you've been told."

Jack was right, but she'd watched all the TV she could stand and was down to her final magazine. Despite the aches and pains plaguing her battered body, she was going stir crazy just laying here. "I think I might go mad if I have to stay cooped up in this bed while everyone else is downstairs."

Sighing, Jack sat down next to her. "You never were a very good patient."

"I don't have *time* to be a patient. I can think of a million things that have to get done. Suitcases don't pack themselves, and Livy needs a bath—"

"All of which Abby, my mother, or I can do."

She huffed out another breath and closed her eyes. "Bumming around here gives me too much time to think," she confessed. "I keep replaying last night over and over... Everything could've ended so differently." She took his hand and pressed his palm to her cheek. "If you hadn't come when you did..." Her eyes watered as she remembered the helplessness of being chained in the room. "You saved me, Jack. You almost died saving me."

He brushed his thumb along her skin. "We're both still here, right?"

She nodded. "Because of you. You ran into a burning building for me."

"And I would do it again." He traced her tender chin with gentle strokes and pressed his forehead to hers. "I'd do it again, Alex," he repeated.

She played her fingers along his neck as his breath shuddered out. "What's wrong?"

He shook his head. "I thought you were—I thought

447

you were dead. You were so limp."

"Shh," she soothed as she wrapped her arms around him. "We're both still here, right?" She gave him back his own words, and he smiled as he nodded.

Livy's screech of laughter echoed up the stairs, followed by Abby's warning that the tickle monster was coming to get her.

Alexa smiled. "That's the best sound in the world. Hearing my sister's voice again. That alone makes last night worth it."

Jack kissed her. "Agreed."

"Thank you." She touched his cheek. "Thank you for bringing Abby home."

"I didn't do it by myself. We all did it together." He eased back.

"But you've been the one by my side every step of the way." She fiddled with the end of his t-shirt, still worrying. "This isn't over for her. She went through so much. Eventually there will be a trial. She's still in danger."

"No, it's not over," he agreed as he played his finger through her hair. "But she's home now, and she's strong. She has you and Olivia. We'll find her a good therapist when we get back to LA, and we'll take care of her security so she feels safe. Everything's going to work out. It'll be all right."

She nodded as she stared into Jack's eyes, believing for the first time in too long that everything might be okay. Livy's delighted screams carried up the stairs again, and she grinned as Jack did.

His cell vibrated at his hip, and he checked the incoming text before he put his phone back. "So, what do you say? You wanna get out of here?"

"Yes, I definitely do." She yanked away the light blanket she'd been covered with since Carol, Abby, and

Livy had tucked her in after her bath.

"Then let's go." Jack bent low and scooped her up carefully. Her legs screamed as the weight of his arms pressed the bandages into her raw wounds; her ankle throbbed in her cast as her foot dangled, but she didn't care.

"You okay?"

She rubbed at the worry line creasing his forehead as he frowned. "I'm perfect. Take me away. Take me anywhere but here."

"That can definitely be arranged." He walked them down the steps and headed for the front door.

"Where are we going? I thought we could give your mother a hand."

He bypassed the chaos in the kitchen and continued on. "You said I could take you anywhere."

"Yes, but..." She rested her head on Jack's strong shoulder as he took the outside steps and started along the path through the tall marsh grasses. The setting sun was warm on her skin, and the salty breeze uplifting. A few minutes in the fresh air couldn't hurt.

"Doing all right?"

"Mmm." She smiled. "This is a perfect idea."

"I have one on occasion."

She lifted her head as she caught sight of the pretty little table draped in a white cloth set for two at the edge of the dock. A fat, periwinkle candle flickered bright in a hurricane glass next to the vase that was bursting with bold pink hydrangeas—her favorite. "Oh, Jack. It's beautiful."

"I'm glad you like it."

"I love it." She kissed his cheek, touched that he would think of such a sweet gesture after the chaos of the past few days.

"I thought it would be nice to have dinner here, since

449

tomorrow's our last night on the Chesapeake for awhile." He set her gently in her chair and propped her foot on a stool with a pillow. "How's this? Are you comfortable?"

"Yes, thank you." The water was dark blue and choppy in the steady winds. Carol's beautiful, silver-rimmed china glowed in the pastel hues of twilight. "I'm going to miss being here. I love your parents so much… and the house and the bay."

Jack took his own seat across from her. "We'll be back. I know my parents plan to come out to Los Angeles after everyone's settled in."

They'd be back to Kent Island? She wasn't so certain. And where would she, Livy and Abby settle? They would probably stay with Jack for a few days while they figured out security measures for Abby, but after that… Should she put her house on the market and take the job offer that had come in Friday afternoon? Would she and Jack work things out the way she so desperately wanted them to? There was so much up in the air, but now Abby was safe and life could begin again. "I don't know… I'm not sure…" She didn't want to bring up the numerous questions needing answers after he'd gone to such trouble to create a beautiful evening. Their problems would be waiting for them tomorrow morning when they got up to face the new day.

"What?" He pulled a large plastic bottle from a small cooler tucked by his side of the table.

"Nothing." She shook her head. "It's nothing."

He studied her for a minute before he lifted the bottle to her wine glass. "Water?"

"Uh, please."

"I thought we should keep it alcohol-free. You might need to take a pain pill later."

Her heart melted as she stared into his gorgeous blue eyes. "I appreciate it. I'm trying hard to stick with ibuprofen. I don't want to be all loopy around Livy."

He nodded. "Are you hungry? We have fresh lobster salad with greens and the homemade rolls mom makes that you like so much."

More of her favorites. Her eyes filled, and she blinked. "Jack." She reached for his fingers and held on. "I can't remember a more special evening."

He raised her hand to his lips and kissed the deep scrapes in the center of her palm. "I love the way you get weepy when I surprise you. And it never has to be much—a flower, a simple dinner. How many opportunities did I miss? How many times could I have made your eyes go soft over the years—the way they are right now?"

"I..." She closed her eyes and swallowed as his mouth moved to the pads of her fingers.

"I have something for you." He brushed her knuckles along his cheek and placed her hand on the table. "I thought maybe we would eat first, but I think right now is perfect."

She blinked, still undone by his tender gesture and sweet words. "You didn't have to—you didn't have to get me anything."

"I didn't." He opened the wicker picnic basket she recognized from their day out on the boat and met his eyes as he pulled out a stack of stapled papers tied with a periwinkle ribbon. "Olivia and I made you something."

"You made me..." Her lips trembled as he handed over the gift she recognized as one of Livy's homemade books. There was nothing better than one of her little girl's creations. "I don't even know what to say. Jack, this is amazing."

"Can I read it to you?"

"Yes, of course." She untied the ribbon.

"Let me slide my chair over." He scooted around to

her side of the table and took the book from her hand so she could look at the pictures while he read her the words. "'Once upon a time there was a prince.' The guy had to be a prince," Jack interrupted himself as he looked at her. "Olivia insisted."

"Well, of course." She grinned as she studied the blue stick figure on the paper.

"Okay, back to the story." He cleared his throat. "'The prince was young and liked to play football and go to parties and eat cake and ice cream.' Olivia's part again. I thought it was better for her to draw a birthday cake instead of a keg."

"Mmm, yes. That was very wise."

"Anyway…" He turned his attention back to the book. "'The prince liked to eat lots of cake and ice cream until his mean coach told him he wouldn't be able to play with his football anymore if he didn't pass his classes.'" He turned to the next page. "'That night, the prince went to the enchanted land of knowledge—the library—and his whole life changed. Sitting behind the royal check-in desk was the most beautiful princess he had ever seen. She had pretty blue eyes and long black hair, and although he'd never met her, the prince knew he loved her.'"

Alexa sniffed and wiped at her eyes as he turned to the next sheet with two smiling stick figures—one with yellow hair and blue eyes and one with scribbly black hair and blue eyes. "'The prince and princess were happy for a very long time.'"

He flipped again. The stick figures on this page had sad faces. "'Until one dark night when the prince lost his mind and made the princess sad.'"

"Jack." She covered his hand.

"I'm almost finished." He gave her fingers a gentle squeeze. "'The prince and princess didn't see each other again for a long, long time, but he missed his princess and thought of her every single day.'"

The next page had three stick figures—two with yellow hair and the princess with her black hair—and two animal figures, one of which had something in its mouth. "'Many years later, the princess flew on a unicorn to the land of Los Angeles and saw the prince again. The princess brought along a very special surprise—a new princess named Olivia who looked just like the prince. He fell in love all over again and took the two princesses to his castle and bought a royal dog named Mutt who liked to ruin the prince's socks.'"

Alexa laughed through her tears. "Look how she drew Mutt eating your sock."

"She's damn clever." He turned the page. "Just a couple more... 'The prince and two princesses had to fly on the unicorn again to meet King Grampy and Queen Grammy. They had fun at the king and queen's castle, until the prince and princess made each other sad again.'"

He turned to the last page where all three figures had smiles, and the furry dog too. "'The prince didn't want to be sad anymore. He didn't want to spend any more days without the two princesses he loved very, very much...'" The words ended there, as did the illustrations. Jack set the book on the table and reached for something in the picnic basket. He faced her again and smiled. "Don't worry. The story isn't over yet." He lifted the lid on a rectangular box, and she gasped as she stared at the necklace she'd been missing since the moment she yanked it off.

"You fixed it," she whispered, and tears spilled down her cheeks.

"The princess told the prince that she was very confused, but the prince didn't want her to be. He wanted her to know that he loved to remember their special days in the enchanted library." Jack unfastened the clasp. "Please let me put this back on."

Overcome, she wiped at her cheeks and nodded as he secured the necklace where it belonged. "I've never missed anything so much." She clutched the triangular pendant and leaned forward, touching her lips to his. "Thank you."

He held her close for a moment before he eased back and brushed the hair from her forehead. "There's more." He smiled. "The prince loved to remember their special days in the enchanted library," he repeated. "Because they were some of the best moments of his life, but he loved the possibilities of the prince and princess's future even more." He reached in his jean pocket and pulled out a simple, one-carat, square-cut diamond ring.

Her eyes flew to his. "Jack," she whispered as she held his gaze.

"Years ago, I told you I wanted forever with you. A lot has changed since then, but not that. I love the shy, serious girl who knocked me off my feet when I walked into the library, but I can promise you I love the mother of my child impossibly more right now. I don't want to live in the past, Alex. I want to build a future—our future. Please say you'll wear this and be my wife."

She stared at the gorgeous, funny man who'd risked everything to save her, the man she'd yearned for since the day he left. This was their second chance. "Yes. Yes, I'll marry you, Handsome Jack."

"Thank God." Grinning, he slid the ring on her finger and pulled her against him for a long, deep kiss. "Let's go tell everyone." He lifted her gently in his arms.

"In just a minute." She pressed her hands to his cheeks. "We didn't finish the story."

"We didn't?"

She shook her head. "Nope. You forgot to say 'and they lived happily ever after.'"

He smiled. 'And they lived happily ever after'. He kissed her once more, and they started up the dock to the delighted screams and laughter of their daughter catching on the wind.

ABOUT THE AUTHOR

Cate Beauman is the author of the best selling series, The Bodyguards of L.A. County. She currently lives in Tennessee with her husband, two boys, and their St. Bernard, Bear.

OTHER TITLES BY
CATE BEAUMAN

www.catebeauman.com

Made in the USA
San Bernardino, CA
17 July 2013